Veiled Empire

Veiled Empire

NATHAN GARRISON

HARPER
VOYAGER
IMPULSE

An Imprint of HarperCollinsPublishers

EPub Edition MAY 2015 ISBN: 9780062418258

Print Edition ISBN: 9780062418241

10 9 8 7 6 5 4 3 2 1

To Kathryn

PART I

Chapter 1

BLOOD HAD ALWAYS made him smile, but not today. The girl had ruined it for him.

He tore his gaze from her crumpled form, bringing his hands up before his face. Sunlight cut through the trees, illuminating the warm red life of his enemies as it streamed down his forearms and dripped from his elbows. The surge of satisfaction he normally felt at such a sight turned sour in his gut.

Abyss take you, sorceress.

As the cacophony of battle raged on all sides, he closed his senses to it all, clenching his hands into fists.

"I am Hardohl," he whispered. "A void. Anathema to sorcery. I have trained since the cradle to fight, to bring justice to those who abuse their power."

The mantra was meant to comfort him. But even as the words left his lips, they rang hollow, meaningless. For before his very eyes, he'd seen the truths by which his entire life depended put to the lie.

Impossible...

He forced his gaze upon her. With eyes closed, she lay sprawled on the stony ground, breath labored yet steady. She seemed, now, so small, so frail, so powerless.

Yet . . . he shook. It was not the quiver of anticipation. It was something different. Something new. Something he had not felt in so long that he'd forgotten what it was. It took him a moment to even remember what to call it, and when the word finally came to mind, he recoiled.

Fear.

IN THE GLOOM before dawn, Mevon Daere knelt onto the corpse's chest. Ribs crunched beneath his weight like trampled kindling. He dipped a hand towards the sentry's neck to check the knife wound, which still oozed warm and wet, slick and red. Not his kill—Mevon had no taste for silent work—but it was enough to whet his appetite for what soon would come.

Mevon craved blood, but he did not lust for it. Many of his male peers grew even more aroused by blood than by the sight of a naked woman. And the female Hardohl were worse. Most seemed to thrive on inflicting unnecessary agony. A symptom, no doubt, of a lifetime spent in opposition to their feminine natures.

Mevon was not burdened by either form of perversion. It was not the blood itself that brought him satisfaction, but what it represented: justice delivered, order restored.

Still, he admitted, *life is never sweeter than when ending it.*

A flicker of movement brought his head up. On the cliffs three hundred paces above them, darkwisps fled from dawn's first light, seeking deep fissures in which to wait out the day. The hovering swarms snapped and crackled like caged lightning. So, too, did a storm stir inside of him. His whole body shook faintly as he struggled to keep it contained. The effort would soon be unnecessary, a fact that brought a smile to his lips.

A shadow stepped out of the fog to stand beside him.

"Well?" Mevon said.

"They're right where we expected, Hardohl," Idrus said, his voice muffled behind a veil. "No change in routine. No hint they know we're here."

"And their casters?"

"They've yet to stir from their tents."

Mevon nodded, eager, as they all were, to end this weeks-long hunt. The bandits they tracked were hardly worthy of their time. He and his Fist wouldn't even be here on the edge of nowhere were it not for the special pair that had taken refuge among these criminals.

Sorcerers.

Not one had ever escaped him in twelve years of active duty though hundreds had tried. The pair today would make it a score this year alone, and it was only the end of summer. Each catch impressed his mierothi masters all the more. With luck, his request for a transfer out of this forgotten corner of the empire would be pushed towards approval.

Anticipation leaked out of every pore. Mevon ached for it to begin.

Still...

"Why here?" whispered Mevon.

Idrus silently lifted an eyebrow.

Mevon rose from his crouch, pushing back dark hair from his face. Idrus, though tall, still had to tilt his head back to make eye contact.

"Do their actions make sense to you? They are corralled here. The cliffs at their back, the falls to the south, and there . . ." Mevon pointed north. Two hundred paces distant, the land cut away, as if cleaved by a god's giant axe.

The Shelf. The end of the world.

"Aye," Idrus agreed. "Something feels . . . off."

Mevon grunted and crossed his arms. "It *feels* too easy. Why should that put me on edge?"

"Most things that appear too easy are often traps."

"Exactly. Yet you've seen no such signs?"

Idrus sighed. "No. Nothing."

"If you've not seen it, then it doesn't exist. We'll just have to do what we do best."

"Lay the trap ourselves."

"And kill every last rat we snare."

"Aye."

Mevon stared sideways at Idrus, just now noting the touch of bitterness that had been in his voice. "Don't worry. After today, my promotion is all but guaranteed." He laid a hand on Idrus's shoulder, leaning close. "And we'll all get a chance to let our blades drink."

Idrus looked away, shrugging from Mevon's grip.

Mevon pulled back. "What is it?"

Idrus took a long breath. "Progress, Mevon. Must it always be accompanied by the crunch of skulls underfoot?"

Mevon felt a chill at these words, like an icy mountain wind slashing across a summer day. The storm inside demanded blood, and these fools were thrusting their exposed necks at him. He had never hesitated to do his duty. *Never.* Why now, should Idrus's words disturb him?

"They'll soon notice that the sentries haven't reported back in." Idrus switched tunes suddenly, as he often did. The unspoken suggestion of urgency was not lost on Mevon.

Yet. . .

Idrus must have sensed his hesitation. "Should we nail the last plank on this bridge, or what?"

Mevon clenched his jaw and ground his teeth. The storm threatened to break. *Too soon.*

"Even when it's burning," said Mevon, completing the catechism. "Let no man say I don't finish what I start."

"Wouldn't dream of it." Idrus dashed past Mevon, joining the dozen other rangers concealed behind a copse of oak trees.

Mevon put aside all thoughts and breathed deeply, catching a salty scent from a Shelf-borne breeze. He stretched, feeling his thick yet flexible leather—once grey but now stained a mottled brown—conform to his muscles like a second skin.

He grasped his weapon and lifted it from its scabbard,

fixed across his back. Bringing it forward, Mevon twirled the double-bladed staff in rapid, whistling figure eights. Black and glossy, like obsidian, and adorned with thorns corkscrewing around the thick rod, Mevon's *Andun* came alive in his hands. Its twin edges, keen and bent into the shape of diamonds, bore the engraving of its name.

Justice.

Which it always delivered.

Mevon launched forward—walk into run into dash. Rocky soil passed beneath him in a blur, his boots pounding with each step. Speed brought him to his first victims.

Two men sat on a log, eating breakfast. Mevon slashed. His outstretched blade passed cleanly through both necks. Surprise masked both faces as the heads sailed through the air. The metallic scent of fresh blood drowned out the musk of sweat and the savor of fried sausage.

He followed through, blade drinking as it passed through the gut of a woman. Her entrails spewed upon the ground. Pained screams, like the shrieks of a mountain cat, broke the silence.

Two bandits swung axes at Mevon. He jabbed, impaling the first, then swept the rod up and caught the second man's haft. Mevon shot out a hand, closing it around the man's throat like a vise. The flesh crunched between his fingers like mud and broken twigs, and the body went slack. Mevon hurled the deadweight forward twenty paces, where it crashed into a tent, collapsing it.

Mevon looked down into the stone bowl carved out of the cliff's base.

Three hundred bandits looked back.

Come and get me.

With a cry, they brandished weapons and rushed at him.

He counted four heartbeats. Then, after forcing a look of panic onto his face, he whirled away into the forest. Somehow, he managed to keep the storm in check.

Only a little while longer. . .

Mevon zipped behind the first trunk thick enough to hide his bulk. He strained open his ears, anticipating that haunting sound of—

~snap-hiss-scream~

—his most cherished refrain. The Elite of his Fist, positioned in pincer formation, firing their first volley. Their enemy dying by the score.

The charge towards his position stalled as the mob turned, without order, to face these new threats. Mevon knew he was forgotten. Eighty men in full armor now commanded the bandits' attention. He spied his Fist's lines of dark green armor to the north and south, the front ranks a wall of heraldic shields, the back wielding crossbows fit for bringing down armored horses.

Mevon, once more, raced towards his enemy. Ten paces from their line, he finally unleashed the storm.

The world slowed. Mevon's acuity sharpened. Every breath, every flick of an eye, every muscle twitch—he could see it all.

Now, time to do what I was born for.

Thirteen arrows sped past his shoulders, released from the bows of Idrus and the rangers at a hundred paces. Each found a throat or eye or heart. The line of bandits wavered just as Mevon stepped among them.

He slashed at an upward angle, bisecting a bandit from hip to opposite shoulder. He watched in glee as great swaths of blood filled the air, coating his face, arms, and chest.

Step.

His *Andun* twirled in a vertical arc and sliced off the faces of men on either side of him.

Step.

He spun and eviscerated two on his left. Mevon smiled as they dropped their weapons and wrapped hands around their abdomens in a futile attempt to hold in their gushing organs.

Step.

He chopped downward, breaking an overhead block and cleaving through skull, neck, and breastbone. He vaulted over the falling corpse and tugged free his blade.

Step.

Three bandits lunged at him, the first coordinated assault yet. Mevon circled around their blades in half a breath, swiping to hack off their legs at the knee. He left them writhing.

Their screams joined others, a dissonant chorus that filled the rocky enclave. The battle became like a song. No—a symphony! His blades sang the melody, ringing out in a low, buzzing roar that grew in intensity with each severed soul, while cries of panic and agony from his enemies created a bittersweet harmony, all backdropped by the pounding rhythm of his Fist's relentless advance.

Beautiful.

Then, he felt it: a tingling, like a cloud of insects on the edge of perception, pulling his attention forward. The two casters were energizing. Soon, they would begin flinging sorcery at his Elite.

He sprinted, stepping on or through any who stood in his way and swinging his *Andun* in wide arcs. Blades scratched across his limbs, but few managed to pierce both armor and skin. He barely noticed the pain.

He came free of the crowd as the first spell flew.

An orb of blue flame exploded into the southern rank of his Elite. Two of his men staggered at the impact, and one fell. Men from the second rank pulled the injured man back. Another took up the downed man's shield and assumed the spot in front within two beats.

Despite this setback, his men held their lines on both sides. Crossbows continued to fire, and longswords snapped like wolf's teeth, devouring those rushing into their jaws. Their shields, without exception, were smeared with blood. Already, both sides had advanced a dozen paces, each step behind them a blanket of shredded flesh.

Mevon raced forward. The casters stood apart and he made for the leftmost one, a male. The other, a female, seemed to be struggling. Her hands moved, but she had yet to cast a single spell. *What holds you? Fear, perhaps?*

It doesn't matter—your time will come soon enough.

The male saw Mevon and waved a hand in his direction. The ground between them began to churn and crack as threads of darkness snaked towards him. They reached up towards Mevon, like black claws closing onto prey—

—and vanished.

The caster jolted from the backlash, fear and panic sprouting on his face. Mevon laughed. *Never encountered a Hardohl before, have you?* He had no idea what went through sorcerers' minds the moment they discovered their magic was useless against him.

Mevon closed. The sorcerer aimed his palms at his own chest and gestured towards himself, dashing backward twenty paces in an instant. A strange residue, like dust the shade of midnight, marked his passage.

Mevon was almost impressed. Almost. Most of his targets simply folded up helplessly once they realized what he was. This one, at least, promised to make it sporting.

Good.

The caster raised his arms wide. Rocks and pieces of strewn camp equipment lifted into the air and careened towards Mevon. He ducked, dodged, and smacked away every makeshift projectile, never ceasing his forward momentum.

Face flushed with effort, the sorcerer waved towards a man-high rock, nudging it into motion directly in Mevon's path. Then, he turned and began gesturing backwards once more.

Mevon leapt. The boulder tumbled beneath his feet. In a single motion, he released his *Andun*, grabbed a pair of heavy-bladed daggers at his belt, and flung them forward. He aimed not for the sorcerer but for a point directly behind him.

The man appeared from out of his shadow-dash exactly where Mevon had anticipated. No—not exactly, but a hand's width to one side. *Scorch me!* Mevon had intended for the twin blades to pierce the man's arms, rendering them useless. Instead, one dagger missed entirely.

The other struck deep into the caster's heart.

Mevon silently berated himself for the throw. He would have liked to bring both of them in alive in order to face public execution. His mierothi masters loved such displays, especially Emperor Rekaj. Mevon didn't loiter, though, sparing barely a glance for the falling body, and not a moment's regret. One still remained, and one rat on the Ropes was better than none.

He kicked Justice up into his hands and trotted over to the girl. As of yet, she had made no hostile moves. Perhaps she would come quietly. He stopped a dozen paces away, soothing the storm to a low rumble.

"By order of the emperor," said Mevon, "you are under arrest for violation of Sanction." He stepped forward and lowered his voice in pitch and volume. "Don't be a fool. You know you don't have a chance of fighting free."

He stepped again. Her hands were paused halfway through some complex spell. Pointless, but she didn't seem to know it. A fierce defiance showed on her face, and she stood straight and firm. He admired her for it but was amused all the same.

"Perhaps I am a fool." The sorceress glanced at her dead compatriot. A single tear rolled down her cheek. "But you, Mevon Daere, aren't as clever as you think."

What? How does she know—?

She gestured forward. A wave of dark energy shot out and wrapped around Mevon, not quite touching him.

He smirked, waiting for realization to dawn on her. Instead . . .

He sank to the ground. Lassitude stole into every muscle, and he crumpled, limp and slack-jawed. The storm vanished like a puff of mist before a gale. Hot bile coated his throat as his stomach emptied. In shame, he even lost hold on his bowels.

"How?" he tried to say, but failed. All that came out was a pathetic, guttural moan.

This can't be possible . . . can't be. . .

"The truth," she said. "It's not as simple as the mierothi have led you to believe."

Ruul's light, he wanted to kill her! More than anything, more than any desire he had ever felt, he ached to wrap his hands around her throat and watch the light fade from her eyes.

She held him there, he knew not how long. The moment stretched. Beats became marks. The fetid aroma of his own vomit nearly choked him. He felt like gagging but lacked the strength for it. He was entirely powerless, entirely at her mercy. His hatred for her deepened.

What are you waiting for?

To his surprise, no killing blow came. He couldn't imagine why she would hesitate. As awful as he felt, he was sure he wasn't dying, yet no answer was forthcoming. Rather—eventually—her breaths became labored, and her arms began shaking. A moment later, they dropped to her sides.

The spell receded from Mevon, and strength returned at once. He jumped up. Crossed the distance between them in half a beat. Lashed out a fist.

A single word she had spoken echoed in his mind. *"Truth."*

The blow was aimed to crush her face in. He diverted it at the last moment, glancing against her temple instead. She flew several paces and sprawled on the ground, unmoving.

The battle at large ended quickly. The discipline, coordination, and raw brutality of his Elite proved the victor over numbers. Decisively. His mind barely registered the last vestiges of resistance being cut down without mercy.

He stood, looking down at the girl.

And shook.

GILSHAMED STOOD ON the fortlet's battlements, studying the stones held in the cradle of his hands.

A breeze whipped his golden hair across his face, carrying the mingled scents of ash, sweat, and charred flesh. Men milled below him, excited banter drifting up from the victors. Those in chains sat numbly in silence. Casters—those with the strength left to stand—bustled about, administering healing to the wounded and dousing the last of the flames blazing through the barracks. Behind him lay a rolling landscape nestled between two soaring segments of the Godsreach Mountains. Gnarled trees like ancient hands poked up, bending over to grab with short, sharp leaves any who dared pass too close.

But it was the stones in his hands that consumed his attention.

One was warm, smooth, and glowed at its center. Solid

and strong. *Life.* The other was cold and brittle and dark. Were he to clench his hand into a fist, it would crumble to flakes and be carried off on the wind. *Death.*

The first filled him with elation. Jasside had made it; alive, and now in Mevon's care. Well, not in his *care* as such, but at least in his *presence.* And, for Gilshamed's purposes, that was enough.

The second filled him with sorrow. Or, rather, it should have. The hope held in the first, however, pushed out all thoughts of despair. What time did he have to mourn the dead? Death came to all, eventually. Most men could do far worse than to make their death meaningful, to die for a cause greater than oneself.

And what greater cause could there be than that of freedom?

Gilshamed snorted. *O, great pondering. The favorite pastime of we who linger on, staggering through so many human lifetimes as if they were naught but a candle's flame—faint illumination, all too quickly snuffed out.*

He sighed, dismissing his pointless cogitations. He had work to do.

Gilshamed placed the stones back into the pockets of his white robe and gazed at the yard below. A familiar figure strode towards him.

"Hey! Golden boy!" called the man. "Care to lend a hand? Or are they too busy there beneath your robes?"

Several of the shepherds barked laughter at this, darting glances back and forth between Gilshamed and the source of the jest. Though they carried naught but a quarterstaff, these men and women—some actual shepherds in truth—had conducted themselves superbly in their first engagement with Imperial forces.

Gilshamed waved. "Ho, Yandumar. I would not worry overmuch about my hands whilst yours are as filthy as a beggar's."

Yandumar sauntered towards Gilshamed's perch, the corner of his lips reaching for his ears. Tangled grey locks swung down past the man's blocky shoulders, and mischief shone in his emerald eyes. A bushy grey beard hung down to the center of his chest. He stood head and neck taller than most men, only two fingers short of Gilshamed's own height, and carried an arsenal of weapons about his person that jangled with each sure step.

"Filthy? Ha!" Yandumar held up his hands for inspection. "This is what us mortals call 'hard work.' Ever heard of it, old man?"

"Indeed I have, yet it appears our respective definitions are somewhat disparate."

Yandumar was treading a ramp that led up to the wall where Gilshamed was standing. "You call what you do hard? All that silly hand waving? Don't know as I'd use that word to describe it. Maybe something like—"

" 'Impressive'?"

" 'Ostentatious.' "

"Is that so?" Gilshamed grinned. "Do you even know what that word means?"

"Eh? Well . . . , no. Not really. But I'm sure it fits you perfectly."

Yandumar stepped up next to him, and Gilshamed laid a hand on his friend's shoulder. His other arm swept over the pentagonal courtyard, the scene of their first victory. "I think that with results like this, we have earned the right to some measure of pride. How many met their gods today?"

Yandumar's visage became grave. "Of our men, only four gave their lives."

"And of the garrison?"

"One. Poor fellow looked fine, so he was passed up for healing. Later, he just dropped dead. Must've been some kinda head wound." He perked up with a crooked smile. "Then we have the daeloth."

They both swiveled their heads. Six corpses had been dragged into a line, their forms charred·and smoking. Daeloth: half-breed spawn of mierothi. They looked human at first glance, but their mahogany skin and the scales on their backs set them apart. Bred for combat, they utilized both sorcery and martial aptitude to command the empire's armies and to ensure that no one ever forgot who the true rulers of this shrouded continent were.

Yandumar growled laughter. "Your tangle with them was . . . uh . . . Oh all right, I'll say it. It was impressive. Mighty impressive. Shepherds are already saying you smote them bastards like the hand of Elos himself!"

Gilshamed looked back, remembering the bright yellow lightning forking out from his fingertips, striking down each daeloth in its red-and-black armor, yet leaving the men around them untouched. The power they commanded was feeble, and their skill was a flaccid thing. None had so much as singed him with their counterattacks.

"Of course," continued Yandumar, "I don't suspect they were too difficult an opponent for ya', eh? You got in plenty of scraps with full mierothi back in your day, after all."

Gilshamed looked down; his eyes lost focus on the world around him. "Yes."

A key turned in his mind, unlocking a door that now flung wide open. *Elos guard me* . . . Into this room his inner eye dove, awakening ancient memories that had long lain dormant.

The War of Rising Night, as it was known to his people, the valynkar, burst forth into a collage of vivid images. Images of fire and blood and war. Images of victory!

But soon they seemed to melt like fresh paint under rain, becoming something else entirely. Ice and fear and darkness.

Defeat.

Gilshamed quivered as the depth of his failure crashed into him. As remembrance came of allies fallen, hopes crushed . . .

. . . loves lost . . .

Gilshamed retreated from the room in his mind and slammed the door. *No more, please. I cannot bear it right now.*

"You alright, Gil?"

The words snapped him back to the present. Over several beats, his eyes regained clarity of his surroundings. The pain from his deeply buried memories faded away like mist before the rising sun, and a smile sprouted on his lips.

"Fine, Yan. I am fine now. I was merely reminiscing."

"Right. I forget how your kind gets sometimes. Makes me glad I'll never live for thousands of years."

Gilshamed nodded, beginning between them a long moment of silence. Over the last six years, he had grown to cherish such times. Yandumar, he suspected, shared in this feeling. With consternation writ plain on his face, Yan finally said, "You about ready to finish this day's business?"

Dread welled up inside Gilshamed as he took up the yoke of his next task. "Get everyone outside the walls but ensure the prisoners have an unobstructed view."

"Aye." Yandumar trotted down the ramp, heading towards their troops to begin administering the orders.

Gilshamed remembered the stones lying nearly forgotten in his robes. "Oh, and Yan," he called. Yandumar paused and spun back. "I am happy to report success on our other endeavors. Jasside has initiated contact with Mevon."

Yandumar appeared thoughtful for a moment but said nothing. He merely nodded before turning away once more.

In three marks, the yard was cleared. Yandumar corralled the former inhabitants of the fortlet just outside the open gates.

Gilshamed lifted his eyes to the center of the compound. He had averted his gaze from the structure there up to this point, and had noticed most others doing the same. Something about it just seemed . . . wrong.

And it was—which was why he had come here to do what must be done.

The towering needle stabbed the sky, impossibly thin. When looked at directly, it appeared a deep grey, seemingly of harmless stone and lacking in mark or adornment. When viewed in the peripheral . . . a swirling silver mien of chaos, like a black-and-white-tile mural. Only the tiles flickered between colors so fast, they blurred in a dizzying display. The mierothi had outdone themselves in the creation of the voltensus, these towers that monitored all sorcery in the empire. Their dark god Ruul must surely be pleased, for the five constructs served as his eyes and ears. And perhaps . . . something else?

Time to find out what.

He had prepared a speech, something inspiring, telling of the valynkar people and how they had been wrongfully banished nearly two millennia ago. How the mierothi, cowering from the world behind the Shroud all this time, had reigned in tyranny long enough. How his return must surely herald their inevitable downfall. How . . .

But the words fled from his mind as his eyes took in the voltensus. There was something foreboding about the tower, inimical even. As he examined it, he was overcome with the sensation that even as he gazed at it, the tower was studying him, too.

Is it possible this thing is alive? Even . . . aware?

He shook himself. No time to waste. He spared a glance for the assembled mass, all of whom were staring back at him. Yandumar stood foremost among them. His face projected an aura of confidence, of faith. Gilshamed drew strength from it. *My friend, I am unworthy of you.*

Eying the stone roof of the nearest guard tower, Gilshamed arched his back, flexing muscles that only his people possessed.

From his spine sprouted wings.

They shone with a brilliant light, illuminating the stunned faces of all gathered below. Focused now, he launched himself skyward. His ethereal wings fluttered silently and lifted him up to land on top of the guard tower.

Here, at last, he found his voice but decided to save his grand speech for another day. He simply said, "Bear witness, you privileged few. And remember this day."

Retracting his wings, he pivoted to face the voltensus. He swept away his fear and pushed his will into its place. Will, after all, was the true essence of sorcery. The incantations, the waving of hands, the rituals—nothing more than means of focusing one's will.

He opened himself to the spirit of Elos, and energized.

Power flooded into him, sweet yet raging, begging for release. It seemed to emanate both from inside him and from everywhere else all at once. He pitied those who never had the privilege of tasting this pure manifestation of light.

The voltensus loomed before him. Gilshamed extended both hands towards it and pushed.

The needle groaned and quivered as his sorcery slammed into it. But it did not topple. Not even close.

Gilshamed pulled back his power and recharged. He pressed forward again, but delicately, probing. With thin tendrils, he brushed against it, like the tickle of a feather.

There had to be a weakness somewhere. Nothing crafted by the hands of men was without flaw . . .

There you are.

It was a hairline crack, nothing more than the space between mortals and their gods. It was enough. He honed his power into razors of will and shoved it into the fracture.

And something pushed back.

Gilshamed recoiled. It *was* alive. More than that, it was aware. Aware, and startled by his intrusion. No, not startled. *Terrified.* He could use that, exploit it. He would not let it get away, not when he was so close.

He charged forward, pressing against the presence once more. This time he did not pause but forced his way deeper. The entity writhed and raged, but its fear made it weak. Gilshamed sliced and scraped and hammered with his power.

The being strained, shook, and finally . . .

The voltensus burst, a million molten fragments careening in all directions.

The concussion threw Gilshamed from the tower. The dying soul lashed out, striking deeply, seeking to drag Gilshamed down with it into the abyss. Even as he fell, his physical state forgotten, Gilshamed fought with desperation to withstand this assault. He wrestled for control of his own life, his own soul, all against a being with nothing to lose.

Somehow, he held on.

With one last scream, like the horrified cries of a legion of tortured children, the entity tore away into death. Gilshamed felt himself immediately revived. Whole, once more.

And then he slammed into the ground.

The air fled from his lungs, and darkness closed in around his vision. *Hold on . . . just a little longer. This is a moment of triumph. I can't . . . I won't. . .*

Pulling on his last reserves, he forced his mind to stay active, his eyes to stay open. He sucked in one breath. Then another.

Someone was shouting. A face floated in front of his, indistinct. Over time—he knew not how long—his senses sloughed towards coherence once more.

Yandumar hovered over him, his beard hanging down to tickle Gilshamed's face. His friend patted him gently and called his name.

The sky above swirled with strange swaths of darkness. Gilshamed shook his head, thinking them black spots in his vision from the blow to his skull. But no, they lingered still. *Ah, darkwisps.* Thousands retreated in all directions from the empty husk of the voltensus.

A chill shot up his spine, and he knew then what the voltensus truly was.

By Elos! What have the mierothi done? What has Ruul?

All his careful planning, the years of scouring this continent for knowledge and allies—none of it had prepared him for this.

"Gil? You all right?"

Gilshamed blinked up at Yandumar. "Fine," he croaked. "Just fine. Help me up. Please."

Yandumar obliged, hefting him into a standing position with welcome tenderness. "You sure you're all right? You took a nasty fall there."

Gilshamed clung to his companion for balance. "I am well, Yan. Truly. The injuries to my body are the least of my concerns now."

Yandumar furrowed his brow and studied him. Slowly, he shook his head. "If you say so."

Gilshamed looked over the prisoners. Awe and wonder clung to each rapt visage. A good start. But the voltensus . . .

"Never again, Yan." Gilshamed lowered his eyes. "We must revise our plans."

"Of course."

One voltensus destroyed. It would have to be enough. They had the empire's attention now and would make use of this opportunity as best they could. Other portions of his grand scheme were in motion, not least of all Jasside's task. It could still work. It *would*.

Ideas floated about, unformed. He left them to stew. There would be time later.

"Yandumar?"

"Yes?"

"Help me to a bed?"

"Right."

VOREN'S BRUSHSTROKES BEAT a steady cadence against the canvas, pausing only to dip into globs of vibrant paint to be renewed in color, in life, in power. Power to translate reality into dream, dream into emotion, and emotion—transcending comprehension—into its own newly expressed reality.

He sat back on his padded stool, satisfied, for the moment, with his work. He was balanced upon a round ledge that thrust out towards the center of a hemispherical glass window twenty paces in diameter. Through it, he viewed the landscape south of this place: palace, fortress, and—to Voren—prison. It sat at the crown of Mecrithos, the heart of the empire.

Having mastered the style of perfect representation centuries past, Voren was attempting a new technique. He played both artist and observer, both inspiration and interpretation, soaking in and squeezing out, simultaneously.

Thus, the western horizon, where the mountains had recently swallowed the sun, became a maelstrom of fire into which jagged boulders wept tears of stone. The eastern sky, faded to night, became needles stabbing through black waves. The ochre plains became a wellspring of blood. The cliffs nearest—just outside the palace grounds, where darkwisps had begun emerging for their nightly revelries—became a web of ghostly chains.

Something new emerged on the scene, drawing Voren's attention. It was a pinprick of yellow light dancing on the cliff's edge. Curious, he narrowed his gaze on the object.

A brightwisp? Here? By Elos, where did you come from?

He had not seen one since—gods, it must have been half again a millennium, not long after the mierothi had eradicated the last sorcerer carrying vestiges of his people's valynkar blood.

How had this brightwisp survived all this time? It

must have drifted alone, scared, avoiding all contact, a journey worthy of its own grand telling, he was sure. The creature grew brighter as it approached. Voren's breath caught in his throat.

Have you something to tell me? Some last secret to share? Have you been carrying it all this time?

But then he saw the darkwisps. In their cavorting, a mass of them had drifted into the brightwisp's path.

They were intertwined now, swaying in a most macabre dance. The two disparate entities repulsed from each other, the brightwisp bouncing back and forth as darkwisps, each in turn, drew closer. But the lone point of light was surrounded, with nowhere left to retreat, and the hovering clouds of darkness, despite flinching as they neared, spun inexorably into a tighter and tighter circle.

It was only a matter of—

The darkwisps surged forward, spitting arcs of black-purple energy between them. And yet, the brightwisp . . . expanded. Not content, it seemed, simply to fall prey, it exploded in a shower of sparks, sending tendrils of a familiar power through its assailants.

Voren blinked against the sudden flash. When his vision cleared, two darkwisps fled the scene of destruction. All others, as the brightwisp, were no more.

A stone took hold of Voren's gut, and tears carved rivers down his cheeks. He shook, wondering why he felt so deeply for such a creature. *It is scarcely alive, much less sentient. Why, then?* Was it the loneliness of its journey? The despair of its death? The symbol of a past best left forgotten?

How much it reminded Voren of himself?

Metal on wood rattled against his ears from behind. Voren swung his waist-length hair, midnight blue and silky, around and quickly dried his face. He breathed deeply, composing himself, as the main door to his chambers—his cell—opened.

A single figure entered, wrapped in a dun-colored cloak.

"Voren," the figure said. "It is good to see you."

"Draevenus?" Voren said. "I did not think you would be here so soon this evening." He descended the stairs holding up his perch and strode towards his guest. Of all the mierothi, this was the only one Voren did not mind paying him a visit.

Thumb-sized scales of deepest purple framed a pale, boyish face. These scales, Voren knew, encompassed the whole of every mierothi body, granting them an appearance more akin to fish than men. Deep crimson irises and whites that were anything but—green or blue or silver, depending on which way the light hit them—gazed up at Voren amiably. Fingerless gloves ended in thick, sharp claws.

"I can go if you are busy," Draevenus said.

"Nonsense. You are always welcome to what pitiful hospitality I can offer."

Draevenus smiled, revealing pointed teeth. He snatched a bottle off the wine rack near the entrance. "Yes, you have only the *third* best wine in all the empire. Pitiful indeed."

Voren couldn't help but laugh, amazed at how quickly

his tears were forgotten. He stepped up to his cabinet, extracting a pair of glasses. "A drink before we begin?"

"Need you even ask?" The mierothi handed over the bottle as if presenting gift. Voren took it and poured.

They settled into padded chairs across from each other at Voren's table and raised their cups. "A toast," Voren said. "To the least offensive mierothi I know."

"And to the most tactful valynkar I know."

Sharing a grin, they each drank deep.

"Now," said Voren, "what questions do you have for me?"

"Tonight, only one. But I truly don't know how long your answer will take."

"It's to be that kind of question, is it? In that case, I demand you tell your story first."

"And if I refuse?"

"I'll be forced to take drastic measures." Voren leaned forward. "I'll only serve you the empire's fourth best wine."

Draevenus's eyes widened in mock alarm. "Well then . . . a story it is."

They both burst into laughter.

When they had composed themselves, a feat aided by several long sips each, Draevenus waved an arm towards Voren. "What kind of tale would you like to hear?"

Voren smiled. "Tell me about innocence."

The mierothi paused, taking a few deep breaths. "I was in the Agoritha plains a few years ago. A bit of a bland-looking country, but peaceful all the same. I was walking through some nameless town looking for supplies. Out of nowhere, I felt something collide hard with my leg.

"I glanced down to see this little girl flat on her bottom in the middle of the lane, rubbing her forehead. Poor thing was dazed enough, but when she looked up to see who she had run into, her face took on a look—and I'll never forget this—that was both confused and angry at the same time, like I was something from a dream and had no right to be in the actual real world.

"Her mother snatched her up in an instant, of course, apologizing as much with horror as she did with reverence. I almost told her not to worry, no harm done. I'm not sure if it would have made any difference."

"What happened next?" Voren asked.

Draevenus waited several long beats before replying. "You asked for a story of innocence, Voren. If I continue, the tale will no longer fit that criterion."

The pleasant tingle he felt from the wine evaporated in an instant. Voren knew that death was the least of the punishments given for striking a mierothi and that most town guards would, in order to prove their zeal, enact such sentences before the offended party could even blink.

Voren set down his wineglass. Draevenus's orations were the only window he had to the outside world. He'd had enough of stories for one night. "Tell me your question."

Draevenus stared, clicking his claws against the table. Moving with all the speed of a man on his deathbed, he grasped his wineglass, brought it to his lips, and drained the remaining liquid. Voren felt dread welling up, stronger with each passing moment that remained in silence.

At last, the mierothi licked his lips. "You've told me just about everything that you know about the valynkar over these last few months. All that is left to know is this: If your people gained the ability to return to this empire, what would they do?"

Voren closed his eyes, struggling not to succumb to the depths of his youth, of the time before he had become a prisoner of the mierothi. It was not difficult. Such memories were few.

"I do not know," Voren said. "It seemed I understood my people little, even back when I was among them. With nearly two millennia to set us apart, I cannot even begin to fathom what they might do."

Draevenus tightened his jaw into a humorless grin, exhaling loudly through his nose. "I see."

"I am sorry. I know that was probably not very helpful."

"No, no, it was a truthful answer, which is more useful than baseless speculation. To be honest, I did not know what I was expecting." He stood.

"Leaving so soon?" Voren asked.

"Yes. And I am afraid this will be my last visit for quite some time."

"Why?"

Draevenus sighed. "It is difficult to explain. Something has begun, and I must now be about . . . other tasks."

"I trust all is well?"

Draevenus ground his teeth. "We shall see."

"I am sorry to see you depart," said Voren, surprised by the truth in those words. "I have grown fond of these visits of yours. You, out of all your people, at least have the wit to carry on a decent conversation. And you have made a most . . . peculiar student."

"True enough. Sadly, my education regarding your people is at an end. Though it was enjoyable while it lasted."

"Well, I hope you learned enough to satisfy your curiosity. If I may, what was it, exactly, that you were hoping to discover?"

The question was tame enough, by Voren's estimation, but seemed to impact Draevenus more thoroughly than intended. The mierothi's eyes glazed over, looking through Voren into a world of introspection that could only be guessed at.

After a half dozen beats, Draevenus shook his head. "I tend to take the long view of things, Voren."

Voren waited patiently for more. When it became apparent that no further explanation was forthcoming, he ventured softly with, "Our kind often do."

The austere visage now facing him reminded Voren that, despite his youthful appearance, Draevenus was nearly as old as he. And the weighted throwing dagger, which Draevenus danced absently across the back of his knuckles, reminded Voren that he used to be the most feared assassin on the planet.

Voren gestured at the blade. "Planning on putting your old skills to use?"

Draevenus's eyes flashed. The dagger vanished up a sleeve. "No." Then, on the very threshold of hearing, he added, "Not if I can help it."

"I see. Of course, I have found that, in many situations, such choices are often beyond our control."

"Control. That word . . ." Draevenus shivered. "It can break the world . . . Bring the heavens crashing down . . . *Burn* the very heart out of you . . ."

Gods above and below! What could you possibly *be heading into?* Whatever it entailed, Voren did not envy Draevenus his journey. His own status as a prisoner of modest privilege seemed, at the moment, a paltry burden.

Voren reached for the glasses and wine bottle. "Here Draevenus, one more drink before you go?" It was, on short notice, the only distraction he could think of.

"No time now. I am sorry." Draevenus turned to leave.

Voren, unthinking, held out a hand, as if to grab ahold of his companion. *Companion?* The idea that a mierothi—*any* mierothi—could claim this title in his mind drove the very breath from his lungs. In that moment, Voren realized that in nineteen hundred years of imprisonment he had not encountered a single other soul whom he would consider a friend. The thought of Draevenus's leaving began tearing a hole in Voren's long-held defenses.

"Draevenus?" he called tentatively.

The mierothi swung back halfway, raising an inquisitive brow.

Voren swallowed before continuing. "Be well on your travels, my . . . friend."

Draevenus nodded. "Keep your head down, Voren. If I don't make it back, before this is all over . . ." He trailed off, as if he had caught himself about to reveal some dire secret. But no—he was staring at something ahead of him. Voren stepped to the side in order to see what held his attention.

Emperor Rekaj stood in the doorway.

"Draevenus," the emperor said, his voice like stones raked across a woven basket. "I thought I made it clear that you were no longer welcome here."

"I'm leaving right now, Rekaj," Draevenus replied.

Voren, in silence, examined the two mierothi males as they regarded each other. Rekaj stood a hand taller than the younger Draevenus, though still twice that short of Voren's height, and possessed a face with none of the younger mierothi's smoothness. Draevenus quivered, ever so slightly, like a pressed coil waiting to release. A hunter crouched for the killing leap. Rekaj, too, seemed to notice this stance. With one hand stroking the long dagger at his belt, the emperor laughed.

"Best get to it then, boy." Rekaj stepped aside, waving towards the open door behind him.

Draevenus sighed. "Until next time, Voren." With that, he strode from the room, slamming it shut behind him.

Leaving Voren alone with the emperor.

"Most honored one." Voren bowed at the waist until his torso was parallel with the ground, hoping the brush of mockery in his tone went unnoticed.

"Why was Draevenus here?" asked Rekaj. "What business did he have with you?"

Voren frowned. "He . . . . merely wished to say good-bye."

"Good-bye?"

"Yes."

The emperor furrowed his brow at this but waved a dismissive hand. "No matter."

A knuckle rapped on the door, and one of Voren's daeloth minders poked his head in. "Emperor," he said, "I have word from—"

"Stuff your message!" Rekaj said. "And you tell the council that *they* await *my* pleasure, not the other way around!"

Eyes wide, the daeloth jerked a nod and departed.

Gods, please, do not lose your temper. Voren shuddered, remembering the last time he had witnessed the emperor's wrath unleashed. Thankfully, it had not been aimed at him. This time, however . . .

Best be exemplary in manner. Just in case.

"Emperor, I am, as ever, your humble servant," Voren said, careful to refrain from even a whisper of insubordination, glad his subtle insolence from before had been missed. "What was it you wished to see me about?"

Rekaj breathed deeply, seeming to calm somewhat, Voren hoped. "Yes. There is one small matter I wish to discuss with you." He brushed smooth his black-and-red-silk attire—the vestments of his station. "There was . . . that is to say, did you feel anything unusual today?"

Voren fought the urge to shudder. He'd never seen the emperor so perturbed and did not know what to expect. "Unusual? How so?"

"As in . . . sorcerous disturbance."

Voren thought to the recent event between the wisps.

Could that be what he was referring to? It did not seem likely.

"No," replied Voren after a few moments. "I felt nothing today that could qualify as 'disturbance,' sorcerous or otherwise. What is this all about?"

The emperor ignored the question, clasping his hands behind his back, and began strolling aimlessly, eyes glazed over. Voren knew better than to disturb him during one of these fugues, for he was well familiar with what was happening behind Rekaj's blank expression.

Reality had to be placed on hiatus, after all, if one wished to access ancient memories.

Something happened, something new. Yet, it is connected to something so very old? None of the possibilities reassured him. Voren did not need to access his own memories to know there was little from his past he would wish to see returned.

The emperor swiveled back to Voren, features firmly back in the present. "Tell me one thing, then. Have you entered communion lately?"

"Communion? No, of course not." He chuckled, half from nerves, half from disbelief. "I would have no one to talk to, naturally. Unless, of course, one of my kin somehow found a way through the Shroud." The sheer absurdity of the suggestion drove him into even greater fits of laughter. "Whatever would compel you to ask such a thing?"

Rekaj narrowed his gaze on Voren. "Nothing. Mind your place. It is *not* to question me."

Voren's mirth was swept away like feathers before a

storm. Feeling a chill start to creep up his spine, he bowed his head in obeisance.

The emperor stormed out. Voren was left alone, and an abundance of questions swirled in his head, none of which he could even begin to answer. Whatever had happened, it meant *change*. Voren had almost forgotten what the word meant, so absorbed as he was in playing the harmless, obedient prisoner. But how long can such a mask be worn before the act is no longer a fiction?

Shame flooded his soul as he realized just how empty it had become.

VASHODIA STROLLED ALONG the Chasm's edge at the cusp of night. She soaked in the burgeoning darkness like a lizard did the sun on a cold day. She was separated from the brink by a mere finger's width, but she feared neither falling nor the hungry maw of depthless shadow below.

It was her home, after all.

She spied her destination and began skipping along. She held apart the folds of her robe, which was so dark as to seem a part of the night itself. It was, in fact, enchanted just for this effect. No, not *enchanted*—such a word was used by the ignorant, which was everyone but her. Rather, it was *augmented*. Yes, a much more accurate description.

The path before her ended abruptly, cleaved by a deep ravine a dozen paces across that bent and twisted its way up into the barren hillsides to the east. Without hesitation, Vashodia marched off into the void.

Falling, she energized briefly and formed a cushion

of air below her feet as thick as stone—no, again she corrected herself. It *was* stone. There. She crafted ropes and tethered one end of each to the cliff top, and the other to the platform upon which she now stood. Her descent slowed. She lengthened the ropes to allow for brisk yet controlled passage down.

Though the night was dark, it was not pure. Not even close. It was a passive thing, beset by two moons and a cacophony of stars. Vapid, hollow.

The darkness into which she now passed was everything night was not. It . . . filled, with intention and rapacity. The dark energy gathered here, thick as foam, made her giggle in delight.

At last, Vashodia reached the ground. A vast cavern opened up, the ends so distant even her mierothi eyes had trouble discerning its scope. What filled it, though, not even humans could fail to see.

Darkwisps. A hundred thousand at least.

"Knock-knock," she said in a high, singsong voice. "Anybody home?"

The normally dormant creatures buzzed into a frenzy of activity at her intrusion. They spun through the air, converging on a point several paces in front of her. They stopped, though, afraid to come closer.

They had learned that lesson the hard way.

She reached into her robe and brought forth two spherical objects. They were the size of her fist and crafted from a dull metal, closer to the look of burnished stone than the glint of a sword. She tossed them on the ground. The hovering mass of darkwisps flinched back.

That will do you no good, my little friends.

Vashodia spoke, and though her voice seemed that of a young girl—matching her face and the size of her body—her tone left no doubt that she was, in fact, commanding.

"Come, darkwisps.

"Come, death-sighs of watered souls.

"Come, machines of a sundered past."

Vashodia paused and giggled once more.

"Come to your new home, you naughty little things."

The spheres opened up, revealing a hollow center. The mass of sparking creatures began slowly descending, contracting.

"Are you watching?" she said. "Ruul? Elos? Can you see?"

Darkwisps now flowed like a stream into the spheres.

"Ah, but what use is sight if you are lacking in *vision*?"

They drew in on themselves, collapsing into a point like a flake of ash, and huddled inside.

"And so, the first day ends. A day long striven for. And all the boys and girls dance to every twitch upon their strings. But who holds those strings?"

The spheres reached their capacity and closed. The remaining darkwisps scuttled away, as if in relief that they had escaped her prison. This time, anyway.

"NO ONE!"

The spheres jumped to her hands and disappeared once more into the pockets of her robes.

Finally, she whispered, "And isn't that the cruelest joke of all."

Chapter 2

MEVON STARED AT the back of the sorceress's green robe, stained now by dirt and sweat. The summer still held strong this far north, and despite the high elevation of the mountain passes, the past two days of riding had seen them all drenched and reeking by noon. Now, as they left behind the narrow trails and descended onto plains of ochre grasses, the days would grow even warmer, and the welcome gusts of glacial wind would cease.

The Fist spread out, like fingers long clenched now unfolding. Mevon could see the tension wane as the men expanded into a broad circle, each mounted man now with room to breathe without fear of inhaling someone else's stench. Quake, his loyal draft horse, tossed his ash-colored mane in approval.

He and his captains stayed in the center. Ahead of them rode four of his Elite, crossbows held in a manner that would only seem casual to the untrained eye. Between them, the sorceress. His low-burning fury flared as he watched her sway on her borrowed horse.

Her arms were tied behind her. Dirty blond hair fell down her back, straight and long. No one would ever call her fat, but her short, plump form hinted at a softness that he did not consider unpleasant. Nothing about her seemed threatening in the least.

Still, Mevon had yet to speak to her.

He was not a slave to fear, as so many were. No, that had been beaten out of him at a young age by his masters. Once he learned just how little anyone—casters especially—could do to harm him, fear became a thing only the weak knew.

He had been four when he first witnessed the death of a sorcerer. The man had been pitted against one of the older students. A test for one, a lesson for the rest. Mevon never forgot what he saw that day, and spent every moment of the next six years in eager anticipation of his own trial. His first kill. And in the thousand since then, his courage had not faltered. Not even once.

Until now.

She was . . . impossible. A caster's inability to directly affect a Hardohl was one of the few truths he knew to be indisputable. What had she done? How had she done it? Why had she done it to *him*—he felt sure he had been specifically targeted. What possible repercussions would there be for his kind, and the empire, if her secret was revealed? Mevon shuddered. He wasn't sure he wanted to know the answers.

He had two days to decide. By then, they'd be in Thorull, and she'd be taken out of his hands to be executed.

And Mevon, for the first time in his life, did not know what to do.

He stared at the woman's back and let his rage boil.

"Planning on shaving with that, Mevon?" asked Tolvar, riding up on his side.

Mevon jerked in his saddle. "What?" He followed his captain's gaze down to where his own hand rested, knuckles white over the handle of one dagger. Somehow, he had drawn it without realizing.

"I think not," said Arozir. He gestured ahead to the sorceress. "I would bet he means to finish what that blade began."

The weapon was the very same one Mevon had used to kill the sorcerer. He did his best to ignore the amused faces of his captains as he slammed the dagger back into its sheath. "Why I ever chose you two, I'll never know. At least Idrus pretends a little respect."

The ranger captain shrugged.

"We were a package deal, that's why," Tolvar said. "Being cousins, 'n' all."

"And a bargain at that," added Arozir.

"Only cost a few drops of that precious Hardohl blood to seal the deal."

"Though quite a bit more of ours."

Mevon remember the day of their trial well. He'd already trounced several applicant groups without a scratch, and had nearly given up on finding suitable men to join as his personal Elite. These three changed all that. Unarmed, he had faced them, and Idrus had managed to break his skin with a well-timed dagger throw. Such a move was only possible because Tolvar and Arozir, abandoning all sense of self-preservation, had thrown themselves at Mevon, wrapping themselves around his legs to keep him distracted.

"Aye. But it sure was worth it, eh?"

"Of course, Tolvar," Arozir said. "The last twelve years we spent sloughing through the woods, chasing criminals, and fighting off insects would have been so different from our fate had we remained in the army."

"Exactly. We'd have been doing all that, only without this fancy armor."

"And fancy weapons."

"And fancy women."

"And—wait. What women?"

As the two devolved into an argument over pay grades and the price of a "lady's" company, Idrus leaned in and whispered in Mevon's ear, "Let me remind you, though close relations to each other, they are rather distant from me."

"No reminder is needed," Mevon told him.

The truth of that was evident enough. Where Idrus was tall, lithe, and dark-haired, the other two were stocky, with heads topped by curly flame-red hair.

"Oh, come now," Arozir still argued with Tolvar. "You know the real reason we joined the Elite was because of the daeloth."

"Of course it was. Idiots couldn't strategize their way out of a stack of hay."

"And we'd much rather hunt casters down   "

" . . . than take orders from them."

Mevon grunted agreement.

"It's no wonder the empire has such a problem with bandits," said Arozir. "From lowest lieutenant to the supreme arcanod himself, the army's officers have failed to embrace what should be common sense to any fighting man."

Tolvar grinned. "'Know your enemy, else fall prey to the unseen danger.'"

To this, even Idrus acknowledged agreement.

Mevon sighed. As ridiculous as his captains' talk was, it had clarified much for him. He knew what he needed to do.

He tapped his heels into Quake's flanks, urging his mount into a trot. The four Elite nodded at Mevon as he drew close.

"Give me a moment," Mevon said. "It's time she and I had a . . . chat."

"Aye," they called. They flashed him knowing smirks and rode off to join the perimeter.

Mevon was alone with the sorceress, for the first time since she . . .

He shook his head and took one last look around to make sure no prying ears were in range. He had prepared a series of questions, but as he drew alongside her, they vanished from his mind. His pulse quickened as he remembered the image of her body standing, arms raised and holding her spell over him. Of his face pressed into the moist soil.

Of his weakness.

He leaned towards her, heat rising. "What did you *do* to me, woman?"

She swung her head to face him, took a deep breath, and smiled. "Jasside," she said. "Jasside Anglasco." She looked away, nose in the air—like she was a lady of some merchant family and offended by his presence. "Since you didn't bother to even ask my name, why should I bother answering you?"

"Because I can make your life very . . . unpleasant while you're in my care."

"Could you?" She leaned back, as if to get a more thorough view. She studied him, her eyes like honey on burnt bread, and twisted her plump lips in a gesture that said "unimpressed." "Being a killer is one thing, even if you enjoy it. But a torturer? Rapist? Murderer? I'd think even you would hesitate to cross those lines."

He clenched his jaw. "Three days ago, you would have been right." He spied her neck, so pale and fragile. He fought the urge to snap it like a twig. His hand twitched towards her, and he had to concentrate to keep from reaching out. "But I've learned things about myself since then. Now . . . ? Who knows what I'm capable of?"

He heard her sniff sharply. *Ah, am I getting through to you now?*

Jasside dipped her head. "Very well. I will tell you what you wish to know."

Mevon waited, shaking, and hated her all the more for it.

"Your blessings," she said. "I presume you know how they work?"

"How? No, not exactly. I just know they make it easier for me to do my job."

"Easier to kill others, you mean. Easier to live through injuries that would claim the lives of ordinary men."

"Yes—fine. What of it?"

She hid her face from him. In a whisper so low Mevon wasn't sure he was meant to hear it, she said, "Children with the power of gods . . . is there anything more horrifying?"

Jasside turned back. Unshed tears pooled in her eyes. Her lips quivered with an emotion Mevon knew well: rage. He looked down at the dagger in his hand, which had again removed itself from its sheath without his realizing.

Of course. The sorcerer.

"Your partner," Mevon said, "the one I killed. What was he to you?"

She trembled, sending a single tear down her freckled cheek. "He was my half brother. Though, we grew up together after—" She choked off her speech. Her jaw set, and she plunged forward without further hesitation. "But you were asking about your blessings. Well, when I was a little girl—"

Mevon clamped his hand down on her upper arm. She let out a sound like the squeak of a dying mouse. "Stop dissembling," he said. "Tell me what I want to know."

Jasside glanced frantically from his hand to his eyes as her breath became short and labored. Most casters panicked when cut off from their power, so her reaction didn't surprise him. He held her a few beats more, just to get his point across, before letting go.

"There is a gap in your natural defense against sorcery," she said, breathlessly. "And your blessings are the gateway."

"I find that difficult to believe."

'Then think, Mevon, for once in your life. And don't just bark the explanations given to you by those holding your leash."

"Watch your tongue, sorceress, else I'll rip it out."

She raised her chin. "Then my secrets die with me. If I'm on my way to die anyway, it's no burden for me to ride in silence the rest of the way."

Mevon, summoning willpower from the depths of his soul, slowly sheathed the dagger. "Abyss take you, woman." But he did wave for her to continue.

A look of satisfaction crossed her features but vanished quickly. She shrugged. "That's all I know, really. You're more familiar with the blessing process than I. You figure it out."

Her advice seemed genuine, even heartfelt, and he surprised himself by taking it.

For once, he *thought*.

Blessings were first bestowed upon infants within days of arrival at the Hardohl academy. They manifested as visual markings upon the back: white rose and black thorns. There was more, Mevon knew, something about blood binding and subdermal inscriptions, but he had never cared to pay attention to the specifics.

He only knew that two men prepared and bestowed every single blessing.

Emperor Rekaj, and his pet valynkar, Voren.

Does one of them know about this weakness? Or, worse . . . had they put it there?

Mevon clenched his jaw and narrowed his gaze on Jasside. "Where did you learn how to do this?"

She smiled. "I saw someone else do it first. And I *am* a fast learner."

"Who?"

"A mierothi. I never learned her name, but I watched as she was attacked by a Hardohl and did . . . what I did to you."

"Who was she? What did she look like?"

"She was short, almost childlike. And she had an amused if somewhat cruel smile on her face."

Mevon cringed. All Hardohl had a standing order to kill on sight one particular mierothi. He had no idea what she had done to earn the emperor's ire, but he knew more than one of his peers had disappeared after chasing rumors of her whereabouts. He knew her, even if Jasside did not.

Vashodia.

If she knows, then . . . who else? All of the mierothi?

More questions than he had begun with swirled around in his head. More fears. *The possible implications of this knowledge. . .*

No. He was letting his thoughts run wild, chasing darkwisps into the Chasm. He would do nothing until he knew more. But how could he? Who could he ask? They would put him on the Ropes for voicing the least of his questions.

He had no choice. He would keep silent.

And Jasside? Well, as she said, her silence was soon guaranteed to be permanent.

A FETID MIST drifted up from bog, coating skin and bark alike in its slick stench. Yandumar didn't mind, though, since the Imperial forces sent against them skirted the patch of marshland. Just as he had predicted.

Imperial tactics haven't changed much since I've been gone. Thank God for small blessings.

Yandumar lifted up from his crouch, wincing as his knees cracked. He knew it was a good thing he had found Gilshamed when he had. Another few years, and his old bones wouldn't have enough fight left in them to see this through. Not that such a thing would have stopped him. He took a vow, after all. And a vow made by one of his people never went unfulfilled.

But it would have been much more uncomfortable.

He glanced over at the valynkar, who stood with eyes closed, still as stone. With hair an impossibly golden gold, and skin so perfect it looked like porcelain, the unfamiliar observer would be hard-pressed to tell him apart from a statue. Yandumar had often seen him like that at night. Conserving his energy. He could still cast without the sun, it just took more out of him.

The Timid Moon flared to life above them. Gilshamed opened his eyes. "It is time," he said.

Yandumar ran his fingers through the grey beard hanging to the middle of his chest. "Right. So, how's this going to work again?"

Gilshamed shot his head over, locking his eerie golden eyes on him. "Did you not pay attention when I explained to the others?"

"I was listening—I promise I was! But all that wizardry talk sounds like monkey babble to me. No offense."

Gilshamed sighed. "Very well. I shall endeavor to explain in terms even a monkey could understand."

"Ha! Fair enough."

Gilshamed pointed to the object in Yandumar's hand, a metal sphere. It had a band around it with a hinge on one side and a clasp on the other. "That is our link." Gilshamed held up his own hand, which held an identical device. "So long as we both have possession of these, I will be able to direct my sorcery on you, as if you were me."

"All right, I think I got that part. What exactly will you be doing, though?"

"I will maintain several effects at once, actually. First will be what I call 'light bending,' which will render you all but invisible. Second, a set of temporary blessings, granting you strength, speed, agility—"

"Yeah, yeah, I know what blessings do. What else?"

"Must you always interrupt?"

"Only when you're boring."

"In that case, you can stay ignorant of the last, possibly lifesaving boon I plan on granting you."

"That's fine. I remember what this one is."

"Do you now?"

"A shield against sorcery, right?"

"Well, something like that, yes. I must warn you though—the protection will not be absolute."

"Knowing you, it will be more than enough. And then some."

"Either way, it is best to be quick about your . . . tasks."

"Ha! No need to coat it in honey. We're about the business of murder tonight."

"Assassination. There *is* a difference."

"Only in motivation. I'm sure their corpses won't care about the distinction."

"We can argue semantics all night, but I would rather we get started soon. The other groups will begin their attacks shortly, and synchronizing our efforts is paramount to success."

Yandumar smiled. "You love this, don't you? Being able to cast again at will?" He didn't blame the ancient sorcerer. He felt just as elated, if for different reasons.

"I admit to a certain enjoyment of this new freedom. Since we destroyed the voltensus, the empire cannot now see or track our activities. I intend to exploit that advantage to its fullest."

"Right, then. Seems like we got us some daeloth to kill."

Yandumar stood and drew a pair of bastard swords from their scabbards seated crosswise on his back. He shared in Gilshamed's eagerness. After so long waiting, drawing steel against his enemy had never felt better.

"One last thing, Yan. When you are done, unclasp the link."

"Why? What will that do?"

"It will . . . signal to me that you are finished."

He was lying. Yandumar could always tell. After six

years by each other's sides, there was nothing they could hide from each other. Still, he knew enough not to press Gilshamed, trusting that his friend had ample reason for his actions.

If I can't trust Gilshamed, I might as well just give up on our cause right now.

Without another word, Yandumar saluted Gilshamed with a raised fist and sprinted off into the night.

He bounced from trunk to trunk, speeding towards the location the scouts had given him. He crested a small rise and was able to catch a glimpse of a clearing three hundred paces distant. The Imperial camp. *If you're planning on doing something, Gil, now would be a good time.*

As if the valynkar could read his thoughts—and he wasn't entirely sure he *couldn't*—Yandumar felt the sorcery take effect. Like a warm wind swirling around him, he watched as his hands first appeared ghostly, then disappeared altogether.

"Scorchin' weird. But, at least it's effective." He'd have to watch his noise, though. He forgot to ask if this effect would make him silent as well as unseen, and would have to assume otherwise.

Yandumar trotted down the hill, careful to avoid stepping on any branches. A mark later, three Imperial soldiers came into view ahead of him. Despite the darkness, he could see them clearly. He hadn't even thought to ask for night vision, but Gilshamed, as always, thought ten steps ahead. *You clever old man.* He marched within twenty paces of the sentries without so much as a head being turned in his direction.

Stepping carefully now, he edged into the company's camp. Over three hundred soldiers slept upon bedrolls in neat rows arranged in a pentagon. No fires were lit. Standard practice was to keep light and noise to a minimum when actively tracking hostiles. In the empire, the only thing that qualified as "hostile" were bandits. Usually. And, usually, such tactics worked.

Too bad we ain't your typical band o' rogues.

Yandumar lingered on the thought, chuckling silently as he shuffled into the center of the camp.

Here, six tents were erected. One for each of the five lieutenants, officers who controlled a platoon of about sixty soldiers each, and one larger structure housing the company's commanding captain. All daeloth. All targets. As Yandumar crept closer to this middle tent, he began to hear voices and could see flickering silhouettes spawned from candlelight.

He froze as he realized there were more than six people inside. Who else would be attending? Though he could not make out any guards outside the tent—the daeloth must think themselves protected within their circle of troops—it was possible that they had stationed some inside. The sergeants maybe?

Bright bloody abyss, like I need any more complications. They needed the sergeants alive if this crazy plan had any hope for success. He'd have to exercise . . . restraint.

Yandumar sheathed the sword in his left hand and drew instead a blunted mace. He forced himself back into motion without any further delay. He didn't want to dwell on what he was about to do. No use second-guessing. That led only to hesitation, which would likely get him killed.

As his hand brushed aside the tent flap, the blessing took effect. Gilshamed, again, delivering with perfect timing. Strength flooded into his limbs, and he blazed with new energy. Every detail of the scene laid itself out. He analyzed threats, sorted his targets, observed weapons, noted states of awareness, and rehearsed the next few moments in his mind.

It took all of half a beat.

Three men stood near the entrance, sergeants indeed by the rank on their shoulders. Yandumar struck the rightmost on the jaw with the pommel of his sword. The leftmost he swiped in the temple with his mace. Yandumar barreled forward, ramming the top of his skull into the nose of the middle sergeant. Blood sprayed, but not fatally, as the three men toppled. Yandumar lunged past, intent on his next round of targets.

Seven men at the center, rising from their seats. Two more on the far side.

Yandumar threw his mace. It sailed past the center group and crunched into one of the sergeants. The soldier folded around the weapon and crashed into the man behind him, the two crumpling in a heap.

Yandumar rushed on the seven. He swung his sword, candlelight flickering off the silver blade as it tore through the throat of a daeloth. *Sweet blessed Creator, I've missed this!* He noted, with amusement, that he was no longer invisible but knew that it didn't matter anymore. Gilshamed's blessings were all the advantage he needed.

His shoulder slammed into a lieutenant. The armored figure careened backwards, tumbling into a compatriot.

Another daeloth slashed a double-edged shortsword sideways. Yandumar caught the woman's wrist, wrenched it around—with a satisfying crunch of bones—and drove her own blade into her gut.

The master sergeant arced a longsword down towards Yandumar's head. He brought up his bastard sword, one-handed, and parried. That familiar, vibrating ring of steel on steel sounded in the close quarters. His attacker stumbled backwards. Yandumar lunged, fist forward, connecting with the man's sternum and doubling him over. He brought his knee up and smashed it into his cheek. The sergeant fell limp at his feet.

The captain and the last of the lieutenants still standing had backed up to the tent's outer wall. With fierce grins, they pressed their hands forward. Dark sorcery twisted towards his body.

Yandumar froze. His mouth went dry. The air squeezed out from his lungs. He stood, not in a tent, but in a forest. Thirty years ago just past sunset. Surrounded by three daeloth assassins.

God . . . no. Please. I don't want to remember. . .

But Yandumar knew that he would never forget that day.

He also knew that he *must* never forget.

He remembered clearly the smell of his own flesh cooking beneath his armor, blood and bile, the screams of rage coming from some otherworldly monster—but no, that was his own voice—as he ripped apart their bodies with sword and dagger and, eventually, his own nails, digging and tearing and clawing even after their corpses had long ceased moving.

Now, two bastard spawn of the mierothi bent destruction towards him once more. Their grins persisted . . . right up until their sorcery deflected off the shield surrounding Yandumar. The spells careened into the two other daeloth he had knocked over earlier, shredding flesh and bone. Their death screams shattered the ice holding him in place.

He leapt at the two in front of him and swung sideways, three decades of pent-up fury behind the blow. The top half of both of their skulls spun into the tent wall, smearing blood and brain matter.

Yandumar panted, half-crouched and covered by the expelled gore of his enemies.

"Not revenge," he said. "Not . . . Please, God, forgive me. Just trying to balance the scales a bit. Set things right."

He turned to leave, and with a start, realized he was not the only one standing in the room.

One of the sergeants stared at him wide-eyed. "Who . . . who are you?" he asked. The man stood with one hand on the hilt of his still-sheathed weapon.

He was the one on the far side, who had been tangled up in the man he'd thrown his mace at. Luck, that he'd been overcome with fascination, rather than duty. *A sign? Hardly. Things don't work like that anymore.*

"Salvation," Yandumar said. "Or not. You'll soon be forced to pick between them. I suggest you choose wisely."

He took out the link and undid the latch.

Nothing happened.

He turned the open sphere over in his hands. *What did Gilshamed say was going to–?*

An all-encompassing light ripped across his vision, blinding him to all else. A sensation like being dipped in boiling water accompanied a wind that shrieked and tore at his eardrums. The moment stretched out, pain rising, and with it, panic.

Then, as quickly as it began, the sensations vanished. Yandumar looked around, blinking in the sudden darkness, and from it a voice spoke out. "Are you all right, Yan? Are you hurt at all? How do you feel?'

"Scorch it, Gil! What was that? You said it would be a signal, not . . . not . . .''

"Yes, sorry. I was afraid you would not agree to this little test."

"Test?" He grabbed Gilshamed by the shoulders and shook him. "I had no idea what was going on. I thought I was dying!"

"Dying? No, no, there was little chance of that. But I had to ensure your safe retrieval from the encampment without further altercation."

Yandumar sighed and released the valynkar. "That's . . . well . . . thank you. I guess."

Gilshamed drummed two fingers on his cheek as he ran his ancient eyes over him. "Yan, is something the matter?"

Yandumar grunted. *You always see to the heart of things, don't you?.* The thought tasted more bitter than he expected. "Will we never escape our pasts?"

Gilshamed smiled and put a hand on Yandumar's shoulder. "Perhaps not. But, together, I think we may get the chance to confront them. And is that not, after all, the better path?"

"We'll see."

Gilshamed seemed to take that as affirmation, for he lifted a hand skyward and released a ball of brilliant yellow fire, which lit the night for a league in all directions.

Their scattered forces moved into position surrounding the four now-leaderless companies. Gilshamed unfurled his wings, their own source of luminescence, and launched himself into the air.

"Give them hope, my friend," said Yandumar at the back of the retreating figure. "This land could surely use some."

VOREN SET DOWN his quill and crumpled up the parchment. A waste, but the tragedy that was his latest attempt at channeling his emotions did not bear viewing by any other soul. It joined several other pathetic excuses for poetry, a few disharmonious compositions, and a painting aborted after only a few dozen brushstrokes.

The departure of Draevenus had left him empty. The mierothi's companionship had grown to be something Voren treasured, waking him up from so many centuries of lethargy. Not even the best of his art had made him so aware of what it meant to be alive. To connect with another sentient being, even on something so simple as the history lessons he had been giving, was so much closer to "living" than anything else he had done since his capture. But now that Draevenus was gone, the awareness of that need lingered without an outlet for it.

Abyss take him for ever knocking on my door!

Even as he thought it, Voren knew the sentiment lacked bite. Draevenus's presence had been the best thing to happen to him in this palace.

But his dull compliance with an empty existence no longer sufficed, and he was plagued by a recent urge to capture . . . something. He could not quite define it, which, of course, was the main drive behind his need to so do. This frustrating ignorance was only made worse by the change happening in the mierothi around him. Change that he knew nothing about.

And his desire to ascertain its heart raged in him like an infection.

Voren picked up the quill once more, but the muse remained firmly fled. Rather than dip in the stone inkwell on his oak writing desk, he placed the feather down again. He was, after all, just lingering in anticipation of his appointment. What need to mar any more fine pages?

So instead, he paced. For nearly half a toll, his sandaled feet wore ruts along a well-trod path of white-marble tile, until finally, blessedly, the hinges of his door began squealing.

Voren bowed. "Emperor Rekaj, how good of you to join me on this fine evening."

Rekaj strode in, a haughty smile already plastered across his visage. Voren's heart sank. That look rarely meant good news. *So much for the direct approach.*

"Voren," said the emperor. The name dripped off his tongue like poison. "What, exactly, is so fine about it?" He gestured out the window, where thick clouds rolled down the cliff's side, blocking all sight beyond the palace grounds.

Voren presented a nonplussed smile. "Merely being polite, of course. I assure you, no disrespect was intended."

"Yes, well, we all know what they say about intentions, good or otherwise."

Voren opened his mouth to reply but closed it again when Rekaj turned away and strode deeper into his chambers. He silently thanked Elos for the reprieve. It gave him a few moments to reformulate his strategy, which, so far, had been failing miserably.

He waited with patience honed from over nineteen hundred years of practice, as the emperor moved about Voren's receiving chamber, passing a contemptuous gaze at everything his eyes fell upon. A bare hand, scale-backed and clawed, waved at the four statues grouped in pairs between the central pillars.

"Such . . . craftsmanship," Rekaj said. "It's almost as if, with a touch of color, they could come to life . . . stand among us once more."

Voren bowed his head slightly. "By your own grace were the finest stone artists in all the lands commissioned for the work."

"'Lands' indeed. I had almost forgotten that this continent once consisted of over a dozen nations. And all of them protected by these, your people's greatest 'heroes.'"

Not the word I would use to describe them. They

may have all *began* as paragons of virtue, but how they ended . . .

Voren's memories awakened, of their own accord, as Rekaj stepped up to peruse each statue.

Analethis, the Champion. He faced a hundred tyrants and felled each one with naught but his blade and the light of freedom in his soul. Until, that is, he ended up replacing one of them, carving out his own kingdom of blood and fire, which sent a third of the civilized world into turmoil.

Murathrius, the Mediator. He had a tongue of quicksilver, which bridged many a conflict with a lasting peace. But in response to a perceived slight, he whispered false tales of the queen's infidelity to the king of Panisalhdron. The king slew her and her entire house, plunging the nation into a civil war that lasted a hundred years.

Heshrigan, the Arbiter. She founded the League of Justice, who traveled the world over, providing unbiased judgment in disputes great and small. And quickly wore out their welcome. Eventually they began forcing their own, perverse brand of justice on any and all, falling out of grace with even the Valynkar High Council. Heshrigan herself was accused, at the end, of more than a thousand murders, deaths she claimed as righteous executions.

Rekaj fixed his gaze on the last statue. He pressed his face so close that his breath brushed cloudy residue across the polished surface. He brought a hand up, almost as if he intended to caress the chiseled face. "Well," said the emperor. "I don't think either of us can ever forget such a figure as this."

Ah, yes. Him.

Voren gulped, struggling in vain to repress this memory hardest of all.

Gilshamed, the Bold. He gathered together the nations of this land and led them in battle against the rising tide of the mierothi hordes.

But in the end, he failed. The entire mierothi population, cut down to just under a thousand by a century of war, chained their sorcery in ritual sacrifice. The resulting conflagration, which later became known as the Cataclysm, pushed the very soil half a league into the air and erected the Shroud. Through it, none could enter, and none could leave.

"There was much turmoil during their lives," Voren said carefully. "I, for one, am thankful that such times are long past us."

"Are they now?" Rekaj said. Then, shoulders slumping, he added in a whisper, "Will they ever be?"

Voren, though careful to let nothing show on his face, let a smile loose in his mind.

Details would come, but now, at least, he could surmise the shape of the change taking place. Some new conflict in the empire. And if it put the mierothi into such states of fretting, it must be serious indeed.

Upheaval meant opportunity for renegotiation. Great upheaval? Change he dared not speak and scarce hoped to dream flicked across Voren's thoughts, like smooth, round stones skipping over the surface of a still pond. He had to clamp down hard on a rising bubble of longing and—dare he even think it?—ambition.

Voren sensed malevolent regard and glanced once more at the emperor. Their eyes met. Voren shivered as if struck by winter's wind, the full weight of the malice behind Rekaj's gaze now focused on him alone.

"Is there . . . is there anything else . . . any other way I can be of assistance to you?" said Voren.

"Oh, indeed you can."

The emperor stepped lightly towards the door.

"A new Hardohl recruit was discovered recently. One of our phyzari out in the western territory found and birthed the infant though she was unable to save the poor mother, of course."

Voren shivered again. "Of course."

Rekaj pulled open the door. "The girl will be here in a week. Your escort comes the day before."

"The blessing will be . . . prepared, as usual. In this, as always, I am your faithful servant."

The emperor smirked but said nothing. Then, he left.

Voren sank to his knees, then toppled forward to press his hands into the slick floor. Salty tears smacked the tiles between his shaking fingers.

"Abyss take you, Rekaj."

Now, at least, he knew why the emperor had insisted on dredging up history. Not merely to stoke the memory but to remind him of failure.

Voren's failure.

And . . . his choice.

For soon, Voren would come face-to-face with their haunting echoes.

Chapter 3

"MAKE WAY, YA' flea-ridden gutter scum! Get outta the road! Can't y'all see we got a scorchin' Fist coming through?"

The sergeant in charge of the gate watch continued shouting as Mevon cantered towards him. Six soldiers with crossbows patrolled the gatehouse wall, and an equal number were on the ground, pushing with the shafts of their halberds at those citizens deemed too slow in evacuating the roadway. Their full-bodied chain mail jingled beneath orange-and-yellow-striped tabards, which bore the oak-tree crest of the Thorull city guard. Mevon whistled once; Quake lifted his bridle-free head and drew to a halt alongside the sergeant.

"Evenin', Hardohl." The sergeant raised his right fist to eye level. Mevon returned the salute. "What can I do for ya'?"

Mevon spared a glance to ensure his Fist had begun

filing under the archway. "You can start, sergeant, by telling me where the rest of your watch is."

The sergeant huffed, then threw his arms out in a helpless gesture. "With, uh, respect 'n' all that, where the bloody abyss have you been?"

"Doing my job. Now answer the question."

"You mean you ain't heard?"

"Obviously not."

The sergeant exhaled, whistling in the process. "Well, no official word's come down, mind ya', but we heard of some scuffle out in the east. Got all the scale-backs red-cheeked 'n' cranky, if you know what I mean. Four outta every five got shipped off to lock the situation down, and the rest of us are left here pulling double duty at half strength."

Mevon rubbed his chin. Four out of every five—over two and a half thousand troops—was serious indeed. Had someone finally cornered those abyss-taken bandit lords? The three hundred he'd wiped out had belonged to them, surely, but represented only a fraction of the rogues, thieves, and highwaymen capable of being called upon by the self-proclaimed rulers of the Rashunem Hills. Mevon smiled, thinking of the clash that would unfold if, indeed, the bastard pair had finally stirred too great a bee's nest with their schemes. How he wished he could be there to see them fall.

Green flash in his peripheral vision, and he turned towards the gate to see Jasside passing by, her eyes searching in his direction. She had been within earshot of Mevon's conversation with the sergeant. She jerked her head away, but not before Mevon glimpsed her upturned lips.

"If I was you," continued the sergeant, "I'd be gettin' on to the fortress, quick-like."

"I intend to."

Two whistles urged Quake into motion. Mevon threaded his way into the cavalcade and passed under the gatehouse archway. After five beats trotting through the tunnel, he emerged into the northern quadrant of Thorull.

The smell hit him first, the stench of a hundred thousand souls, squeezed together like grapes in a winepress. A wall of noise next struck his ears like a thunderclap, displacing a half month of silence save the clip-clop of hooves and the solitude of his own thoughts.

Mevon patted Quake on his right shoulder, and the horse accelerated, passing several rows of Elite and sending one basket-laden citizen scampering to vacate his path. He soon came abreast of Jasside. Arozir and Tolvar rode at her flanks, and they inclined their heads to Mevon, a gesture he returned.

He addressed his captains. "You saw the gate?"

"Aye," said Arozir. "Idrus already raced ahead to find out what's happening."

"Good." He had expected no less. "Until we know more, keep the men on a short leash."

Tolvar sighed dramatically. "If we must." He raised his voice so that those around could hear. "So . . . maximum of, say, ten pints?"

"Right," Arozir said. "And four whores."

"And two tavern brawls . . . but only if they win!"

A dozen of the closest Elite chuckled and let loose a

mock victory cry. Mevon could not bring himself to join in the merriment. Jasside, her face wholly unreadable, had fixed her gaze on him. He stared back.

"Give us some room," Mevon said. "I'd like a last chat with our prisoner before she's taken out of our hands."

"Aye." Tolvar turned his head around as both he and Arozir pulled back on their reins. "You heard the man, slow your asses down!"

"They're horses, not asses!" someone called.

"Horses, too, then!"

"And I'll throw saddles on your back and let your mounts take a ride if you don't hurry up!" added Arozir.

"Don't you mean *slow* up?" yelled a different voice.

"Who said that? Why don't you . . ."

Their banter continued, but Mevon left them to it, their voices fading into background noise. He and Jasside now had space enough to talk in peace.

She smirked at him. "Back for more?" she asked.

"So it seems."

Their last conversation had ended with Mevon's wandering away, lost in thought. He had not spoken to her again in the days since.

"Good," she said. "I'd hate to think that you planned on washing your hands of me."

"I . . ." Mevon had thought to do just that. He shook his head. "We shall see."

She let out a *hmph* and turned away, a perfect image of apathy. It was a sham, though, and they both knew it.

"What game are you playing at, sorceress?"

"Whatever do you mean?"

"Some conflict is unfolding to the east of here. Why should that please you?"

She shrugged. "I'm on the way to my own execution, aren't I? The empire's woes are among the few things that can still bring me pleasure."

"So that's it then? Are you just like every other criminal I've known, throwing empty defiance in the face of the justice when it finally catches up to you?"

"Don't talk to me of justice!" The words left her mouth like fire, and her eyes blazed, belying the charade. She took a deep breath before continuing. "You claim to serve its cause, but you don't. You, Mevon Daere, know *nothing about it!*"

Mevon had to stop himself from growling at her. "I'll not have such words spoken to me. I know nothing, do I? My earliest memories involve lessons in the ways of justice. My devotion to it is unequaled among my peers. Ruul's light, I named my scorching weapon after it!"

She lowered her voice to a pitch Mevon almost considered dangerous. "Please. You kill because you enjoy it and enforce a cruel mockery of the term based on the whims and fears of your masters. You know not devotion, only blind obedience."

Mevon, his composure shattered, felt his jaw hanging wide. *Nobody* talked to him like this. And with such words as to drive even a gentle soul to violence, he truly, for one brief moment, lost control.

Scores of heads turned to him, eyes wide, as he began laughing.

It was not a gentle thing, nor was it devoid of hysteria.

Perhaps two dozen beats it persisted, until finally he was able to bring himself, in increments, back under control. Jasside's visage held to a mask of horror for its duration. Only as he wiped away moisture from the corner of his eyes did she also make an effort to compose herself. It didn't matter. The deed was done, and Mevon now knew everything he needed to know about her.

He looked into her eyes, holding them trapped. He searched her soul, and felt . . . nothing. "A few days ago, such words might have incited me to a regrettable reaction. Now? Just be glad I no longer feel the constant urge to snap your neck."

She made a sound very close to choking, then nodded—a gesture too meek to be part of her act.

They rode together, a cloud of silence hanging between them. Their procession turned once to skirt the edge of the northern quadrant's market square. Two more turns would bring them to their destination. Two more turns until he was free of her forever.

Midway through the row, Jasside surprised him by speaking once more. In a whisper, she said, "Mevon, why do you fight?"

He lifted an eyebrow as he studied her. She faced forward, eyes downcast, chin pressing towards her chest. What angle was she trying now? "You know why: justice."

"Yes, but *why*?"

"I . . ." Mevon shook his head. "It's what I've always done, what I was born to do."

"To what end? What purpose does your justice serve?"

"Isn't that self-evident? Justice is its own end." He

swept his arm in an arc. "Look around you. Would civilization be possible without men like me standing between it and chaos?"

"No. But, is it the order that you protect or the people within it?"

"What difference is there?"

She sighed. "Oh, Mevon, all the difference in the world."

Mevon shrugged.

"You asked me to look around," Jasside said. "Well, now I ask—no, I *challenge* you to do the same. There." She pointed. "Look, and tell me what you see."

Mevon tilted his head in the direction indicated. "What? It's just a few musicians playing to the crowd."

She forced a smile. "Is that all?"

"Want me to write you an essay? What more is there to tell?"

"I'll tell you what I see. I see three men playing fiddle, skin-drum, and wood-flute. The song is lively. The fiddler is singing the melody. It's about a shy, pretty farm girl, unable to choose between lovers and causing all sort of trouble for it. The crowd is full of people just off from their day's labors, eager to ease their tired backs with an ale in hand and a song in the air. I see the tears in their eyes, unshed yet brimming, for the song tells of innocence, of peace, and allows them, for a few brief moments, to forget that they live in a land that has all but forgotten these things.

"*That* is the difference. You don't see it because you're not one of us. I don't blame you, though. I guess it's not your fault. Not really. They've had their claws in you since birth."

Her words sank into him, each a lance of ice to his soul. He rubbed his chin. *Is she right? Am I truly so set apart from the very people I risk my life to protect?*

More importantly: *Does it matter?*

The thought gnawed at him as the two of them followed the front half of the Fist into the first turn. Too soon, they made the second.

The fortress at the heart of Thorull loomed before them. Its blackened stone walls soared nearly twice as high as the city's outer perimeter. The tips of crossbow bolts peeked out of half a hundred murder holes, and halberdiers by the scores stood at attention along the gated entrance.

Idrus waited just inside. As the Fist moved off to the stables and began dismounting, Mevon grabbed Jasside's reins and whistled once, which brought them both to a halt two paces from his ranger captain. "Report."

"It's bad," Idrus said.

"I gathered that. The watch sergeant told me they stripped four out of every five soldiers stationed in the city. Any more word? Have the country garrisons been affected as well?"

"It's worse than that. The general is in there with the prefect, and it sounds like they may be mobilizing the entire Host."

"The prefect? You mean this isn't just a military matter?"

"Afraid not."

Mevon turned as his other two captains rode up alongside them. "You heard?"

"Enough of it," said Tolvar. "Scorch me, looks like it'll be a short leash indeed."

"Very," Mevon said.

"I feel for the elegant ladies of the Feathered Dollhouse." Arozir sighed. "They may have to wait a bit longer for our most dubious presence, I'm afraid."

"Right." Mevon turned to Idrus again. "Anything else I should know before I head in?"

"Well . . . there is one thing, but it might be nothing."

"Tell me."

"It's about the other Hardohl. They seem to be . . . missing."

"What? Both of them?"

Idrus raised his hands in a gesture of helplessness. "That's all I know. It might be I heard wrong."

"Not likely." Mevon dismounted. He reached to lift Jasside out of her saddle, a mere featherweight bound at the hands and ankles by coarse ropes. She had an oddly thoughtful look on her face as he reached with a knife to undo her lower bindings.

"You're taking her with you?" Idrus asked.

"I might as well. The sooner she's out of our hands, the better."

All three captains gave each other pointed looks, as if they were concerned parents deciding whether to let their child out for the evening. Mevon did his best to ignore their "affections," since such instincts served so well on the battlefield. After a few moments of that eerie silent communication they seemed to cherish, they nodded to each other.

"Very well," Arozir said.

"Be careful in there," added Tolvar.

Idrus guided a hand to Quake's neck and guided the horse away. Tolvar and Arozir followed, leading their own mounts. Mevon grabbed Jasside by the upper arm and marched her up the onyx steps to the prefect's receiving chamber.

He came to the thick door and cast a glance at the two daeloth guards. Three purple lines, like ragged claw marks, adorned their black tabards, marking them as members of the prefect's own darkwatch. One quickly turned to grasp the handle, saying, "You're expected."

Mevon marched in without hesitation.

" . . . simply don't know what we're dealing with."

The words came from a familiar figure: General Masri Genrasco, the daeloth commander of all forty thousand troops stationed in the prefecture. She was dressed in the typical armor of her kind: thick steel, jagged, meant to appear imposing in stark shades of black and red. Blond hair curled toward her jawline, looking odd, as ever, against the mahogany skin all daeloth possessed. On the back of her neck and hands, scales glittered in azure globelight.

Prefect Hezraas stared her down. A feat, considering how short he was, even for a mierothi. Whatever retort he had planned died on his lips as he swung his gaze towards Mevon. "About time you got here."

"Honored one." Mevon bowed his head, then forced

Jasside to her knees and stepped in front of her—a formality indicating that she was unimportant and could wait until more pressing matters were discussed. "I hear there's some trouble?"

The prefect barely glanced at Jasside. "Your penchant for understatement is ever amusing, Daere."

"What's going on?"

Masri nearly growled. "It's the voltensus. Someone . . . destroyed it."

"*What?* How is that possible?"

The general looked searchingly at Hezraas, who flopped down onto his cushioned throne. The prefect fidgeted with his embroidered silk pants. He grumbled under his breath for a few moments, rage evident in his eyes. "We don't know," he said at last.

Mevon frowned. The voltensus was a crucial part of Mevon's job, for without it, there was no reliable way to detect sorcerers who were casting without a legally purchased Sanction. Of more immediate concern, though, was the fact that he thought the things were indestructible.

Clearly not.

"I see," Mevon said eventually.

"It gets worse," said Masri. "We sent almost two full battalions in to contain matters, but over the course of two days, we lost contact with my field commanders."

"All of them?"

Masri's face went blank, a sign, Mevon knew, that she was struggling to rein in her fury. "Every last one."

"I'm sending most of our remaining forces," Hezraas said. "The bastards will find themselves in an ever-tightening cage." He pounded a fist on the arm of his throne. "They will not escape us!"

Mevon frowned at the prefect for his childish display. *Feeling the pressure from Mecrithos, are we?*

"Also," Masri said, "we're fairly certain these insurgents have a cadre of powerful sorcerers with them. So, we'll need you to—"

"You presume to give me orders, daeloth?" said Mevon.

The general's eyes widened as she casually dropped a hand to the shortsword at her hip.

"This is *my* order," said the prefect. "And you'd better deliver. Both of you. All eyes are on us, and if either of you screw it up . . ." Hezraas hissed, spraying spittle through gritted teeth. "Just know that whatever price I pay will be magnified tenfold to you."

Mevon eyed Masri coolly, a look she returned, but they both provided Hezraas with an expected nod of understanding and obedience.

"If I am to go," Mevon said, "then I take it the rumors concerning my peers are true?"

"What have you heard?" asked the prefect.

"Only that they're missing. What's happened to them?"

Masri and Hezraas shared a silent glance. Slowly, they turned back to face Mevon, and for the second time he heard those infuriating words: "We don't know."

Mevon clenched his jaw. *Too much coincidence. All of this reeks of a guiding hand. Someone has been planning these events for a long time.* He felt his eyes instinctively drawn down and behind him. *She couldn't have had anything to do with it, right?*

"What do we know about our enemy, then?" he asked.

"Next to nothing," said Masri. "But I did receive a brief commune from a lieutenant. He died only moments after beginning his message, but he did manage to scream something about assassins and made a brief mention of a 'midnight sun,' whatever that means."

"So basically, we're in the dark," Hezraas said. "That's why I need you. I'm giving you free rein, Daere. Bring me the heads of the leaders and scatter the corpses of any who follow them."

Mevon smiled. "As you will." *Oh, the reckoning that will come.* He began to savor his inevitable triumph and the river of blood that would surely flow.

The prefect's eyes moved at last to Jasside. "And who is this?"

"Oh." Mevon turned to her. "This is my . . . ."

The word "prisoner" died before reaching his lips. It was her expression: Jasside's face was . . . aglow. The look she bore was unmistakable. Inexplicable.

Pride.

Then, like pieces of a blacksmith's puzzle sliding into place, it all made sense.

A powerful force destroys the voltensus, presumably with efficacious sorcery.

The only other Hardohl in the vicinity vanish without a trace.

A mysterious girl confronts me, doing the impossible,

*which captures my attention as surely as snow in winter.
And, from the beginning, she knows my name.*

You knew *me! You were* sent *for me!*

A blade of ice shot up his spine. *Oh . . . gods. . . .*

Why?

He became aware of alarmed stares from both the general and the prefect. " . . . informant," he finally said. "My informant. I believe she knows something about what's going on."

"Good." Hezraas rose, smiling hungrily. "Very good. I'll question her myself."

"No! I mean," he said, seeing Hezraas's strained expression, "that I'll need to keep her with me. If she's in as deep as I think she is, I must have her close to answer any questions that arise."

"Hmm. All right. I can see your need." Hezraas sat down again. "You'd better not disappoint me, Daere."

"Have I ever?"

The prefect grinned.

Mevon turned to Jasside, a new heat rising in him, and her smug face only stoked its flames. He grabbed her arm, lifting her to stand, and began marching out.

Mevon whispered in her ear, "Whoever sent you *will* have answers, and they had better be good."

She smiled up at him. "Oh, Mevon, you have no idea . . ."

GILSHAMED STEPPED TO the edge of the outcropping. He peered down on the crowd gathered below. His followers ringed the edges of the clearing, and in the center stood the prisoners. A combination of awe and terror had kept them from putting up a fight, but now, as they continued their march up into the Rashunem Hills, they were becoming restless. Gilshamed's troops could no longer manage so large a burden.

By day's end, they would be prisoners no more. One way or another.

All eyes clung to him, waiting for his declarations. He decided not to bring out his wings again. No bright lights. No booming voice from the sky. He had used such tactics once before and knew they would lose efficacy if attempted again. No, they needed something different now. Something to make them feel as if Gilshamed were truly one of them. Something . . . heartfelt.

Gilshamed smiled to himself. *I can do heartfelt when I need to.* He cleared his throat.

"Soldiers of the empire," he began in tones loud enough for all to hear, "look around you, and tell me what you see."

He allowed a moment for them to swing necks left and right, minds searching for the answer Gilshamed desired. He did not let them flounder. "I will tell you," he continued. "I see farmers and shepherds, bakers and butchers and blacksmiths, former soldiers and former whores. All citizens of your same empire. But all fighting for *me.*

"None of you ask *why* they are fighting. I can see, though, hidden within your eyes, that you already know."

No few number of heads dropped at this. Shame, after all, was a powerful tool. But Gilshamed did not mean to use it exclusively. These people did not need reminders about friends and family who have been hauled away to toil endlessly in the mines and tunnels, or made playthings of the mierothi and their bastard-spawn daeloth, or those who had become virtual slaves to the great merchant families that squeeze human flesh dry to line their own pockets, all without a breath of regulation.

No, what they needed was a cause to call their own.

"I have traveled the length and breadth of this continent for years, observing life among its people. Wherever I went, the story was the same. Every man, woman, and child feels utterly powerless.

"That is why you put on the empire's uniform, take up your swords and shields, and stand your walls. It is the only way, even as small and empty as it is, for you to reclaim some sense of power, some notion that you are not being constantly ground underfoot by forces so much greater than yourselves."

Gilshamed shook his head, sighing. "For this, I do not blame you."

Drooped heads shot back up again. Bodies leaned forward, ears straining to catch his words. The small rustling and whispers that accompanied any crowd ceased, blanketing the clearing in utter silence.

Gilshamed drew a breath. "BUT WHAT DOES IT MATTER!"

The crowd rocked back on their heels.

"Surely," he continued, beginning to pace back and forth along the edge of the outcropping, "our cause is doomed. What chance do a few thousand have against a million-man army that can descend on us like an avalanche? What chance against the sorcery of the mierothi themselves, which makes that avalanche seem but a snowflake?"

He stopped, turned to the crowd, and lowered his voice to just above a whisper. "Then again, what good are a million men if they are in the wrong place? What good a measured response, when our hidden allies strike from the shadows? What good the mierothi's potent sorcery, when we will have means of negating it?"

Excited chatter erupted from his audience's former silence. Such a promise had never before been delivered, never dared to be dreamed. Gilshamed knew that he had them now. He raised his hands, silencing them once more.

"So I offer you this. If any of you wish to leave, to go back to your empty life of servitude to an empire that cares for you naught, I will not stop you.

"But if you wish for the remainder of your days upon this world to have meaning, if you wish to fight for a worthy cause, if you wish to feel truly powerless no more, then pledge yourself to this revolution." He cast one last, long glance over the crowd. "You have until the end of the day to decide."

Gilshamed pivoted away, descending the back side of the rock outcropping. He kept a smile on his face as he treaded down the short path to the waiting command tent.

Even before he pushed aside the flap to enter, the thick aroma of alcohol hit his nose. Yandumar was sunken into a chair, his feet propped on another. A pewter mug filled with ale was in his hand. Half of its contents seemed to be dripping down the man's beard.

Gilshamed raised an eyebrow. "Celebrating something, Yan?"

Yandumar's glossy-green eyes eventually managed to settle on Gilshamed's face. He chuckled but did not smile, and raised his mug. "To our new recruits!"

"And how exactly do you know that my speech achieved the desired effect?"

Yandumar drained the rest of his ale in one long gulp, then belched. "It's the great Gilshamed we're talkin' 'bout here. You could convince a pig to eat bacon, even after 'splaining what it was."

A freshly tapped cask rested on a table near the entrance. Gilshamed nudged it gently, easily determining that it was over half-empty. He frowned over at his friend. "Yan, do you remember where we met?"

"You mean that dusty tavern in the middle of nowhere? What about it?"

"You were well into your cups that day, and have been many a day since. But I have never once seen you this drunk before. What is going on?"

Yandumar sighed. "Today is the thirty-third of Sepuris."

Gilshamed's eyes flared. "Your family . . ." Today was the anniversary of their deaths. "I had not realized."

Yandumar waved the sentiment away. "Don't beat yourself up about it. I've always tried to keep these little pity parties to myself but couldn't manage it this year. Not now that we've kicked things off. I'm afraid we'll be keeping even less from each other than before."

Gilshamed stepped over to his friend. He touched his

hand upon Yandumar's shoulder. "Either way, I am truly sorry for what happened to them. If there is anything I may do for you, please do not hesitate to ask, my friend."

Yandumar nodded. Gilshamed remained by him, offering his support and comfort.

So often, words expressed were actually the least appropriate thing in the world. Times like this reminded Gilshamed of that. Despite both of their propensities for the superfluous, this stillness, this silence, it fit them, filling the empty spaces in their souls with that which naught else could.

Yandumar peered down into his empty mug, then tossed it to the side. "It is good, though," he said, straightening in his chair, "to be reminded of why you fight."

"Indeed it is."

"And you know," Yandumar said, a bit of his old self already starting to return, "this road we're on feels good, don't it?"

Gilshamed marveled at the resiliency displayed by Yandumar, which, at times, put his own to shame. Without such an attribute, he doubted any of their success thus far would have been possible. "Treading the path of justice often grants such feelings, especially while rectifying an evil so pernicious as this."

"Gotta be careful, though. The line between justice and revenge is thin, especially when you've lost a loved one."

"Yes . . ."

The words sent Gilshamed plunging into distant memories. Not a flood of images this time, but rather a single frame, holding the likeness of a valynkar woman. She had hair of violet and a smile that melted glaciers. The woman he loved. The woman he lost. The woman he had not spoken of to anyone, nor dared to allow his thoughts to dwell upon. This solitary window was all he had left of her, all he could allow himself to keep locked inside, for the pain of her loss still ached like a hammer-blow to his soul.

And with pain came the rage. The rage he felt towards the one responsible for her fate.

Gilshamed flinched as Yandumar's hand came down on his shoulder. "Who was she, Gil?"

A protest of ignorance sprang onto his tongue, but he clamped his lips shut. It was no use. "Am I really so transparent?"

"Only when you think of old things. Old, painful things. Your face looks like I feel when I think of my wife and children."

With solemnity, Gilshamed closed the window, sighing as the image of his one and only love faded away into oblivion. "She was my life-mate. I do not . . . that is . . . I suppose I should have told you before now."

Yandumar let loose a warm chuckle, the kind Gilshamed knew meant that all was well. "I understand why you didn't. Still, we need to keep an eye on each other. Now especially, since things are in motion that we have little hope to control, we must keep our motivations in check. I know you'll be there for me. I just wanted to let you know that I am also here for you."

Gilshamed smiled, placing his hand on Yandumar's

shoulder, their embraces now intertwined. "You constantly surprise me. It seems I may never learn all there is to know about you."

Yandumar dropped his hand, grimacing briefly before he turned away. "Just don't go digging too deeply, Gil. You may not like what you find . . ."

To this, Gilshamed did not know what to say.

VOREN STEPPED FROM the carriage, blinking, into the newly risen sun. The image jarred him. On principle, he avoided sunrises, for they could hardly fail to conjure memories of his early days of confinement. Days when he still harbored thoughts of his redemption, of his own light rising and conquering the darkness once more.

So foolish to think such is still possible.

He felt a tug on his wrist as the man next to him jerked the band that connected them. A band made of human flesh. "C'mon, Voren," said Kael, much as a man might address a hesitant pet. "No point in dawdling."

Voren, sighing, stepped to keep pace with his keeper. Kael looked as old as Voren felt, with thin hair and an even thinner beard the shade of new snow. His appearance, however, was doubly deceiving. At first glance one might guess him at around seventy years of age. However, the man had nearly four decades on this estimate. But neither of these numbers was the slightest indication of the man's physical ability, for he was a warrior still and could fight better than most men even a quarter his age.

All thanks to me.

A wind roared overhead, but they were saved from its bite by a wall of towering boulders on either side of the faded game trail. Distant Mecrithos could be seen sporadically through gaps in the stones, a dark wave widening as it spread down the mountain's slope. North of the city, an endless sea of grasses rolled to the horizon, appearing as if on fire by the sharp angle of the sun.

The four daeloth acting as his protection walked by twos, both fore and aft of him. They wore not the heavy armor of the empire's officer corps, but rather padded leathers overlain with chain mail, all black. These were not mere daeloth, but adjudicators. Voren had no illusions about their purpose. They were not here to protect him but to subdue or kill him if he tried to escape. Their garb, weaponry, and tactics were straight out of *Methodology of the Sorcerer-Assassin*, written by Draevenus himself.

Voren began sending a silent prayer to Elos for his friend's journey, wherever it might lead him, but then thought better of it. The god of the valynkar was not in the habit of casting a compassionate eye on the mierothi.

There are times when I wonder if he still looks favorably upon me.

Their little group marched in silence save the scuffle of their feet on the rocky path. Voren knew this trail well, having trod it countless times. They rounded a bend, and the entrance to a cave came into view ahead. The lead daeloth marched in, with only the slightest hesitation as they passed under the jagged stone teeth marking the entrance.

In mere moments, light had become a memory, and a thick odor, reminiscent of moss and bile, filled the air. Despite having been here on numerous occasions, Voren still nearly choked with each intake of breath. The cave closed in around them, stifling sound and thought. Each adjudicator conjured a ball of blue fire to illuminate their path.

Periodically, the lead daeloth would motion Kael forward, and the Hardohl would march to stand in place whilst the rest of them passed. The sorcerous wards here held out all intruders and could only be passed with the aid of a void such as his keeper. Voren, so many centuries ago, had insisted upon such protective measures.

After some time, yet all too soon, they arrived at their destination. A simple wooden door stood before them. They paused just outside. Kael pulled the handle, dispelling the last ward standing between Voren and the chamber beyond. The Hardohl held open the door with a foot as he slipped the band off Voren's wrist.

"In you go," Kael said.

Voren nodded, then walked inside. The door closed softly behind him.

Free now.

He smiled, truly alone and unhindered for the first time in nearly a year, lacking the suppression of both a Hardohl's touch and the wards affixed in his chambers back at the palace. He energized, savoring the torrent of raw power that filled his whole being. *This* was life, not the paltry existence he endured on most of his other days. *Oh, to be able to hold this sweet, scathing essence at will again*. Voren could think of few things greater.

He opened another door, this of smooth grey metal, using sorcery to pull the heavy bulwark which had no handle to speak of. He stepped inside the room beyond.

His elation dimmed.

A soft turquoise light bathed the chamber in luminescence. Round and a dozen paces across, the room had but a few tables in the center. Around the edges of the room were twoscore figures, held floating upright in individual alcoves filled with a glowing, viscous fluid. In stasis, as they had been for time unending.

Valynkar, one and all.

Voren steeled himself, and set to work immediately. He approached the first stasis pod, which held a middle-aged valynkar male with oky blue hair. Voren produced a glass vial from his robes and held it up to a small tube jutting out from the wall. This tube connected with the subject's inner elbow, inserted intravenously into the main artery. A small wave of magic coaxed a stream of blood down the tube and into the vial. Once it was filled, Voren stemmed the tide and stepped to the table at the center of the chamber. He poured the contents of the vial into a large stone bowl.

He proceeded to the next prisoner and repeated the process. Down the line, one after another, he drew from them all, slowly but surely filling the stone bowl with the mixed lifeblood of his kin.

Each new face threatened to open the locked cell of his memories, but he was sure to keep his eyes averted, mind firmly on his present task and naught else. Pain rested there, behind iron bars in his mind. He had no desire to revisit a time when they had called him "friend."

At last he came to the final static soul. More than any of the others, he could not afford to rest his eyes upon her. He kept them firmly downcast as he extracted her blood. Or, tried to, anyway.

As soon as the red trickle began, a most peculiar thing occurred. None of the others had so much as flinched, but she . . . she began swaying.

Then, she started twitching.

The motion intensified, becoming a violent thrashing. Her head rocked back and forth, swirling her hair into tangled violet threads.

Her face pressed forward through the motion, and her lips parted the vertical seal of liquid. In a cry so hollow, so wracked in misery, as to make his heart skip, she let loose a single word: "Why?"

He stumbled backwards, the vial falling from his hands to shatter on the floor. He stared up at her, frozen. *This isn't possible. You are all locked away into perpetual dreams . . . perpetual nightmares.*

Voren surged forward and pushed her head back into the pool. Now, as his gaze lingered on her face, he could no longer keep the cage of his ancient memories shut.

He pictured himself in his youth, not yet even a century old, as the War of Rising Night dragged on. He and his band of equally impetuous valynkar, tired of being told they were too young to fight, forming their own strike force.

Lashriel coming to him, like an older sister, begging him not to go.

Voren looking into her eyes, emotions burgeoning that were anything but brotherly.

His zeal, in time, winning her to his side . . . but merely as an ally. Nothing more.

Their early successes, disrupting the mierothi supply lines.

Then, the trap. And their capture.

The choice granted to them all. One by one, his compatriots refusing the mierothi, spitting defiance in the face of certain death.

Voren's decision, that led them all . . . here.

Voren shook his head, escaping his cage and slamming the bars shut behind him.

He turned from her, the woman he loved but could never have, for she had already been mated to another. Among the valynkar, such things were never broken. The pain of choosing between death or eternal nightmare was an agony he would not wish upon anyone, yet it paled before even a single moment of this unrequited desire.

Ignoring the glass shards at his feet, Voren stood and returned to the center of the room. Thirty-nine would have to be enough. The infant Hardohl would not suffer from such a minor lack.

A small dagger rested on the table. With it, Voren sliced open his palm then pushed his hand down into the blood-filled bowl.

Voren began energizing.

The chamber filled with a thick humming, a vibration in all senses, as the sorcerous power of his kin's souls awakened, magnified by the blood-scything, every last drop of essence pouring into Voren, and through him. Ecstasy washed away all traces of guilt, every last bit of . . . everything.

Gods, imagine what I could do with this power . . . if only I dared. But Voren never *had* dared. He might be able to secure his own escape, but his kin would be left behind in Rekaj's clutches. And without Voren, the emperor had no use for them.

His thoughts became jumbled as he drew in more power—now almost a tenth of the capacity available to him. Such magnitudes of energy begged to be used, to scorch and burn, to take control, and he needed the utmost of his concentration to keep it bent to his will.

Voren forgot all else as he extended his other hand over the jar of ink and began preparing the blessing.

Chapter 4

THE FOREST LAY about them, twisted trees wilting in the late-summer heat. An underbrush of yellow grasses and shrubs blanketed a parched landscape, ground pocked with clusters of drab boulders and patches of soil too dry to sustain much more than weeds. Mevon thought it a fitting place for his enemy to meet their end.

They rode into a rough clearing, and he held up a hand. "We'll make camp here."

"Aye," said Arozir and Tolvar in unison. They dismounted, setting off a clatter of motion as the rest followed suit.

The days and leagues had taken their toll, showing in the faces of every member of the Fist. Even the rangers, ever at home in the wilderness, had circles under their eyes from too-brief rests and long stretches in the saddle. They had made good time, though. Tens of thousands of rank-and-file troops had begun their marches well before them, but the Fist had outpaced them all. For those masses were merely the walls of the trap.

Mevon and his Fist were its teeth.

The scenes they had already visited were gruesome indeed. First the voltensus, a shattered ruin, confirming the rumors of powerful sorcerers among their quarry. Whoever they were, they were bold. Mevon almost admired them for that.

More chilling were the sites of supposed ambush, where daeloth bodies had been found. That, and not much else. Where the rest of the soldiers had disappeared to could only be guessed at. Eight sites and not a trace of them, leaving Mevon in the dark as to their numbers and capabilities.

They had left a trail well enough, though. And Mevon had not hesitated to follow.

Mevon hopped down from Quake, then helped Jasside off her mount. One of the Elite guided both horses away to the picket lines now under construction.

Mevon glanced down at her, then tilted his head for her to follow. Together, they began circling the campsite. "Tell me again," he said, "of this rebel leader."

"Searching for a weakness?" she said with a smirk. "You won't find one."

"Let me be the judge of that."

She shrugged. "He is smarter than you, by far. Whatever plan you come up with, be sure that he has prepared for it. Your defeat is certain."

She had displayed nothing but cooperation since their departure from Thorull. Her one defiance showed in her descriptions of this "golden man," the one to whom she claimed loyalty. He assumed that such words were intended to instill fear in him, or perhaps some caution, but they had the opposite effect. A prize, as this man surely would prove, was not one Mevon intended to share with others.

"We shall see, won't we?" he answered at last.

Her façade remained in place, for now, a smile and upturned nose and an air of nonchalance. Whatever paltry acting lessons she had been given seemed to give her enough confidence not to realize how pathetic her attempts at subterfuge were. All the better. Mevon played her game, letting her think she was effective in her deceptions.

"Your confidence would be admirable, were it not so misplaced," she said. "I don't know where you get it from."

Mevon stepped over a fallen log, then reached behind to help Jasside over. "I was taught by the best."

"One of your old masters at the Hardohl academy?"

Mevon nodded. "Master Kael. It was no secret the other masters were afraid of him. He was something special. Didn't look like much, but he could fight any five students at once, even the oldest ones. Never lost, so far as I saw."

"Let me guess, he took a keen interest in you from a young age? Said that you were special?"

Mevon peered at her sideways. "Yes. How did you know?"

She flashed a crooked smile. "Like I said—a guess.

Though, if he's even half of what you make him out to be, I can see where your arrogance stems from."

"Is it still arrogance if it's justified?"

She shrugged. "Some would say so."

He grunted. "Kael taught me everything he knew. The lessons he gave me far exceeded the instruction received by my peers. When I graduated, he said I was the best he had ever seen. No one disagreed with him."

"And this peerless review extended to your tactics as well?"

"He taught me to surround myself with men who knew their business in that regard. I am a weapon, and best suited to that task alone."

"The task of killing, you mean."

"Yes."

They strolled in silence, making half a circuit around the camp before she spoke again.

"Have you decided what you will do about me and my . . . ability?" said Jasside.

Mevon hesitated. He'd thought much on the subject but had failed to come up with any satisfying resolution. "After this is all over, I will turn you over to the prefect as I had originally planned."

"And simply keep quiet about my secret?"

"What would you have me do? It's not as if I can confront the emperor about this."

She took a long breath. "What if you could?"

Mevon furrowed his brow. "What?"

"If you *could* confront the emperor, what would you say?"

"I . . ." *had never even thought of it,* "don't know. It's just not my place."

"So you are afraid of the mierothi then? Good. I was beginning to think there was nothing you feared."

"It's not fear, but respect. They are this land's rulers, and all must bow before their authority."

"Why?"

Mevon rocked his head back. "Excuse me?"

"Why should they be allowed to rule unopposed? Why not someone else? Someone . . . better?"

"And your glorious master thinks he is this 'better man'?"

"And what if he does?"

Mevon released an amused grunt. "Then I pity your cause. From what you've told me, I gather that your lord is ruthless and possessing of arrogance that would make even Ruul seem humble. He would make no better ruler than we currently have, and probably far worse."

Her mouth opened, but no sound came out. His words must have pinched a nerve. This unexpected turnabout proved most satisfying. Her face scrunched up in thought, and it was a score of beats before she spoke again.

"In truth," she said, "I am not his closest confidant. That post belongs to another. As to my master's plans, his desired end state, all I know is that the mierothi will no longer be the undisputed power in the empire."

The truth of her words was belied by her quavering voice. She *didn't* know. An interesting development if she was indeed ignorant of the final goals of this golden man.

He added "manipulative" to the list of adjectives in his head describing him.

"So," Mevon said. "This 'revolution' of yours . . . I take it some deep-seated hatred for the mierothi is fueling your cause?"

Carefully, Jasside replied, "I suppose that would not be inaccurate."

"And your master, his strife with them is greatest of all?"

"Perhaps. But each of us, to some degree, has reason for joining."

"What's yours?"

She turned away, a tear rolling down her cheek, and sniffed. Softly, she said, "The unjustified death of someone I loved."

Mevon frowned. *And by my own hand, nonetheless.* Then he paused. She had become a rebel before he had killed her half brother. It must have been someone else. His actions had probably only confirmed her decisions.

Their path had now completed its revolution, bringing them back to where they started. Mevon was rescued from further conversation by the thump of approaching hooves. In moments, their source rode into view: Idrus, along with two other rangers, returning from their reconnaissance.

Mevon turned to wave Tolvar and Arozir over, but the pair was already on the way. Their steel boots dragged up close as Idrus, on his lean steed, came huffing to a stop.

The ranger captain motioned his companions off, then vaulted from the horse.

"Bad news first," ordered Mevon.

"There is but one road into the valley," Idrus said. "A narrow canyon passage guarded by five hundred alert and entrenched soldiers. They are protected by stakes and bulwark fortifications, and have a killing field a hundred paces deep. At least a dozen casters stand at the ready, with all kinds of nasty wards laid about the place. Any frontal attack would cost us dearly and awaken the hornet's nest beyond."

"And the good news?"

Idrus smiled deviously. "Our enemy is confident that no other path exists. With patience, and a bit of rope, we were able to create our own trail into the valley."

Mevon, though facing Idrus, kept his attention in his peripheral vision for Jasside's reaction. So far, her mask held: a thin smile and eyes that gave away nothing.

"Excellent," Arozir said. "Looks like our rebels are in for quite the surprise."

"Aye," said Tolvar. "Bastards won't know what hit 'em."

"Tonight we rest," Mevon said. "And most of tomorrow as well. Come the next nightfall, we cut off the head of this rebellion and feast on its bleeding corpse."

As his captains moved off to inform the Fist, Mevon spied a twitch of Jasside's lip. But the setting sun had cast her face in an odd light, and he was unsure if the movement had been towards a frown or a smile.

He wished he knew what it had been . . . and, either way, what it meant.

"They are close," said Gilshamed.

Yandumar, seated on a flat grey stone around a low fire, glanced over his shoulder at the valynkar, who had come up behind him. In his hand was a smooth object that glowed at the center. Jasside's soul-stone. Each day he had watched as Gilshamed took its reading, measuring the progress of Jasside and Mevon. Each time, as he confirmed their continued approach, a part of him marveled that this crazy plan was actually working.

The rest of him was filled with dread.

"You think tonight, maybe?" he asked.

"Possibly," said Gilshamed. "Though, as hard as they've been pushing, I imagine Mevon will want to give his men a rest first."

Yandumar nodded, turning back towards the fire. "Let's hope he takes the bait."

"He will. Your faith in Kael is greater than mine. I should think you most intrepid regarding this stage of our plan. Should I, instead, be worried?"

"Ha! No. That old geezer came through. In more ways than we'll ever be able to count."

"Ah." Gilshamed stepped forward and sat at his side. "Then it is yourself that you doubt."

Yandumar sighed, slumping forward. "Right, as ever. You know, Gil, you should try being wrong once in a while. Might do ya' some good."

Gilshamed shook his head, voice turning solemn. "I think not. I have had enough of failure. Underestimating my adversaries . . . misplaced faith in my allies . . . no. No more."

"Don't worry. I'm sure you've thought of everything this time."

Yandumar settled his gaze on Gilshamed. Those golden eyes reflected the dancing firelight, sight lost in memories. His usually regal posture sagged in a mirror of Yandumar's own, and his leather-wrapped feet kicked absently at a clump of grass. Yandumar noted these details and more, his mind grasping at everything, anything, trying to keep busy so he wouldn't think. *There are things I haven't told you. . .*

He sat up, stretching his back to a satisfying ripple of vertebrae. "Still, we're not gods. We can only do our best and . . . pray."

Gilshamed drew a sharp breath, snapping back into the present. "True, I suppose. Does the God of your people lend strength to such endeavors?"

"Yes. At least, I'd like to think so. As long as our intentions remain pure." In truth, he didn't know. So much was lost. He and his kin, the people of the old nation of Ragremos, did their best to live according to the teachings of the First Creator, fragmented though the scriptures were. It was not always easy deciphering truth from the scattered passages. *Oh, the vows we have taken. . .*

But they tried, and prayed that trying was . . . enough.

"Would you two shut up already?"

The woman's voice broke his thoughts. Both he and

Gilshamed jerked their heads up to face the speaker, who sat across the pit of flames. Her throaty laughter accompanied the *shhkkt* sound of her whetstone as it sharpened her favored daggers.

Gilshamed addressed her. "This may be the last moment of peace we have for quite some time, Slick Ren. Let us spend it as we may."

Slick Ren slid the blade into a sheath situated crosswise under her breasts and drew its twin. Her curve-hugging leather attire, the shade of blood, held a score of daggers of various sizes and purposes. Both her plump lips and her slicked-back hair matched the hue, though the latter held a streak of grey—the only indication of her forty-two years of age.

"You go right on and do that," she said as she set to work sharpening the new blade. "While we sensible folk actually prepare."

The bandit queen of the Rashunem Hills had a point. Yandumar, however, had no desire to conduct such pre-battle rituals. Usually, he would. Not this time. He planned to fight, but did not wish his edges to cut too deeply.

Gilshamed turned towards his tent, and Yandumar followed with his gaze. "As you can see," said Gilshamed, "my own preparations are under way." As he spoke, a man passed through the golden flaps towing a cart, flanked by another pair who carried shovels. Before the entrance folded closed, Yandumar spied another dozen men working inside.

"Risky business, that," Slick Ren said. "Better hope it pays off."

"You're not backing out now, are you?" Yandumar asked.

She fixed her icy eyes on him, smiling. "Our kingdom was founded on risky plays. I have every confidence that this game will be no different. We'd not be involved otherwise. Isn't that right, Derthon?"

Mention of his name brought her brother's gaze up. He sat cross-legged at her side, silent, as always. They both had their share of brains and brawn, but when it came to voicing thoughts, he let her take permanent lead. Yandumar had never heard him speak. He wasn't sure if the man could.

Derthon nodded once, then bent his eyes down again. He returned to rubbing an oiled cloth across his sword, a sleek, curving, single-edged work of art. The blade was impossibly sharp and never dulled, enchanted, most likely. The man wore no clothes, at least not what normal people would consider clothing, but his entire body was wrapped in linen bandaging. Beneath, Yandumar did not know what would be found.

"I am glad to hear it," said Gilshamed. "We all stand to gain much from this. Though some"—his eyes flicked to Yandumar—"more than others."

"So long as we get around to killing some of them mierothi bastards," Slick Ren said, "I'll help you fetch lost pups from wells all you want."

Yandumar jumped up, glaring down on her. "That's not what this is about."

"Tell yourself whatever you want to," she said, pointing with her dagger. "So long as you remember our deal."

"We will," said Gilshamed, standing alongside him. "But let us not count victory before battle has even begun. I suggest we all get some rest tonight." As if on cue, the sun flashed, then disappeared behind the Godsreach Mountains. Gilshamed continued. "I will notify you all at once as soon as Jasside makes contact. Until then . . ." He bowed, as if at some royal court, and departed for his tent.

Slick Ren and Derthon both rose as well, slipping blades into their respective sheaths. The brother stepped away, but Ren lingered.

"You know," she said. "I never like to step into battle feeling . . . unfulfilled." She raised an eyebrow. "How 'bout you?"

Despite himself, he smiled. "Tempting." *Scorch me, isn't that the truth!* "But . . . maybe some other time."

She chuckled and sauntered away, lips turned down mockingly. "What a shame. I've always had a thing for beards . . ."

Her allure trailed away along with her words, and Yandumar sat once more by the fire. He closed his eyes, running fingers through his beard.

God, please, give me this one. Give me tomorrow. Let it all go . . . according to plan.

The fire blazed up. Yandumar shivered.

VOREN WATCHED TWO students spar through an open window. True blades—not blunted practice swords— blurred as young hands swung with all the force they could muster. His eyes could barely follow the thrusts, parries, slashes, and a dozen other moves, the names of which he did not even know. Dust puffed into a cloud as their feet kicked and danced across the courtyard. The fighters were the youngest of the bunch, little more than toddlers.

The clanking of steel continued for a score more beats, until one finally got the upper hand on the other, cutting across his opponent's forearm. The injured child dropped her weapon. The boy, thinking the contest over, smiled and drove his blade for a finishing thrust. The girl's hand shot out to intercept the small sword. Blood spurted out from between her fingers. She yanked hard, pulling the boy towards her, and punched him in the jaw. He stumbled. She wrestled him to the ground and executed a move that caused bones to snap. She wrapped her arms around the boy in a choke hold. In moments, his struggles ceased. Only when she failed to let go of his limp body did the master, watching nearby, step in and pull her off.

She scampered off and found a towel, wiping the blood off her arm. No more flowed. The injury had already healed.

The boy was slower in recovering. It took him almost two full marks before he stood again. He stretched a few moments. They both took up their blades and faced each other once more.

"Enjoying the show?" Rekaj asked. His voice grated both nerves and eardrums.

"Just reminding myself of the benefits of what we do," Voren said.

The emperor let loose a rasping cackle. "If it helps you sleep at night . . ."

Voren sighed. *I am not able to sleep much at all, these days.* He had grown to fear it. Every time he closed his eyes, nightmares plagued him. Darkness and chaos. A vortex, raging, and himself falling into its heart.

A softly spoken "why?" echoing endlessly in his head.

The emperor stepped up next to him. Voren braced himself for the inevitable mockery.

"We do the best we can, you and I," said Rekaj. "For the good of ourselves and the empire. For the good of all."

Voren stared. He wondered, briefly, if the emperor he knew had been replaced by the good twin out of a fairy tale.

Rekaj continued. "Only time will tell if our efforts mean anything."

The mierothi's face betrayed no hint of amusement. Voren swallowed. "Time. Of course."

Why does it feel like my own is running out?

The door to the sterile, cramped room creaked open behind them. They both turned. A cart was wheeled in, pushed by the mother phyzari, the highest of her profession. She closed the door behind her, then gestured to the cart. "She's ready."

Voren stared down at the infant girl. The newest Hardohl. Not a single strand of sorcery could touch the babe. But, like beauty, her special ability was only skin deep. Unfortunately, the mierothi had discovered ways around that.

"She's fully dosed, Kitavijj?" asked Rekaj.

"Yes, emperor." The mierothi female began preparing her medical instruments. Voren did not know what most of them did. He supposed it didn't matter. "The herbs are fully in effect. She won't feel much."

Voren's stomach began to churn. He tried to ignore it.

Rekaj turned to him. "You first. Are you ready?"

Kitavijj brought a scalpel over the child's spine. Voren turned away, grasping hold of the prepared blessing and his spiked chisel as an excuse to keep busy. "Ready."

He forced himself to think of something, anything, as the mother phyzari conducted her final preparations of the babe. His thoughts drifted again to the strange behavior of the mierothi. All of them. He still didn't know what had made them so antsy, and his ignorance weighed on him. He would have to press for answers soon.

The voice of Kitavijj brought him around. "Quickly now, Voren."

He turned and stepped up to the cart, blessing in hand. He did his best to ignore the child's pained whimpering. He opened the jar of glowing ink, dipped his instrument in, and set to work.

He'd done this countless times. No—he *had* counted them, he just didn't like to contemplate the number. His only respite was the fact that the movements were second nature. He let his hands work while his brain remained elsewhere. He scratched the blessing, little by little, into the exposed vertebrae, praying to Elos to keep his nausea at bay. The child's rising wail did not help matters.

After three grueling marks, the ink in the jar dried up, and the last of the inscriptions fell into place. Voren wiped the sweat from his brow. "Done."

The flesh began reknitting before his eyes. Kitavijj

moved in and placed instruments to keep the wound open. "Emperor," she said.

Rekaj moved forward. His tools were nearly identical to Voren's, a blessing raped from the same number of mierothi as there were Voren's kin trapped in stasis. He had seen them. They wandered the palace grounds, aimlessly, eyes glazed, ever confused, as if a wall had been erected between them and reality. Voren thought his brethren had the better part of that deal.

Two blessings then, working separately, yet in harmony. Their combined efforts, plus a lifetime of training and indoctrination, turned simple voids into unstoppable killing machines. All perfectly loyal to the empire. He shuddered, placing a hand to his stomach.

Rekaj set his spike to the child. "Get out, Voren. Your face offends me, just now."

Voren nodded, not even caring about the insult. He rushed out of the room.

The hallway was empty, save Kael. The man gave Voren a strange look, but he ignored it. He turned away and fell to the ground, spewing the last two days' worth of meals onto the floor.

"Something the matter?" Kael asked.

Voren shook his head as he wiped the bile from his lips. *Why is this affecting me so much?* He had never reacted this way, not since the first few times. Not since he had still clung to hope like a child to the hem of his mother's dress.

He knew what had caused the change.

Draevenus, why did you have to make me remember? Why did you have to make me care?

Chapter 5

DEAD SENTRY'S BLOOD on his fingertips and the storm on a low rumble. Mevon smiled. *How fitting that things should end as they began.*

From the shallow cliff top, Mevon peered over the rebel camp. Hundred of tents and nearly as many fires lay nestled in the valley. All but a few outer sentries, such as the one at his feet, had retired for the night. Their enemy was too reliant upon their natural defenses. This would be almost too easy.

Idrus shifted at his side. "Their work begins."

Mevon nodded, though in the absolute darkness of night's coldest toll, the movement could not be seen. Invisible. Just as the rangers now moving into the twelve tents that stood between him and the center, blades drinking deeply yet silently, carving him a path in blood. His eyes settled on the large rectangular structure less than two hundred paces away, its golden canvas still shining in reflected firelight.

"That's where they are?" he asked.

"Aye," Idrus said. "The leaders. Four of them."

He'd set the ranger captain to watch the place this night, the very same night they had initially discovered the camp. He couldn't wait. He suspected the rebel leaders were somehow in contact with Jasside. So, he'd fed her the lie of his plan, and before she went to bed, gave her a surprise in her evening tea. The sorceress would sleep like the dead for a day at least. Whatever signal she was supposed to give the enemy would come far too late.

"Ears open," Mevon said. "Let me know the moment the feint begins."

"With pleasure."

All of the Elite had followed them up the rope ladder, but rather than join Mevon and the rangers, had instead skirted ridges around to the far side of the sprawling encampment. Their diversionary assault should begin—

"Now," said Idrus. "Time to nail the last plank on this bridge."

Mevon rose from his crouch. "Even when it's burning." He took three long strides, then leapt forward.

Off the cliff.

His gloved hands tightened on the rope as the ground rushed up to greet him. He slowed, smashing against the cliff face. His suit scraped on rocks and mud as he descended, far too loudly for true stealth. His boots thumped into the stony soil.

No shouts of alarm. No curious faces poking out of tents. The rangers had done their work well tonight.

The tent lay ahead, and his targets were within. He

raced forward. Speed was his ally now. He pulled Justice into his hands. As he approached, he finally heard what Idrus had nearly a mark before: the sounds of distant battle. The slaughter had commenced, Tolvar and Arozir conducting a symphony of death.

Let your blades drink well, my friends. I surely shall.

He rushed at the command tent.

"GILSHAMED! UP!" YANDUMAR cried.

Gilshamed rolled out of his cot, energizing and drawing his sword protectively.

"What?" he said. "I have received no—"

"They're attacking right scorching now!"

By Elos, we're not ready! Why tonight? Surely Mevon's soldiers must be too worn for an assault. And why had Jasside not sent her signal? He wiped sleep from his eyes and stumbled into the tent's main chamber.

Derthon was there, ready, at ease. But both Slick Ren and Yandumar were scrambling to tighten weapon straps.

"You both have your links?" he asked.

Yandumar nodded.

"Of course we do. We're not idiots," Slick Ren spat. "Are *you* ready?"

Gilshamed took a deep breath. "Yes." He cast a several layers of weak wards in rings around the tent. "It seems—"

He gasped, speech forgotten, as the farthest ward winked out of existence.

"Gil?" Yandumar said. "You all right?"

He staggered as the next ward vanished.

Gilshamed felt like a boulder was pressing on his chest, driving the very air from his lungs. The sensation intensified as the closest ward was voided into oblivion.

He could not speak. It was all he could do to lift a hand and point.

"What?" asked Yandumar.

Derthon saved them all in that moment. The bandit king lunged, sword flashing out, in the direction Gilshamed had pointed—

—just as a rent was torn in the wall, and Mevon himself poured through the gap. The Hardohl's blade was caught on the outstretched sword and halted. Both Yandumar and Slick Ren had been in its path.

And like that, battle was joined. Gilshamed soothed his rapid pulse, knowing that had Derthon been half a beat later, all their efforts would have been for naught.

He poured his sorcery through the links into both Slick Ren and Yandumar, and slowly backed away.

THE STORM HOWLED. Blades rang out on all sides, and Mevon laughed. *Gods, they stand!* He couldn't remember the last time enemies had lasted more than a heartbeat against him.

Mevon recognized his opponents at once. Slick Ren and Derthon, bandit lords. He was glad he hadn't been too late. Their deaths would bring him greater renown than any dozen casters.

The only mystery was the greybeard.

And I'll solve that one when I finish with these two.

Derthon parried Mevon's sideways slash, the force knocking him back several paces. Slick Ren darted in, daggers flashing towards Mevon's eyes, and the grey-beard swung a three-headed flail at his knees.

Mevon stepped towards the greybeard, kicking his wrist. He lifted his *Andun* and parried both of the woman's daggers.

Derthon stepped forward again, perfectly balanced. He struck high. Mevon blocked with his rod and swept the lower blade forward. His opponent twisted away.

Mevon felt the air move behind him on both sides. He ducked and spun, slashing low as blades passed over his head. Both sides of Justice sank into flesh, spitting blood from wounds on Slick Ren and the greybeard. It wasn't without cost, though, for the greybeard's flail connected with Mevon's jaw and wrenched his head around.

Mevon sprang back, surprised that a blow had even been landed on him.

All three advanced on him. The two he had wounded did not so much as falter. *Impossible!* He had cut deep into their thighs, enough to leave them hobbling. He spied their wounds, which were not bleeding nearly as much as they should have been.

They attacked in tandem. Mevon spun his weapon in front of him, a defensive move. It deflected their blows and bought him a beat to think.

The caster. Mevon had seen him when he first entered. Where was he now? He could feel the tingling, like a hive of bees risen to anger at either ear. The man was powerful, more so than any Mevon had ever come across, and he was somehow enhancing those he fought against. No other way for them to give him so much trouble.

Slick Ren darted in, but Mevon saw it for a feint. Both males struck from the sides as she pulled up short and flung her daggers at him.

Mevon deflected the thrown knives with one set of blades and parried Derthon with the other. Unfortunately, that left the third assailant unopposed, and the greybeard's flails wrapped around his *Andun*. The old man yanked hard.

Mevon pretended to stagger off-balance, but then threw himself into the pull. The greybeard's face showed surprise as Mevon slammed his shoulder into it, breaking the nose in a spray of blood. The grip on the flail's handle was lost. The old man stumbled back, grasping for Mevon blindly.

Mevon grasped back. He grabbed hold of the man's tunic and, with one hand, flung him towards Derthon.

The bandit king twisted to the side. His queen appeared next to Mevon, as if out of nowhere. Her new daggers slashed, cutting into Mevon at his right abdomen and shoulder. One caught on his collarbone and held fast.

Mevon inhaled the pain from his wounds and looked down on her. He grunted amusement. Her eyes widened as she realized her mistake.

Mevon flashed out his hand, gripping her throat.

A strange sound, like gargling, erupted from behind, and Mevon turned to see Derthon throwing himself forward in a rage. Like he had with the greybeard, Mevon threw the woman. This time the distance was too close for Derthon to dodge, and the two collided, falling to the ground in a tangled heap.

The greybeard was up again, and he made to stand over his compatriots. Past him, and in the next section of the tent, Mevon could see a man seated cross-legged on the far side of a large rug. Golden hair. Golden eyes. From him emanated sickly-powerful waves of sorcery.

You.

Ignoring the others, Mevon dashed toward the sorcerer. The greybeard raced to intercept. Mevon jabbed at him as he ran, forcing the old man to draw up short and swing both swords in a desperate parry.

The move threw the greybeard off-balance, allowing Mevon, with a kick, to send the old man flying backward. The bandit lords scrambled after Mevon, but he turned away and sprinted at the sorcerer.

Three steps away, he heard the air whistling behind him. Mevon ducked at the edge of the carpet as twin daggers whipped over his head.

He pressed his foot down on the rug, preparing his *Andun* for the killing blow.

His foot hit the surface of the carpet—

—and continued to fall. Mevon saw the golden man wink as the rug wrapped around him, and he plunged into darkness.

Chapter 6

"WILL YOU BE needing any more of my services?"

Voren, sprawled sideways in a chair, looked up from his wineglass. The courtesan stood near the door of his chambers. She leaned toward the exit, lips pressed into a thin line. Voren didn't blame her for wanting to depart so quickly. He had used her more roughly than normal.

He waved absently and turned back to his drink once more. The door opened, then slammed shut behind him.

Voren sighed. She had been a welcome distraction, but no woman's charms could hold his dread at bay for long. Neither could the wine. Even the exhaustion generated by vigorous exercise did little to keep his mind from dwelling on things he would rather forget.

He drained his cup and reached for the bottle. It was empty. And the last one he had in his chambers. He hadn't the patience to send for another. Besides, he knew there was only one thing that could truly bring him solace.

Voren stood and walked towards his closet of artistic supplies, only slightly unsteady on his feet. He pulled open the folding doors and stepped inside. The lightglobe spread its illumination; one of his own creations, not the hideous blue- or purple-hued imitations made by dark-blooded casters. Shelves line the walls, filled with paint jars and sketching tools, blank canvas, brushes in a hundred varieties. More. The sight of it all put a small surge of joy within him. *Yes. This will do the trick. It always has*.

He picked colors at random. He grabbed easel and canvas, a handful of brushes, and marched up to his perch.

Night held. Moonlight slanted across the land, casting long shadows. *What time is it?*

The answer came as a small round light blossomed before his eyes, outshone by the true moon but brighter than any star. The Timid Moon was an object of much debate. The valynkar claimed it was the Eye of Elos, opening to peer upon the planet. The people of the empire mostly ignored it. The nation of Panisalhdron declared the time during which it was visible the period of truest beauty and inspiration. The land of Sceptre had several rude gestures reserved exclusively for its arrival.

Voren stood, enraptured, lost in the sight. He lost track of time. Finally, the Timid Moon sputtered and winked out. Voren shook himself, unsure where the two tolls had gone, and finished setting up.

He knew, now, what to use as inspiration.

He dipped in and began.

The true moon was several lengths above the horizon

when he started, providing his only source of light. Voren left the other lightglobes in his chambers unlit; moonlight was the perfect reflection of his mood. He worked, pouring himself out onto the canvas, barely glancing at the square block of white. His brushes seemed to choose paints and dance across the surface of their own accord.

When he finished, the moon had just ducked below the far eastern mountains. He sat back, panting, and allowed himself to view what he had just created. Or, tried to. It was too dark to make out more than vague impressions.

Voren descended from his perch and returned half a mark later with a small lightglobe in hand. He sat down, tapping the globe to activate it. The painting sprang to life before his eyes.

He rocked back. The stool tipped over, spilling him onto the floor. His torso hung over empty space, a drop of almost a dozen paces staring up at him. With care, he pulled himself back onto the stool and willed his eyes to gaze upon his creation.

The backdrop was a desert. Dry, cracked clay. Barren. A harsh sun beat down. Voren could feel his throat becoming parched. In the center was a pale figure. Dark blue streaks, like floating tentacles, ran out from a round face, which was half-concealed in shadow. Globs of something tarry and black leaked down from its heart. The figure was crouching, holding hands to its ears.

A hundred objects surrounded it. No—a thousand. Voren looked closer. His breath caught as he realized they were fingers, pointing at the figure in the center. Accusing. Angry. One had a body attached, with decidedly feminine features. Violet hair curled around a shoulder. A thick ray of light bent out from the sun, forming its own digit of blame, falling in brightness the farther it reached.

Voren sat, paralyzed. Cold sweat formed on his brow. Breathing became difficult. Vision turned murky as drops flooded into his eyes.

Too much. Too much at once.

He knew of his own frailty. He had never been able to form for himself that shell of protection most people had. Things . . . got to him.

Draevenus's leaving, the emperor's mockery, Lashri-el's reaction in the chamber, something going on that he had failed to unearth . . .

Guilt.

His people's oldest stories, now considered fable or myth, told of a time when valynkar had been human. Then, touched by Elos and gifted with magic, wisdom, patience, and long life, transformed into beings of purest beauty. Almost like the story of the mierothi and their encounter with Ruul. Almost.

Their particular form of remembrance had been instilled to prevent madness. For who could stay sane with a hundred lifetimes drifting through their head? Only at will could the oldest memories be brought to the forefront again. Then, once sorted through and dwelled upon, returned to their haven.

Now, it seemed his own were leaking through to his waking mind. Long-buried guilt rested just below the surface, poking up without his guidance. Was it his conscience? Or his sanity? Both possibilities filled him with despair.

And my art . . . It was the one thing left to him. The one thing that never failed to center him, to banish the specters of his worst fears and regrets. And now, it seemed, even that had been taken from him.

Voren stood and lifted a hand. Began swinging it towards the painting.

He stopped. *What's the point?* The piece was merely a symptom. He was starting to obtain an understanding of the cause.

Voren picked up the canvas and marched down to his bedchamber. He hung it on the wall, replacing a portrait of himself. It would serve as a reminder. In the coming days, he knew he would need it.

Nothing new came to him. No plans. Not even the vague formation of an idea. He only knew that, somehow, something had to change.

I will be powerless no more.

MEVON AWOKE AS water was thrown at his head. He spluttered and shook, trying to banish the fat droplets swimming down his face. As his senses returned, he realized just how parched he was and instead held out his tongue to catch as much of the moisture as possible.

Blessings did much for Hardohl, allowing them to push their bodies well past what would kill normal men.

The basic requirements for food and water, however, were not among their many boons.

Mevon tried to move but found that he couldn't budge so much as a finger in any direction. He flexed against his bindings, rattling the loops of thick chain constricted around his body. A steel stake had been driven deep into the ground at his back, and the chains were attached to it.

He blinked several times, adjusting his eyes to his surroundings. A dimly lit tent surrounded him. *The same one we fought in?* No, it was round and black. He searched, but could find nothing else in the room besides him, the stake and chains . . . and the bandit lords looking down on him with curious eyes.

"You are one hard man to put down," Slick Ren said.

Mevon still felt the itch from when deadly poison had raged throughout his body. Slick Ren's daggers had been coated in the stuff. The wounds had healed closed, and the poison was purged from his body by his blessings, but they had done their part. He had been weakened nearly to the point of death just long enough for his captors to strip him down to his breeches and bind him utterly.

"You two," Mevon said, glancing from Slick Ren to Derthon, "have made a grievous mistake."

"Only time will tell, of course," said the woman. "Me? I'll hold off judgment until this has all played out."

Mevon grunted. "You're running out of time then, Slick Ren. My men are still out there, and a vast cordon of Imperial troops is tightening its grip on these hills as we speak."

She laughed. "Oh, the regulars won't be giving us any trouble, I assure you. As for your men . . ." her eyes darted to Derthon. He held open a flap of the tent and motioned a group of figures inside. Nine men garbed as Imperial soldiers guiding three others in shackles. Idrus, Tolvar, and Arozir.

Mevon studied them with wide eyes, a blade of ice stabbing between his shoulders.

"Deepest apologies, Hardohl," Idrus said. "Somehow, they knew our plans. They countered us perfectly."

"What happened? Where are the rest?"

"Captured." Tolvar spat at the feet of the bandit lords. "Every last one of us."

"They dug deep pits around the entire camp, then covered them with wood planks and sod," Arozir said. "After we began our assault, the bastards pulled the logs out, and we were stranded on an island, surrounded by dozens of casters."

Mevon narrowed his gaze on Idrus. "Surely the rangers at least got away?"

Idrus shook his head. "Turns out the tents they entered were empty save a lingering alchemical powder. One breath inside, and they each fell into sleep."

Mevon lowered his head, closing his eyes. "I see."

The prisoners and their guards shuffled out of the tent, and Mevon lost himself in thought.

His plan, turned to ashes at first contact. It didn't seem possible. It should have been the last thing his enemy suspected, but they knew just how to counter it. Not just blunted, or even rebuffed, but turned on its scorching head.

Jasside. That woman. She was to blame. Her bad acting had turned out to be brilliant. It had convinced Mevon that her faith in her allies was a deliberate charade, when that was exactly what she had wanted him to think. He hated her. Hated being manipulated. Hated the golden man and the bandit lords and the greybeard and all who followed them.

But mostly, he hated himself.

Possibly the first lesson he received, even before teachings on justice and obedience, was that defeat was intolerable and failure worse than death. He had held that lesson close, wrapping it around his soul. He viewed the entire world through lenses made of the certainty of victory. Not once had the glass shattered.

Until now.

"So," he whispered, "this is what failure feels like."

He couldn't stand it. How he wished he could get ahold of a blade. Something sharp and pointed, so he could throw himself on it. Such was as he deserved.

It didn't seem like he would get the chance. Nor could he even fight back. He had barely enough room to breathe, and his limbs were twisted in such a way that he had no leverage, no way to even begin breaking free so that he could fight, dying if he had to but taking his price in blood even as he fell.

He had only one choice left to him, really. They had kept him and his men alive for a reason. He might as well find out what they wanted.

The tent flap opened again and three now-familiar figures strode in.

GILSHAMED KEPT HIS eyes locked on Mevon as he entered the tent. Yandumar stepped through on his left, his eyes wide, face strained with his efforts at self-control. On his right came Jasside.

She stopped on the threshold, shaking. She stared at Mevon a few beats in silence.

"Jasside?" Gilshamed asked. "Is everything all right?"

She shook her head. "I can't. I just . . . can't. I'm sorry."

She turned and fled from the tent.

"Wait—"

Yandumar grasped his arm and turned him back. "She's had a rough month. Let her be."

Gilshamed took a breath and nodded. "Very well." He turned his gaze to Slick Ren and Derthon. "Some privacy, please?"

"He's all yours," Slick Ren said. The siblings slipped out of the tent, letting the flap swing down behind them.

A moment began that stretched in time, in which he and Yandumar examined Mevon, and the Hardohl them. None spoke. None moved. Barely a breath could be heard as the smell of mingled sweat filled the close confines.

At last, Gilshamed cleared his throat. "Mevon Daere, it is good to finally meet you. Especially now that you are no longer trying to kill us."

"Oh, I'm still trying to kill you, but you seem quite adept at turning my efforts"—he shook the chains holding him—"into dust."

Gilshamed laughed at that, and Mevon returned a look of incredulity. *If he's skeptical of my amusement, then this will really turn his world around.* He turned, indicating his companion. "This is Yandumar, a former Elite captain under the Hardohl Kael."

This introduction had the desired effect. Mevon eyes flashed wide, blazing scrutiny on Yandumar.

"My name is Gilshamed, of the valynkar."

Somehow, Mevon's eyes widened even further. "Impossible. The Shroud—"

"Has been pierced," he said, smiling. "Just not from the outside."

Mevon regarded him, staring murder for several beats before answering. "I've heard rumors of a . . . tunnel?"

"Yes, far to the northwest of here, buried deeply underground. It seems your empire is no longer content with ruling only this land." Gilshamed waved his hand wide. "But that is not why we are here."

"Why then?"

Gilshamed smiled. "We are here for you."

He was expecting a series of possible reactions from Mevon upon hearing this. A shrug, however, was not among them. Gilshamed narrowed his eyes, searching the Hardohl's face for clues to his inner self.

Despite nearly four millennia of practice, he could discern nothing.

Eventually, though, Mevon sneered at him. "Your pawn of a sorceress has already made that clear. What do you want with me, then?"

"We wish to recruit you to our cause, of course."

Mevon's breath seemed to catch in his throat, and Gilshamed felt himself mimicking the reflex. The moment hung like a slice of frozen time.

Mevon's laughter shattered the ice.

Gilshamed turned to Yandumar, hoping to find . . . something. An answer, perhaps. Hope. All he saw was despair as the Hardohl bellowed, sucking in another lungful of air to lend continued exuberance to his cackling.

Finally, the laughter tapered off. Gilshamed drew himself up straight. "I can see why that amuses you. You are the empire's most fearsome instrument of death, after all, held in high regard even among your peers. By all accounts, you are a man who not only excels at killing but also thrives on it. What reason could you possibly have to turn against the mierothi?"

Mevon arched an eyebrow. "Is this what all of Jasside's babble was about? Were her words somehow supposed to prepare me to accept your offer? Gods, what fools you are."

"No, Mevon." Gilshamed leaned forward. "She was merely meant to make you ready to listen."

"That so? Well, here I am. Say what you have to so we can be done with this charade."

"No." Gilshamed placed a hand on Yandumar's shoulder. "It will not be I who convinces you of anything."

YANDUMAR STARED AT Mevon, motionless. *You've waited long enough, Yan. Don't screw this up.*

His gaze must have lingered too long. Mevon's face grew impatient. "Well, old man?"

Yandumar took a deep breath.

"Thirty years ago, I was an Elite captain, serving under Kael. You knew him well."

"Yes," said Mevon, as if it had been a question. "He was like a father to me."

"If so, then I'm glad. Old bastard owed me a favor."

"What do you mean?"

"I was only twenty-two at the time. Gods, how naïve I was back then . . ." he trailed off, closing his eyes as memory took hold. He could smell the burning flesh, taste the blood and salt of his tears. "Our Fist was out on assignment, tracking down Sanction violators who had been hiding out up north near the Taditali vineyards. It was in the hottest time of year, in the hottest part of the empire. We had all been taking a break in the shade. A messenger came for me. Told me I had visitors, sent by the emperor himself. I was nothing special. No reason to have that tyrant's attention. I should have known what was coming. But I went. Alone, as instructed. Still armed and armored, though. Scorching scale-backs were too arrogant to think that little detail could make a difference."

Yandumar opened his eyes. Mevon's gaze was locked with his, and he seemed scarcely to be breathing. Good. At least he was paying attention.

Yandumar continued. "Three daeloth greeted me, there in that lonely glade. They were adjudicators, and their message was simple: Your wife and two oldest children are dead, and now . . . it's your turn." He saw the question in Mevon's face. "Why? My wife was pregnant, full term, and . . ." he paused, struggling, " . . . not a lick of sorcery could touch either mother or baby."

Yandumar watched Mevon's face, saw the wheels turning behind those green eyes. Eyes so very like his own.

"I discovered what Imperial doctrine was regarding voids that day: taking them—taking *you*—to be trained in their academy, turned into loyal killers. But those daeloth discovered something else: how terrible a father's rage can be. It was their final lesson."

Mevon opened his mouth, but it was several moments before words came out. "Are . . . are you saying . . . ?"

"Yes . . . son. I am." Yandumar stepped forward with an iron key in his hand. He put it to the locks securing Mevon's chains. "And I will prove it to you."

It took longer than he expected. The chains were wrapped tightly around the majority of his body and were meant to hold against the strength of a Hardohl. When the last link fell to the ground, so did Mevon, slumping. Denying him food and water had been necessary, but Yandumar still cringed as Mevon—*My son!*—struggled to keep from collapsing.

He moved forward again to help Mevon stand.

Mevon grasped his tunic, pulling himself up. He stood still. Caught his breath.

He pushed Yandumar away violently and scrambled for the exit. Gilshamed stepped aside. Yandumar hurried out after him.

What?

Mevon stared. There were no guards encompassing the tent. No wall of steel and flesh to keep him contained. He almost felt insulted.

He could see his men though, disarmed and sitting

under guard a hundred paces away. Intact, as his captains had said. He wasn't sure if they had been forced to lie on that point. Not that he expected them to.

Something else stood closer. He had dismissed it at first. It didn't make sense. Quake was saddled and ready, and a soldier held out the reins in Mevon's direction.

"You can go, if you want," Yandumar said behind him.

Mevon spun. "What game are you playing?"

"No game." Gilshamed emerged from the tent but stayed well out of the way and remained silent. Yandumar took a step forward, his hands open in a gesture of peace. "We won't stop you and your men from leaving. But first, will you hear one more thing?"

Mevon grabbed the reins and shoved the soldier away. "What can you possibly say that would convince me to join you?" The words came out in a shriek. *What is happening to me?*

"Just this." Yandumar took one last pause, a deep breath. "Ragremos Remembers."

A hammerblow seemed to crush the air from Mevon's chest. His blood turned colder than the Frozen Fingers of the deep south. His eyeballs threatened to pop out of his skull.

"Where?" said Mevon. "How?"

"You were eighteen," Yandumar said. "At your graduation. Kael handed you your *Andun*, then leaned in, and whispered, 'Tell no one, and never forget these words.' Then, he said, 'Ragremos Remembers.' He said that because I asked him to. Because I couldn't be there to say the words myself."

Mevon heard a rumble rise from behind him. It was faint at first, only a few voices. They had heard what Yandumar had said, and now repeated the words.

"*Ragremos Remembers. Ragremos Remembers.*"

It continued, becoming a chant and rising in volume. He thought he recognized some of the voices.

"Don't you see, son?" continued Yandumar. "All of this has been for you." He stepped up to Mevon and laid a hand on his shoulder, locking eyes. Eyes an identical shade of green as his. The face an aged mirror of his own.

Mevon shook. *I . . . I had a family?* The notion jarred him. He was married to duty and fought alongside his adopted brothers. He wanted nothing else. *Needed* nothing else. A dead mother and siblings he had never known had no place in his life or his heart.

But he felt his blood rising all the same.

The chanting grew louder.

"This is what happens to all Hardohl?" Mevon asked.

"Aye," Yandumar said. "Think about it. Have you ever met a void that wasn't carrying an *Andun*?"

Mevon didn't need to think long. "No."

Yandumar shook his head. "Of course not. The emperor is much too practical to let a resource like you just lie around without being used."

"*Used.*" How that word stoked his rage. He had been loyal and obedient his whole life. Efficient, deadly, just as they had trained him to be. Yet, in the end, little more than a tool. *Rekaj, you have much to answer for!* He spotted Jasside in the distance, eyes rimmed red. *Much.*

The whole valley now echoed with resounding cries.

A third of his Elite had risen to their feet, lending their voices to the crowd.

He looked at Yandumar. The evidence seemed thin; yet, somehow, Mevon knew it for truth. They could have lured any Hardohl into their trap, but they hadn't. *They did it for* me. *And at enormous risk to themselves, no less.* That, to him, was proof enough. The man's claim . . . he could not deny.

But to turn his back on everything he had ever known? It was not something he had ever fathomed. He peered down the inevitable roads that led from this place, this decision. Veering destinies. One would pit him against the only family he had, fighting for people who had betrayed and used him. The other?

Mevon smiled. "Revolution, huh? Sounds dangerous. Bloody." His men seemed eager enough. In truth . . . so did he. If nothing else, it promised to be a fight for the ages, and he could not conceive of a more worthy foe than the mierothi.

And if Mevon wanted to have *any* chance at discovering true justice, he could not turn back. Not from this.

"Though I will not lead my men into anything blindly, for now . . . you can count us in."

Yandumar's face lit up like a lightglobe. He clapped Mevon hard on the shoulder and held out his other hand. Derthon appeared. He placed Mevon's *Andun* into Yandumar's open palm. The old man then presented it to Mevon. "Ragremos Remembers," he said once more.

Mevon took hold of Justice. He faced his men and held it up over his head.

The chanting stopped. Silence struck the valley like a hammer.

Mevon shouted, "Ragremos Remembers!"

Thousands erupted into cheering.

Mevon, finally, returned Yandumar's embrace. "This saying . . . you'll have to tell me what it means."

"Of course, son. Of course. I have so much to tell you."

PART II

PART II.

Chapter 7

THE WOODS WERE quiet and still, but Draevenus remained wary. He, of all people, knew better than to trust that silence meant emptiness.

In the wilderness, it usually meant the opposite.

His hands worked automatically, placing another trip wire, and pulling it to just the right tension before securing the tie. Soon, he would be vulnerable, and such precautions served to ease his mind. No sorcerous wards though. They drew more attention than they were worth.

And attention was what he always strove to avoid. Now, more than ever.

He had been traveling southwest out of Mecrithos for three weeks, avoiding the main roads in favor of lesser paths. The forest here was taller, thicker, and greener than the patches of trees visible from the capital's thick outer bastion. Wilder. He felt more at ease here than he did in any city or town.

Draevenus circumnavigated his campsite, giving his web of traps one last check. He had spent several human lifetimes inventing new ways to cause death. Doing the opposite was vastly more difficult. He checked twice to make sure he saw nothing that would give him away.

Ready.

He sat down and leaned back against a tree with his legs crossed. He had always been a creature of solitude. Assassination, by its very nature, broke down life into its most rudimentary physicality. He could not even get close to anyone without noting the places where pulsing veins strayed closest to the skin. Yet here, in these woods, he felt a stab of loneliness. It took him awhile to determine its source.

Draevenus shook his head. *Oh, Voren, what did you do to me?*

It had been centuries since he had last called any of his mierothi kin a friend, and no humans could overcome their fear of him. Only a single valynkar, just as lonely as he was, finally staked a claim within him. Draevenus wished he could have lingered longer but knew that he had work to do that could not wait.

He closed his eyes. Breathing deep, he energized for half a beat and grabbed hold of just enough power to do what he needed without drawing notice. He hoped.

In his mind, Draevenus formed his will into a sphere of darkness. Slowly, it flattened out, spreading into a thin disc. A portal. He took his consciousness, his truest self, and stepped through.

Into communion.

An expanse of static white, unending in all directions, came clear in his mind's eye. Pricks of darkness dotted his view, like the night sky reversed and spread out on a vast plane.

Here, he had no body—unless he wished to—but he could still move as he pleased. He floated upwards to get a clearer view. The dark stars each represented a caster. The largest ones stood for his kin, while those less substantial indicated daeloth and any others with diluted mierothi blood.

Placement of the spots in this place depended upon physical location. There, ahead of him, the thickest cluster of them stood for Mecrithos. Nowhere in the empire was there a greater concentration of mierothi and other casters.

No. That wasn't quite true. *Don't think about that. Not yet.*

He floated forward, leaving behind the representation of the capital. He sought another. She would be found farther ahead, currently near the continent's edge. Draevenus could almost feel the leagues passing by as the occasional blotch of darkness came and went.

Only a few dots now remained between him and the void beyond, and he began to feel resistance to his movement, pressure and a kind of buzzing. The Shroud. Invisible, here as in the waking world, but it still proved an impervious barrier to anything wishing to get in. Or, get out.

By Ruul, what fools we were back then.

His eye spotted what he was looking for. A single negative star, alone, darker than all the rest. And larger. He brushed up against it, then pulled back. As he waited, he formed for himself a body, clothed in a simple black robe. He might as well be presentable.

A mark later, the star pulsed, and he felt another's presence in communion with him. In beats, she had formed herself a body, complete with a form-hugging gown and a glass of wine in her hand.

Draevenus looked down on her. "Sister. I trust you are not too busy?"

Vashodia smiled. "For you? Never. But do make it quick. Paen just broke the seal on a cask of his father's private reserve. It's going to be a rousing evening."

If he had a real spine, a chill would have just climbed up it. Even after all these centuries, he still disliked the notion of his baby sister getting . . . intimate. With anyone. Especially given her appearance.

"Very well. I'll try to be brief," he said.

"And you're doing a marvelous job so far."

He sighed. "How are things progressing out there?"

"Splendidly." She took a sip of her wine. "All the little puppets are dancing their steps in tune."

"And your personal marionettes?"

She shrugged. "Satisfied, for the moment."

Draevenus nodded. "You will let me know if the need arises for more . . . direct involvement?"

"There won't be. I've planned far too well for that." Vashodia's face held confidence, as always. And, as always, he couldn't help but wonder what madness lay hidden there.

"Sister . . . you can't—"

"What? Drop a pebble on a mountaintop and expect the planet to change its turning?" She laughed. "Yes, dear brother. Yes I can."

Draevenus sighed. He formed a small black dagger and began dancing it across his knuckles. Silence hung between them. Vashodia took another sip.

Be brief. "I'm going after them," he said. "Will you not reconsider?"

She laughed again, but the tone held no mirth this time. Instead, it cut to his bones. "Don't be such a sentimental fool."

"But she's—"

"Nothing to me!"

Draevenus stared at her. Even here, there was fire in her eyes. *Do you see me the same way? I am tool as well, just like everyone you touch?*

He shook the thoughts loose from his head. Such thinking led only to despair, and he'd had enough of that in his life to know how pointless it was.

"Well, I'm going. With or without your assistance. Be so kind as to keep me apprised?"

Vashodia scrunched her face up. "Fine. But don't dawdle about on your little sideshow. We can't have you missing the grand finale, now can we?"

"No guarantees. I'll be alone, after all. Anything could happen."

She arched an eyebrow at him. "Is this some pathetic last attempt to garner my sympathy?"

He shrugged.

Her face lit up. "It worked! I give you my most heart-felt blessings, dear brother. Go and make Ruul proud."

"That's cruel, Vash. Even for you."

"Ah. Right. I take it you and our beloved 'deity' still aren't in each other's good graces?"

Draevenus tossed the dagger to the side. It vanished in a puff of black mist. "No. We are not."

She stepped up and patted him on the cheek. He glared at her. She giggled and retreated a few steps in mock concern for her safety, then held her hands behind her back in a gesture of utter innocence. She almost looked convincing. Draevenus fought the urge to smile. Failed.

Nothing more need be said, so he nodded once to her, then turned away. He began dissolving his body, and with it, his perceptions of communion. He said nothing as she faded. She forbade him from saying good-bye, and from expressing what was always on his heart. She couldn't stop him from thinking it, though.

I love you, dear sister. Take care.

The white void vanished, replaced by a foggy darkness. Draevenus inhaled. Real air. He blinked open his eyes, taking stock of the forest around him.

Something was wrong.

He leapt into a crouch, daggers in both fists. He didn't energize. Not yet. He could summon what power he needed at a moment's notice. His blades were usually enough.

He held his breath, closed his eyes, and listened. There it was again. A faint sound. Rustling, and something else. A whimper?

He rushed in the direction of the noise, keeping low and silent. His eyes darted. Muscles bunched, ready to spring in any direction.

He came within sight of one of his outermost traps. Something was lying there, tangled and bleeding.

A boy, no more than ten years old.

Scorch me!

Blades went back in their sheaths as he rushed forward.

THE HONEY BLOOMS filled Voren's nose with their scent, sweet yet subtle, their vines hanging down over the hedgerows. He strolled past marble benches and carved stone friezes, potted shrubs and dwarf trees of every variety imaginable, and beds of flowers in colors so vivid, his eyes watered if he stared too long. Sparrows and bluebirds chirped a symphony as they flitted about, snatching up insects in their beaks.

The palace gardens were his favorite place. Were it not for the dark cloud hanging over his thoughts, he would almost be content.

Voren lifted his eyes to the stark face of the Imperial Palace. "Is it not humorous how something so beautiful as to make Elos weep can rest under the gaze of that which is most foul?"

Kael grunted. "Feeling poetic are we?"

As ever, for his outings, the aged Hardohl marched at his side, attached at the wrist by his fleshly tother. His very presence was a reminder of Voren's fears and regrets.

"Always," Voren replied. "But I shall try to refrain from boring you too greatly."

"Good."

They turned a corner, passing beneath branches pruned into an archway and dotted with white blossoms, and began down a path lined by sentinel hedges. The tall, verdant plants, trimmed at sharp angles, blocked all light from the setting sun. Voren realized belatedly that they had entered the hedge maze.

"Did you want to turn back?" Kael asked. The question did not surprise Voren. He usually avoided the maze. It was the one place in the gardens that he did cherish.

"There is no turning back," said Voren. "Not now. We might as well see our way through."

"Whatever you say."

They marched on. Kael lagged behind a step and let Voren choose the path, which he did without hesitation. After a few turns, however, they came to a dead end. Voren quickly backtracked, choosing the opposite path from their last juncture. After a few more splits, they came again to another aborted path, and Voren was forced to retreat once more to their last intersection. The very next turn ended in a solid wall of hedges.

Voren felt the heat of both frustration and embarrassment rising. It didn't help matters when he spied Kael's undisguised amusement.

"Well, I suppose you know exactly how to traverse this place, then?" Voren said.

"Eh?" Kael said. "Well, maybe I do."

"Then tell me, Kael. Tell me how to get out of this mess. Tell me!"

The Hardohl stared at him, eyes blank, for several beats. "We ain't talking about this maze anymore, are we?"

Voren closed his eyes, taking a deep breath. He shook his head.

"Come on," said Kael.

The old man stepped forward, tugging Voren along at a gentle pace. He maneuvered through several turns with confidence. A few marks and half a dozen intersections later, when they had yet to come to any dead ends, Voren admitted to himself that the Hardohl most likely knew his way. When he voiced this observation, Kael merely shrugged.

"How do you do it?" asked Voren. "How do you take every step with such assurance?"

"Simple. I actually know where I'm going.

"And why."

Voren eyed Kael sideways. "And how exactly is that supposed to help me?"

"Did I say it was?"

Voren gritted his teeth. He held out his hand, feeling the branches scrape across his fingertips as he walked.

"You upset about the child?" Kael said.

Voren cringed, remembering the terrified squeals of the infant. "Partly," he said. Voren realized he was shaking.

"Thought so. You get like this every time you inscribe a blessing."

"Do I?"

"Twelve times in as many years. Same reaction."

Not quite the same. Not this time. "Is it worth it you think?"

Kael smiled and grunted. "I'd be long dead if you hadn't done the same to me."

"True. I just wish the procedure were not so barbaric."

Kael held up his arm, pinching the flesh of his forearm between his fingers. "Only way past our defenses."

Voren allowed himself small smile. At least the child had healed itself after they were done. At least the screams had finally ended.

"What else?" asked Kael.

"Hmm?"

"You said 'partly.' What else is bothering you?"

Voren exhaled, loudly and slowly. *How can I tell you of it all? Of centuries spent keeping everything inside? Of a love I could never have and a hate I could never act upon? Of an unexpected friend who, without meaning to, did just about the worst thing imaginable to me? How can I speak of my guilt and pride, which are both, inexplicably, tied to the same event?*

Yet somehow, when he next opened his mouth, it all came out. It was jumbled at first, as he kept skipping backwards and forwards in time in an attempt to explain all the relevant history, but eventually he got his points across. When he finished, Voren felt as if a great weight had been lifted from his shoulders.

Kael had remained silent throughout his avalanche of

words. "I think I hear what you're saying, but what is it that you *want*?"

"I am done," Voren said. "I want . . . *out*." He stopped, shocked yet relieved to finally hear those words escape his lips. "What would you do if you were in my place?"

Kael studied him. Voren held his breath. After several long beats, the Hardohl nodded, as if coming to a decision, then turned and began walking forward once more.

"Change," Kael said. "It's never easy."

Voren knew that. Change had led him to this. But he also knew that he could not go back to the way it used to be. "I'm prepared for whatever hardships may come."

"Are you now?" Kael chuckled. "So, what would *I* do? I suppose I would have to have a goal first. Then, a plan."

Voren remained silent, his attention now rapt. *My goal is freedom. But my plan?* He had no idea where to start.

"You would need allies," continued Kael. "And you would have to know their strengths and weaknesses. Same with your enemies."

The trail brightened ahead. They were coming to the end of the maze.

"From a position of powerlessness, it's best to make your adversary underestimate you. At least at first. Until it's too late."

They passed beneath another archway of shrubbery, emerging into a red-stone courtyard on the far side of the gardens.

"And one of the best strategies is to turn your enemy's own assets against them."

Kael, voice lowered now to a whisper, added at last, "And even if you don't think you can win, you might as well bring as many of the bastards down with you as you can."

Voren nodded. "Thank you, Kael. I appreciate the advice, and . . . your discretion."

Kael shrugged.

Voren, however, smiled. He had an ally now, which was a far greater victory than he could have hoped for in so short a time. Now, he had a chance to change things. Change that would be of *his* choosing, not anyone else's.

He cast his gaze up at the palace once more. This time, he felt no dread. He only wondered which of the mierothi would be most susceptible to manipulation.

JASSIDE DRAGGED HER feet across the rocky floor of the tunnel, the echo of her steps amplified by the too-close walls and ceiling. A score of people scuffled along nearby, a mix of shepherds, bandits, and converted Imperial soldiers. No one spoke. Conversation was prohibited while on scout duty, which was the reason she had volunteered for every shift she could these past ten days of flight.

Absolute darkness held them in its embrace. Even for her it was suffocating. To combat it, the group huddled within her sphere of influence, wherein she gifted each person with night vision. While they kept their physical senses alert, she maintained forward wards capable of detecting danger in any form.

The empire didn't know about this network of caves.

Thank God Slick Ren and Derthon had, else the Imperial army—which closed in soon after Mevon arrived—would have trapped and slaughtered them all. The revolution wasn't quite ready to deal with a threat of that magnitude.

Two casters normally accompanied each lead element, but Jasside worked alone. She did the job a pair usually struggled with, and still had enough mental capacity to send back periodic reports through commune, distract herself by mapping the tunnels, and keep prepared a few nasty spells for any shadow beasts or darkwisps they came across. She'd already put that last to use on a dozen occasions.

The stench of long-unwashed bodies mingled with the ever-present fungal aroma of the caves. Jasside reached to a chain around her neck and brought a box the size of an infant's fist to her nose. She inhaled deeply. A strong floral scent filled her nose. She released the trinket, letting it jangle against a string of others attached to the necklace. She had made them all herself. Jasside cherished its return, for it had been taken from her when she was captured.

By Mevon.

No. Don't think about him. Just stop.

But she couldn't.

Jasside replayed the scene in her mind, over and over, watching the daggers fly from Mevon's hands. Watching one sink into Brefand's chest. Watching his body fall, already dead.

Brother, forgive me. I was too late. I should have been faster. I'm sorry. So, so sorry. . .

But she'd done what was asked of her. Completed her mission. The outcome was everything Gilshamed had wanted. He and Yandumar had been pleased with her performance. She was *useful*. The weeks of maintaining her façade, all while facing her half brother's killer, had drained her, body and spirit alike. But it had all been worth the pain.

Right?

Someone tapped her on the shoulder.

She jumped, barely managing to suppress a squeak. It was only Orbrahn, her replacement. She had to stifle a spike of envy at the sight of his face. She had never seen him pushed to his limits but had heard tell that he was strong. Very strong. Stronger than some daeloth, if the rumors could be believed, though she didn't see how that was possible. He had, apparently, been a crucial factor in several battles already.

Well, you're not the only one who can prove their worth.

He gave her a wry smile, saying nothing, and shooed her away. Jasside forced out a stoic grin in return. She slowed, encompassed by a shuffle of humanity as the scout patrol exchanged personnel. She felt Orbrahn energize and let her own spells diminish.

Most marched backwards through the tunnel, eager to find friends and family. Jasside simply stood still. Both groups soon passed out of the range of her senses, and she exhaled loudly, glad for the peace and isolation.

Her thoughts again drifted to her half brother, and she struggled to hold back the tears.

Loud footsteps rang out behind her, coming nearer.

Jasside turned to face the interloper, turning her sorrow into annoyance. She energized a moment, then recast night vision on herself. Her breath caught as she saw who approached. He was the last person she wanted to see.

"There you are," Mevon said. "I've been looking everywhere."

His voice conveyed familiarity, even friendliness. Such tones she had only heard him use with his captains, and rarely at that.

She pivoted and began tramping forward. Stiffly, she said, "Is there some way I can be of service, Hardohl?"

Mevon chuckled. His long strides carried him to her side, and he had to shorten his steps after that to keep pace with her. "No need for that, Jasside. Call me Mevon."

Jasside entertained the notion, briefly, of running. But she knew she couldn't escape him that way. She slowed her steps instead. "Very well."

"And no," he said, "there's nothing I need from you. You've done so much for me already."

"Glad I could be of use." *Please just go away.*

Mevon shook his head. "I still can't believe you would put yourself at such risk."

She gritted her teeth. "The payoff was deemed worthy."

"Oh, aye. But what you had to endure? What you had to sacrifice?" He grunted. It seemed . . . respectful.

She fought down the rising bubble of mixed sorrow and hate. She'd kept her mask on for so long around him, letting it slip only rarely, and briefly. She hadn't the energy to resurrect it now. *Why can't you take a hint?*

And yet, he didn't; he went on, oblivious. "I've been in battle countless times, but I always had a plan. Was always certain of victory. You? You entered knowing you would fail, and that your only hope of survival was thin and rested squarely on my shoulders.

"That takes courage. The kind I've never seen before."

Jasside stopped breathing. She looked up at him. His face seemed sincere. She exhaled slowly but could think of nothing to say. She didn't trust her voice just now anyway.

She pressed her lips together, hoping it looked like a smile, and nodded. Mevon appeared to take it as affirmation.

Scorch you, Mevon! She wanted to let herself hate him, but could already feel the fire of her fury starting to ebb. It was easy to hate a monster. Even one cajoled into being an ally. Why couldn't he have stayed as he was? Why, now, did he have to start showing a little humanity?

They marched along for several marks in silence. How they must have appeared as young lovers out for a stroll. How much that thought disgusted her.

"I have a proposition for you," Mevon said after a time.

"Yes?"

"When you disabled me with that spell, it was the first time you used it?"

Jasside shrugged. "It's not like I've had someone to practice it on."

"You do now."

Her eyes widened. "What?"

"We'll likely run into mierothi at some point. They may know the spell. I'd like to see if there's any way to defeat it, or at least find a way to lessen the impact of its effects."

"I see." *So, I'm to be used by you still.* She sighed. It was for the good of the revolution. She could put her feelings aside for that. Again. If she had to.

"Also," Mevon said, "there's a good chance we'll end up fighting other Hardohl. You might be glad of the practice. It could prove invaluable."

Her mouth went dry. She hadn't thought of that. *He* had. And now that the idea was in her head, she could see the advantages. She could get better, faster, even learn how to hold it longer. Maybe next time, her failure wouldn't lead to a loved one's death.

Twice was enough. I can't survive a third such lesson.

"Yes," she said at last. "A fine idea. When should we start?"

"Soon. According to Slick Ren, we'll be out of these tunnels in a few days. Times will be busy when we emerge."

"Has Gilshamed revealed his plans?"

"Not yet. He'd better do it soon, though. I don't like being left in the dark."

Nor I.

He turned to go, appearing troubled. She thought to call to him, give him some encouragement. *Don't be a fool, Jasside.* Perhaps she didn't hate him with as much passion as she had a toll ago—he had reached out to her, after all—but she wasn't about to lie to herself.

Mevon had yet to earn her forgiveness. And Jasside, most certainly, was not ready to give it.

THE CAVES HAD become dim again. Gilshamed energized fully and conjured a score of tiny suns, casting them to the roof of the tunnel. They spread in both directions. One remained directly overhead, illuminating those marching nearby. The dying sun faded before the brilliance of the new, for it had been cast three tolls ago, long forgotten by Gilshamed. He only became aware of the need for replacements because he was looking for someone and had been having trouble making out faces.

Now, he could see clearly.

Yandumar marched just ahead, chatting with Slick Ren. The majority of his time seemed to be spent either in her presence or in his son's. The man smiled. Never stopped, in fact. Gilshamed had given him his space, knowing that he himself would have trouble focusing on someone else's needs at such a time.

But it had been long enough. Now, Gilshamed needed answers.

He strode to the pair. He did not try to mask his approach, nor his demeanor. Yandumar met his eyes at a dozen paces and cut off his banter with Slick Ren. She turned, eying Gilshamed with scorn.

Gilshamed matched their strides. "A fine evening to you, Elrenia. May I have a word with Yandumar in private?"

She smiled, puckering the faint scar under her right eye. "Of course, Gilshamed." She made to step past him.

She stopped and whipped a hand towards his throat. It came up short. The distance between was occupied by the tip of a dagger.

"But call me that again, I'll take a strip of your hide from navel to neck."

Gilshamed swallowed. Nodded.

"Evening, then." Slick Ren dashed off.

Gilshamed glared a moment after her departing form. "I can see the appeal, Yan, but is she truly worth the risk?"

Yandumar laughed. "I don't know, Gil. She's wearing my resolve down. It might just be a matter of time. Ha!"

Gilshamed flashed a grin he knew looked halfhearted. Yandumar seemed to pick up his mood quick enough. "Alas, that's not why I came to talk to you."

"I know."

Gilshamed studied Yandumar's face, and said, "Ragremos Remembers?"

Yandumar twitched.

"Why did you not tell me sooner about this?"

"The time wasn't right."

"How so?"

Yandumar ran fingers through his beard. "It's complicated."

Gilshamed scoffed. "Complicated, I can handle." *Something out of my control, however. . .*

"You know what my people did way back?"

Gilshamed nodded. The nation of Ragremos, a warrior society, invaded its neighbors in a blitz campaign, achieving almost total victory in a few weeks, which was far too quickly for valynkar arbiters to step in and stop them. The only remaining resistance was a small group of tribesmen, harrying Ragremon forces in the swamplands. Accounts varied, but it was said the Ragremons drove the tribes into the deep swamps, lands untamed and unmapped, thinking them as good as defeated.

History, of course, proved otherwise.

When the tribe reemerged months later, decimated to only half again a thousand, they were transformed, and wielding a new, dark sorcery with wild potency.

The mierothi had begun their rise.

It did not stop there. The armies of Ragremos capitulated before them, electing servitude over annihilation, and became the core of the mierothi military machine. For half a century, their entire nation served as their most elite warriors, the strong right arm to mierothi sorcery.

"Yes," Gilshamed said at last. "I remember well your people's ferocity in combat. And . . . that you were pledged to the other side."

"And so, our words."

Of course. "What do they mean?"

"After your kind were banished, the rest of the continent fell easily. The mierothi began a . . . consolidation."

"Which is?"

"They moved people around. Mixed 'em up. Outlawed the mention of nations and peoples. In only a few generations, the past was buried. That was their final victory."

"But?"

"But they left us alone. Let us stay unified as a people. We'd served them so long, and so faithfully, I guess they figured they had nothing to worry about.

"But they were wrong. Well . . . *will* be wrong. Some-day."

Ah. The fog begins to lift. "I presume that there is a vow in place?"

Yandumar nodded.

"And that, once invoked, your entire nation will rise up to correct the mistakes of your ancestors?"

He nodded again.

Gilshamed smiled. "Well, what reason not to share something like that? Such allies to our cause will surely tip the balance in our favor."

Yandumar grimaced, half turning away. "I . . . had to be sure."

"Of what?"

The aged face seemed almost ancient in that moment. Perhaps it was. The weight of a nation, and centuries of its traditions, rested on his shoulders. Yandumar sighed. "Of the resolve of the revolution. Of finding Mevon." He paused. "Of you."

Gilshamed couldn't stop the rising bubble of fury from entering his voice. "Me? Why ever would you doubt my resolve? Have I not proven, by my very persistence, my dedication?"

"Never said I doubted that. Just had to make sure all of this at least had a chance of success. I won't invoke our vow lightly. If I do, and we fail, the mierothi will hunt us to ex-tinction, and this land will lose its best hope for freedom."

Gilshamed waved a hand towards Yandumar, indicat-ing his acceptance. His companion seemed to breathe a little easier.

He considered the implications. He had machinations in place around the continent, movements he had set in motion that would provide ever-increasing pressure and distraction upon the empire. Having a hidden force of efficacious warriors would provide an enormous enhancement to his plans. He smiled, thoughts forming for their eventual use.

His friend pulled him up short, however. "But that's not the real reason I didn't tell you," said Yandumar. "I actually hoped you'd never find out."

Gilshamed whipped his head around. "What?"

Yandumar ground his teeth a few beats, seeming to mull over his thoughts. "What will you do, Gil, once this is all over? If we win, that is."

"I . . ." He forced his face to appear introspective. In truth, he knew exactly what he would do. The endless years he had spent wandering the world, searching for a weakness in the Shroud, had given him ample time to fantasize about his eventual victory.

He could not give his true answer. He suspected that it would set Yandumar against him. Perhaps permanently.

"Once I am satisfied the land is in good hands, I will depart."

"Truly?"

"I would have no reason to stay."

"Ah, but what about your people?"

Gilshamed furrowed his brow. "What of them?"

"The truth will get out eventually. Once, they were settled here. If they learn about the demise of the mierothi, and about the way in, do you really think they will stay away forever?"

"Perhaps not. But why should that distress you? What about the return of the valynkar has you troubled?"

Yandumar grunted. "Because while my people may have had a part to play in the rise of the mierothi, your people set the stage for their victory."

"What the abyss are you talking about?"

"I'm talking about your scorching arbiters!"

Gilshamed frowned. "They maintained peace among the lands. I don't see—"

"How, Gil? How did they maintain peace?"

He cleared his throat. "We maintained a policy of intervention against any invasive use of force, which was quite successful. There was not a single full-scale war in the first three hundred years I sat on the council."

"Yes, because the nations stopped defending themselves. And why should they? They had you to do it for them."

"And you consider that a bad thing? Kingdoms were allowed to spend resources on other advancements instead of pouring all they had into defending their borders."

"And when the mierothi came, all were helpless to stop them. Your arbiters didn't make a lick of difference then."

Yandumar's pronouncement drove a spear into Gilshamed's soul. *By Elos, could he be right! Why have I not seen that possibility before?* Perhaps his true plans regarding victory would have to be altered after all.

It was a half a mark before Gilshamed replied. "I see. I take it you seek . . . assurances?"

Yandumar deflated. Whatever anger he had been saving for this encounter seemed spent. "It's not you, Gil. Scorch me, at least you're *doing* something about all that. I just want to make sure we don't trade one set of tyrants for another."

Gilshamed felt a chill at these words. "Of course, my friend. Of course. But let us not count our scars before the battle. I think we should be focusing ourselves on the tasks right in front of us rather than one in the murky fog of could-be."

"Ha! Right you are." Yandumar exhaled loudly. "Sorry, Gil. Just had to get all that off my chest."

Gilshamed clapped him on the shoulder. "Worry not. It is these tunnels, I think. They weigh on your soul."

"Heh. I'm glad we'll soon be out of them."

"Yes." Something caught his eye over Yandumar's shoulder. A figure, hunched and cloaked, had suddenly turned around. Gilshamed tracked his movements a few beats, but as they were headed in opposite directions, the distance soon became too great to maintain visual contact.

Odd.

But he thought no more of it. Here, among his followers, Gilshamed had no reason to fear.

ONCE FAR ENOUGH away, Mevon shed the cloak and straightened his back, marching towards the rear of the snakelike column. Everyone gave him a wide berth. None dared to actually glare at him—at least not where he could see—but he sensed their disdain anyway. Before being trapped, his Elite had carved a chunk out of their hide. Many had lost friends. Most weren't yet sure of his allegiance.

The fact was, neither was he.

He knew how to follow orders. He'd done that his entire life. But, being told how to carry them out was different. And he surely didn't like being left uninformed. He could endure, for now, if he had to, but only for his father's sake.

Father. . .

Strange to even think that word. Stranger still being around the man. Mevon had never had a father, never needed one, and alien emotions kept rising to the surface whenever they talked. It felt . . . good. They had much in common, which made their conversations far more comfortable than Mevon thought possible. Yandumar reminded him of Kael.

Kael, you crafty bastard. His old mentor had betrayed him. Next time they met, Mevon meant to genuinely thank him for that. Somehow, Gilshamed had been in contact with him, and Kael had shared with the valynkar how he thought Mevon would attack. The old Hardohl had, after all, taught Mevon everything he knew. Lucky, now, that his guesses had been close to the mark.

Things would have turned out quite differently, otherwise.

Mevon strolled past the last cluster of rebels. He found himself alone, in a gap between the main body and the rear guard.

A score of beats later, Mevon came upon his Fist. He turned and began walking forward with them.

Idrus, Tolvar, Arozir, and twenty-five others all turned out to be more than just brothers in arms. They were blood. Ragremons. His people's old warrior mentality still held, and a large percentage of the populace entered into military service, preparing for the day when their vow would be invoked.

He'd told them everything. They deserved the truth. It hadn't taken long to convince them. His kin nearly jumped at the chance, and the others were fully swayed after a few days. They were loyal to Mevon above all, and after hearing his history, became filled with nearly as much rage as he. Mevon was glad. He didn't know what he would have done if some had elected not to defect.

Unbidden, his captains came to him. They all had business to discuss.

"What did you find?" said Mevon.

"Morale seems high," said Tolvar. "Nothing but victories so far, and astonishing ones at that. For now, they have every confidence things will continue this way."

"Good. Arozir?"

"The organization is solid. They have twice the materials they need and planned resupplies already in place. Also, there is a cadre of skilled craftsman along with enough raw goods to make and repair anything that could be needed for an extended campaign."

Mevon rubbed his chin. "I figured they would. Idrus?"

"Total troop count tallies up to six thousand one hundred and nineteen, not including us. Almost twenty-nine hundred of that are recently recruited Imperial soldiers. Two thousand are bandits. The rest are part of the original movement, a group calling themselves 'Shepherds of the Sun.' They're a mix of people, mostly farmers and ex-soldiers, but I should note that there are ninety-one casters among them."

"That many?"

Idrus shrugged. "Sanction is rather harsh on their kind. I'm only surprised there aren't more already a part of this movement."

"There likely are."

His captains gave him questioning stares.

"Gilshamed," said Mevon, ignoring their looks for the present. "What do you know of him?"

"He's straight out of the scorching legends," said Tolvar.

Arozir grunted. "It's still hard to believe it's him. The same person."

"Anything useful?" Mevon asked.

Idrus cleared his throat. "By all accounts, he was a leader among the valynkar, and personally led the armies that stood against the mierothi. It's likely he sees this revolution as a way to redeem his past failures."

"I agree. I only wonder why he's here alone rather than at the head of a valynkar army."

"Who knows?" Tolvar said.

"The world beyond the Shroud is a mystery," Arozir said. "Could be the valynkar don't have the capacity to wage war anymore. Maybe all they can do"—he waved a hand forward—"is this."

Mevon considered a moment. He reviewed what he had learned so far, and the words overheard most recently between Yandumar and Gilshamed.

He breathed deep. "We'll have to stay alert. This Gilshamed is hiding secrets."

His captains all nodded without hesitation. They had seen it, too.

"So," Idrus said. "What do we do for now?"

"For now?" Mevon paused. "We follow orders."

"Aye," they said in unison. That, at least, they knew how to do.

They wandered back to their places among the Fist. Mevon walked alone with his thoughts. There was one thing he hadn't told them. One thing he couldn't. He didn't want to share his suspicions with anyone else until he knew for sure.

But Gilshamed wasn't the only leader of the revolution harboring secrets.

Father, whatever it is, don't let it stand in the way of our justice.

Chapter 8

DRAEVENUS DROPPED THE straps of the litter carrying the injured boy and held out his hands. The relief he first felt at seeing the village turned to stress as its inhabitants surrounded him with wary, militaristic movements. He remained silent, not wanting any trouble. He'd let them make the first move.

The biggest man of the lot was at their center. Burnt-orange hair, fading to gray in places, rimmed a bald pate and swept down into a full beard. He wore well-fitting clothes, drab and stained as those of a lifelong farmer, yet a frame of bunched muscles could be seen beneath. He motioned for the rest to halt a dozen paces away, then gestured, sending some into flanking positions. Others ventured farther out, as if scouting the surrounding woods.

The big man spoke first in a commanding voice. "Who are ya' and what are ya' doin' with that boy?"

Draevenus forced his stance to stay relaxed. "Just a traveler, sir. Just passing through. I found the boy caught in a . . . a trap of some kind."

"He's injured?"

"Yes. I did what I could to keep him alive and get him here quickly."

The big man rubbed at his beard while examining the boy. After ten beats, he nodded, then turned to a trio of men standing close by. "Go to the search groups and tell 'em we found the boy."

"Aye," they replied in unison. They dashed off in different directions without a moment's hesitation, sparing only one last curious glance at Draevenus.

The mayor turned to a stout, middle-aged woman. "Kaera, will ya' look after the boy until his folks get back?"

The woman said, " 'Course I will, Abe!" and snatched up the two nearest men. They approached and relieved Draevenus of his burden, each muttering a "God bless ya'," which he accepted as humbly, if awkwardly, as he could.

The big man waved the crowd off, and they all turned to head back to their homes, though most first threw a grateful nod in Draevenus's direction. Draevenus walked up to the man. "If you've the time, sir, I was hoping to share a few words? In private?"

The man squinted at him, trying to see his face most likely. After a moment of scrutiny, which lasted just long enough to make Draevenus uncomfortable, he made a sound that was half grunt and half cough. "Aye, stranger. We can talk." He turned, waving Draevenus after him.

He followed the man through the small village. He saw perhaps a hundred longhouses, walls of dark timber and roofs of thatch. The homes meant for extended families all glowed cheerfully with evening hearth fires. The smell of cooking food, which wafted from each open door and window, set his stomach to rumbling, reminding Draevenus that he'd had nothing but dried trail rations for weeks.

They came to a blocky building near the center, much smaller than the houses. A wooden sign with the words MAYOR'S OFFICE was nailed over the threshold. He followed his host inside. A layer of dust covered a chamber furnished with only a desk and a few chairs, and a single door led to what appeared to be a jail cell. No fire burned, giving the space a slight chill. Draevenus was glad for this detail, for it gave him an excuse not to shed his cloak.

The man extended a welcoming hand. "Abendrol Torn."

Draevenus shook it. "Nice to meet you."

Abendrol frowned and began muttering to himself. Finished with the obligatory greetings, the man cleared his throat. "Caster or herbalist?"

"Excuse me?" Draevenus said.

"You fixed that boy up somehow. So which is it?"

Draevenus gritted his teeth. "Caster."

"Hmm. Not very good at it, are ya'?"

This one is sharp. "At healing? No. My skills lie elsewhere."

"Ha! I can see that." Abendrol scooted sideways

behind the desk and sat in its wooden chair. He gestured for Draevenus to sit across from him, which he did.

They mayor cleared his throat again. "You ain't a Sanction runner, now are ya'?"

A burst of laughter escape his lips, but Draevenus composed himself in a blink. "Ah, no, good sir. I am not."

Abendrol stared a few beats, an eyebrow raised. "Good to hear. We don't need that kind of trouble round here. We've had enough in recent times."

Finally. "Oh?"

The mayor waved a hand. "Bah! You don't wanna hear our small-town woes. I just wanted to thank ya' for bringing back Enod—that's the kid. He's a cousin of mine. Of sorts. Abyss, go back a handful of generations, and everyone in this village is related."

"I take it family is important to you?"

"Ain't nothing more. Folks take care of each other round here. After all, nobody else is gonna do it. Not in this empire, anyway."

"It must be nice, being able to rely upon one another. Keeping each other safe. Not at each other's throats all the time."

"I take it your family ain't the same?"

Draevenus sighed. "No—not anymore. They were, once. Long ago."

The trapdoor in his mind creaked open, and he fell into the void beyond.

Memories sprang forth, each an image but so much more than that. Draevenus felt the cold water as he and his sister played in a stream, smelled the woodsmoke and seared meat as father cooked their evening meal, heard his mother's voice singing him to sleep, tasted his own tears as all the fighting men left the village armed with their spears and bows, their faces already those of the walking dead (but at the time he had not recognized it for what it was), and how he wished he could go with them but he was just too young and someone had to look after the women and children, and the march afterward that soon became a desperate flight into strange and dangerous swamplands, and all the village elders arguing about what to do night after night, and when all hope was lost, a voice coming to them, carried on the wind, promising salvation, whispering the truths (lies) of a god embracing his chosen (forsaken) people, then the change and the pain and the wonder and the power and the glory and what followed . . .

Blood.

So much blood. Staining his hands, splashing hotly across his face, flowing and pooling, breaking him over and over. He told himself he didn't mind. It was for his people, for his family.

But then his people broke his family. Broke themselves. Called it progress. Called it necessary. Called it—

Something moved towards his face. Draevenus reacted on instinct.

He grabbed the wrist, then wrenched down and across. His other arm pushed on the man's shoulder, doubling him over. He kneed the man in the face, hearing the nose snap, smelling blood. He swept a foot behind the man's knees and yanked back on the shoulder. The mayor sprawled backwards onto the wooden floorboards with a thud.

Draevenus shot out his hand, aiming for the throat as he threw himself down upon the man's chest.

Something in the eyes stopped him. Not fear—that had never given him pause—but resignation.

Draevenus froze, hovering over him, a breath away from a killing blow. Their noses were nearly touching. And he had no idea what to say or do.

Abendrol coughed, holding his hands open beside his face. "Apologies. I meant no disrespect. I didn't know. Please . . . honored one. Please."

Draevenus sighed. *So much for avoiding notice.* He swept back his hood. "No need. It is I who should be apologizing." He stood halfway, extending a hand.

The mayor looked askance at the hand a full half dozen beats. Finally, he grasped it, allowing Draevenus to pull him up. He shuffled to his seat again, holding one hand to his broken, bleeding nose and keeping his eyes on his guest. He couldn't seem to put words to his lips.

Draevenus resumed his seat, folding his hands over his lap. "I could do something for the nose. It's nothing, really. A simple casting, even for me."

"I'd not have ya' expending yourself on me, honored one."

"I said that's not necessary. Call me Draevenus."

Abendrol jerked in his seat. The assassin sighed.

"You've . . . heard of me," Draevenus said.

"Only by reputation."

"Yes." Draevenus lowered his eyes. "It seems I may

never escape it." And what he planned to do would do little to change things. Would make them even worse if his fears played out. But it was . . . necessary. *Peace may come, someday. But not before something changes. Not before I change it.*

He only wished he could see the end of his road. Catch a glimpse, at least. Instead, he kept seeing the start of the journey, of the memories that had led him down this path.

Draevenus became aware of the scrutiny given him by the mayor. He met the man's gaze.

"You brought the boy back," the mayor said. "You brought back a part of our family. You didn't have to." He paused. "You're different than the others."

Draevenus nodded. "A change is coming. I'm sure you've heard the whispers. Ready your people. Your vow . . ."

Abendrol shivered.

"Remember me, though," continued Draevenus. "Remember that not all of us are . . . monsters."

"I will."

Draevenus stood. "There is one more thing. I'm following some people. A large group. Thirty daeloth and about three hundred men. Have they passed through hereabouts?"

The mayor let out a sound nearly like a growl. "Yes. They were here."

"How long?"

"Departed about a week ago, I think."

"Seven days!" He was farther behind than he thought.

Saving the boy had delayed him more than he could afford. Was it the right choice? He didn't know. His goals always seemed to conflict with each other.

Redemption, after all, was not an easy road to tread.

Nor should it be.

He left the village without another word.

VOREN SAT IN a cramped alcove on the second floor of the library. The stone structure was one of a half dozen outbuildings along the road that led from the main gate of the palace grounds. Though it boasted the largest collection of written works in the empire, Voren found it lacking. He remembered the floating cities of his people, each holding a score of libraries all containing a hundred times as many books and scrolls, tablets and tomes.

As a youth, he had spent a lifetime's worth of days among those rainbow shelves, lounging by the quicksilver fountains, devouring histories and mythologies and folk legends and fictions. Sunlight would illuminate the endless pages by day, and the glowing bulbs of the evervine by night. It was a simpler time. Peaceful.

Gone now. Swept away like a child's sandcastle before the tide.

Voren chuckled. The sound held no humor. He had been fifty, just off his mother's breast, the last time he had seen an ocean shore. His eyes had still been full of wonder then, for he had not yet learned the true nature of the world, and of that which that hides in all men's hearts—

Darkness.

"Don't worry," Kael said. "He'll come."

Voren sat up, rubbing the glower from his face. He nodded. "I am not worried about him showing. He is a slave to habit, as are we all. The cages we craft for ourselves always prove the most comforting. And the most difficult to escape."

Kael grunted.

Voren reached a hand, patting Kael's forearm. "Thank you for this. Without your help, I would not even know where to begin."

"Yeah. Fine. Just don't try to drag me into anything . . . questionable."

Voren curled up a lip. "I shall endeavor to abstain from mischief."

The snow-haired man grumbled but turned back to perusing his book without further comment.

Voren raised his eyes, searching for their quarry. It was early still, and the man was nowhere to be found. There were about fifteen other people in the library, mainly off-duty daeloth and other guards, but a few others were likely members of Mecrithos's wealthy society, of those merchant families rich enough to afford passage into the palace grounds.

One figure ambled through the rows of shelves. A minder trailed in his wake. The mierothi male's face was glued to a brightly colored picture book, the kind drawn for children. Drool fell down his cheek, which the attendant periodically wiped clean. His eyes were wide, glazed, empty.

Voren shivered. He hated seeing one of them. "Enlightened," they were called. The story circulated that their minds were elevated to another realm of thought, a higher plane of existence. Voren, however, knew the truth.

He peeled away his gaze and redirected it to the open book in his lap. He read for some time but soon found he could not concentrate on the words, so he turned to peer out the window by his shoulder.

The day promised rain, and an icy one at that. With fall in full swing, the days continually grew colder. A hundred leagues south, the Agoritha plains had already seen its first snow. Voren hoped it would not cause a change in their target's plans.

Squads of darkwatch guard, mixed humans and daeloth, marched in formation up and down the broad avenue. One of the Blade Cabal stood sentinel bisecting the palace gate, the diamond-shaped edge of his *Andun* poking up over a shoulder. Archers and crossbowmen by the hundreds occupied vantages along the outer wall and atop the other nearby structures.

Voren sighed. *It seems all I do is look out through windows.*

They surrounded him: in his chambers, his memories, his art. Even the written word was a kind of window, a view into the mind of the author, a glimpse into the untempered schism of the soul.

I have had enough of simply looking. He smiled as a mierothi, the one they had been waiting for, walked through the entrance of the library. *Time to start opening some doors.*

Voren brought his book near his head, feigning absorption in the text. A few beats later, he heard a throat being cleared.

He looked up. "Chronicler Truln?" he said.

The mierothi stared at him blankly. "That's my spot."

"It is? My apologies." Voren stood. "We will make room for you, of course." He flapped his hands at Kael, who shifted to the next seat with a grunt. Voren took the seat just vacated by the Hardohl. He smiled at Truln.

The chronicler's face held a look of bafflement. "I . . . uh . . . that is, I didn't mean . . ."

"Yes? Is something the matter?"

Truln pressed his lips together, draining them of what little color they contained. He swallowed. "Ah . . . no. I guess not." The mierothi took a few deep breaths as he planted himself in the open seat. He grabbed the top book off a stack on the adjacent table and began reading, ignoring the unwanted company.

Voren bent his head back to his own book. He waited a few beats, then leaned over to retrieve a sackcloth from the floor under a table stand between his and Kael's seats. Loosening the drawstring, he spread the contents across the stand: hard bread, sliced cheese, and sections of salted sausage. Kael produced two fist-sized flasks of wine and handed one to Voren.

As Voren and the Hardohl began crafting miniature sandwiches and gobbling them down, chewing more loudly than was necessary, Truln turned towards them, a look of alarm slowly spreading across his face.

"You can't do that here," the chronicler said. "Food and drink are strictly forbidden in the library."

Voren finished chewing, swallowed, smiled. "Oh, come now. This alcove is secluded, out of sight of those pesky librarians. We will not be caught."

"Yes, but the crumbs, and the grease—"

"We brought napkins." Kael produced several on cue, handing one to Voren. "What harm is there in a little snack while reading?"

"I . . . well—"

"And we brought enough to share." Voren waved a hand over the food. "If *you* were partaking, surely no one would dare speak out against it." He raised an eyebrow into a hanging question.

The edge of Truln's lips curled up over the next several beats. His gaze met Voren's. He nodded.

"Excellent," Voren said. He divided the makeshift meal, sweeping a third of it into a cloth and handing it to Truln. He also passed over his flask of wine. He waited until the chronicler had taken a bite and washed it down before asking, "What are you reading?"

"Sarian Thress's *History of Rebellion in the Empire*," Truln said.

"What for? Surely your own Chronicles detail those events far more accurately than any human's could?'

Truln smiled, sitting up straight. "Accurately? Of course. I am the chronicler, after all, not just some historian."

Voren returned the grin.

"As to why?" continued Truln, "Despite the fanciful causality, faulty recollection of events, and, often . . ." he paused, looking around and lowering his voice, ". . . anti-

Imperial sentiment, I find the, uh, different viewpoints helpful in crafting a more complete picture of events."

The chronicler sat back in his seat. He breathed rapidly, as if he had just finished running. Voren suspected that the man did not often string so many words together at once. Not, at least, by tongue.

Voren gave the mierothi a few more moments to recover. "Fascinating. And prudent, of course. Especially considering"—Voren gulped—"current events."

The hook was cast. Voren had been able to piece a fragment of a picture together concerning what was going on in the empire. Agonizingly sparse in context, the crumbs of information came to him from disparate and murky sources. Even Kael, his supposed ally, had only grumbled a few brief phrases on the subject. Truln, however, had already proven more informative than all the others combined, and, with a few nudges, would give him everything he needed.

And more.

"Yes," said the chronicler. "I am trying to determine . . . patterns. The rebellions of the past all seemed to follow a similar progression. But this one?" He shook his head and shrugged.

"Breaking the cycle, I take it?" said Voren.

Truln frowned. "You have not heard?"

"Oh, the emperor has been keeping me informed. Well, trying to anyway. You know how busy he is. And not much of a storyteller, either." Voren leaned forward. "But you? Reading your works, I am constantly awed by your eye for facts both great and small, each woven together to form a perfect picture of history. It would be truly a privilege to hear your version of events."

The words had the desired effect. Truln puffed out his chest and fought against a childish grin. Voren sat back, leaning his chin on his fist, and kept his gaze pinned on the mierothi.

Truln cleared his throat. "If we disregard the unrest and squabbling during the first century of our empire, each outbreak of violence has been reactionary in nature. Our current rebellion has been decidedly proactive in contrast. The pure audacity of destroying a voltensus . . ."

Voren nearly failed to stifle his gasp.

" . . . as their first act indicates a staggering amount of forethought, for its loss has rendered our forces impotent in tracking them down. Already two battalions, along with a Hardohl and his Fist, have gone missing, presumed dead, and the entirety of the prefecture's soldiery is wandering aimlessly through the woods, chasing wisps.

"Though the prefect insists he can handle affairs, both the governor and arcanod of the western territory have ordered additional assets into the region. And what's more, the adjudicators are nearly in full panic mode dealing with whispers ranging across the empire. Whispers of change. Whispers of . . . freedom."

Voren exhaled. "And this all points to what, exactly?"

"A mastermind, Voren. Someone with the genius to plan, the patience to put into motion, and the charisma to hold it all together. Someone dangerous. Someone new. At least . . . at least I hope so." Truln shivered.

Voren felt the all-over prick of bumps rising on his skin. *Someone new. Yes, let us pray that that is true.* This revolutionary leader sounded chillingly similar to someone he used to know. Someone Voren prayed he would never meet again. Just the thought of such an encounter set him to mimic the chronicler's shaking.

Stop this nonsense, Voren. He is gone. No use fretting about the impossible.

But he could not stop. And the impossible became a certainty, a horror constructed of guilt and dread and shame. His palms turned slick with rancid sweat. Breathing became a labor. He managed to nod, appearing engaged as Truln continued, but he caught no more of the words.

He was too busy fleeing the windows in his mind.

THE DARKNESS RECEDED at such a slow pace that Mevon wasn't sure, at first, if it was actually happening. Not until he saw the glow off Yandumar's grinning teeth did he even become aware of the change. A breeze brushed their faces, banishing the stale cave air, yet it was as if a strong tailwind were pushing them forward, quickening their steps towards the escape they all so desperately craved. Then, as the tunnels made one last bend, he caught orange light baking the earthen exit ahead.

The small group seemed to exhale as one, a breath held far too long, and with far too much tension, finally released. An excited murmur arose. Laughter. Mevon understood. Even he was relieved to see this long night end.

And get on with the business of justice.

"Now ain't that a welcome sight," Yandumar said.

Mevon studied his father's face. So similar, despite the marks of age, yet alien all the same. The man never ceased smiling, it seemed, always holding to joy. And though Mevon was aware of its source, he did not comprehend its intensity, its relentlessness.

Part of Mevon wished he could find it comforting. He was awed, true, but more baffled than anything else. Despite their alliance, and their bond of blood, Mevon didn't know how to bridge the chasm that rested between. Neither, he suspected, did his father. He took solace in the fact that at least they both wanted to.

Which is good enough, I think. Better than the alternative.

Mevon turned to Idrus. "Scout ahead. I don't want any surprises."

Idrus nodded. He flipped hand signals to the other dozen rangers, and they bounded forward at a run, securing veils over faces and readying bows in hand.

Haughty laughter floated towards Mevon. He glanced past his father to where Slick Ren was waving her own men forward. "There's no need, Mevon," she said, the words dripping from her overly sensual mouth like honey. "These woods belong to us. We are expected."

Fifty bandits sauntered towards the light, seeming to mock his rangers with their casual pace. They jostled and joked with one another, leaving their weapons sheathed. The odd couple at Mevon's side, and Derthon trailing three paces, were all that remained of the crowd of moments ago.

Mevon inclined his head to Slick Ren. "I'll take the precaution anyway. Complacency will get you killed if you practice it too often." The image of his first encounter with Jasside floated to the forefront of his mind. "Your own men even paid that price. I should know. It was I who . . . collected."

"Oh?" She smiled. "Those were not my men."

"Weren't they?"

"Hardly." She flicked her wrist, dismissively. "They were a recent acquisition. Men who weren't happy with our takeover of their territory. The fools thought to eliminate us and set themselves on our throne. They thought themselves clever, thought their conspiracy a secret, thought we wouldn't dare have them killed.

"They thought wrong."

Mevon didn't like her tone. "Masters of your own little world, are you?"

"Little? Is the empire really so ignorant of our dominion?"

"What's that supposed to mean?"

"Oh, child. One out of every five bandits in the empire answers to me and Derthon. This entire territory is ours, and every rogue lord and lady beneath the Shroud knows our names."

The numbers, if they were true, staggered Mevon's conceptions. "So your men traveling with us are just—?"

"Our vanguard, yes. Our most loyal and able core."

Mevon frowned. He'd hunted bandits as a matter of course his whole adult life. Sanction runners inevitably sought refuge among them. Being allied with them now already left a sour taste in his mouth. Knowing the true depth of their influence made his stomach twist.

It must have shown on his face as well. "Why so tightly wound?" Slick Ren added a *tsk tsk* sound. Mevon almost laughed at the ridiculous gesture. "That can't be good for one's health. Wouldn't you agree Yanny?"

Yandumar blushed at the affectation. He took a moment to compose himself before saying, "Aye, son. There's nothing to worry about. Gil's had this all planned out for a while now."

Mevon clenched his jaw. "So I've heard."

"Problem, young one?" Slick Ren said.

"Just that I've yet to be informed of this master plan. Gilshamed had better let us in on it if we've any hope of success."

"Soon, I think," Yandumar said. "Tonight, even, if all goes well."

Not soon enough. "You'll have to forgive my skepticism," said Mevon. "I've seen little that inspires absolute faith in our chosen leader, such as seems to come naturally to the rest of you."

Yandumar looked down. Softly, he said, "We've saved each other from so much, I guess I don't really think about it much anymore. In all my years, I've never seen anyone so committed."

Yandumar locked his gaze on Mevon. "And besides, he brought you and me together. If that don't inspire you, I don't know what will."

"Proof will," Mevon said. "Proof that he isn't insane."

His father's eyes flashed wide. "What do you mean?"

"He's been away a long time, if the stories are true. And by your own admission, he's done little except try to find his way back in all the centuries since. Tell me that doesn't hint at obsession. At . . . imbalance."

His father's face transformed. Truth hitting hard. Painfully. So quick did it dissipate that Mevon almost doubted it had ever been. The old man shook his head and barked laughter. "Gil is many things, son. Driven? Yes. Able, competent? Abyss yes. The best man for the job? Absolutely. But insane?" He shrugged. "It's all . . . ?" He paused, lifting his head as if struggling for the right words.

Slick Ren piped in. "A matter of degrees?"

Yandumar smiled at her. "Yes. Exactly. Degrees."

She patted Yandumar's bicep, staring at Mevon. "We're all a little psychotic in our own little ways. Gilshamed has just had more time than the rest of us to develop his . . . peculiarities."

Mevon frowned, troubled by something he couldn't quite place. "You know him that well?"

She glowered. "Well enough."

Something in her tone told Mevon he should refrain from further questioning. But, he was never one to obey the whims of his conscience. "How is it, exactly, that you and your brother came to be his allies anyway? You never did say."

She glanced back at Derthon. He met her eyes. The pain in that gaze was evident to even Mevon. After too long a moment, he signed with his hands to his sister. The movements were different than those used by his rangers, and Mevon could not discern what was passed between them. Still, she nodded, breathed deep, and flicked her glossed eyes back to Mevon.

"My brother . . . he's like you, Mevon. Or, he was, once. It was long ago. He lost much of what he was, all in the name of duty."

"Like me?' You can't mean he was—"

"Hardohl. Yes. Yes he was."

Mevon looked to his father. "You said Imperial protocol was to eliminate the family. Ensure there were no ties, no loyalties other than to the mierothi and the empire." He swept his eyes across Slick Ren and Derthon, then settled them again on Yandumar. "How can this be true?"

His father's mouth moved without sound. The old man looked to Slick Ren for help. "I was grown when our mother had him," she said. "They tried to track me down, but I was already an accomplished thief and assassin by then. After three groups of daeloth met their end by my hand, they stopped sending more."

Mevon followed her mournful gaze towards Derthon. "What happened?"

"His first assignment was part of the mierothi's dirty, secret war. They sent him to kill one of their own."

Mevon closed his eyes, holding his lids together for several beats. "Vashodia."

Slick Ren nodded, her eyes downcast. "She . . ." a tear rolled down her cheek. "You want to know why my brother wears bandages as his only attire? You want to know why a Hardohl is as helpless as the rest of us against sorcery?

"That *bitch* . . . she took off his skin."

Mevon turned, staring at Derthon. His gut writhed with the very thought of what had been done to him. Rage surged, a tempest of molten ice.

He recalled his time in the academy, and the young student whose name he'd forgotten. Seven years his junior, yet already considered a prodigy with the longsword. Irises like the eastern sky in twilight. *Gods, is it you?*

Derthon stared back. His eyes, once glimmering with life, with guile and cunning, now held only emptiness. A promise of nothing save a swift death.

Mevon felt his steps slow of their own volition. In beats, Derthon had caught up with him.

He thought, briefly, of laying a hand on the man's shoulder, but decided against it. They were too alike, and Mevon knew such a gesture would be wasted. Instead, he leaned in and whispered, "They'll pay. You and I . . . we will make them."

Normally unreadable, Mevon was surprised by the sudden intake of breath and the twinge of Derthon's eyes. The man's facial bandages scrunched in what might have been either smile or grimace. It didn't matter which. Mevon had reached him.

It felt good.

Wherever the conversation might have gone from there, Mevon would never know. The exit loomed. A shining ray of light welcoming them back into the world at last. It was a short climb out of the pit. Mevon clutched to the wooden slats nailed into the soil and pulled himself out into daylight, savoring the warmth on his skin and a lungful of the cleanest air he could remember.

Idrus stood waiting for him.

"What is it?" Mevon asked.

Idrus sighed. "Trouble. You'll want to see this for yourself."

YANDUMAR BURST THROUGH the front door of another house. Silence. Stillness. No difference from the others.

The dust here was thick. Thicker than he'd come across so far. And putrid. It was like walking into a carpenter's shop set inside a corpse-littered battleground. Every breath made him want to cough, sneeze, and gag simultaneously.

He steeled his stomach and set about his search of the house. It was bigger than the others, indicating the family might have been one of the wealthier in the region. A dining room set with silver utensils and crystal glasses confirmed the suspicion. The table was stained a dark mahogany, and the chairs matched, though all but one were tipped over. A full meal was set. Rotting now. Three days? Four? He shook his head and moved on.

He bound up the stairs. Candleholders, not lightglobes—apparently they weren't *that* rich—lined the hallways, cupping melted stubs of wax. A peek inside several open doors revealed empty, undisturbed rooms.

It was the closed door at the end that drew him.

He tried the handle. Locked. He stepped back, and then rammed his body forward, shoulder slamming into the door. Wood crunched and splintered, and the door swung violently inwards.

Yandumar inhaled. He fell to his knees, stomach writhing. The smell had intensified tenfold.

Through watery eyes, he scanned the room. A large, netted bed dominated the center, with dressers and a mirror stand and a porcelain washbasin along two walls. Glass shards littered the ground beneath two broken windows. And in between them, a scattered pile of what looked like ash. Shredded cloth, in a half dozen colors, surrounded it.

Yandumar rose shakily. He held his breath as he walked to the ash. Standing directly over it, he leaned down and sniffed.

He nearly fell unconscious from the rank, suffocating odor. He retreated from the room, then the house, holding his breath until he got outside. He calmed himself and looked around the village.

Figures moved in and out of every building in sight. Mostly Ren's men, but a few of his own. Elite, too. His son stood at a cobbled intersection, arms crossed, neck craned to examine the edifice dominating what could only be considered the town square. Yandumar lifted his eyes. A rectangular block of silverstone rose ten paces from the ground, tilted at a slight angle. Like its name suggested, it had the shine and hue of silver but the feel and purpose of stone.

The valynkar had built their floating cities out of the stuff. This chunk must have fallen during the war, riven from the city as the mierothi attacked. He guessed the town built up around it, but was surprised that it even existed. The mierothi had conducted entire campaigns to eradicate every last trace of their hated nemesis, as if even their ghosts could do harm to the fledgling empire.

Paranoia. That's all that is. Yandumar shook his head as he made his way over to Mevon. *A trait that seems to define their race.*

The three captains got to his son first. Yandumar knew them, of course. Their families anyway. Arozir and Tolvar were part of the Torn clan, and Idrus of the smaller Chant family. None were close to the Daere line, but his always had been a select bunch. He'd traced back twenty generations and found that each Daere man had produced only a single male offspring, which kept the line pretty narrow.

When Kaiera had gotten pregnant with their third, the midwives had been sure it was a boy, their second such. It had seemed like they'd finally had a bit of luck. The visit to the district's phyzari was supposed to be a formality . . .

He shook himself, banishing the memories. He caught only the tail end of the reports.

" . . . have it pretty well secure," Idrus was saying. "But they didn't know what to make of it. Not that you can blame them."

"No," Mevon said. "I suppose not." His son's eyes settled on Yandumar, and they exchanged nods. "It's the same everywhere. Have you seen it?"

"Firsthand, unfortunately." Yandumar spat to the side. "Ain't pretty. Only wish it made a lick of sense."

Mevon sighed. "I know what you mean." His gaze shot to the side. Yandumar followed, spying a large group approaching, Gilshamed foremost among them. They would arrive shortly.

Yandumar studied Mevon from the corner of his eye. He was proud of what his son had become and glad he hadn't been so far drowned in mierothi doctrine to recognize the truth for what it was.

Like I have any idea what truth even is anymore.

He'd been so sure, so righteous in his beliefs, so disdainful of anything falling outside his tidy notion of reality. But he'd seen too much in the last thirty years to be sure of anything anymore. He could only do his best to hold on to what little sanity he had left and finish what he started.

After all, if a man broke a solemn vow—a promise to himself as much as anyone else—could he even still call himself a man?

Mevon cleared his throat. "So, father. What do you think happened here?"

As much as hearing the word "father" warmed his heart—he even felt the involuntary smile spring forth onto his face—Yandumar couldn't help but notice the uncertainty in his son's voice. It seemed he wasn't the only one still trying to figure out . . . everything.

Yandumar shrugged instead. "Don't know. I've seen villages emptied before, the population brought to the tunnels for labor. But that was far away, and . . ."

"Not like this?"

Yandumar shook his head. "Not like this."

Mevon unfolded an arm, swinging it towards the newcomers. "Let's hope they can shed some light."

Gilshamed arrived, leading a dozen sorcerers and sorceresses. Yandumar recognized Jasside and most of the others. Leaders, all. He watched Gilshamed's eyes became glued to the silverstone, his face lost in an entranced state Yandumar knew well. He turned to Jasside instead, giving her a smile and nod.

She returned the gesture, which he was glad to see. She'd been almost a ghost while in the tunnels, and what little he'd seen of her had been curt conversations over meals before she collapsed into a bedroll in exhaustion. *You don't have to keep proving yourself, girl. You're already the best of us. Why can't you see that?*

"Yandumar," she said warmly. Her gaze flicked past him, and her eyes and voice both took a dive. "Mevon."

Yandumar turned to his son as Mevon returned her greeting in flat tones. A hint of a smile appeared as he said her name. Jasside's face held no humor.

Oh son, be careful. Whatever you think or hope might be there . . . isn't. The cold shell that was his son had begun to thaw now that he was out of mierothi clutches, but the process was slow. He knew that Mevon didn't yet understand the human heart.

Yandumar only hoped he could chisel away at the remaining ice before it was too late.

He turned back to Jasside. "Village is empty. Ain't got a scorching clue what happened here. Any insights?"

She looked around, drumming the fingers of one

hand on the other. After a full rotation, she said, "There's a strange residue here. Magical." She turned to the other casters. "You feel it?"

A chorus of nods. One sorceress, tall with platinum-blond hair, said, "Yes. It's just like when Gilshamed destroyed the voltensus."

Jasside frowned. "I wasn't there, Calla. What happened?"

Calla shook her head. "I don't remember exactly. When it happened—when the tower exploded—we all kind of . . . blacked out."

"But you're right," said Orbrahn, who somehow stood as if lounging. "The feeling is the same. That much I remember."

Jasside appeared thoughtful a few moments. "Hmm. There might be a way . . ." She trailed off, sudden excitement blooming on her face. She spun to face the casters. "Can I get some of you to harmonize with me? Four should be enough."

After some shuffling, Jasside made her way to a clear spot in the avenue. Following her were Calla, two other sorceresses, and Orbrahn. The boy made eye contact with Yandumar and winked.

Yandumar glared back at Orbrahn, feeling a growl rise in his throat.

Mevon stepped up next to him. "What are they doing you think?'

Yandumar shrugged, exhaling his anger. "Don't know. Never been all that interested in how magic works."

"In the past, neither was I." Mevon tilted his head toward Jasside. "But ever since she . . . ensnared me, I've been curious."

Yandumar nodded. He hadn't wanted to send her, but Gilshamed had insisted. Said it was the only way to ensure Mevon was ready. But the price . . .

"Tell me something, Mevon."

"Yes?"

"Had it been any other way . . . had we simply approached you, tried to convince you to join us . . . would it have gone the same way in the end?"

Mevon brought one of his hands up to rub his chin. His eyes looked out on nothing. The moment stretched.

"No," he said at last. "I think I would have laughed at you. Then, probably, I would have killed you."

Yandumar shivered. It was the answer he was hoping for, but he wasn't sure it would be enough to help him sleep at night.

Mevon shifted. "I think they have it."

Yandumar looked up. The four casters stood facing Jasside. He couldn't see anything happening, but they all had looks of concentration on their faces.

"There is a dark energy," said Jasside, in a trance-like voice. "It is everywhere. It fuels us. Some say it wars with the energy of light." She shook her head as if she were underwater. "I don't know. What I do know is that it has . . . memory. There!"

Her body trembled. She arched her back and thrust her chin skyward. Her arms shot out stiffly to the sides.

Yandumar almost didn't hear the soft steps approaching from behind.

"What?" said a familiar voice.

Yandumar turned. Gilshamed stood rigid, his horrified eyes locked on Jasside.

"What is she doing!" Gilshamed darted forward.

He made it two steps before Mevon intercepted him, clutching the valynkar by the shoulders.

"She trying to help," Mevon said. "Said she could find out what happened to the village."

"No," said Gilshamed. "She's invoking powers she cannot even begin to understand, much less control." He shrugged out of Mevon's grip. "Go touch her, Mevon. Stop this before it is too late."

Mevon looked at Yandumar, searchingly. *Like I know what the abyss is going on?* Still, Yandumar knew Gilshamed, and had never seen such a frantic look on his face. He nodded at his son.

Mevon bounded forward. He closed the distance in a beat and reached out to Jasside's hand.

All five casters slumped immediately. Jasside would have fallen had Mevon not caught her and held her up. Yandumar noticed the absence of a humming sound that he had not even known was there.

He stalked over to Gilshamed. "Mind telling us what that was all about?"

Gilshamed was frowning. "She was looking through time. Only the mad attempt—"

"I knew what I was doing," Jasside said, breathing hard.

"No. You did not. Where did you even learn to do that?"

"I worked out the method years ago. I'd never had the power required to attempt it before now. Nor a reason to. What's so dangerous about it?"

Gilshamed glared at her. "Six thousand years ago, one of my people thought to play with time. While attempting little more than you were today, one of our cities was knocked out of the sky." He paused, taking a deep breath. "For every one that was able to fly to safety, a thousand more were trapped within the city as it fell."

Jasside made a study of her feet. "I'm sorry. I . . . I didn't know."

Gilshamed's face softened, and he exhaled loudly. "I suppose not. In the future, could you run any experiments by me before attempting them? I do have some . . . experience."

Meekly, she nodded.

Yandumar stepped up to her, laying a hand gently on her shoulder. He offered her a consoling smile. "I don't suppose you saw anything before you were cut off?"

Her face twisted, somewhere between victory and fear. "Actually, I did."

"You know what caused all this, then?" asked Mevon.

She nodded. "Darkwisps. Thousands of them."

GILSHAMED STOOD ALONE in the command tent. He hovered over the maps, staring, but not seeing. A light-globe he had crafted bathed the room in golden light. His shadow on the wall writhed as the tent billowed in the wind.

He slammed a fist into the table.

"Darkwisps," he said to himself, "consuming entire villages. What else could I have missed?"

And the girl had been hiding something. He could tell. What she saw in the vision had terrified her, but she had not revealed all of what it was.

"Just one more thing of which I am ignorant."

Gilshamed punched the table again.

He had ample time to plan for every eventuality of this revolution during his exile, and pulling souls to a cause—*his* cause—had always come naturally to him. The oppressed outnumbered the oppressors ten thousand to one, and countless men and women would rise up at his calling. He had hoped that alone would have carried them to victory.

Yet every step forward showed him how little he actually controlled things.

Something was out there, lurking in the darkness. Not the mierothi, not the darkwisps, not the enemy he had chosen or the possibility of death. It was a broken memory, a collage of shattered images whose meaning is lost in the chaos of itself. The shadow on the horizon of perception.

Uncertainty.

He pounded the table once more, jarring the metal figurines, as if he could obliterate his own doubt with brute force.

As much as he embodied the ideals of his people, a

perfect portrait of a true valynkar, there was one trait he possessed that was considered aberrant.

The will to act.

"If only we had not squabbled among ourselves. If only we had united as a people and stood together against them . . . nothing could have stopped us.

"How differently things would have turned out. For everyone."

"Thought you said bad things happened to anyone messing with time. Yet here you are, wishing to change the past."

Gilshamed turned. Yandumar stood just inside the outer flap.

"How long have you been there, Yan?"

Yandumar shrugged. "Long enough. Listen, you can't beat yourself up about the past, especially when the mistakes weren't really your fault."

"I know." Gilshamed sighed. "It is just—"

"No more, ya' hear? We gotta look forward now. We all need you, and being distracted ain't helping things none."

Gilshamed bowed his head, gritting his teeth yet feeling a smile overcome him all the same. "Again, you remind me why I keep you around."

"Ha! And don't you forget it."

No need to worry about that, friend. Forgetting is something I can never do.

"They're all waiting, Gil. Can I let 'em in?"

"By all means."

Yandumar lifted up the flap and whistled. Figures

began filing in. Gilshamed waited patiently, righting all the figurines knocked over by his outbursts.

"Welcome," he said after the last had entered, "to this, the first official war council of the revolution."

"About time," Mevon said. His captains grunted agreement. "Any reason you waited so long?"

Because I do not answer to anyone, no matter how potent an ally they may be.

But Gilshamed just smiled. "Forgive me. I am a patient man and sometime forget what it is like to be—"

"Human?" said Mevon.

"Just so."

Mevon did not seem pleased by that response.

"Also," continued Gilshamed, "we were not before in a position to enact any plans. Now, we are. Now . . . we *will.*"

He turned his attention on the bandit queen. "Slick Ren, I asked you sometime ago to do a favor for me. Please inform the others what it entailed."

A wry grin slowly spread on her face. *Clever girl.*

"You asked me to send men to watch the mierothi. All of them in this prefecture. Study their movements, their schedules. Learn their routines and"—she snorted laughter—"their weaknesses."

"And they have succeeded at this task?"

"Yes. Quite thoroughly, I might add."

"Excellent. Then we move forward as planned."

He scanned the faces in the room, witnessing the fear and excitement and determination sprouting in various degrees upon each. They knew what he was about to say. It almost did not need to be uttered.

"We are going to eradicate the mierothi in this prefect. All of them at once."

Silence hung as his audience absorbed the news.

"How?" Mevon asked.

"In ten days, there will be a meeting in each of the five cities. It occurs on the same day every month. Three mierothi in the district capitals, and twice that in Thorull. We will divide our forces and hit them all simultaneously."

Mevon clenched his jaw, staring dangerously at Gilshamed. "You're mad."

Gilshamed was prepared for such a divisive response, but its vehemence still sent a shudder up his spine. "Think about it, Mevon. They think we are still on the run, cowering in fear before the empire's supposed might. The mierothi think themselves safe. What better time to strike than now?"

"I . . ." Mevon shook his head. "I don't like the idea of splitting ourselves. Any attack on the mierothi has a much better chance of succeeding if I am there."

"You will be. In Thorull. But news of our first blow will spread quickly, and the others will become alerted, defensive. It *must* be this way."

Mevon glanced around, looking like he was measuring the others' sympathy. He must not have found the support he hoped for. He turned his head back to Gilshamed and gave a reluctant nod. "Fine. How are we going to divide our forces? And who will lead them?"

Gilshamed breathed heavily. "Now, Mevon, you will see why we thought it important to recruit not just you, but also your men.

"You see, when it comes to planning and executing raids and ambushes, particularly against casters, there are none better in this world than the Elite. And your Fist has proven to be peerless in this regard."

Mevon turned to his captains, eying them each in turn. One after another, and without hesitation, they each gave him a nod. He turned back. "Very well. But I only have three captains, and there are four locations."

"Is there not some among your Fist who are prepared to lead should your captains fall? Some being groomed for the task?"

"Ivengar," Tolvar said.

"Aye," Arozir said. "And Ropes."

Idrus nodded. "Those two together can do as good a job as any of us."

Mevon rubbed his chin. "All right, but how should we man each expedition? Each mierothi will have no less than fifty men guarding him at any time, four of which are daeloth. This will be no easy task."

"One squad plus three rangers to each," said Tolvar.

"And three casters for communication and distraction," said Arozir. He arched an eyebrow at Gilshamed.

Gilshamed faced Jasside and Orbrahn. "I trust you two can choose suitable candidates?"

"Yes, Gilshamed," Jasside said. Orbrahn nodded with a shrug.

Idrus turned to Slick Ren. "How many of your men are at each site?"

"Twenty, for now."

"They have crossbows?"

She nodded. "And deadly with them at fifty paces or less."

"Good." Idrus faced his fellow captains. "Think another two hundred will do?"

"Aye," Tolvar said. "Veterans, if possible. Can't have anyone freezing up."

"All right," Mevon said. "Get Ivengar and Ropes and flesh out the rest of the details tonight." He swung back to Gilshamed. "That about covers the other locations. What's the plan for Thorull?"

Gilshamed smiled. "In Thorull, we will show the mierothi the true depth of our resolve." He raised a clenched fist in front of him. "And tear off the veil that has long hidden this land."

Chapter 9

DRAEVENUS STOOD IN the middle of the rut-worn road, smelling mud as he leaned on a gnarled shepherd's crook. His ragged cloak flapped madly in a wind that chilled his bones as it whistled through the evergreen forest behind him and turned the field of knee-high grasses into a sea during storm. The sun was but marks from reaching full noon.

He'd chosen this spot carefully. After finally catching up to those he sought, he'd dashed ahead—their route was no secret—and spent the night preparing the grounds, memorizing every tree trunk and blade of grass and boulder. Sharpening his blades and his senses.

Let my arrangements be all in vain.

He feared, however, that such hopes were the hopes of fools.

The stench of unwashed bodies drifted on the breeze to his nose, just beats before the mud-muffled sound of hooves reached his ears. Half a mark later, the first horse came into view from the shadows of the trees three hundred paces to his front.

Draevenus coiled every muscle but did not budge a finger.

A two-horse team pulled every wagon, a daeloth for a driver, and a score of bedraggled bodies in the beds. All men. None seemed particularly unhappy, making Draevenus wonder what lies had been told them. The train reached its end, fifteen wagons all told, just as the lead driver seemed to acknowledge the existence of someone in his way. He didn't make to slow down. Thirty paces separated Draevenus from them.

Draevenus slammed the staff into the ground. The spells he had stored there released, shaking the ground for half a klick in all directions.

Horses reared, shrieking. Some bolted, while others froze in terror. The cries of startled men rose in cacophony, drowning out the efforts of the daeloth who were attempting to bring their animals under control.

It took half a mark, but at last the drivers had the horses settled. The general rumble of voices died down. Dozens of stares beamed at him, alternatively frightened and angry. Most of the angry ones were from the daeloth.

Draevenus cleared his throat, then called out across the narrow field. "I would speak to your leaders. Now, if you please."

The command had the desired effect. Thirty daeloth, two from each wagon, emerged and stepped to the sides of the road. They approached with caution. Hands were on weapons, but none had yet drawn. A cluster made their way to the front.

One stepped forward, skin like chocolate bark and hair a fop of coal-turned-ash. He looked to be about four hundred, well past retirement age for a daeloth. All but a few, the trio closest, were on the opposite end of the spectrum, looking like they'd been out of training a handful of years only.

Draevenus, his head still concealed beneath his hood, addressed the foremost daeloth. "You speak for these?"

"I do."

"What's your name? Rank?"

"Tursek Grenalsco. None here have any rank though I was once a general. Who the bloody abyss are you?"

"Who I am does not matter. I am here to make you an offer."

Tursek arched an eyebrow. "Oh, really?" He stepped closer. "That was a neat trick you pulled with the groundquake. It might have impressed some of the younger ones, but I've been around awhile. I could probably replicate the effects myself with enough time. So, tell me, why should I stand here and listen to you one beat longer?"

Tursek drew his sword and began energizing. Twenty-nine others followed suit.

Draevenus sighed. "War is coming—"

"Doesn't concern us."

"Oh, but it does. Some have already turned their attention to your little outfit. Some who want to put a stop to what goes on in Verge."

Tursek froze midstep, eyes widening. "How—?"

"*I* know. Will you hear my terms?"

The daeloth leader sagged, looking back at the other veterans. One shrugged, another shook his head, and the last simply stared.

Tursek turned back. "What is your . . . offer?"

At least they are willing to listen. Better, so far, than I had anticipated. "Leave now. All of you. Leave these men in my care. Do not return to Verge or attempt to communicate with any of the phyzari there. Early retirement."

"In exchange for what?"

"Your lives."

Tursek scoffed. "You are one against thirty. Who are you to threaten us?" He shook his head, signaling with his hands ~six~flank~ on either side. "I think we will follow orders instead. I don't care how good you thi—"

His words cut off as Draevenus flung off his cloak. Tursek's expression widened as he appraised Draevenus. The blackened chain mail, dark bands of leather holding twoscore throwing knives and no less than six long-bladed daggers, a body coiled like a serpent, a face of serenity, the visage of a legend—these things, Draevenus knew, all took their toll on the aging daeloth in the span of a heartbeat.

Tursek stopped in his tracks.

"Last chance," Draevenus said.

Tursek sagged farther than before. Eyes full of resignation stared. Blinked.

Maybe this won't come to bloodshed after all?

The next moment gave lie to the hope.

Having received no further orders, the flanking

daeloth each casted: a prebattle self-blessing. Standard procedure. It drained their reserves. They all began recharging as they surged forward at a speed greater than that normally achievable by mortals.

Not fast enough.

Draevenus grabbed a throwing knife in each hand and hurled them out, one each at the groups to the sides. They were bunched close as they approached. The center daeloth reached up a sword to deflect the spinning steel.

At impact, the spells stored within the small hunks of metal discharged. Swaths of hungry, dark power raked out in a deadly sphere. The air thrummed with virulence. A dozen throats cried out as the energy scored their bodies, consuming. Then . . .

Silence.

Tursek and the three veterans casted direct spells at Draevenus. He energized and motioned backwards, shadow-dashing two hundred paces into the folds of the forest behind him. Their spells churned grass and soil and stripped bark from trees, crackling with hatred. The rest of his opponents began moving forward.

Raw sorcerous capacity had never been his strength. Such gifts fell to the likes of Vashodia and Rekaj, as well as others now in positions of affluence. But what he lacked in power, he made up for in speed and efficiency.

Energizing to full in under a beat, he blessed himself, feeling a surge of strength, speed, and awareness bolster his body. Though weak among the mierothi, he was still far more powerful than any daeloth, and the blessings he gave himself reflected the disparity.

Of course, the act gave his position away. Nearly a score of spells careened towards him. Dark lightning, blue-purple spheres or jets of flame, flattened discs of razor-sharp air—all standard castings, learned within the first two years after emergence. His opponents had no imagination.

Draevenus energized again as he dodged the spells. He crept forward. Tree to tree. Staying in shadow. He reached the edge of the tree line and peered out at the daeloth. They had spread out and were moving cautiously towards the forest.

Draevenus picked up a stone to which a thin, invisible wire had been attached. He aimed behind him and pushed with sorcery. The stone flew. The wire pulled, releasing a dozen catches to a dozen traps stacked against the tree line. Small objects, glinting in sunlight, flew towards his adversaries.

Eight daeloth flung themselves onto the ground. One was too slow. He raised a blade to deflect the projectile. Draevenus saw him wince as it made contact.

The object bounced off sword and chest and fell harmlessly to the ground.

Tursek shouted, "It's a diversion! Up fools!"

Draevenus flung two more knives toward the veterans. As they sailed, he drew a pair of long daggers and shadow-dashed forward.

His blade sank into the heart of the slowest one. He gestured at the ground, casting. A wall of flame and smoke rose up, obscuring him and the scrambling daeloth. He sprinted, his speed enough to impress even Hardohl. A foot of thick steel—enchanted to never dull or break—swung with the strength of a bull and with perfect accuracy was more than sufficient to decapitate his next opponent.

Five paces beyond, another met the same fate, this one having risen as far as his knees before losing his head.

The sound of his thrown knives exploding behind him announced at least two new victims. Screams rising, just as quickly extinguished.

The next daeloth in line managed to lift a sword in defense. Draevenus swung out his right hand, batting it away, and drove his left dagger up through the jaw and into the brain. The blade caught on the skull, so Draevenus left it behind and drew another.

Three more.

These last had recovered. The middle one readied his sword, while the outer pair thrust a hand forward, discharging a beam of pure, destructive energy. He leapt, and the beams scythed beneath him.

The middle daeloth thrust his sword to impale him, and simultaneously cast a web of crackling sorcery. Draevenus had no way to alter course, so he plunged straight into it.

One of his charms activated. The sensation of icy burning grabbed hold of his chest, where the device lay pressed against his skin. Draevenus could feel the power of his enemy's spell diminish as he passed through. Pain lanced across his whole body but not enough to damage or disable.

Draevenus kicked aside the sword with an armored

boot, then landed on the daeloth, his momentum crashing them both to the ground.

Twin swords swung down on both sides. Draevenus turned the one on the right, leaning that way to avoid the other. Not far enough. The tip scraped across his ribs. He heard the metallic clinking as the links of his chain mail parted, and a gash two fingers deep spurted the first of his blood.

He pressed his right hand down, cutting across thigh and groin. His left foot kicked up and shattered the wrist of the one who had cut him.

He rose, spinning. Slightly off-balance, he aimed both daggers for throats. He didn't miss.

Coming out of his spin, Draevenus drove both blades down into the skull of the daeloth he had landed on.

Draevenus sensed the castings and felt the familiar sensation of sucking air. He cartwheeled to the side as the first pair shadow-dashed through his wall of smoke. Their blades passed bare hands away from where his head had been.

He sheathed his daggers and righted himself as the next two came through. Hands thrust out, he intercepted them midair with twin arcs of dark lightning. Their bodies writhed and jolted, slamming into the ground mere paces away. He kept casting another beat to ensure they did not stand again.

A body crashed into him from the side.

They flew, skidding along the ground and colliding with the first pair. They all tangled together in a mess of limbs and torsos and armor and weapons. He pressed against the ground, righting himself.

Two more shadow-dashed out of the forest. He side-stepped the first, scoring a dagger against the daeloth's abdomen. The second slammed into his back, forcing him, once more, to the ground.

Two more arrived in a swirl of darkness.

The next few moments were a frantic scrabble. They had him surrounded. Six against one. Draevenus spun and dodged, kicked and parried, ducked and slashed.

And prayed.

He took a wound across his right cheek and left ear, barely brushed aside a swing that would have severed his thigh, and felt steel penetrate skin on his left side shoulder and ribs, as well as both calves.

In desperation, Draevenus gathered power into his fist and slammed it into the ground. The shock wave lifted his attackers, pushing them back several paces. He aimed for a dark spot in the forest and shadow-dashed into it.

He pulled his hood forward and squatted behind a thick trunk, willing himself to silence, stillness. The trees were tall, thick, and the shadows deep. He had only to wait for them to enter.

He felt them approach. They stopped at the tree line, sending aimless spells crisscrossing through the woods. Trying to flush him out. Draevenus did not move a muscle. Not even when a jet of flame passed less than a pace away.

Slowly, their feet began scraping against the under-brush.

Draevenus smiled.

They thought to hunt him, but it was he that did the

hunting. He stalked to within paces, undetected, not a breath of sorcery to aid him. In under a mark, he had effected four silent kills.

Two left. They discovered, too late, their missing companions and came together, standing back-to-back in a small, sunlit clearing.

The need for subtlety past, Draevenus energized fully and cast a volley of arrow-like projectiles at the pair.

The first . . . shredded. His body was replaced in an instant by a cloud of blood and bone and splintered armor. The second managed a hasty shield. This absorbed the energy of the spells. For a few beats, at least. The daeloth was outmatched, however, and the shield soon failed, its owner succumbing as had the first.

Draevenus marched towards the wagons. Halfway there, he stopped. He'd heard a scraping sound in the grass. He went over to inspect.

Tursek was there, dragging himself along a trail of blood that leaked from his rib cage.

"I'm sorry it had to be this way," Draevenus said. "If I could have accomplished my goals without bloodshed . . . I would have."

Tursek spat blood towards Draevenus. "You'll not find Verge so easy to penetrate."

I like that he thinks thirty-to-one odds is considered easy for me.

Draevenus looked down at himself, at the wounds and blood, far too much of which were his own. "I'll admit I'm a bit . . . rusty. Unfortunate as this encounter was, it served well as a reminder of what I once was. What I need to become again if I'm to succeed."

"So glad our deaths could help . . ." Tursek coughed, winced, sucked in a rasping breath, " . . . prepare you."

Draevenus closed his eyes, taking several calming breaths.

"Tell me, then," began Tursek. "You said there's to be a war. Which side are you on?"

"The side of sanity," said Draevenus. "And . . . hopefully, someday . . ."

He felt the energy gathering in Tursek's palm. Without opening his eyes, he stomped down on the daeloth's wrist. Bones crunched under his heel. He swung out his hand and tore out the man's throat with his claws.

" . . . peace."

SNEAKING INTO THE city had been the hardest part. Though, even that difficulty had been assuaged by the reduced garrison.

Mevon thought it all too easy.

And, like he did with such things, he remained wary for the turning of the trap.

"They approach, Hardohl."

Mevon glanced up at the speaker. She was dressed in the armor of a daeloth, the markings of a lieutenant upon the shoulders. The former owner of the steel suit lay in a pool of her own blood. The remainder of her squad rested around her. Bound and gagged, half of them unconscious, the Imperial soldiers seemed a pitiful lot. Wide eyes stared, disbelieving, at the sword points aimed for their noses.

"Good," Mevon said. "Let me know when the last carriage passes under the archway."

His ally in the daeloth armor nodded down at him.

Besides the dozen men standing alert in the borrowed garb of Imperial soldiers, a hundred other men sat crouching on the parapets. Ahead lay the western quadrant of Thorull, which was slowly being illuminated by the rising sun. The park lay behind.

Mevon didn't like being separated from his Fist, nor reliant upon so many others. In this situation, though, he could think of no better way to achieve victory. Gilshamed's plan, however well thought out, was not without risk. The valynkar seemed more focused on sending a message than minimizing casualties. Yet, in the end, Mevon had swallowed it. He'd offered scant advice, fearing little of his input would be accepted. He had been right.

His own part, significant as it was, seemed, somehow, less than it could be. Less than it *should* be.

Perhaps it is not too late for one little change.

"What's your name again, sergeant?" Mevon asked.

"Bellanis," she said.

"Bit young for a sergeant."

She shrugged.

"Also rare, isn't it, for a woman to become a career soldier? Then to betray that life for one of rebellion?"

Bellanis turned to him, lifting the visor of her helm

to reveal a face both youthful and hard. "What do you want, Hardohl?"

Mevon grunted in amusement. "A . . . modification to your orders."

She stared, seeming to consider a moment. "Well?"

"When it starts, keep everyone on the wall."

She narrowed her eyes. "What for?"

"I'm used to fighting alone. It will be better this way. For all of us."

She closed the visor and turned back to the east. The sound of booted feet, marching in unison, could now be heard. "Aye," Bellanis said. "We've got enough bows for it. Just don't go getting yourself killed."

Silently, he thanked her.

He felt better. Somehow. What he was about to do was something he needed a clear head for, and looking out for the safety of allies would only hinder that.

Time for the mierothi to start paying for their crimes.

Perhaps not Rekaj himself, but all of them were agents of his regime just the same. All were guilty. The mierothi community was too small for any to be truly ignorant of the multitude of violations their race committed.

Once he'd learned the plan, Mevon had spent much of the last ten days sparring with his Elite, practicing with Jasside, and simply thinking. To *say* one was going to fight against everything he had ever believed had been, in retrospect, as easy as cracking eggs with a mallet. To actually *do* so was something else entirely.

Mevon had to make sure he was ready. Ready to shed the blood of his former masters. Ready to stand up against a tyranny so pervasive as to be invisible, obscured beneath a veil of contempt, fear, and control.

Mevon clenched his fists—his wielders of justice—before his face.

Ready?

He thought of his mother, bleeding to death on the very birthing bed that had brought him into this world. The brother and sister drowned in the nearby lake of their hometown. His father, forced to flee the continent, yet never forsaking a vow to return and set things right.

He thought of the mierothi who had caused it all to happen.

Ready.

Mevon inhaled deeply as the first of the darkwatch marched through the gate beneath him.

JASSIDE FELT HER mouth go dry as the first carriage rolled into view. As she looked south and west, the vehicle rumbled towards her position from the right, four daeloth walking at its corners and fifty armored men marching both fore and aft.

A brief gap, then the second such group began.

Six mierothi and their darkwatch guard. Are we insane to even try?

Her stomach fluttered. What beauty the park might have held on any other day was invisible to her eyes. With the top half of her head poking above the parapets on the north side of the enclosure, she focused on tracking the movements of their enemy through the nearly bare branches of the park's trees. She tried, and failed, to keep her breath even as she glanced back at those gathered behind her, giving them a silent gesture to let them know to be ready.

Many of the middle-aged casters had balked at Gilshamed's choices. Not the older ones, though. They knew who was best for the job and, as they put it, there was no use getting your breeches in a bunch if you didn't agree.

Forty-one casters huddled in a mob behind her. She made forty-two. It seemed a good number though she couldn't say why. She'd harmonized often enough before, though never with so many at once, and never with such stakes.

She glanced to her right. About half a klick away, another such group lay in wait. One member short of her assembly, they were led by Orbrahn.

Orbrahn turned to her. Over the distance, they made eye contact. He flashed a confident, charming smile. She returned the gesture, sure her own lip twitch had been far from reassuring. Still, the exchange gifted her with a dollop of confidence.

Whatever else, she would do her part and prove to them all how indispensable she truly was. *Oh mother . . . if you could see me now . . . you would be so proud.*

Jasside breathed deep and waited. The third carriage lumbered into view.

YANDUMAR STARED AT Slick Ren. "That some kinda joke?"

"I don't jest about these sorts of things, dear," she said. "You have an answer for me or not?"

Rake in hand, he examined the pile of leaves at his feet. A piece of metal poked out of one side. He quickly covered it up with a fresh batch.

"This ain't the time or place, Ren." He tilted his head toward the sound of the marching hundreds. "In case you didn't notice."

She laughed. He couldn't help but smile at the sound, like the twitter of birds in the morning. The way her lips curled, showing just a hint of teeth. "Oh, Yanny, this is precisely the time for it. When better than just before facing almost certain death?"

Yandumar looked past her to Derthon, the only other soul in the vicinity. All three of them were wrapped in long cloaks made bulky by what they wore underneath. The man glanced up from his own rake. Yandumar flashed him the hand-talk for "help."

Derthon signed back "on your own."

Yandumar grunted.

He peered south. One of the doors to the fortifications was ajar, an overeager face poking out of it. Yandumar frowned towards him. The man started, then withdrew.

"Keep raking, dear," Slick Ren said. "We can't be giving our position away too early."

Yandumar grumbled under his breath and resumed the mindless movements. "If I said yes, what would that make me?"

She brushed her hair out of her eyes, a gesture he knew meant that she was thinking. "Not . . . not king. My brother already has that post, and he does not wish to give it up."

"So . . . what? Emperor then?"

"Yes! And I would be Empress. How marvelous."

"Ha! I'd think a thousand or so mierothi might not take kindly to our use of those titles."

"Well then, we'll just have to kill them all, now won't we?"

"I love it when you talk dirty to me . . ."

THE WARMTH OF the rising sun on his back filled Gilshamed with joy. Today, finally, the blood of his true enemy would be shed. And this was just the beginning. So much more did he have prepared. The mierothi would crumble before the combined efforts of his will, his might, and his cunning.

Nothing will stop me.

He ignored the hundred soldiers crouched on the wall around him, focusing instead on listening. The sound of marching steps drew nearer. Now, though, a sudden diminishing in volume. The signal from the watchers was almost unnecessary. Gilshamed knew the foremost group had halted.

Gilshamed energized. In three beats, he was bursting to capacity, filled with the holy fire of Elos. He rose as the first carriage loomed into view, black like the horses that pulled it. He extended his hands forward, focusing his power, gathering all he had.

He aimed for the center of the carriage, and just as the door opened, he released his spell.

Like a flare from the sun, light and fire burst forth in a wide beam. The carriage, the mierothi inside, the daeloth at the corners—these all simply melted. The horses and a score of the closest men burst into flames.

Gilshamed slumped on the parapets, sick yet somehow satisfied by the smell of roasting flesh. As his nearby allies jumped up and began loosing their bows and crossbows, he gathered his strength.

"Now," said Bellanis.

Mevon unleashed the storm.

He gathered his legs up beneath him and launched himself off the wall. He took hold of his *Andun* as the ground rose to meet him. Two daeloth marched at the rear of the carriage. His feet kicked towards their heads, crushing skulls with a crunch. Still descending, he swung Justice sideways at the vehicle.

The wood shattered. Mevon kept pushing the swing through until, with great pleasure, he felt the blade pass through flesh. The scent of blood hit his nose, and he smiled.

I may reject the reason I was made a killer, but I don't think I'll ever lose my passion for it.

He hit the ground and immediately sprang forward again. He thrust to the right, impaling the third daeloth. He drew a dagger with his left hand and sliced across the throat of the fourth, the cut deep enough the leave the head dangling by a thread.

Bolts and arrows from his friends on the wall flashed down. Darkwatch fell by the dozens.

Mevon raced forward, casually cutting down any that drew too close. More came anyway, and he chopped them down, too. Finally, through the press, he came to the next carriage.

He couldn't see any of the four daeloth, nor the mierothi. Strange. He took two steps and leapt onto the vehicle's roof. He lifted his *Andun* and thrust down.

The carriage exploded.

Shards of wood and metal shredded into him from below, and he fell. Shrapnel careened at his face, slicing across his cheek and nose. Blood sprayed into his eyes. Blind, he swung, hoping to make contact with whoever had been in the carriage.

His torn feet hit the ground, and he staggered, nearly falling to a knee. He pushed the pain into the back of his mind as he wiped the blood from his eyes. He stood.

A powerful spell was cast. Close. Mevon turned to see a dark, robed figure standing less than two paces away.

Hezraas.

Mevon growled. He slashed at the mierothi.

The prefect sprang forward.

Mevon had never been punched so hard in his life. He skidded backwards, falling to hands and knees. His lungs felt like they were being squeezed in a vise. He could feel at least three broken ribs, and his heart yammered in panic.

His vision darkened.

JASSIDE SWALLOWED HARD. She turned to the others, tried to speak, but found she could not. Instead, she energized, pulling in just a whisper of energy. Holding out her hand, she clenched her power, feeling it squeeze out like mud between her fingers.

Over several beats, her sorcery took on a sort of rhythm, a thrumming, like a pulse only faster than the beat of a hummingbird's wings. The other forty-one casters mimicked her actions. First, they each gathered a small pool of energy. Then, set it to pulsing. Like hers.

With agonizing slowness, the others matched the cadence of their sorcery to hers. She felt the first one snap into harmony.

Forty more to go.

YANDUMAR THREW DOWN his rake and ripped off the cloak, revealing the armor beneath. His usual assortment of weapons surrounded his bulk. He reached down into the leaf pile and drew forth a bulwark shield and one of his favored bastard swords.

He glanced over at Slick Ren and Derthon, as they made similar preparations, then past them, to where half a thousand of his allies were pouring out of doors set in the stone foundations of the park's southern wall. Former Imperial soldiers led the way, a long, thin line of shields and armor. Behind them came a mass of bandits, shepherds, and other warriors of the revolution, wielding axes, spears, dueling staves, and countless varieties of blunt and thrown weapons.

Yandumar smiled at Slick Ren. "Ready to do some killing?"

Her return smile, and the glint of sunlight off her bared daggers, was all the response he needed.

The three of them turned to the enemy line as their allies came abreast of them. Together, they charged forward.

Yandumar peered up and down the spread line of the darkwatch. Front and back, each three hundred paces distant, were already a mess of destruction. The middle milled in confusion. As they closed the gap, a hissing sound grew louder in his ears.

The barrage arced over Yandumar's head, launched from bowmen hidden on the rooftops of the buildings just outside the walls of the park. The darkwatch formations, just forming tight ranks against the threat of ground assault, withered under the volley of more than four hundred arrows. Men fell, screaming.

Yandumar felt his pulse rising as he rushed towards the nearest group of guards.

GILSHAMED UNFURLED. HIS wings glowed. He launched himself skyward, the sun blazing at his back down into the eyes of his enemy below. Eyes that smoldered with hatred as they locked on him.

That's right. Focus on me. I can take it.

Gilshamed cast a barrage of fireballs. They moved slowly, spreading out to strike near the location of each carriage. Each hit a barrier a few paces overhead. Three sets of red eyes glared as the mierothi erased their hasty shields and launched counterattacks. The daeloth joined them.

Gilshamed shaped his power into a bubble-like shield of his own. Over a dozen attacks struck him within two beats, battering at his protection.

It held.

He had no strength remaining to strike back, though, so he kept up his shield, continuing to float over the battlefield. He had their attention. And with it, bought the time his allies needed.

Hurry, my friends. Hurry.

MEVON SHOOK HIS head, holding on to consciousness. His whole body burned as his blessings worked to heal his injuries. He sucked in a breath. The storm had vanished as soon as he had been hit, and Mevon stoked his fury into retrieving it.

Hezraas stalked towards him.

"So it's true," the mierothi said. "You *did* turn traitor."

Mevon coughed, spitting blood onto the grass. He staggered halfway up. "To betray you," he replied, wheezing, "would require that I first owed you loyalty. By the shed blood of my mother, brother, and sister, I owe you NOTHING!"

Talking, he now saw, was a mistake; he had not fully caught his breath. Though only a handful of beats, the wasted time had also allowed a flood of darkwatch to converge upon his position.

Mevon cartwheeled backwards, avoiding the first falling blades. The mob descended on him like a pack of ravenous wolves. They had heard the prefect's words: TRAITOR! Mevon could tell that they lusted for his blood, frenzy and fury twin glints in their eyes.

Unfortunately for them, Mevon found the storm again.

He danced back, spinning, not bothering to parry. Though sharp and held by strong, skilled hands, the weapons could not pierce his armor, too fast and fluid were his movements. The *Andun* in his hands came alive. Each arm that extended a weapon toward him was caught and severed by the twirling blades.

Still he retreated, leaving a dozen injured men writhing on the ground, clutching their bleeding stumps. The mob had thinned, but they still clamored for him. Deciding to take them off guard, he suddenly reversed direction, charging headlong right into the thick of them. His weapon swung out in deadly arcs again and again. They had pressed too close together in their pursuit and now had no room to dodge or deflect his strikes. For his efforts, Mevon received half a dozen shallow cuts, but ten of the darkwatch fell, never to rise again. Their dying bodies crashed into those behind them, and Mevon stood, for one fleeting moment, in a serene bubble of perfect stillness, perfect solitude.

His eyes quickly scanned. *Only fifteen left.*

They came, heedless of the danger as they flung themselves at him. The bodies already piled at his feet made a coordinated assault impossible. They didn't seem to care, coming instead in ones and twos and threes.

Fools.

Mevon channeled his rage into Justice, assailing any that came near with a savagery few had ever seen, and none had lived to tell about. If they tried to parry, he poured in his strength, breaking through their defenses and cutting them down. If they tried to dodge, he slowed and altered the blow, catching their twisting bodies and cutting them down. If they tried to rush as a group, he would swing wide and long, cutting them down. Again and again they rushed at him, striking without regard for their own safety, and Mevon would step forward, over and over, plunging his bloody blades into their bodies.

At last, the final darkwatch lunged recklessly. Mevon stepped to the side and swung upwards through the man's abdomen. Red mist filled the air. The two halves of the body tumbled down to join the tangle of corpses already strewn in an assortment of grotesque positions.

The prefect, flashing his pointed teeth, sauntered towards Mevon. He stepped absently over his dead and dying guardsmen and drew a pair of twisted daggers.

THE OPPOSING LINES slammed into each other. The sound of the impact throbbed in Yandumar's ears. Sweat and spit flew, and men screamed in rage and fear and pain.

The darkwatch lines held. Despite being heavily outnumbered, they were showing why they had the honor of guarding the lords of the continent.

Yandumar barreled forward anyway, his shield knocking over the two darkwatch in front of him.

Into the gap formed by Yandumar's fallen opponents flew Slick Ren and Derthon. Her knives snicked about, finding throats and hamstrings and groins and major arteries. Derthon—*My God that man can fight!*—became a whirlwind of death. Around him, heads and limbs flew in a shower of blood.

The gap widened, and Yandumar led the charge through. He grabbed hold of one of his commanders. "Take your men east!" Yandumar said, pointing.

"Aye!" said the old veteran.

"The rest of you, with me!"

Yandumar guided the men around. They drove deep to the west before slamming into the exposed flanks of the darkwatch formations. In a dozen beats, the battle lines blurred into a score of isolated skirmishes. The enemy fell. But for each one killed, five or six of his allies did as well.

They had the numbers, but victory would be costly.

And yet Yandumar drove farther west, pulled by something he could not explain.

JASSIDE SHUDDERED AS another snapped into harmony.

Thirty. Almost there. . .

THE ATTACKS ABATED. Gilshamed allowed himself a breath, thankful for the reprieve. The mierothi were relentless, blasting him with a hundred varieties of sorcerous destruction. He had managed to hold back their attacks, but only barely, and he could feel his energy reserves draining rapidly.

He looked down, wondering why they had stopped.

A chill ran up his spine as he realized what they were doing.

Each of the three mierothi had paused to harmonize with the four daeloth nearest them. His defenses were already strained. With the added power . . .

He pooled what energy he could in a beat and cast a beam of light down at their positions. His enemy thus blinded, Gilshamed made his retreat. He cast light bending on himself and glided, invisible, to the ground.

Jasside . . . Orbrahn . . . hurry. It's your time, now. Show me that my faith in you has not been misplaced.

Blood covered Mevon. The substance, warm and sticky, matted his hair, soaked his armor, dripped from his limbs, squished between his clenching fingers. It pooled on the ground, still oozing from the circle of bodies. The men of the darkwatch had given their lives to protect their master.

And judging by the look on the prefect's face, their sacrifice had meant nothing to him.

Hezraas continued advancing, his gaze boring into Mevon, his mouth twisted in scorn. The blades in his hands twirled with a flourish.

"Impressive, I must say," the prefect said. "I've never seen such wanton slaughter from a single man, even among those of your station. I can see now, looking into your eyes, that you enjoy all this killing, these lives snuffed out by your hand."

"I am nothing but what your kind made me," Mevon said. He rammed his *Andun* into the ground. Stepping forward, he drew his ivory-hilted daggers.

"Yes, such a good dog you have been. So well trained and obedient." Hezraas paused to snicker. "But, as everyone knows, when a pet becomes rabid and begins snapping out at his masters . . . well, I'm afraid the beast must be put down."

"You're welcome to try."

The prefect grunted. "There will be no trying, traitor. I will end you quickly, then aid my brethren in exterminating the rest of your pitiful allies. Your rebellion is finished."

Mevon raised his daggers into a fighting stance. "Enough words." He pounced forward.

Sneering, the prefect launched himself towards Mevon. Four blades met in midair. The twisted metal of Hezraas's knives flashed up with such speed, such strength as to knock Mevon's daggers out of his hands. The prefect's face filled with confidence and bloodthirsty glee . . . which was exactly how Mevon *wanted* him to feel.

Scaled hands darted forward. Mevon twisted at the last moment, but the knives still pierced through the armor and into his flesh.

Pain blazed into his right buttocks and left abdomen a hand above his waist.

Mevon smiled.

The pain was slight, tolerable. Surface pain. Not the deep throbbing of a mortal wound.

Hezraas's eyes widened. His self-blessing had indeed given him both strength and speed beyond that of Mevon, but it could do nothing to change his mass.

And Mevon weighed a lot more than the prefect.

They collided. Mevon continued barreling forward, falling atop Hezraas, grasping for his throat. The prefect abandoned his now-ineffectual knives and darted out his clawed hands to intercept Mevon's.

Their hands clenched together, Mevon's massive heft pressing down upon the dark figure. Like this they remained for several beats, straining, grinding their jaws. Slowly, slightly, Mevon felt himself rising, his grip being pressed back by the mierothi, his wrists bending.

"You mentioned the blood of your mother and siblings, traitor," Hezraas said through clenched teeth. "What of your father? Did his death mean so little to you?"

Mevon, now red-faced with exertion, glanced up. What he saw filled him with hope. "You must not have known, then. The empire's assassins were not quite as thorough with him. I'm afraid that little oversight"— Mevon ceased pressing, instead pulling the Mierothi up into a standing position—"will be the death of you."

The tip of that now-familiar bastard sword plunged through the prefect's chest, exploding out the front in a gush of dark blood.

Hezraas cried out with inhuman, guttural shrieks. Yandumar swept his other sword horizontally, removing the source of the dissonant screams.

"Ya' looked like you could use a hand, son," Yandumar said.

Mevon smiled. "Thank you . . . father."

THE LAST CASTER came into parallel with her, and Jasside quivered in ecstasy. Though she only held a fraction of their power, it was still more than she had ever controlled, more than she had ever dreamed of holding.

She stepped up, gaining a full view of the battlefield. The chaos and death that greeted her nearly drove the joy from her. But her experiences over the last several months had forced her to grow more than the first two decades of her life combined. She surveyed the carnage, and with forced serenity, found her targets.

Pulling from the energy sources of the forty-one casters behind her, Jasside filled herself with all she could hold.

She groaned, leaning against the parapets. "My God," she whispered.

She shook herself and formed a spell. The first mierothi was dead ahead.

For you, mother. And for you, Brefand. "And now . . . my redemption begins."

The bolt of lightning that struck from the sky darkened the entire park for one brief moment. The crack that sounded left her deafened. Where the mierothi had been standing was . . . nothing. Just an ashen smear for a score of paces in any direction.

Three beats later, a maelstrom of dark energy consumed the spot another mierothi had been. Orbrahn. Jasside allowed herself a smile that she had struck before him.

She turned her gaze to the last mierothi, positioned in the very center of the park. Pulling half her energy, she casted, pushing the ground up beneath his feet. The mierothi and his daeloth flew skyward fifty paces in a jumble of dirt and stone.

With the other half of her current pool, she formed hundreds of razor-sharp discs of pure, volatile energy. She sent them forward. They chopped through the bodies of her airborne enemies, slicing them into countless bloody chunks.

She watched the shower of flesh fall for four beats. Slowly, the din of battle began sounding as her hearing returned. Clusters of darkwatch still fought her allies, killing them in droves.

She had ended the mierothi threat here. Now Jasside narrowed her focus and set to work ending the battle.

GILSHAMED SURVEYED THE handiwork of his followers. The effectiveness of the linked caster groups was, he admitted to himself, quite impressive. Jasside and Orbrahn, after annihilating the mierothi, had used a surgical application of sorcery to end the remaining groups of darkwatch. Those two were now lying on the ground. A linkage of that magnitude, he knew, would leave them drained for days.

Mevon and Yandumar stood talking beneath the

hanging boughs of a willow tree. Their animated gesticulations indicated they were replaying the battle, congratulating each other on their kills. There had been a barrier between them—understandable, given the circumstances—but it was obviously gone. Truly, the two were now father and son. A new bond formed in the heat of bloodshed. He hoped it would be enough to ensure . . . cooperation.

The troops had suffered worst, but Gilshamed had expected that. Of the five hundred committed to the ground assault, less than a hundred remained. They had bled for their cause. They would not have had it any other way.

It is well. More will come. What we have lost today in manpower we have gained back in reputation tenfold.

Already, as casters moved around the field of broken bodies, administering healing to those who could be saved, curious civilians had flocked to the scene. His men had orders to keep them out but not to prevent them from seeing. Or from witnessing that which was mounted on stakes at both of the park's gates.

Mierothi heads.

The crowds would talk. The word would spread. The revolution had killed six mierothi, and all of their guards, in broad daylight, in the middle of the prefecture capital. A flying, golden man had weathered the worst the mierothi could conjure, and men of every station—from lowly peasant to unstoppable Hardohl—had joined in the battle.

Yes. Let news spread. Let the emperor shake in fear of what we have done. Let him know that this is just the be-

*ginning and that this empire is veiled no more. Its people
now know their oppressors are not invincible. Someone
has stood up to them and prevailed. Spectacularly.*

Gilshamed, arms crossed, allowed himself a smile.

A man rushed through the eastern gate, wearing a
haggard look. He looked around frantically for a moment
before his eyes fell across Yandumar and he bolted in that
direction. Gilshamed moved closer as the man gave a
report.

Gilshamed came to Yandumar just as the man saluted
and rushed away. "What is that about?" he asked.

Yandumar turned to him. His shoulders slumped as
he said, "Scout from the eastern city gate. There's an army
approaching."

"How many?"

"He said that the hills were buried beneath them,"
Yandumar said.

"Masri," Mevon said. "And her host. It has to be."

Gilshamed's spine went cold. *Forty thousand . . . we're
not ready to face that. Not yet.* "Give the order. Full retreat. Out the western gate."

"On it," said Yandumar. "Let's move!"

VOREN SWEATED BENEATH his grey furs. The crowd below
huddled together, bundled in coats and hats and gloves to
stave off the chill of late autumn, red noses visible on those
closest. The masses blurred all the way to the palace gates,
a swaying sea of brown and orange and yellow. Close to
fifty thousand souls by Voren's estimation.

They came because they were told to. Because the emperor had commanded that the compound be full, so that as many ears as possible could hear what he had to say. Voren wondered, with no small amount of trepidation, if this had something to do with the revolution. When the voltensus had been destroyed, the palace had been full of angry mierothi. But now . . .

Now, it was not anger on their faces, on their lips, in their behaviors and stances. It was fear. Cold, mortal fear.

Voren bent his head next to Kael. "What do you think happened?"

Kael, ever dour, had on the blankest expression Voren had ever seen on the man. The very lack spoke volumes about the Hardohl's effort to conceal his true feelings. *Ah, but what is it, exactly, that you are trying to hide?*

Kael slowly turned his head and eyes up to Voren. "Don't know. It's serious, though. Rekaj don't hardly ever make public speeches."

Voren nodded absently, scanning across the balcony to where the council stood. No one spoke, the mood too dour for even the most basic of civilities. Only Truln held something on his face other than shock. The Imperial chronicler seemed to be taking mental notes. Voren stepped over to him.

"Good to see you, Truln. You reckon this is a day for the Chronicles?"

Truln blinked rapidly. "Uh, hello, Voren. Yes. Yes I do."

"Why is that?"

Truln opened his mouth, then shut it quickly. A long moment passed before he was able to re-form words.

"Just wait for the emperor's announcement. It should answer . . ." he paused, frowning. "You'll understand soon enough."

"Of course," Voren said. "I suspect his speech will prove most enlightening."

Truln stared at Voren, wide-eyed. He pressed his lips together, shook his head, and said no more.

Voren peered at the rest of the council but dared not approach any of them. Few looked on him as anything other than a leashed pet, and the tether connecting him to Kael did not help the image. No, now was not the time to speak to them. But he could watch.

Kitavijj, the mother phyzari. Head of the group of mierothi women who monitored every birth in the empire, keeping careful tabs on the number of casters born, as well as finding every last void. Finding, and ensuring no questions remained. No loose ends. No witnesses. Her jaw hung open, and her glazed eyes gazed unflinchingly onto the ledge.

Lekrigar, the high regnosist. His order was devoted to the furthering of knowledge both magical and mundane, conducting experiments of every kind. Horrific, gut-wrenching experiments. He sat, arms crossed, legs twitching up and down in a staccato beat.

Jezrid, the marshal adjudicator. His network of listeners and hidden daggers had been running ragged chasing rumors of dissent, only to find themselves blindsided by the very real revolution popping up in the one place they hadn't bothered to look. He stood rigid, jerking his head and body around at every sound, as if expecting assassins to jump out at any moment.

Grezkul, the supreme arcanod. Over a million men under his command. Yet even he could not control the look of despair that plagued his features.

They each collectively inhaled as the emperor strode onto the balcony.

Rekaj stepped up on the podium. He swept his robes around as his eyes glared over those assembled behind him. Voren felt a lump forming in his throat as that piercing gaze passed his position.

The emperor sneered, then turned to face the crowd.

"Listen, you mewling masses. Listen and heed this warning. Today, the blood of my kin has been shed. Eighteen of my brothers and sisters breathed their last upon the mortal plane. Murdered by insurgents. By people just like you.

"What have I to say in response? Just this. Anyone involved in this rebellion will be hunted down and exterminated. Anyone helping them will by flayed alive. Anyone whispering of their deeds with smiles on their lips will instead find smiles on their throats. Anyone so much as thinking of aiding them in the smallest way will be burned alive."

Rekaj paused. The words sank into the crowd, and a hush fell over them, making a graveyard seem a boisterous place. Voren felt his pulse racing, his breath become shallow and strained. *Well done, Rekaj. If I am any indication, you have put the fear of the gods back into them.*

The emperor, however, was not finished.

"My agents tell me that there are sympathizers among us, even now. Right here in this crowd. Never let it be said that I am not a man of my word."

With that, he raised his hand, forming a fist, then let it fall.

It began with the bowmen. Stationed atop the outer walls as well as the roofs of the buildings in the causeway, they released a barrage aimlessly into the crowd.

Guardsmen poured out of every gate leading to the square, formed lines, and began advancing. They cut down all in their path, and as packed as the area was, no one had any chance to run.

I take it back. You are a fool, Rekaj. The biggest fool this world has ever seen.

The council, as one, stepped up to the edge of the balcony. Voren sensed them energizing. *By Elos, no!*

The emperor leading them, the six mierothi cast their spells into the screaming, desperate crowd.

Tornadoes of dark energy, swirling with destruction, churned through the seething mass of flesh, ripping bodies and spraying skin and blood and bone and pulpy chunks of human meat into the air. This excrement fell upon others, claiming even more victims.

Voren turned away, his stomach wrenching. He fought to keep its contents down. He closed his eyes and tried to will away the sounds of death and panic below him.

His efforts to block out the world only served to plunge him into nightmares of memory.

Voren's mind conjured the scene. A familiar one. The

one he strove to run from every time his mind's eye was opened.

The day of the Cataclysm.

He saw himself, bound, as were twoscore of his kin. His brothers in arms who had all fallen into the mierothi trap. Lashriel tied up at his side. She was praying.

Vashodia, Rekaj, and Gandul—the second emperor—arguing. The entire nation of the mierothi gathered around them. Finally, Gandul sighing and nodding. Vashodia scowling. Rekaj twisting his mouth in suppressed glee.

They took their places. Emperor Gandul initiated, and the thousand surviving mierothi harmonized with him. It took almost a toll to finish.

When they had linked, all eyes turned to the ten thousand captured soldiers, bound together in a massive mound of wood and hay. The stench of oil. A hundred torches touching within beats of each other. Blazing. As grand a funeral bier as ever there was. The sickly-sweet smell of roasting human flesh. The choking smoke.

Blood sacrifice. To empower the casting.

And oh how it had.

Voren's memory blanked out, and when it returned . . . the world had changed.

Gandul was dead. The land was shaking. The enemies of the mierothi had been swallowed up, the Chasm now their grave. The sky became an electrified web as the Shroud first fell into place.

And Voren's shackles were removed.

He had shaken his head to the accusing stares of his kin. *I do this to save you. How can you not see that?*

Lashriel had said nothing. A single tear had fallen, carving a ragged river down her dust-strewn cheek. Then she turned away.

Maybe one day, you will thank me. Maybe one day, you and he may find it in your hearts to forgive me.

Voren blinked. Save for him and Kael, the balcony was empty. The slaughter of the crowd had diminished, and the square was a scattered mess of broken bodies, bone and flesh and bloody swaths of shredded clothes. The stillness of death hung over like a miasma. Anything living had long since fled.

But my day of redemption has not yet come.

Perhaps it never will.

Chapter 10

SNOW FELL, AND Draevenus set fire to the last wagon. Ten gathered around him to bask in the warmth of the blaze.

He would not call them good men. Those volunteering for their particular brand of service were rarely men of high moral standards. Greedy, lustful, scum of the world—these were the words that usually came to mind. Most did not belie this conception.

These ten, though . . . Draevenus would not entrust them with much. But after spending a week among those he had freed, they were the best he had to work with. Men, he hoped, who would at least keep their word.

At least so long as he paid well.

Draevenus threw down the last of the coin sacks that had belonged to the daeloth. "This should keep you for a while. Spend it well."

They dug in, greedily, dividing the contents among themselves. Perfectly evenly, he was sure.

Once the gold had all disappeared into each man's preferred hiding place, one of them had the courage to ask a question. "You ready to tell us what the abyss this is all about, honored one?"

Draevenus sighed. When he had first taken over the convoy, he had told them that he had saved them from a fate worse than death and that their only hope of survival was to do exactly as he said.

Fear, greed, curiosity, and deeply ingrained obedience had all served to keep them in line. Now, however, he owed them the truth. Most of it, anyway.

"When you were chosen for this," Draevenus said, "what were you told it was for?"

They all chuckled. "Them daeloth said some horny mierothi women needed fresh studs to keep them entertained for the winter," said one of the men.

"Said we'd have every luxury imaginable, so long as we kept them satisfied," said another.

"And once they grew bored with us, a fat purse o' gold for our service." This drew another round of laughter.

Draevenus gritted his teeth. *So close to the truth, yet still so deceiving.* "A hard bargain to reject. But this was, of course, a lie."

Grumbles of "thought as much" and "I knew it!" and "told ya' so" were murmured among his listeners. "What *was* waiting for us, then?" the first one asked.

"A dark fate. One that may well be worse than death. But this I cannot say for certain, for I have never experienced either, myself."

The mutterings took on a bleaker, quieter tone.

Finally, one man, the youngest of the bunch, asked, "Why did you save us?"

Draevenus sighed. How much to tell them? "I can't reveal too much, you understand. When you do not arrive, people may come looking. They likely have already been sent. If I tell you my plans . . ." he raised his arms, a gesture of helplessness.

A chorus of nods answered, urging him to continue.

"Still," he continued. "I didn't want to leave you unaware of the danger. Nor without means of surviving the winter.

"You see . . . I," Draevenus paused. "I need your help."

Confused, they looked at each other. "What for?"

"I've spread three hundred men among the towns and villages of this region. Ten different locations. They have enough money to last a week. You ten have the rest of it. Long-distance travel is suicide this far south with winter already in its fury."

Though not men of brilliance, realization was slowly dawning on their faces.

One of them piped up. "You want us to stay here and keep the rest in place. We get it. Still don't answer why, though."

Draevenus closed his eyes. "If all goes well, I may need you to fulfill part of your original service arrangement. Though not in the way you might expect."

Silence fell as befuddlement struck their faces. He could almost see their imaginations running rampant with possibilities of both the tempting and spine chilling varieties.

"And if you do as I ask, you will find yourself with the deep, personal gratitude of a mierothi . . ."

Lean them over a precipice. . .

" . . . and, of course, a fat purse of gold for your . . . service."

. . . and push them off the edge.

Draevenus lined them up and shook each of their hands, gathering their solemn oaths in the process. When the last had passed, he said to them, "You've each given your promise, and you have mine in return. So long as I draw breath, and so long as you keep your end, I will fulfill this bargain."

He reached down and took up his travel pack and took two steps away from the fire. "Oh, and if any man chooses not to keep his word, and decides to take the money I have already given you and run? I will hunt you down and kill you. And when it comes to the business of death, there is no better, in all this world, than I."

Smiling, Draevenus left them, heading deeper into the woods. Farther south. Farther towards danger. Farther towards the hope his people so desperately needed.

AROUND THE FIRE were gathered his fellow victors, all basking in the glow of each other's company. Yandumar couldn't remember the last time he'd felt anything like it. The joy, camaraderie, the gratefulness to be alive—he'd missed it all.

There was too little of it these days, and not just among

the soldiers of the revolution. It was as if the whole continent held its breath, waiting for the bad times to pass,
forgetting what it was to celebrate—to live.

Now the ripples of their victory were spreading out.
Hopes and dreams were newly awakened from their long
sleep, manifesting into conscious thoughts of freedom.

And so, they came.

They'd left Thorull with less than nine hundred, and
by the time all the groups had rendezvoused, they numbered greater than four thousand. The four other raids had
succeeded, numerically, far greater than the main group.
Mevon had lost only six of his Elite, and less than a hundred other soldiers paid the final price. For that, twelve
mierothi, forty-eight daeloth, and six hundred darkwatch
met their end. A good exchange by any measure.

But their losses were dwarfed by the number of new
recruits. They now stood at fifteen thousand, just in the
main army, with almost three thousand more operating
as listeners, recruiters, spies and scouts, and supply runners. Gilshamed had also dispatched a few hundred special messengers, sending instructions to the sleeper cells
prepositioned in every corner of the empire.

And even with all that, this surge of fresh troops was
only the beginning.

Yandumar smiled as he thought about what came
next. About what would happen at the end.

"Thinking about your lady friend again, father?"

Yandumar started. Mevon had crept up on him
though he had no idea how a man of his size managed

that. His son sat on the fallen log next to him, holding a plate brimming with steaming meat. The savor of the aroma drove his belly to grumbling.

"Ha! I don't think she'd take too kindly to you calling her 'lady,' son. And no, it wasn't her I was thinking about."

"What then?" Mevon took a mouthful, which consisted of nearly half a leg of turkey.

Yandumar sighed. "Been thinking 'bout the end of all this. When we done what needs doing, and all my promises have been fulfilled."

"Promises? You mean the ones you made to Gilshamed?"

Yandumar tensed up. "Yes. Of course."

"What is it? What's wrong?"

Abyss take your perceptiveness. "Nothing. It's . . ."

He stopped, as a woman had walked up and halted before them. Yandumar was thankful for the interruption. "Bellanis?" he said. "What can I do for ya'?"

She blinked over at him. "Oh! Yandumar. Hello." Though it was hard to tell in the firelight, Yandumar thought she was blushing. "I just came to, um, congratulate Mevon." She turned back, locking eyes with his son.

"Yes . . . Bellanis," Mevon said, as if trying out her name. "Thank you again for heeding my instructions at Thorull."

"Of course." She cleared her throat. "I watched you the entire battle. The way you fought . . . it was spectacular."

Mevon smiled. "Thank you."

Her eyes flashed over to Yandumar. *I know how to*

take a hint, darling. He stood. "Well, I think it's about time I got some food myself. You two enjoy yourselves." He stepped away, and Bellanis immediately took the seat he had just vacated.

Watch yourself, son. This one has claws.

He laughed as he realized that was probably exactly how Mevon preferred them. Not that he blamed him. Yandumar liked his women the same way. Kaiera had had a temper to make the emperor cringe and a right hook to back it up. And Slick Ren . . .

Kaiera, dear. I'll never stop loving you. Though you may curse me for a sentimental fool, I think I'm ready to let you go. Now, maybe, I could love someone else without tarnishing the memory of our time together.

He spotted Slick Ren at the next fire over, smiled, and began heading her way.

He was almost there when Jasside stepped in his way. She opened her mouth to speak but before she could utter a single word, Yandumar noticed her eyes flit past him to where Mevon was sitting. Mevon and Bellanis.

A look of outrage flared. It was quickly replaced by one of confusion. Then wonder. Then anger. Then sorrow.

Scorch me, the mind of a woman is a terrible thing. Yandumar cleared his throat. "You need something, Jasside?"

She almost jumped out of her skin, as if she had forgotten Yandumar was even there. "Yes. Sorry. I just wanted to give you the western-perimeter report."

"Shouldn't you be giving that to Gilshamed?" Yandumar pointed to the valynkar, who was standing with one hand on Orbrahn's shoulder, gesticulating broadly with the other as he relived the events in the city. "He's usually the one who handles you casters."

"He's"—she pressed her lips together—"occupied, at the moment."

Yandumar sighed. "All right, I'll take it then. What's the status."

"All pickets report clear. There's been some trouble integrating the new recruits into rotations, but that should be worked out with time."

"Sounds like you got your hands full. Just how many new casters do we have?"

"One hundred and ninety-seven."

Yandumar let loose a low whistle.

Jasside shrugged. "What did you expect? With the mierothi dead, there's no one to issue Sanctions. And without the ability to cast freely, they're all without means of income. It was either us or go rogue."

"Or both," Yandumar said, eliciting a chirp of laughter from her. He stepped past her, patting her on the shoulder. "God bless ya', Jasside Anglasco."

Slowly, she said, "And God bless you too, Yandumar Daere."

Yandumar turned back to her and they shared a smile.

Her eyes turned black. She stopped breathing, and her spine went rigid.

Yandumar stepped to her, grasping her by the upper arms. "Jasside? What is it?" Commune reports usually came by brush message. Forcing something through like this was only done in an emergency.

Not good.

A sudden hush fell. Yandumar looked over to Gilshamed's fire, and saw Orbrahn in the same state as Jasside.

She came to, blinking and gasping. "Trouble," she said.

Mevon appeared at their side. "What kind?"

Jasside took a deep breath and stood upright, shrugging off Yandumar's grip. "One of our casters reported a disturbance. Their wards . . . vanished."

Yandumar felt a chill that had nothing to do with the nearly freezing temperature. "Voided?"

She gulped. "Has to be."

"Where?" Mevon asked.

"Straight west of here, two klicks out."

"And him?" Mevon pointed to Orbrahn, who was now coming around as well. "What section was he monitoring?"

"He had the eastern perimeter."

Mevon marched over towards the other fire, waving them after him. Yandumar followed, Jasside at his heels.

Mevon rushed into the circle of firelight. "Gilshamed, we're under attack. Focus your defenses to the east."

"What?" said Gilshamed. "How did you know? Orbrahn is just now saying . . ."

Mevon hushed them all with a sharp gesture. Just audible over the crackling flames was the sound of distant screaming, and the unmistakable clamor of battle.

"By Elos . . ." said Gilshamed softly.

Yandumar stepped up. "Go, Gilshamed. You can make the difference while we organize."

Gilshamed ground his jaw a moment, but at last he nodded. He unfurled his wings and blasted into the sky, heading east.

Mevon stepped up to Jasside. He brushed her upper arm with a tenderness that shocked Yandumar. "Jasside," said his son. "I need you now."

She looked back at Mevon with wide eyes and shivered. "Of course."

Yandumar grasped Mevon by the forearm. "Be careful, son."

Mevon leaned in close. "Try not to engage them fully. I may be able to . . . persuade them. Somehow. I just need time."

"If you can, then do it. And quickly."

Mevon nodded to Jasside, and the two rushed off.

Yandumar turned to Orbrahn. "Time to save our asses. Again."

Orbrahn smiled wryly. "Not to worry. She's still pleased with our progress."

"Shut your scorching mouth! Now let's go!"

JASSIDE CLUNG TO Mevon's back, which felt like stone beneath her grip. Quake's hooves churned the soil, propelling them at breakneck speeds through a forest dappled by moonlight. Her pulse raced along with them.

Sooner than she had expected, they came to the picket. Jasside searched for the casters on duty, spotting one she recognized and three she did not. "Calla?" Jasside said. "You sent the report?"

"Yes, sorry about punching the message through. I thought it was urgent." Calla fixed her eyes on Mevon. "Seems I was right."

Jasside nodded. "You did well. Where did it happen?"

Calla pointed west. "Keep going that way. We spread out more wards, and they kept vanishing at the same spot. Looks like they aren't moving."

"Of course they're not moving," Mevon said. "They're waiting for me." He reached to pat Quake on the neck.

"Wait," Calla said, stopping his hand. "Just the two of you?"

Mevon arched an eyebrow. Jasside could feel the confidence rolling off him in waves. *Don't put too much faith in me, Mevon. Or in yourself.* She glanced back at Calla. "Go into commune and keep watch on me. If you feel . . ." She paused, taking a deep breath. "If you feel me die, pull everyone back. You won't be able to face what will come for you."

Calla gulped, then nodded.

They shot away, but more slowly than before. Mevon seemed to be exercising caution. "Jasside?" he said.

"Yes?"

"Thank you for being here with me."

Stunned, she couldn't speak. She started to nod, then, realizing he couldn't see her, patted his shoulder instead.

"This will be hard enough, as it is," he said. "Having you at my side . . . I don't know. It's . . . comforting I guess."

You sure do know how to sweet-talk a girl. Jasside coughed to clear her throat and to make sure her voice still worked. "I'm the most qualified. Still, if you wanted to, we could have brought more to help us."

"No. I don't think that would do," he said. "Besides, that's not the kind of difficulty I mean."

Jasside furrowed her brow, unsure what he meant by that. He sounded . . . hesitant? *Don't you dare. You didn't falter when you threw that blade into Brefand's heart. Now is not the time to start second-guessing.*

"I will do what I can," said Jasside. "All that I am able."

Mevon turned his head. She saw his jaw bunch and grind, but further conversation was cut short.

Quake stopped. On the other side of a narrow glade bisected by a low, babbling brook, three figures stood, illuminated by the light of the moon. Across each of their backs was strapped an *Andun*.

Jasside quivered.

GILSHAMED SWOOPED LOW, shooting flame out in front of him. The enemy squad jerked backwards. His spell scorched the ground in front of them, doing no harm, but it bought a group of his troops the moment they needed to withdraw.

He longed to gather his strength and melt their flesh from their bones, but he had not the time. He flew on, soon coming to another group of his allies, leaving a wake of their own dead behind as they retreated. He spotted the line of Elite and sprayed a hail of sorcerous arrows at them.

They bunched up, ducking behind those enormous bulwark shields. Gilshamed's attack spattered into them but did not penetrate.

Abyss take that armor! The enchantments imbued into every piece took the bite out of his spells. And they were sturdy enough to withstand what made it through.

Gilshamed shook his head as he battered at another group of the enemy. *What did you expect? We used sorcery to kill mierothi, so they send those best suited to the killing of casters. Why did you not plan for this kind of attack?*

His anger at himself abated slightly when he saw one of the Elite fall before his onslaught. He cast another spell at the downed man, engulfing his body in flames.

His satisfaction was short-lived. Arrows streaked by, one cutting across his cheek. He had been too busy to keep his shield active.

Gilshamed resumed it now, casting a broad web of light out into the forest and scanning for the bowmen. Nothing. Even in the midst of battle, those rangers could avoid being seen if they wished.

He ascended, seeking more allies to aid. He spotted a large group of the enemy charging down a hill at his troops. A beat later he saw a second cluster of his soldiers about to be overrun. His spine chilled as he realized he could not help them both in time.

Save whom you can. Show them their faith in you is not misplaced. Gilshamed set his jaw and flew towards the first group.

He aimed his spells not for the Elite themselves, but both below and above them. The ground before their feet he churned into thick mud a few hands deep. Their charge stalled as they struggled through the muck. His second spell pulled at a gathering of boulders, sending them tumbling down the hill. The stones crushed half of the enemy squad. The rest retreated.

Gilshamed looked towards the second group, still two hundred paces distant, just as the Elite began cutting into them.

He saw movement. Men running, not in retreat, but straight into the enemy.

Yandumar, leading some of Mevon's Elite.

They crashed into the enemy, knocking several to the ground. Blades thrust out. Shield struck upon shield, an impact that Gilshamed could feel even from this distance.

The clash lasted but a few beats. Gilshamed counted six enemy Elite retreating at full speed, leaving more than twice that many of their dead behind. The squad lead by Yandumar seemed intact.

Gilshamed landed near them, dismissing his wings. "Mevon picks his men well, I see," he said loud enough for them all to hear.

"That he does," Yandumar said. He turned to the Elite and pointed into the distance. "You got me to him safe. Now go. You have your orders."

Mevon's Elite raced off without another word.

Yandumar turned on Gilshamed. "I've had conflicting reports. Some say there are thousands of them out there. You've had a better view than any of us."

"Not thousands," said Gilshamed. "They are less than a thousand for sure, likely closer to five or six hundred."

Yandumar nodded. "We're pulling everybody back. Clustering at a strong center. Casters are next to useless individually, so I had Orbrahn and the others all do that linking thing."

Gilshamed raised his eyebrows. "Excellent thinking." He turned to survey the field. "It looks like the first wave of attacks are finished."

"They'll be back. Soon. And with tactics adjusted to our defenses."

Gilshamed sighed. "Get back to the center, then. They need a strong commander right now." He unfurled once more and craned his neck skyward.

"What will you be doing?" Yandumar asked.

"What I can."

Once more, Gilshamed launched himself into the air.

MEVON HALTED TEN paces from the three Hardohl. The distance between them seemed so small, yet felt like a chasm nonetheless. No one moved—not so much as a muscle twitch—but Mevon knew that each of them stood upon the cusp of violence.

The storm rumbled within him. For once, he was not glad of its company.

He studied his brethren. *No. Not my brethren. Not anymore.* The thought drove up inside him a swell of . . . something. It was an unfamiliar feeling. Like a piece of him had just been murdered.

Killing mierothi had seemed difficult at the time, a leap off a cliff into unknown waters. But this? This made it seem easy in retrospect. This was falling into an eternal abyss, knowing the end would come without warning, and without mercy, and that by the time it came, he would welcome it gladly.

And their silence only widened the void.

Mevon eyed them, these three among many whom he had declared enemy by his change of allegiance. He did not regret the decision. Not until now, at least. Now, he didn't know what to think, what to feel. Now, as only once before, he hesitated.

"Mevon," whispered Jasside. "We must hurry. Our friends depend on us."

Friends?

Yes. I suppose I do have those now.

He turned, peering down upon her. For the first time, lit by pale moonlight, he took in the heart shape of her face, the deep chocolate of her ever-so-slanted eyes, the way her hair tumbled over one shoulder. Now, when he felt vulnerable like he never had before, he saw her beauty. And he saw the courage she possessed to overcome her fear and stand at his side at a moment such as this.

Courage of a kind he'd never had.

He smiled. Not his usual smile, the one only spawned by memories of blood, but a different kind of gesture altogether. He saw the shock on her face as she realized what he was doing.

Mevon squeezed Jasside's hand gently, somehow invigorated by the exchange, then turned to face the other Hardohl once more.

He cleared his throat. "It seems that you wished my presence." He spread his arms. "Here I am."

The one on the right, of similar build to himself only smaller, leaned forward. "Yes. Here you are."

"What do you want with me, Naeveth?"

Naeveth smirked. "Me? Nothing. These two wanted to see you for themselves. Hear you try to defend yourself. I already knew you were a traitor."

"I am not a traitor."

"You killed two mierothi. How is that not treason?"

"Because our loyalty was bought with blood and lies. Such actions permit—no—*demand* retribution. Demand justice."

Naeveth frowned. "What madness are you spouting now?"

"Think, Naeveth. We grew up together in the academy. How many of our fellow students had identical stories to our own? How many supposed orphans?"

Naeveth narrowed his eyes but said nothing. Mevon knew what he was thinking: all of them.

"And how many voids have you met who were not counted among our order?"

Again, silence. But again, Mevon could practically see the word dancing across Naeveth's mind: none.

Mevon took a deep breath. "We were brothers, once. If you could open your eyes to the truth, perhaps we could be again."

Naeveth sneered. "You always did think you were special. Kael's favored student. Always receiving extra lessons that the rest of us could only wish for. Always a little better at everything and thinking you were some kind of

Ruul-given gift to the world." He spat towards Mevon's feet. "You, Mevon, are a fool."

The one in the middle—a bear of a man—placed a hand on Naeveth's arm. "That's enough," he said.

Mevon met his eyes. "Have you nothing to say, Mosnar?"

"What's to say?" Mosnar said. "You've only confirmed our suspicions."

"And what about the truth of our heritage?"

Mosnar shrugged. "The only truth I know is that we have orders. I intend to follow them."

Mevon shook his head. *A lost cause, these two.* He turned to the third figure. She had yet to speak. Though her form was hidden in shadow, Mevon could tell she was short—barely taller than Jasside—with a freshly shaven head. Her face did not look familiar.

"I don't know you," he said. "But I may have heard of you. What is your name?"

She did not move. Nor blink. Mevon could not even discern the rise and fall of her chest. At last, she replied. "I am Ilyem."

Mevon had indeed heard of her. Ilyem Bakhere was known by a peculiar moniker: Ilyem the Uncut. It was said she not taken a single wound in battle, and not for lack of participation. Mevon leaned down to Jasside. "When the time comes, the lady is all yours," he whispered.

She furrowed her brow. "Are you certain?"

He stared at her. Whatever she saw in his face seemed to be enough confirmation, for she nodded.

"And who is this?" Naeveth asked. "This was supposed to be a private . . . discussion."

"She is . . ." Mevon paused, making eye contact with Jasside. " . . . a friend."

An avalanche of emotions rolled across her face, none of which Mevon could make sense of.

"Why is she here, then?" asked Naeveth.

"She is here to even the odds."

Mevon nodded, once, firmly, to Jasside. Then, he stepped away from her.

She took a deep, slow breath, and Mevon felt the familiar tingling of a caster beginning to energize.

Naeveth burst out laughing, and even Mosnar let out a chuckle. Ilyem only responded by shifting her eyes, briefly, to Jasside.

"You," Naeveth said, still fighting to control his mirth, "have truly gone mad."

Mevon stepped to the right. "My only madness is in thinking that this revolution might actually succeed. And that, perhaps, I could convince some of you to join us."

From the corner of his eye, he witnessed Jasside's hands begin their dance. *And now, we'll see if all our practice has paid off.*

It took her only three beats. Her hands shot out towards Ilyem.

The female Hardohl dropped like a sack of grain.

YANDUMAR RAISED HIS shield just in time. The arrow bit deep, hitting right in front of his face, and sent a ripple up his arm. This was the third time those scorching rangers had gotten close enough to take a shot at him. *Seems like they knew who was in charge.*

He'd ordered everyone to the center of the camp. Now they sat, huddled together behind double-thick lines of shield bearers. They waited. Rough estimates told him that less than thirteen thousand remained.

They've cut us deep. So few of them, yet the best the empire can send at us. It could have been worse, though. Had their Hardohl joined in, he doubted he would have been able to drive away the first wave of assaults.

Yandumar looked west. Mevon was out there, facing them. Nearly alone. *No, not alone. And I've seen what that girl can do.* Knowing Jasside was with him brought a small measure of comfort. Not so much as to calm him completely, but enough.

He scanned his forces. Fear ran rampant among them. As far as introductions go for these new troops, he could think of few worse disasters. Some would desert. It was inevitable unless they could salvage not only victory but a spectacular one. And for that they needed a grand gesture. A single defining act that would plant itself firmly in everyone's mind. Anchor them to the cause. Give them hope.

Trouble was, Yandumar had no idea how to achieve this.

Slick Ren and Derthon slid up next to him. They were covered in blood, but little looked to be their own.

"Any news?" Yandumar asked.

Slick Ren shook her head. "Except for those rangers taking shots from out of the darkness, we can't see them anywhere."

"Any sighting of Gilshamed?"

She threw up her hands. "Flying about someplace to the north. Man thinks he can win this all by himself. Idiot."

Yandumar sighed. He shared her sentiment but did not dare voice the thought aloud. The soldiers needed to have faith in Gilshamed, not doubt. Especially right now. "I assure you," he said, adding volume to his voice. "Gilshamed is doing everything in his power to keep us all safe." He peered at Slick Ren, tilting his head slightly, and wished he felt as confident as he sounded.

Slick Ren frowned, then seemed to pick up on his stance. "Of course, dear. Just venting. I hate fights like this. At least," she added, smiling, "when I'm on this end of the game."

"Me too," said Yandumar.

She stepped close to him. Her body pressed up against him, and she leaned her lips up towards his ear. "Have you thought anymore about my proposal?"

He didn't have time to answer. Their moment was broken when Yandumar spotted three men pushing towards them through the crowd: Mevon's captains.

"What is it?" Yandumar asked.

Idrus spoke first. "They've circled around. Their main force is to the west. They're readying to assault en masse any moment now."

Yandumar noted the blood staining Idrus's sleeves and fresh cuts on his shoulder and thigh. "How close did you get?"

"Close."

Yandumar dipped his head in respect. Slick Ren and Derthon did the same. And he remembered what Mevon had said about his ranger captain's powers of observation.

"We'll go out to meet them, then," he said.

Arozir nodded. "Our Fist will form the center. We'll stop them in their tracks and hold them. Protect the casters behind the strongest men you have left and have them flank to both sides."

"Linked, they should be enough to carve holes in their lines," Tolvar said.

Yandumar nodded. "And we'll drive our skirmishers into the gaps." He turned to Slick Ren and Derthon. "That's you and your best men."

She smiled deviously. "And here I thought you'd try to spare me the dangerous assignments, what with our . . . evolving relationship."

"You?" Yandumar raised his eyebrows. "You'd never allow it. And I'd rather save our first argument for a less hectic time."

He turned back to Mevon's captains, ignoring their quizzical looks. "Let's move!"

As soon as Jasside's spell hit—it had taken her only a fraction of the time to prepare since she had first used it against Mevon—both Naeveth and Mosnar turned their heads and stared. The shock on their faces was clearly visible even in the moonlight.

It was only the briefest of moments, but that was all Mevon needed. He dashed forward, flashing before her eyes in a blur of motion. She saw his hand shoot out. It connected with Mosnar's throat with a crunch.

Naeveth recovered, drawing his *Andun*, as did Mevon. The two blades struck together, filling the glade with a queer sound, unlike anything she had ever heard before. It was shrill, like the scream of a mountain cat mixed with the wail of an out-of-tune fiddle, yet at the same time, it reverberated deeply, shaking her down to her bones.

Mosnar fell, and the two spun away into the darkness. Their movements too fast for her to follow, their bodies too similar for her to tell them apart.

She maintained her spell, not pouring all her power into it as she had the first time but keeping a steady flow. She could last marks at best. Though still better than a few score beats, she was not without limits. *Hurry, Mevon.*

Ilyem had fallen with her head pointed towards Jasside. Though the rest of her body did not so much as budge, the woman's eyes darted about, often locking with Jasside's for long moments. What she saw there surprised her. Jasside could discern little fear, only alertness, confusion, and . . . *Could that be awe?*

Jasside's thoughts broke as Mosnar began stirring.

Impossible! Your throat was crushed in. No one can survive that.

But then she remembered the steps necessary to

subdue Mevon and the blessing, which burned away his wounds as she watched, leaving only faint scars behind.

Mosnar lifted himself onto an elbow and sucked in a breath.

Jasside felt her own fear rise into panic. The spell she now held on Ilyem took the whole of her power and concentration. She had no weapons on her.

Naeveth and Mevon came into view, swinging at each other in what could only be described as a dance. Everything became a pale blur as they stepped into a shaft of moonlight.

Mevon, though, still managed to spare a glance her way. He must have seen the sweat pouring down her brow and her frantic gaze directed towards Mosnar. But he could do nothing, for Naeveth stood between him and the others.

Then, she saw him smile. He opened his mouth, and shouted, "Quake!"

Jasside had forgotten about the horse. He came tromping up behind her. The wind from his passing whipped her hair across her face. The enormous mount, without hesitation, tromped over to Mosnar and promptly began stamping down on him.

She watched in morbid fascination as the first blow from Quake's hoof flattened the Hardohl to the ground. The horse immediately followed up with three rearing stomps directly on his victim's head, the last of which splattered skull and brain matter on the ground like a melon caught under a falling rock.

From that, no one could recover. She was sure of it this time.

So it seems our numbers were equal after all.

Jasside turned her head, attempting to track the state of the battle by the twisting shadows and that eerie sound which had, if anything, intensified as their duel raged on. She needed Mevon to finish quickly. To win. And not just because her energy reserves were nearly spent.

Despite the hate she had held on to for her half brother's death at his hands, Jasside realized that she wanted Mevon to live. He had become a different person in the months since they first met. A better person.

And the look in his eyes, just before their battle had begun . . . Jasside knew what it meant. And she could no longer deny that she cared for him. Perhaps, even, as more than just an ally.

She felt a tear swimming gently down her cheek.

Mevon . . . I forgive you.

Naeveth appeared, backing up towards her. Mevon followed soon after, battering down upon the other Hardohl's defenses, which were visibly weakening. Naeveth had a gash across his temple and forearm, and each shook free more blood each time their weapons clashed.

Jasside felt the weariness begin to wash over her. She had a handful of beats left.

Mevon crushed down upon Naeveth. Once. Twice. Three times. On the fourth, Naeveth's guard failed, and Mevon's *Andun* slashed down, severing an arm at the shoulder.

Naeveth reeled back, crying out in pain. Mevon swept his blades down, slicing cleanly through both knees. Mevon fell atop the crumbling body. His face paused fingers away from that of his opponent.

"I'm sorry it had to be this way," Mevon said, almost reverently.

Naeveth, gasping, said, "Abyss take you, Mevon."

Mevon nodded. Then he rose up and chopped down. Naeveth's head tumbled away in a spray of blood.

I am spent. Jasside's mouth was dry and every muscle had turned to jelly. Willpower alone kept her from collapsing, kept her spell from dissipating, but even that was on its last hair-span of strength.

"Mevon," she croaked, barely above a whisper.

Mevon's head shot up. In a beat he took in her condition, looked over to Ilyem, and lunged atop her.

Jasside released her spell, and with it, her ability to stand. She crumpled, more exhausted than she could ever remember being. *But I did it. I succeeded. We won.*

She fought the urge to lie down and sleep. She knew this was only a small part of the battle at large. There was still work to do. She might still be needed.

She struggled up to a knee.

"Rest," Mevon said.

She looked up at him. Somehow, he had already trussed Ilyem up in bindings more secure than she had ever seen, and mounted Quake, his prisoner splayed sideways in front of him.

"I can still help," Jasside said.

Mevon looked down on her. "You've done more than enough already. You, Jasside, are the very best of us. There's no need to prove yourself any further."

Jasside managed a smile, feeling an enormous weight being lifted from her shoulders. "Thank you, Mevon."

He offered her a salute, then whistled at Quake. The horse and both riders disappeared into the gloom of night.

GILSHAMED FUMED. The men he followed had not been heading for the main enemy force. They had been a diversion, intended to draw him out of position. Away from where he could protect his allies.

And they had tried setting a trap. Six rangers. They had almost succeeded. Gilshamed had burned them all to ashes.

He flew south now, back to the army. His army. His tool for retribution. The anger seared him. These Hardohl and their men had disrupted his plans. Set him back. Killed thousands he needed for other things. And now they sought to trick him into missing the battle.

I must be there, to be seen, to be the instrument of our victory. The people must maintain their faith in me if ever we are to scourge this land of my enemies, of all those that declared themselves against me.

Mierothi . . . or otherwise.

Gilshamed swept over a hilltop. The mass of humanity came into view, waged still in a tight, bloody encounter.

Yandumar had done it. The enemy forces were surrounded, cut off into a several small groups and fighting off attacks from all sides.

But even as he watched, the clustered formations of his adversary surged into motion, disengaging from the battle by simply trampling over any that got in their way. A surge of newly dead, on both sides, littered the battlefield in their flight.

Gilshamed flew over their heads. He landed several hundred paces ahead of the enemy's line of retreat, resting briefly to gather his strength. He knew he had not the power stop them all, not even if he were fresh to battle, but perhaps there was one thing he *could* do.

He stretched his arms out to the sides. In a semicircle, welcoming in his fleeing foe, sprang up a wall of fire twenty paces high and as many thick. An illusion, of course, but they'd have to get dangerously close before they realized the flames gave off far too little heat. He cast an aura of light, centered on himself, which transformed the midnight forest into the brilliance of noon.

Gilshamed lifted his chin and, amplifying his voice with sorcery, shouted for all to hear. "Stop! All of you! This battle is finished!"

Everyone froze.

Gilshamed smiled.

Yes. This is the moment we needed. My moment. Now, to plant it firmly in their minds.

The Elite stared him down, murder in their squinting

eyes. He had an appropriate fate in mind for them. He stretched out his arms . . .

But the wall of flames vanished.

Gilshamed jerked around, staggered by the voiding of his spell. "What the abyss . . . ?"

MEVON STRODE TOWARDS Gilshamed, carrying Ilyem in one arm and three *Andun* in the other. His skin tingled after having absorbed Gilshamed's wall of fire. He whistled once, and Quake turned and galloped away, vanishing into the forest in mere beats. Mevon stepped past Gilshamed, giving him a nod.

He laid Ilyem down gently. He then took the weapons and, one by one, thrust them into the ground in a line.

"Mosnar and Naeveth are dead," Mevon said to the gathered Elite. "And I have captured Ilyem."

He watched the enemy soldiers, watched their rage flash hotly for a beat, watched fear and despair rise to take its place.

Mevon bent down to Ilyem and removed the cloth from her mouth. "If you wish to save any of them," he said, "this is your only chance."

Ilyem glanced once at Mevon. Then, she cast her eyes downward. After several beats, she nodded. Mevon helped her to her feet, and she faced the Elite.

"I claim no authority over the other Fists," she said. "But as for mine, I order you to stand down. I urge the rest of you to do the same."

Her soldiers immediately obeyed. A cluster near the center, some two hundred strong, began laying down their shields and weapon harnesses, and unstrapping pieces of armor.

The rest of them, seeing this, stood in shock for several long moments. Eventually, and with obvious reluctance, they, too, submitted. Mevon saw his own Elite move forward to begin removing the gear and apply bindings to what were now considered prisoners.

Mevon noticed a familiar figure winding his way towards him. "Father," shouted Mevon. "It's good to see your head still attached to your shoulders."

"Ha!" Yandumar patted his neck. "This here is too stubborn to give way before any mere blade."

They drew together and clasped forearms. Yandumar eyes flicked past him, and the old man's brows scrunched together. "Something the matter, Gil?"

Mevon turned to see the valynkar, eyes locked on his back, shaking a glare loose from his face. Gilshamed waved a hand dismissively. "It is nothing." He stalked away, saying no more.

Yandumar shrugged. "Probably mad he missed most of the last part of the fight. Had us all worried when he didn't show up for so long."

"I doubt you ever need worry about him," Mevon said. "I've never met a man more capable of ensuring his own preservation."

Yandumar nodded. "I don't see Jasside anywhere. Please don't tell me—"

"Look," interrupted Mevon, pointing into the trees.

Quake rode up. Atop his back was a weary-eyed Jasside, clutching to the horse's mane as though her life depended on it.

"Well done, son."

"You too, father."

Mevon helped Jasside down just as Idrus and Arozir came up next to him. He turned to them, giving them the same greeting he had given his father. "What the status of the Fist?"

"More than half are recovering from wounds," Idrus said. "But the casters made our men a priority, and no one died who could be saved."

Mevon sighed. "How many?"

"Twenty-one," Arozir said. "Including . . ." His voice nearly cracked. Mevon laid a hand on his shoulder. He now noticed what he should have recognized immediately: both men, Arozir especially, fighting to hold their emotions in check.

"Tolvar," Mevon said.

His two remaining captains slowly nodded. Mevon clenched his hand into a fist.

Tolvar, who had been with him since the beginning. A great warrior. An even better leader of men. Gone now. Dead because he had followed Mevon.

And twenty others. Mevon had never lost so many in a single encounter. Not even close.

"You led them into the thickest fighting?" said Mevon, only half a question.

"Aye," said Arozir. "There was no other way to thwart their assaults."

"And how many were saved by your actions?"

"Thousands," Yandumar said. "Had your men not turned back those initial waves, they would have trampled right through us. Just like you planned to do the night we captured you."

Mevon bobbed his head absently. *Another failure that I should have been able to prevent. The best men in this land, doomed by their own bravery. Doomed by me.*

Yandumar moved to stand in front of him, less than half a pace away. "We lost over three thousand tonight. It could have been much worse. Your Fist made the difference."

Mevon frowned.

His father stepped even closer, laying hands on both of Mevon's shoulders. "What you have to realize, son, is that every man and woman in this revolution is our responsibility. Mine, Gilshamed's, and yours. We each did what was necessary for the good of all."

"I know. But those men can never be replaced."

"'Course not. We don't forget the fallen. We honor them by continuing to fight for our cause."

Mevon nodded. "I suppose you're right." He swept his gaze over the Elite prisoners and settled on Ilyem. "One question remains, however. What are we going to do with them?"

REKAJ'S HEAD SERVANT gestured towards the antechamber couch after taking his coat. Voren obliged, seating himself as the deaf-mute man—dressed in brightly colored livery—retreated, leaving him alone.

From the emperor's room, raised voices could easily be heard.

"I said pull them back, Lekrigar. All of them. Even your creatures and the slaves."

"Rekaj, surely this threat cannot be all that serious?"

"It is."

"But that's no reason to put the invasion on hold. You know how Ruul dislikes such setbacks."

"*I* am the voice and will of Ruul. No one else. Need I remind you of the cost of disobedience?"

There was a pause.

"No."

"Good. I trust your forces will be on their way back to our lands before dawn?"

"Y-yes, emperor."

Another pause.

"Your predecessor, though brilliant at her job, suffered from severe insubordination. I would think twice about following in her footsteps."

"Let me assure you, then, that I have no intention of doing so."

A chuckle. "Smart of you. I don't think you would handle exile well."

Voren heard something that sounded liked choking, or a chortle of pain—he wasn't sure. He had no time to contemplate, for the door opened, and the high regnosist stepped in. The reedy mierothi looked down his beak-like nose at Voren, sniffed, and exited the antechamber's opposite doors.

Voren remained seated, unsure whether Lekrigar's

departure indicated an invitation to enter. Not that he had any desire to. Apprehension gripped him, for he still had no idea why he had been summoned, and he was fairly sure he didn't want to find out.

"Get in here, Voren!"

Sighing, Voren rose to his feet, put on his best demure expression, and shuffled into the emperor's presence.

The odor hit him—urine and feces and blood and bile—and an involuntary glance revealed its source: three women, kneeling and chained, covered in the aforementioned matter. Voren cringed as he absorbed the cuts marring their once-fine faces, the dead look in their eyes.

Somehow, he peeled his gaze away, trying to hide his shock and disgust as he approached Rekaj. He stopped five paces away and bowed, eyes trained on the fine scarlet carpet. "You summoned me, emperor?"

Rekaj, his back to Voren, stood at his open window, which let in an icy breeze and occasional flurries of snow. The city spread out down the gentle slope of the mountainside, glowing softly as a million souls warmed themselves by their nightly hearth fires.

The emperor waved his hand across the sight. "Look at them all. Living their lives in peace. Many, even, in luxury. Safe and protected. By *me*." He turned, fixing Voren with a stare. "Yet so many still defy me. Still spit in my face with their whispers and their schemes."

Voren nodded. It took him a moment to realize that Rekaj wanted some kind of response. *Tread carefully.* "They do not understand our kind. They are brief upon this world, and cannot comprehend the grand nature of our struggles and purposes."

Rekaj sighed, turning back to face the city. "You are right, of course. Such small-minded souls can't be expected to fathom the very will of the gods. It is difficult enough for us."

Voren gulped, not knowing how to respond.

"I asked him once, you know, about Elos. Do you know what he told me?"

Voren, eyes wide, shook his head.

"Ruul called your god impotent," Rekaj said, bursting into laughter. "How absurdly ironic."

Ironic? Shade of Elos, what have you learned about your god to think so? "I am in no position to argue his assertion," Voren said. "After all, if Elos had any true power, you think he would have figured out how to undo your god's work."

"Such as?"

"The Shroud comes to mind."

Rekaj let out a puff of amusement. "You assume too much."

Voren lifted an eyebrow. "But if not Ruul . . . ?"

The emperor's scowl halted the voicing of his thoughts. Once again, Voren found himself perched on a precipice far too precarious for his liking.

"The Shroud," said Rekaj, "was a mistake. One I have failed to fully correct. At least a way around has been recently found."

A way around? Suddenly, the argument with Lekrigar he had overheard made sense. He shivered, thinking about mierothi influence spreading beyond the confines of this continent.

Then he remembered how shaken Rekaj had sounded. How afraid. The revolution had the man worried, enough so that he risked Ruul's ire to bring more forces to bear. Voren suppressed a smile at the thought.

"Tell me, Voren, when you look upon the face of your god, what do you see?"

"I . . . I have never . . ."

"No? I thought all your kind gazed upon his face?"

"Yes. Normally. Once every hundred years we are allowed to bask in the presence of Elos. To hear his words of wisdom and reason. To see, with our own eyes, proof to validate our devotion.

"I was ninety-seven when I was . . . when I came to be in your service."

"Ah. How peculiar then. Here we are, you and I, on opposite ends of the fulcrum. I, the only one of my people to have actually seen my god. And you, the only one of yours not to."

Voren furrowed his brow, looking away.

The edge of Rekaj's lip twitched outward. "You disagree?"

Voren shut his eyes. *Too late to hide it now* . . . "We both know that isn't true. You're not the only mierothi—"

"The others," Rekaj snapped, "are dead. Or as good as dead, anyway." He smiled. "And it was no accident things turned out as they did."

Voren cringed. "I know."

Rekaj studied him for several moments. He moved his jaw in tiny circles, and the sound of his teeth rasping against each other put Voren on edge. "My kin," he said at last, "do not. If they did, my rule would be threatened. I wonder . . . can you be trusted with this secret?"

And so, we come at last to why I was brought here. "I have known since the day of the Cataclysm what kind of person you are. Among all the mierothi, living or dead, there are none more ruthless. This secret"—Voren shrugged—"it keeps itself."

Rekaj laughed again, a sound devoid of amusement. "Ruthless. Yes, I suppose I am at that. But my actions, are they my doing? Or Ruul's? It was he, after all, that set our people on the path to conquest, even if he never used such specific words."

"Never used . . . ?" Voren frowned. "I don't understand."

"Conquest was . . . implied. Or so thought our first emperors. A tradition I maintained after their deaths.

"Ruul, however, had . . . other things in mind. Things that, to this day, make little sense."

"Why . . . ?" squeaked Voren, working moisture into his mouth. "Why are you telling me this?"

"You were able to keep one secret. Let us see how you handle another."

Fighting against the urge to shake his head—vigorously—Voren said, "As you wish."

The next moment stretched. Voren couldn't say how long it lasted. The sound of his shallow breathing and the thumping of his heart seemed to play over and over, countless times, becoming a nightmare of rhythm. And yet Rekaj stood rigid, unblinking.

At last, the emperor's lips parted. "Ruul," he said, dragging the word out the length of two breaths. "Ruul has gone . . . silent."

Pinpricks blossomed on the surface of Voren's skin. "How long?"

"Attempts at communication became labored and broken almost two hundred years ago. It has been more than half a century since I've heard even the faintest whisper."

Voren nodded. "That must be difficult."

Rekaj waved a dismissive hand. "My people continue to believe I operate solely on the word of our god. Suffice to say, were this knowledge to be revealed, it would end me far more quickly than would the other secret you are privy to."

"Yes."

Rekaj narrowed his gaze. "I will not allow that to happen."

Voren swallowed the lump in his throat. "Of course."

The look in the emperor's eyes was that of a boy watching an animal caught in a trap, wounded and helpless. Voren shook. He closed his eyes, and he summoned every fiber of his will to hold back his tears.

Rekaj stepped past him, stopping in front of one of the women. He picked up a pair of bloody pliers from a metal tray and forced open her jaw with a firm grip. A single tooth could be seen. Rekaj gripped it with the pliers and slowly twisted it free. The woman choked in pain, whimpering feebly.

"Sleep well, Voren," Rekaj said as he began to undo the front of his robe.

Voren walked rigidly to the antechamber, shrugged into his coat, and fled.

He closed the door to his chambers and immediately headed for his recently replenished wine rack. He knelt in front of the display, passing a hand over the '79 Taditali red—he had no time to savor such a fine vintage—and selected a cheap bottle without even the prestige of a maker's label. He popped open the stopper and filled a glass almost to the brim. Voren lifted it to his lips, tilted his head back, and emptied it in a series of gulps. He refilled and repeated the process.

After his third cup, he set down the glass and began making his way—slightly unsteadily—towards his bathing chamber. He kicked off his boots as he went, then tugged off his coat. He tossed it to the side, where it landed with a crunch.

Voren made it as far as the threshold, eying the porcelain tub with a smile, before he turned around.

What was that sound?

He stepped back to the coat, inspecting it with curiosity. Finally, he bent down and picked it back up, and began squeezing in various places until he heard the crunching noise again.

It did not take long. He reached into the inner pocket and withdrew an envelope.

The front simply read "Voren." He flipped it over. Red wax held it closed, and pressed into it . . .

Ruul's light!

. . . the seal of the High Council of the Valynkar.

Voren's heart began pounding. He tore open the letter.

Voren,
    Make your peace with Elos. I am coming for you.
      —Gilshamed

Voren fell to his knees.

PART III

Chapter 11

THE WINTERS WERE harsh this far south, and Draevenus had not made it as far as he wished to before it became too dangerous to travel. Less than fifty klicks from where he'd left the men he'd rescued, he was forced to hole up in the inn of a small town to wait out the snowstorms and ice storms that ravaged the land.

Though he kept the rest of his body covered, even he knew that wearing a hood indoors at all times would draw far too many questions. Questions that might lead to a whisper in the ear of the local garrison commander. So, instead, Draevenus wore a thick wig, which sent black hair tumbling past his shoulders. He also applied a paste to his face that darkened it enough to hide his pale complexion.

The weather would soon begin warming. The first thaw was but weeks away. He was glad that the need for such hiding, such stagnation, would soon be over.

Time to get on with it.

Verge. He didn't want to think about that place. About what took place there. He'd done all he could throughout the winter to keep himself distracted, focusing on securing provisions for the trek and keeping his body in peak condition. And returning his mind to the place it had been all those centuries ago. A place ready to kill at a moment's notice. A place that didn't think about the consequences and didn't hesitate.

He thought he was nearly there.

Draevenus shoveled the last bite of food—mutton again—into his mouth and pushed the plate away. Within beats, a serving girl came to clear his plate, offering him a smile and a refill on his ale. He declined the latter but returned the former, which caused a spot of pink to blossom on her cheeks. He gulped the last of his ale and set the mug down just as an icy wind blew in from the open front door.

Draevenus studied the lone man who entered. He was tall, with a girth that indicated an appetite a shade north of healthy. The man shook snowflakes from his cloak and from the grey hair he kept tied in a ponytail. He carried a pack with a fiddle case strapped across the top of it.

As he made to sit, he pushed back the flaps of his cloak, and Draevenus saw the unmistakable outline of a sword sheath.

Draevenus tensed up. Only two kinds of civilians were allowed to carry swords: retired darkwatch, and retired Elite.

Instinct gripped him. He'd been staring at the man

since he walked in but had not received the barest of glances in return. And the man had not been conservative with the cast of his eyes.

Bad move, friend. You might as well have announced your interest in me.

The only question was why? No answers came to mind that did not leave a sour feeling in his gut. He was not about to stick around to find out which it was.

Draevenus stood and made for the stairs. His room was on the second floor. Not easily accessed from the ground, yet, if he had to exit quickly, not too far a fall. As he put his hand on the banister, his gaze left the man for the first time.

From the corner of his eye, far past a normal person's edge of perception, he saw the man look his way.

He took the stairs three at a time.

He reached his door, silently padding the last few paces, and leaned his ear against it. He listened for several beats, holding his breath until sure that no one was inside. He pushed his key in the lock and swept in, closing it behind him with care not to make a sound.

He exhaled. "Foolish, Draevenus. Foolish to think you could trust those men. Gold fast loses its allure when an adjudicator has his blade at your throat."

Draevenus should have known what to expect. He had founded their order, after all.

He threw on his cloak and shoved in the few things he had that were not already in his pack. He was ready to go in less than a dozen beats. It was early yet to travel, but he had no choice. If the listeners were already this close, staying in place would only lead to a confrontation. Such would draw far more attention than would the small uses of sorcery required to keep him alive in the wilderness.

Draevenus cracked open the windowpane and peeked up and down the alley. Clear. He dropped his pack, then swung his legs out and lowered himself. With just four fingers gripping the sill, he reached with his free hand to close the window.

He released and landed softly in a crouch. He slipped his arms through the pack straps, lowered his hood to cover his face, and marched out of the alley.

He rounded the corner and stopped cold. A squad of guardsmen crowded around the front of the inn's main door.

The man with the fiddle stood in their midst.

Draevenus averted his gaze. He walked, step unchanging, doing his best to appear not the least bit interested. His right hand grazed the hilt of the dagger hidden up his sleeve.

Maybe they're just checking his certifications? Draevenus had never been very convincing, least of all to himself. His pace quickened.

South was where he needed to go, but the eastern gate was closer. He needed to get outside the town walls as fast as possible. It would be easier to disappear in the woods, and his pursuers would have to be sure of their quarry if they were to chance following in this snowstorm.

In three marks, he came to the gate. No one had looked twice at him on the way, but the guards now eyed him with open suspicion.

"You crazy or something?" the sergeant said. "Don't know if you noticed, but there's half a blizzard under way."

Draevenus gave an exaggerated shrug. "The old lady wants more firewood."

"And she thinks this is the best time to gather?"

"She claims this storm gonna get worse before it gets better. But it's not like we don't already got four days' worth stockpiled."

The sergeant grunted. "Women, huh?"

"You got that right."

A flip of his hand, and one of the sergeant's men lifted the bar and pushed open the gates. Draevenus gave a nod full of sincere gratitude. He looked back once, saw no one watching or following, and ambled out of the town.

"We'll keep an eye out for you, friend," said one of the guardsmen.

"Don't bother," Draevenus called over his shoulder. "I'm gonna circle around and come in a different gate. But thanks anyway."

It wasn't long before the town walls had disappeared behind a sheet of falling snow. Draevenus, at last, released the knot of tension that had gripped his belly since the fiddler had walked into the inn.

Still, I'm not out of danger yet. Feeling invigorated by a full stomach, and a seeping flow of adrenaline, he burst into a jog. He needed the exercise and, more importantly, to put as much distance between himself and those he knew were now on his trail. And to draw closer to his destination. He could almost hear the sands siphoning away, a countdown that he could not afford to let outpace him.

Verge awaited.

Despite the sweat starting to form beneath his attire, Draevenus shivered.

JASSIDE RAN THROUGH the camp, smiling at each patch of newly thawed ground and grateful for the modicum of warmth gifted her by the midday sun. Her patrol had just come in when she heard the news. She didn't want to be late.

Red-faced and sweating, she burst through the ring of onlookers just in time to see it begin.

Mevon stood in the center. All he had on was a pair of breeches. Had she not already been out of breath, it would have been taken away by the sight. Scores of pale scars crisscrossed his frame of rippling muscles. His eyes were closed. Only the faint expansion and compression of his chest let her know he was even breathing.

Three men circled him warily, each fully armed and armored. At a slight nod, they all lunged at once.

Jasside couldn't follow what happened next. Mevon moved too quickly. Two of the men ended up sprawled on their backs, and the third fell to a knee, wincing in pain.

One of the downed men rolled onto his stomach, then pushed himself up. "Check!" he called. "By Ruul, I swear I drew. Check!"

Mevon took on a wide stance and lifted his arms as his captains came forward. Idrus started on the right side and Arozir the left. Ropes, newly promoted, knelt and in-spected Mevon's feet and legs.

A moment later, Ropes stood. He lifted his finger, lips twisted in what might be taken for a smile. "Take a look," he said.

Mevon peered down. He grunted. The end of Ropes's finger was slick with blood. He looked past his captains to the three combatants. "Welcome to the Fist," he said.

A cheer rose from the small crowd. A few casters moved forward to attend to the Elite. These men had once belonged to Ilyem's Fist. They were part of the threescore Ragremons among those Elite who had attacked them, all of whom had defected upon Mevon's speaking one simple phrase.

Ragremos remembers.

This was the last bout. Mevon's Fist was again at full strength.

Jasside waited patiently while the men did what men do: grunting, slapping each other's backs, boasting loudly. She knew not to intrude at a time like this.

The winter had been strange between them. Letting go of her hate for Mevon had allowed something else to take its place. She didn't know quite what it was yet. She didn't know what she *wanted* it to be. But to say what lay between them was better than before would be an understatement.

At first, she thought it enough that his humanity was beginning to overcome the monster she'd first taken him to be. But more than that, his passion for justice let her know that, perhaps, he might be capable of passion in . . . other areas.

At last, the crowd began dispersing. Jasside moved forward to congratulate Mevon.

"Five," said a voice behind her, stopping her cold. "Five is the usual number."

Jasside turned slowly. Ilyem stood, flanked by a pair of shepherds as escort. Though she had no weapons or armor on her, Jasside still knew how dangerous the woman was.

"What do you mean?" Jasside asked.

Ilyem stepped forward, sunlight glinting off her freshly shaved head. "The trial for new Elite. It is usually five applicants at once, not three."

Jasside raised an eyebrow. "What are you trying to say?"

Ilyem gave her half a smile. "Three indicates that the Hardohl either has no confidence in himself or that his standards for the men he allows in his Fist are much higher."

"I see," Jasside said. "And which do you think it is?"

Ilyem stared past her. Jasside followed the gaze to where Mevon was squeezing into his combat suit. "I always wondered why he kept his Fist so small."

Jasside could only shake her head in wonder.

Ilyem turned to march away.

"Wait," said Jasside. Ilyem paused midstep and craned her neck around. "Our offer . . . won't you reconsider?"

The Hardohl stood so still for so long that Jasside was afraid she would never answer. At last, the woman sighed, and slowly shook her head. "I cannot."

Jasside nodded. *One Hardohl on our side has given us unfathomable momentum. If we could have two . . .*

She closed her eyes. It was not to be. Ilyem had made her choice.

"But," Ilyem said, "I will keep my word. You shall not meet me on the battlefield again."

"When do you leave?"

"Tomorrow, I and my Fist will depart. Not including, of course, those who have elected to stay."

In a surge of insanity, Jasside pounced upon an idea that had sprung up in her mind. "It must have been a shock when your men chose us over you?"

Ilyem eyes narrowed, lips pressing together. Jasside thought she saw the woman's cheek begin to quiver and was reminded that she was less than ten paces from a Hardohl whom she did not consider an ally. Out of fear, she almost began energizing. Almost.

"Yes." Ilyem's voice had become like a mirrored pond. "It was. But not nearly so great a shock as was your unique . . . ability."

Jasside's eyes flashed wide. She realized, upon closer examination, that the Hardohl was not in an aggressive stance but a defensive one.

Ilyem was afraid of *her*.

Jasside felt her spine firm up a bit. "There is one thing I would ask, then."

"What is it?"

"Spread the word among your peers. Let them know what you've learned. Maybe—if at all possible—get them to follow you."

"Follow me in doing . . . ?"

"Nothing."

Ilyem appeared troubled.

"You owe us," Jasside said. "For your life, and those of your Elite. You owe us."

The Hardohl ground her teeth. "No, I do not."

"But after everything we've told you? Everything we've *shown*?"

"Your claims are . . . convincing. But I considered the lives of myself and my Elite forfeit the moment we surrendered. Passive treason is the best I can give you."

"Understood. But wouldn't you say the rest of your peers deserve an end to the lies? Shouldn't they get to make their *own* decision based on the truth the mierothi have kept from them?"

Ilyem turned away, and Jasside thought she could almost hear a frustrated growl. "Very well," said Ilyem. "I will consider your request. But I make no promises as to the response of my peers should I even mention it to them." She marched away before anything more could be said.

Jasside breathed a sigh of relief as she watched the retreating back of the Hardohl. It was not quite a yes, but it wasn't a no, either. For the first time in her life, Ilyem might actually think for herself, and maybe—when she realized her life has worth outside the orders of the mierothi . . .

It would be a small miracle, but sometimes that's all we can ask for. I have a feeling we'll need every last one.

YANDUMAR CAUGHT THE cask in the cradle of his arms as it rolled off the wagon bed.

"Fresh from the Taditali vineyards," Paen said. "My father's finest for the esteemed leaders of the revolution."

The smooth-skinned young man smiled down at him. Yandumar tried not to grimace. "Any trouble?"

Paen arched an eyebrow while straightening his silk cloak, a gaudy shade of purple with silver embroidery. "My family does not have trouble."

"What about all the extra guards?" Yandumar pointed to the columns of armed men flanking the caravan. "No one thought it a little suspicious?"

Paen laughed with youthful arrogance. "My friend Yandumar, have you not heard? There's a rebellion stirring up trouble in these parts. Honest businessmen, such as myself, need to take extra precautions to ward against such lawless ruffians."

Yandumar sighed. The kid had come in the middle of winter, offering the full support of not only his family but the entire guild of wine and spirit makers. The campaign had seen few losses over the year's coldest months, and recruitment had soared. With over twenty thousand mouths to feed, the timely logistical support Paen provided had prevented a winter spent huddling in the cold with empty bellies.

I just wish he wasn't such a pain in the ass. Obviously, he couldn't let such feelings show. The revolution owed them big. And none more than Yandumar himself.

"Tell your father, next time you see him," Yandumar said, "that I can't afford to fall any more into his debt. He saved my ass thirty years ago, when I had no one else to turn to, and he's doing it again now."

"Yes, well. My father is ever practical. Upheaval means change, and change means new opportunities for profit." Paen laughed again, a dark tone lacing his voice. "And, of course, he does all he can to please our dearest Dia."

"Ah, yes. How is your . . . cousin, is it?"

Paen's lips twisted in wry amusement. "Cousin, yes. She is well. Fascinated by all the goings-on in the empire these days. Pleased."

Yandumar nodded. He turned to leave, still carrying the cask in his arms. "Thanks for the wine," he called over his shoulder.

"Enjoy!"

Yandumar strolled through the camp, returning nods and friendly greetings to all he passed. So many new faces, so many he didn't know, yet all had come together, all bound under one purpose. He felt a stirring in his gut, just the faintest of twinges, every time he thought about all the people who looked to him to lead and protect them.

How many dreamed the same dream? This dream of freedom. Did anyone even know what that looked like?

I've seen the world beyond. I know what life can be like. Should be like. I only hope our dreams don't end up like all those that came before. Those who struggled and died in hopeless causes. Let this time be different.

Dear God, let us win!

He pushed through the flaps of the command tent. He set the cask down in his section, then strode into the central chamber. Gilshamed stood studying a table that held a geographical representation of the continent. He looked up and motioned Yandumar over as he entered.

"Come, Yan." He was smiling.

Yandumar slid up next to him, looking down. "This the latest?"

Gilshamed nodded. "Fresh communes this morning. Things are progressing perfectly."

Yandumar had to agree. The entire map was covered in marks, each indicating a local uprising of the people. Many were thousands strong. One, on the plains of Agoritha—the breadbasket of the central territory—almost rivaled their main group in numbers.

"Looks like all the groundwork we laid years ago is finally paying off," Yandumar said.

"Oh, indeed," said Gilshamed. "We have created a wealth of opportunities and sown chaos for the empire. They will have no way of knowing where we will strike next and no way to respond in time once we do."

"Do you know *where* that next push will be?"

Gilshamed rubbed his chin. "There are several possibilities. The most promising one will be to strike north and establish a stronghold in Namerrun."

Yandumar frowned. "North?"

"Yes. What is it?"

"I mean, I understand why, what with our allies up there . . ."

"But?"

"But, well, maybe there should be some discussion about it at the meeting?"

Gilshamed flipped a hand. "Fine, fine. I will, of course, welcome suggestions."

Yandumar clapped the valynkar on the shoulder.

"Good. It's not just you and me anymore, scheming away in some nameless tavern halfway between nowhere and lost. There's too much at stake for anyone, even you, to think they can take it all upon themselves."

A look of fury flashed across Gilshamed's face, so briefly that Yandumar was sure he had imagined it. A smile instantly replaced it that was so genuine, so convincing, that he knew it must be false.

Can't fool me, Gil. I know you too well. And I know you have had to carry the entire burden for so long. But that time is past—you have friends now.

He knew why Gilshamed tried to keep the pain hidden, and he loved him for it. Almost two millennia of holding on to anger, on to dreams of revenge—no matter that he had labeled it justice—would drive any man crazy. That Gilshamed had withstood the lure of madness so far spoke volumes about his resolve.

Maybe soon he could share the pressure and expend a bit more energy keeping himself in check—at least for the time being—instead of balancing on the edge of sanity.

We need you too much to have you lose it now.

Yandumar began slipping around the table. Before he had gone two steps, his eyes picked up something on the map he hadn't noticed before. A black flag, the only one present. He pointed to it, asking, "What's that?"

"That," said Gilshamed, "is an anomaly."

"Why? What happened there?"

"Details are scarce. All I know is that no fewer than six adjudicators have been seen in the area, asking questions with the tip of a dagger. And whatever took place there was not of our doing."

Yandumar peered closer. The flag rested in the Fyrdra prefecture, the westernmost in the southern territory—and just north of where the Andean cliffs gave way to the ice fields of the Frozen Fangs. "Hmm."

"Something on your mind, Yan?"

"Not really. I just remembered that some of my old friends lived out that way."

"Old friends? Did you ever try to make contact?"

Yandumar shrugged. "Tried. Couldn't find 'em."

"Well, perhaps they are behind whatever has been stirred up. Who knows, maybe they are helping us without even knowing it?"

Yandumar shrugged, not ready to commit that much optimism. "Any word from Slick Ren?"

Gilshamed quirked a sideways smile. "Missing her already?"

"Don't judge," Yandumar said, holding up his hands. "I'm just worried about her."

"Of all the women in the world, she is the most capable I've ever seen at taking care of herself. And with Derthon at her side?" Gilshamed laughed. "Your concern would touch her, I'm sure."

Yandumar arched an eyebrow impatiently. "Well?"

Gilshamed sighed. "No word as of yet. Their mission will take more time, more finesse than the rest. After all, you know the temperament of bandit lords better than most."

"Ha! Ain't that the truth."

MEVON STOOD WITH his arms folded as he surveyed the training grounds. Thousands, grouped in platoons, were being drilled by Elite. Practicing reactions to commands, movement as one, oftentimes simply growing accustomed to wearing full battle kit for tolls on end.

They had been caught unawares by the enemy once. Mevon vowed it would not happen again.

Most of the new Elite had tried out for Mevon's Fist. Only the best had succeeded. The rest had been tasked as leaders of the new units. It was a sound plan. Though Mevon had little experience with large-scale battles, he'd seen enough men panic and break simply because there was no one in charge nearby to tell them what to do.

Mevon hoped it would all be enough.

The winter had seen them moving constantly. No major battles yet, just minor skirmishes, a few strategic ambushes, and feints in every direction. All attempts to keep the full brunt of the Imperial war machine from bearing down on them. So far, it had worked.

Now, however, it was time to decide what to do next. Mevon turned to his captains. "That's enough for today. Let them rest for the night."

"Aye," Ropes said. Arozir simply nodded. The two moved off. Idrus lingered at his side.

"How are they doing?" Mevon asked.

"Ropes is . . . adjusting."

"Can he do the job?"

"Well enough. He's just not happy about Ivengar."

"Trouble between them?"

"You didn't know, but before you promoted Ropes,

they fought each other for the captain position. Ropes lost."

Mevon rubbed his chin. "I see. What about Arozir?"

Idrus exhaled heavily. "Tolvar's death hit him hard. But he'll be ready when we need him."

"Good enough."

The sun began to set, painting the snowcapped trees harsh shades of orange and casting long shadows over the landscape. Mevon could just make out the deepest shadow of all—the nearest tip of the Chasm, that scar upon the face of the continent that comprised a third of the boundary between the eastern and northern territories, and stabbed partway into the central. Mevon turned from the sight and marched towards the command tent.

He swept inside without pausing. As soon as his eyes adjusted, he became aware that he was the last to arrive. Yandumar was there, standing for the soldiers. And, of course, Gilshamed. Representing himself, as always. For the caster contingent, the young sorcerer Orbrahn.

And, of course, Jasside.

As his eye met hers, she smiled. Mevon could not help but smile back. They'd spent quite a bit of time together over the winter. It felt good being near her in a way he had never experienced before. He was eager to see where it led.

As he moved to stand beside his father, Mevon noticed one last person in the tent. Someone he had not been expecting.

"What's he doing here?" Mevon said, pointing at the intruder.

Paen swept his cape back and executed an exaggerated bow. "Fear not, Mevon Daere. I am merely here to see to the interests that I represent."

"Why? This is a meeting to discuss strategy. You have no place here."

"My benefactors consider this revolution an investment in the future. I must ensure that it remains a healthy enterprise and will offer guidance as befits that goal."

Mevon glared across the tent at the boy. Paen smiled back.

Mevon had never been enthralled with the notion of the merchant families. Too much money controlled by too few people. Too much power and influence bought with the blood and sweat of a desperate populace. The whole enterprise was too similar to the way the mierothi ruled, and now that he was working to undo one group, the other seemed an enticing candidate for his next target.

Justice should be immune to the effects of influence. Equal for all. No man should be able to escape the penalty for his sins based on the size of his coffers or the strength of his army. . .

Mevon surprised himself as he completed the thought.

. . . or the god that he serves.

But he knew this wasn't the time to wage a second war. He sighed. "Very well." He turned to Gilshamed and nodded.

The valynkar raised his brows. "Let's begin then, shall we?"

A chorus of murmured assent answered him. "With spring approaching, movement will become significantly easier. Not only for us, but for Imperial forces as well. As you can see"—Gilshamed gestured to the table—"the empire is in chaos. Many of these groups are in contact with us, some even willing to take direction. But we gathered here are the focus, both as the hope of the people and the thorn in the side of the mierothi. Our fate is the fate of the continent.

"So, we find ourselves at a critical juncture and must ask ourselves: What is the best course of action? How now should we proceed to ensure victory for the revolution and freedom for this land?"

Gilshamed eyed Yandumar, who seemed pleased by the speech. "I am . . . open to suggestions."

Silence gripped the tent as each person contemplated. The purpose of the meeting had been known for a while, and everyone present would have ideas to put forth. They all seemed to be waiting for someone else to go first, however. Mevon himself was content to wait.

Finally, Jasside spoke up. "I, for one, have enjoyed the freedom to cast due to the destruction of the first voltensus. Wherever we end up striking for next, I believe should be preceded by an attack against the region's sensor tower."

"A fine idea, Jasside," said Gilshamed. "Though, once we make such a move, the empire will have strong indications about our intentions."

"What about a feint?" Yandumar said.

Gilshamed gestured for him to continue.

"We send a token force to attempt to destroy another voltensus. Imperial numbers have increased tenfold at the towers, and our attempts will appear weak and disorganized, making them underestimate us. Meanwhile, we take our main force in another direction, maybe even link up with some of the smaller cells along the way, and attack an important target. Maybe one of the territory capitals?"

"I like it," Orbrahn said. "Just like Thorull." He nudged Jasside. "You in for killing some more mierothi?"

Mevon could tell she was trying to hide her enthusiasm for the idea. "Wherever I am needed," she said, looking from Orbrahn to Gilshamed, "you can count on me."

Gilshamed sighed. "I dislike the idea of retracing our steps. It borders on predictability—a situation I wish to avoid at all costs."

"Don't think we can handle it?" said Orbrahn.

"The mierothi are scared, which is a double-edged sword," said Gilshamed. "They have stripped their local military to bolster their own guard, and keep close to each other, cowering in their cities. Though this has reduced the number of men in the field, and made our movements easier, it also makes any attempt to rid ourselves of their filth that much harder."

"Right," Yandumar said. "The death of individual mierothi isn't the point. It's the end of their rule that truly matters."

"Precisely," said Gilshamed. "More of them will die. Of that, you all have my assurance. But as our next move . . . ?" He shook his head.

A hush fell once more as they all turned their minds to the problem at hand. An errant thought began tickling the recesses of Mevon's mind, but it was still unformed, still brewing. He was not yet ready to give voice to it.

Paen cleared his throat. "What about Mecrithos?"

Gilshamed laughed. "I appreciate the enthusiasm, but we are nowhere near ready to take on the heart of mierothi power." He pointed at the top part of the map table. "There, in Namerrun, we have allies, the source of our logistical support, and a populace ready to join our cause. I suggest we make for the plain and establish a base of operations. From there, we can gather our strength, renew our focus on training and recruitment, and systematically plan how to dismantle the Imperial war machine. Perhaps, in a few years' time, we may actually be ready to strike at the capital. But not yet."

"You're talking an extended campaign?" said Yandumar. "Fighting from a position of strength instead of all this sneaking around?"

"Indeed."

Yandumar ran his fingers through his beard. "Well, I do prefer a straight fight. Most of the time . . ."

Gilshamed sighed, fixing Yandumar with an impatient stare.

Yandumar grumbled. "But it seems like we're heading the wrong direction."

"I see," said Gilshamed. He looked around the room. "Any other opinions about my plan?"

"I have no issues," Jasside said. "Careful planning will grant us a greater chance of success, I think."

"I dunno," Orbrahn said. "I think I'm with Yandumar on this one. Seems like north is the wrong way to go."

"Agreed," Paen said. "Those I represent would, I'm sure, wish to remain a *distant* source of support."

Gilshamed sighed, and Mevon thought he saw a flicker of irritation in the valynkar's eyes though it was over in a beat. "Very well. We can shelve the northern approach until we've considered other suggestions. I suppose our options, then, are to finish cleansing the eastern territory or head to the western territory. Now, our raids in this area have been highly effective. Imperial supply lines are stifled, their command structure is in disarray, and their strength in numbers has been cut to a manageable size.

"Yet despite our efforts, and the distractions in every last prefecture in the empire, reinforcements are still heading our way. Staying put and finishing our work here will be greatly rewarding for both morale and momentum, but it will take time and comes with significant risk.

"The western territory has been untouched by our machinations. A surprise attack—"

"No."

All eyes turned to Mevon. They were the first words he had spoken since the debate began, and even he was surprised by the firmness of that single word. As Gilshamed had been talking through his plan, Mevon's mind had worked through its thoughts. He knew now what he needed to do. What they *all* needed to do.

Gilshamed cast a sour gaze his way. "You have a problem with some part of my plan?"

"We cannot go west," Mevon said.

"Well, it does not have to be west. It could be—"

"Not west," said Mevon, ignoring the fury bubbling behind Gilshamed's eyes at being interrupted again. "Not east either. And certainly not north. We are overlooking some crucial facts. Facts that must dictate our path."

"Very well," said Gilshamed, lifting his chin in the air. "Enlighten us."

"First of all, Imperial military strength is far beyond your reckoning. They've been surprised on many occasions, but they've also been biding their time. Once spring hits, so will they. Hard. We won't be able to stand against a full assault by a major force.

"Secondly, these distractions you seem so confident of will soon be wiped out. The Hardohl alone will see to it. Since you saw fit to implant casters into each group, they will be easy to track down and annihilate."

"Have you no faith in our allies then?" said Gilshamed.

"Faith?" Mevon paused. "I'm not much familiar with the word. But I know the empire, and I know what it will do. And I know that every last man and woman involved in these small-scale uprisings is likely doomed."

"Maybe not," Jasside said.

Mevon turned to her. "What do you mean?"

"Before she left, I had a . . . talk. With Ilyem."

"And?" said Gilshamed.

"She said she would consider speaking to the other Hardohl. That she might try to convince them to sit this conflict out."

"Sit it out?" Yandumar said, wonder evident in his voice. "And you thought of this yourself?"

Jasside blushed. "Yes."

"Will she do it?" asked Orbrahn. "And, more importantly, will any of them listen to her?"

"I don't know. But she was definitely scared enough to give it serious thought. Perhaps others will as well."

"Hardohl don't . . ." Mevon stopped himself. He had almost added "*fear anything*" but then he remembered when Jasside had first disabled him. He cringed at the memory yet couldn't help but smile. "We don't change our minds easily. But if anyone can make us see reason, Jasside can."

He locked eyes with her, and something passed between them that he could only describe as a spark. Emotions and thoughts all jumbled and twirling. A sudden intake of breath. Right now, Mevon couldn't even remember quite what he'd said to her, but apparently it had been the right thing.

Yandumar cleared his throat and turned to Paen. "Your family has ears everywhere. They heard anything about the Hardohl and their Elite?"

"I can confirm nothing, of course, but I *can* tell you that my father's guards have recently seen a huge influx of highly skilled applicants. Some of them have *very* impressive resumes."

Mevon eyed Jasside again, nodding to her with respect. And gratitude. Facing his peers once had been hard enough. He did not relish the thought of having to do it again. "That was good thinking," he said. "Thank you."

She cast her eyes down, obviously embarrassed by the attention everyone was giving her.

"But as good as this news seems to be," continued

Mevon, "that only alleviates one of our problems. There is another, more serious issue that no one has mentioned yet."

"And what is that?" said Gilshamed.

"Lightfall Square."

Everyone in the tent seemed to stop breathing as each was suddenly reminded of the emperor's mass execution.

"What was the final death toll?" Mevon asked. "How many slaughtered in response to our actions?"

Gilshamed, to his credit, had the decency to look abashed. "Conservative reports estimate thirty thousand. Some say much more."

"And hundreds more every day face public execution," Yandumar added.

"That's just in Mecrithos," said Mevon. "Who knows how many more are questioned by the adjudicators and disposed of quietly?"

"I won't contest the tragic nature of our situation," said Gilshamed. "But we knew there would be casualties. Sacrifices even. What would you have us do to put a stop to it?"

Mevon glanced at Paen. "As much as I hate to admit it, the boy is right.

"We should march on Mecrithos.

"We *must*."

Mevon looked around. His father seemed troubled, but after a glance at Paen and Orbrahn—who wore identical half smiles—appeared to accept the idea. Jasside's visage beamed at Mevon in what he took as pride. Gilshamed's eyes were downcast.

Slowly, Gilshamed said, "We are not ready."

"Perhaps not," Mevon said. "But we cannot wait any longer. If we drag this conflict out for too long, this empire will become an empty husk filled with nothing but ashes and bones. This may not be your land, valynkar—and it may not even be mine—but it is for the millions of men and women who toil under the emperor's yoke. If there's a chance for it to be saved—for true justice to be had for all—then we have to act now."

"He's right, Gil," Yandumar said. "Scorch me, he's right."

Jasside nodded. "It may well be the last thing they expect. Wasn't surprise the most important criterion for our plans?"

"We carve out the corrupt heart of the empire," Orbrahn said, "and the rest will fall."

Mevon, as the rest, peered upon Gilshamed. He stood, arms on his hips, brow pinched in contemplation. And for one beat, one infinite sliver of a moment, the man who called himself their leader had upon his face a look that Mevon was not expecting.

It was the look of a man who thinks he has made a terrible mistake. A man ready to turn his back on everything, everyone.

And then it was gone.

Gilshamed inhaled deeply, then finally returned everyone's gazes. "Mecrithos it is."

Mevon inclined his head, wondering if Gilshamed was aware of how much he had just given away. "Let's get started on the plan."

GILSHAMED REMAINED IN the tent long after everyone had left. The details had been worked out, more or less, to everyone's satisfaction.

He thought about what waited for him at the end of this journey. About *who*. He fantasized about the look on the traitor's face as he read his letter and despaired.

Soon, Voren. Sooner than either of us expected. Your time will come, and my vengeance will be complete.

VOREN SWIRLED THE wine around in his glass, thinking how blood-like it appeared. The notion turned his stomach, and he found he could not drink another sip. Not that he much cared for mulled wine, even in cold weather, but it was all that was offered here in the emperor's personal viewing platform. Voren only held on to the glass as a gesture of respect to his host.

Rekaj was well into his cups already, and the "competition" had not yet reached the midpoint. Voren glanced sideways at the emperor, who cheered along with the crowd. Voren noted the difference in their shouts and jeers. Whereas Rekaj's vocalizations were full of malice and glee for each new victim, the rest seemed almost a sigh, as if they were saying, *Your pain is at an end. It is time to rest.*

Voren peered down into the pit of the stadium. There, the Ropes.

A hundred-pace square filled with bubbling tar, deep enough for four men to stand on each other's shoulders and still not peer over the surface. A dozen taut lines stretched across. Half a score dangling ropes on every line, each intermittently energized with surges of lightning by sorcerous constructs. Those competing were forced to cross, this after days without food, water, or sleep.

Two were left on the current heat. Voren watched one, about halfway through, incorrectly time a swing. A jolt ran through him and his sizzling body flew into the pit. The last man made it to within two ropes of the ending platform before his grip failed him, and he slipped away into sticky oblivion.

The Ropes were typically reserved for the worst of the empire's criminals, with freedom the prize for any who survived not one bout, but three. Too often, none even made it through one. The names of those who surpassed the trial were practically legendary, for only one man in a thousand made that list.

Another dozen people—men, women, even a child this time—mounted the starting platforms at the urging of sword points. The only thing the victims had in common was their crime: suspected sympathy for the rebellion. This was the ninth round, with eleven more promised before the day was out. No one yet had made it to the far platform.

Voren sat quietly, trying to ignore the looks of desperation, of hopelessness, flush on every set of faces, and swirled wine around in his glass.

"What's the matter, Voren?" Rekaj asked. "Not enjoying yourself?"

Voren tensed. They were the first words spoken to

him. He had wondered ever since the invitation—the summons—had come, what the purpose of this outing would be, all the while dreading to know the answer. Now, it seemed, the wait was over.

He gave a perfunctory smile. "After a while, anything can lose its charm. It is surprising what one can become used to."

He'd hoped to be as vague as possible with his answer but knew he had failed when the emperor scowled.

"Once again, my generosity is lost on you," said Rekaj, his face showing an alarming amount of color. "After all this time, you still make me question if it was worth it to keep you around."

Voren was tired. So *very* tired. The revolution was to be his ticket out of bondage. Instead, it had become just another reminder of the complete failure that was his life.

He had questioned Kael. Though he denied any knowledge, Voren could tell that the man knew the truth. Knew, and was trying to keep Voren ignorant.

Gilshamed was their leader. Voren, for his part, could think of no one worse.

He sighed, casting his gaze at Rekaj with something halfway between apathy and defiance. "Without me, it seems, you would have no one to talk to these days."

A laugh dripping with bitterness sounded from Rekaj. "Leave us," he ordered.

The darkwatch guards, four in all, bowed and departed to the rear. Kael patted Voren on the shoulder before following. Voren flinched at his touch.

After the Hardohl had shut the door behind him,

Rekaj turned in his seat to face Voren. "Do you tire of me so quickly? Is it so exhausting being in my presence?"

Yes. It had been a long winter, full of conversations with Rekaj. Talks that, on the surface, seemed to be about faith, of all things. Yet the unspoken threats never failed to seep through. Voren knew that arousing Rekaj's displeasure would bring about his death.

Voren couldn't seem to stop teetering on that ledge.

He shook his head. *When the truth condemns, a lie will do.* "It is the winter. Too long without seeing the sun. We valynkar are creatures of light and do not cope well with its absence."

"You are a terrible liar, Voren."

"I know."

Rekaj laughed. Almost, there was real humor in it. "Is it Kael? You two have seemed at odds for months. I can have him replaced if you wish?"

Kael was not the problem. *Better the enemy you know . . .* He shook his head. "That will not be necessary."

Rekaj drank deeply from his glass. "Come, then. I can't have one of my loyal subjects moping about."

Voren sighed. Rekaj, of course, was part of the problem. Yet not even the biggest part of it. No, that title belonged to Gilshamed. Voren felt himself going mad, stuck as he was between the two sides of the conflict. He knew Gilshamed wanted him dead. Knew the man would stop at nothing to see it done. And Rekaj?

He eyed the emperor. A flush overcame his body as he realized that he feared the man less than he did one of his own kin. A thought struck him, a moment of insanity that stretched into eternity as he followed the line of thinking to its conclusion.

He began sweating as he realized where it led.

My only option now. How did it come to this?

Voren reached into his coat and pulled out the letter. He pressed it into Rekaj's hands. "I believe this may shed some light on the situation."

Chapter 12

DRAEVENUS CROUCHED BY the path, covered in a layer of branches and concealed beneath a blanket of fresh snow. This far from civilization, he deemed it an acceptable risk to warm himself with magic. It was the only thing that had been keeping him from freezing to death for the last day while he lay in ambush.

He had passed through six villages—the last merely a collection of hovels long abandoned by all save a single half-mad hunter—and had fled every one.

The fiddler was following him.

Now, nothing remained. Not even a hunting lodge or much of a road beyond an overgrown game trail. Here the man would not be missed. Finally, he could be rid of his tail for good.

He just wished the man would hurry up. Draevenus had more important things to be about.

He chewed a piece of dried meat, rinsing it down with

a mouthful from his waterskin, all the while keeping an eye nailed to the small hole in his concealment that granted him a view of the trail to the north. The fiddler had not yet tried to hide his movements. Draevenus did not expect him to start now.

At the very least, this pursuit had kept him on his toes. Kept him alert. Honed his senses. He smiled, knowing that, because of the man with the fiddle, he was more ready to complete his tasks than he would have been otherwise. He would have to remember to thank the man before he killed him.

He heard his prey before he saw him. A high-pitched sound echoed through the cold, still forest: a tune being whistled. Draevenus recognized it. It was a song about a man who leaves everything he knows behind to pursue a dream, one that, in the end, leads to only bitterness and pain. It was called "The End of the Road."

Draevenus thought it quite appropriate.

The man drew close, walking noisily along the trail. Draevenus focused on quieting his breathing. He succeeded. A smile spread on his lips.

Still whistling, the fiddler drew abreast of him and continued marching past. Oblivious.

Perfect.

Draevenus sprang forward, shoving aside snow and the thin branches that concealed him. He energized and cast an immobilizing web at his opponent. If his observations were correct, the man was, or had been, a formidable warrior. Draevenus was taking no chances.

His prey froze more solidly than a block of ice. As

luck had it, both of his feet had been on the ground when Draevenus's spell hit him. If not, the man likely would have fallen.

Eyes darting for hidden threats, Draevenus approached. He circled once, then drew a dagger and thrust it at the man, striking his abdomen with the flat of the blade. If the man had hidden allies nearby, they would have reacted to the move, hopefully revealing themselves in the process.

Only if they cared about his life, that is.

He had to be sure.

Draevenus stepped back and lowered the height of his spell, freeing the man's head from its effect.

"You alone?" he asked.

Working his jaw loose, the man cracked a smile. "'Course not, Draevenus. I'm here with you, ain't I?"

Draevenus did not react. He already suspected the man was aware of his identity. "Who do you report to? How many are coming after me?"

The fiddler raised an eyebrow. "To be honest? I don't rightly know how to answer those questions."

"Don't play games." Draevenus pitched the point of his dagger to within a finger of the man's eyeball. "Cooperate, and I will make your death painless. Now, who is the adjudicator in charge of my pursuit?"

The man stared a moment with wide eyes. Then, he burst out laughing. It was a high, keening cackle, yet somehow quite melodious. Draevenus found it disturbing. Eventually, the man got himself under control, saying, "Oh, don't get me wrong, I'm sure they're after you. But I've had a whole heap of trouble avoiding their like while staying on your backside." He paused to laugh again. "I never did stop to ask their names."

"Lies."

Yet. . .

He studied the man's eyes, working through all he knew about him. About his tactics, his behaviors. He did not seem like the typical listener or crony. Too transparent.

And his lack of stealth . . .

The man raised both eyebrows. The closest thing to a shrug as was possible in his current state. "She said you might be a little incredulous."

She? Draevenus frowned. "Who are you?"

"Chant's the name. Harridan Chant. I'd shake your hand, but . . ." He laughed once more.

Chant. Why does that name sound familiar? "Fine, Harridan Chant, give me one good reason why I shouldn't kill you."

"Because," Chant said, smiling, "you're gonna need some help if you wanna succeed in attacking Verge."

Draevenus froze. *There's no way he can know. Not unless . . . .* "Who sent you?"

"No one *sent* me, as such."

"What do you mean? Speak clearly!"

"I was *asked* to come. *Asked* to keep an eye on you. *Asked* to watch your back."

"By whom?"

"Why, your sister, of course."

RAIN PATTERED DOWN, soaking Yandumar as he sat atop Quake. Mevon had insisted on letting him ride his son's favored steed. He considered himself a patient man but had to struggle to keep his irritation from showing. The knot of tension resting between his shoulder blades refused to dissipate.

"Here they come," shouted Idrus, mounted a short distance away.

Yandumar saw and heard nothing, but his son's instructions echoed in his mind, and he took the ranger captain at his word.

A week gone by, and already they were running into problems. Mevon's entire Fist had accompanied him, along with three thousand more, all mounted. Speed was their priority. Unfortunately, so was stealth.

The split had been no one's idea. Gilshamed had wanted to move as a single group. Mevon, as scores of small units. Both ideas had their merits. Yandumar wasn't sure this compromise was the best course of action.

No, he *was* sure—sure it was the worst possible idea of the bunch. *Why didn't I say something? Why didn't I step in when I knew this plan was scorching idiotic?*

They had argued throughout the night. His son and his best friend had nearly come to blows, and Yandumar had stood and watched.

And did nothing.

He had been tired. Exhausted. Not just from the late toll or the endless debate. His responsibilities weighed on him. His obligations. His vows. Letting someone else make the decision had been the most selfish thing he could have done at the time. Selfish and stupid.

He only hoped it would not cost them all in the end.

Now, he heard the riders approaching, a full mark after Idrus first gave him notice. He swelled a bit with pride as he thought about how well his son had chosen his men. A streak of nostalgia wracked him as he thought about his old Fist, wondering what they were up to these days. He hoped at least some of them were still alive and kicking.

Abyss—if they're still alive, then they're definitely still kicking.

His musing were cut short as the two rangers came round a copse of trees and approached. They drew rein next to Idrus, conferring briefly. The ranger captain nodded once, dismissing his subordinates with a gentle command, before guiding his horse over to Yandumar.

"They've moved on," Idrus said. "South. Looked like they were in a hurry."

"How many?" Yandumar asked.

"Division strength."

Yandumar ran his fingers through his beard. Eight thousand heading south. Away from his destination, but towards his allies. Would Gilshamed receive the brunt of their attention? Or would Mevon? Yandumar couldn't find a single piece of him that was glad that this group of Imperials had moved out of their way.

His force was a diversion. They had come west, skirting the border between the north and central territories. The plan was to hit a garrison at one of the district capitals as a means of drawing Imperial forces away from Mecrithos.

Yandumar thought it might even work.

He prayed that it was true. But in a place deep inside, a place he kept carefully concealed, he suspected it would be a wasted endeavor.

He muttered his thanks to the ranger, then turned to Ropes and Arozir. "Get everyone moving."

"Aye," they said in unison. They'd become better at that, he'd noticed.

At hand signals from the two men, his troops surged into motion, the clopping of hooves muffled by the soft shoes worn by every horse and the damp soil that was covered in a layer of dead underbrush.

He rode in silence for a time. After a while, he turned to Idrus, still at his side. "Tell me something," he said.

"What?" replied Idrus.

"You ever follow an order that you knew was the wrong call?"

Idrus thought a moment. "Yes. But I adjusted my tactics to account for it."

Yandumar nodded. It was answer he hoped for. "I need you to do me a favor . . ."

GILSHAMED RODE STANDING on a flat wagon bed. He made sure to keep himself visible to his followers at all times. Especially now, with so many new faces, it was vital that he remain in their minds, a symbol of strength and hope. If the faces beaming up at him as he passed the marching formations were any indication, he was succeeding marvelously.

The word had been sent out. As they marched inexorably southwest—using the Chasm as a handrail on their left side—people had joined, pulled in from many of the disparate groups that had arisen at his calling. His forces, less than half their total strength, still numbered close to eighteen thousand now.

And yet, no sign of the Imperial military standing in their way. Not even a whisper of the Hardohl. If the reports about Ilyem and the other Hardohl were true, they would make it to the very gates of Mecrithoo before seeing a drop of blood spilled.

Gilshamed, though, did not think they would be so fortunate. A part of him even hoped not.

I have outwitted you, Rekaj. You and all your kin, your filth. Send what you may. It is too late to stop us now.

The inevitable encounter was still weeks away, at the earliest. It had been too long since he had spilled the blood of his enemy, and, strangely, he felt himself longing for it. After so many centuries spent dreaming about his revenge, his patience, it seems, had at last run out.

"Scorch me!" Orbrahn said.

Gilshamed looked down to see the young sorcerer seated in one of the wagon's seats, shaking his head to clear the fog of communion. "What is it?"

Orbrahn sighed. "Another darkwisp attack. Two of our scouts were found. Well, what's left of them, anyway."

Gilshamed sighed, looking towards the Chasm. The soil looked grey and barren, and a cloud of dark dust clung to the ground wherever his troops were marching. "We knew staying this close to the Chasm was dangerous. How many have we lost so far?"

"A few hundred, give or take."

"That many?"

Orbrahn shrugged. "A small price to pay to avoid Imperial entanglement."

Gilshamed knew it for truth. There were no settlements anywhere near the Chasm, which meant no garrisons, no signs of life at all. "Have they always been so . . . active?"

"What, darkwisps? Not always. Been getting worse, though, recently."

"Hmm. I may have to do something about it, then. Once our current goals are completed, that is."

Orbrahn laughed. "That your plan, then? Stick around and help us poor humans who don't know how to take care of ourselves?"

Gilshamed frowned down at the young man. "Honestly? I have not yet decided."

It was a lie, of course. During his long centuries of exile, the majority of which was spent combing the boundaries of the Shroud, he had thought of what he would do. In great detail. Endless solitude had granted him the time to think through every possibility, follow the train of logic from fruition to conclusion. In reality, there was only one possible choice for him to make.

And you, young caster, will never be privy to such knowledge.

"Right," Orbrahn said, the sarcasm dripping. "Well, if I were you, I'd not worry too much about the darkwisps."

"Oh? Why is that?"

Orbrahn smiled. "It will be dealt with in time, and by far more capable hands than yours."

Gilshamed glared at him. "What the abyss do you mean by that?"

His tone was intended to intimidate, yet Orbrahn seemed unfazed. "This land is not the same one you left all those years ago. It has changed. Its people have changed. We don't need some outside influence telling us how to fix our problems. Not anymore."

Gilshamed's mind recalled his conversation with Yandumar nearly half a year ago as they fled in the tunnels. His friend—the only one he had had for nearly half his life—had said much the same thing. Was he truly so obsolete?

No.

"Where, then, would this revolution be without me?" said Gilshamed. "What chance your hope for freedom?"

Orbrahn, like a man waking from long sleep, blinked rapidly and shook his head. "My apologies, Gilshamed. I meant no offense."

It was not enough of an answer. Gilshamed looked around. Several others were within earshot, yet none had voiced their support of Orbrahn's opinion. Neither, though, had they renounced his words.

Gilshamed had made of himself a symbol. His intention was to bind the hearts and minds of the common people, tear off the veil of oppression, and help them see their fate for what it truly was. And then, to offer them an alternative. A life full of meaning. Hope. So far, he had exceeded even beyond his generous expectations.

But what use was there for a symbol after the hope is achieved? What purpose? Gilshamed struggled to come up with a satisfying answer.

Gilshamed looked around again, but this time the bright visages that met his gaze did not bring him joy.

He felt, instead, a growing disdain for them all.

In silence, he glared down at the dark-haired caster who shared his wagon.

With or without this revolution, I will have my revenge.

The thought warmed him. The smile on his face, now, had nothing to do with maintaining his image for those who followed him.

MEVON KNEW THAT the trek would be dangerous. They were lucky, so far, to have avoided contact. His troops had walked along the southern edge of the Chasm for a while, but he grew increasingly uneasy near it, and, ultimately, had steered them away.

The proximity to the vast, gaping wound in the land was not the only thing that made him feel out of sorts. He had never been long without his captains, and despite the best efforts of all the sergeants now under his command, their efficiency and capability paled in comparison to even the least of the men in his Fist. Orders he expected to take effect within marks instead took tolls. When he needed perfection he got mediocrity. Laziness when he needed professionalism.

The business of leadership was not all he had expected it to be, and he now realized just how much of that burden his men—captains especially—lifted from his shoulders.

"You're doing fine, you know."

Mevon turned his head, smiling as orange light from the setting sun gleamed upon Jasside's face. A breeze, carrying the scent of wild grass, had misplaced a strand of her hair. He reached to push it back behind her ear.

"Reading my mind again?" he asked.

"No need," she said. "For as hard of a man as you are, you seem to wear your thoughts freely in your expressions."

"Only around you."

She looked away, blushing.

It was true, though. She brought out a side of him he had never known existed. He looked at her, and he . . . felt.

He used to think that the only time he would ever feel anything was during battle. Then, when he allowed the storm to rage—when blood filled his senses and life and death greeted him with every passing breath—he knew what it was to truly be alive. To truly feel. Around her—with her—the feeling was similar, yet so, so different.

Better?

Perhaps.

The notion gave him pause. He had always craved blood. Always hungered for his next kill. Yet, as he grew closer to Jasside, her presence, her faith in him, made him think that he could survive without it.

What would my life be without death? He couldn't imagine it. Had never wanted to. Never needed to. Even in joining this revolution, his main draw—beyond justice, beyond the claims of his father—had been the promise of a fight like no other. A fight to end them all.

But, even in victory, the thought of what would come after frightened him like nothing else could. The thought of . . . peace.

Not anymore.

He took her hand. The gesture brought a gasp of shock from her, as it always did. She had become better, though, at suppressing her reaction to the sudden loss of her power. Mevon had become better at not taking it personally.

"I . . ." he began, shaking his head. *I am no good at this sort of thing.* "Have you thought of what you will do after?"

"No," she said, the firmness in her voice surprising him. "I take things one step at a time. Thinking that far ahead makes me lose focus on what's right in front of me, on the here and now." She smiled up at him. "And why would I want to do that?"

A feeling, both painful yet exquisite, began to rise within him at her words. He had been with women before, courtesans whose beauty made Jasside seem plain in comparison. Yet, the memory of their faces, their bodies, morphed into something so ugly compared to what he shared with Jasside. And knowing that their relationship had not progressed beyond what it was now— her hand resting within his—gave him hope for what it could become in time. What *he* could become.

"I am the same," he said, and meaning it. "I just thought—"

"What? That this story has a happy ending?"

Mevon and Jasside both turned towards the voice.

"Paen," Mevon said. "I don't remember inviting you to be a part of our conversation."

The boy licked his thumb and forefinger, then used them to slick down his mustache and pointed beard. "I don't recall needing permission."

Mevon gritted his teeth as Paen approached. He remembered that plausible reasons were cited in support of having the boy join Mevon's group, but—being exhausted at the time—he could not say what they were. Something about the kid sent shivers of repulsion through him.

"Tell me then," said Mevon, "why are you supporting us if you think the revolution won't turn out well?"

Paen laughed. "As if happiness could determine profitability. You truly don't know anything, do you?"

"I know how to kill. Does that count?"

"For our purposes," Paen said, "absolutely."

Mevon frowned. He started towards the boy but found himself stopped—not by force, but simply by Jasside's hand placed gently upon his wrist. He looked down at her, receiving a silent look that said, *Not worth it*.

Mevon took a deep breath and continued marching at her side. "Let's hope it will be enough."

"It will be," said Paen. "If anyone is going to nail the last plank on this scorching bridge, it will be you."

Mevon nodded.

Even when it's burning.

WAR ROOM. VOREN had used the words before, but here, now, inside the place, he finally came to an appreciation for what it meant.

He sighed, scanning the barrels full of rolled-up maps and shelves of scrolls holding tallies of troops and supplies. Charts mounted on the walls listed out the command structure, including unit and location, right down to the lowest lieutenant. Supreme Arcanod Grezkul seemed right at home, even more so than Emperor Rekaj.

Voren had never felt more out of place.

He ran his hand along the table, noticing how slick the wood felt, how pungent the oils that kept it preserved. The piece was ancient, possibly older than anyone in the room. Voren did not recognize the tree that it came from. It was a relic from a forgotten time, heralding from the swamplands that the tribe of mierothi people used to call home. Lost now, like so many things.

Carved into the table was the empire. The sculpting was meticulous and thorough, yet bland. To Voren's eye, practicality ruled, not beauty.

And does that not sum up the empire in its entirety?

Rekaj sat at the head of the table. He had a glass of wine, untouched, in front of him. Voren was waiting for him to explain why they were here. *Why* I'm *here.* He tried ignoring the stares and whispers and pointed fingers from the rest of the council members as he trod upon sacred mierothi ground, and thought about how Rekaj had instructed him to act.

Subservient, as always. But playing the demure, helpless figure that he had for so long would not do to support his cause, his new reason for existence. Instead, he must project an aura of confidence, competence, and present himself as an equal, someone with just as much at stake as the rest.

Voren still had no idea how he would accomplish this.

He tried to feel it. Tried to make himself one of them in his mind. Tried not to think of them as the enemy but instead as allies. Not that he had any choice. No, choice had been taken from him the day Gilshamed returned to the continent. If he wanted to survive—and Voren most certainly did—then he had to make this work.

Somehow.

Finally, Rekaj sat forward in his seat. "Done with your whispering?" he asked no one in particular. The room went silent. No one responded. "Good." Rekaj nodded in Voren's direction. "He is here because *I* asked to him to come. Asked, not ordered." He took out the letter and passed it to Grezkul. "This is why."

Grezkul read it silently, then, at Rekaj's urging, pressed it into the next set of hands. The paper made its way around the room until all had read it. Each eyed Voren with curiosity after they had finished reading. Truln added pity to his gaze.

Rekaj lifted his hand, palm up. Voren stood and cleared his throat. "Gilshamed," Voren began. "You all know his name. You know his face. You know what he is capable of. And you know that, had you not found a way to banish all of the valynkar the day of the Cataclysm, he would have defeated you long ago."

No one spoke, but Voren could feel the room tense at

his words. No one liked being reminded of failure, especially mierothi. Most especially *these* mierothi. He gathered his breath, knowing they would enjoy what he would say next even less.

"He is back. Gilshamed is the leader of the rebellion."

Grezkul pounded the table. "I knew it!" He turned to Rekaj with venom in his eyes. "I told you, right after the voltensus was destroyed, but you didn't listen."

"Inquiries were made, but nothing substantial ever came of it," replied Rekaj calmly.

"It makes sense," said Marshal Adjudicator Jezrid. "Gilshamed always did know how to hit us where we were weakest."

Mother Phyzari Kitavijj pointed at Lekrigar. "You let him in, didn't you? I thought you'd at least be smart enough to guard the tunnel entrances, or did you leave that job to those creatures of yours?"

"It matters not how he got in," he said, and Voren could tell that despite his indifferent demeanor, the high regnosist desperately hoped that was true. "What matters is what we're going to do about it now." He shot his contemptuous gaze at Voren. "And I assume that's why you're here, is it not?"

"It is," Rekaj said. "Tell them, Voren."

Voren swallowed hard. *No turning back now.* "We know two things for certain. First, that Gilshamed wants me dead. I don't think I have to explain why."

Amused chuckles answered.

"Second, that there are only two valynkar currently within the Shroud."

When he said nothing further, Grezkul slapped the table again. "Enough with the dramatics. Whatever it is you came here to say, tell us!"

"Don't you see?" Truln said. "Only two of them. Our biggest problem is not knowing where the rebellion is. Where their *leaders* are."

The room became still.

"Of course," Kitavijj said. "Communion."

Voren nodded. "That is what I bring. What no one else can."

He studied the looks that came his way, watched them morph from what they had always been to something different. Something other than contempt.

Respect will come. This will do for now.

"So what are you waiting for?" Jezrid said.

"Nothing." Voren smiled, projecting confidence he did not yet feel and unity that make his stomach turn. He closed his eyes and energized briefly. When he opened them again, he stood in a sea of pure darkness.

And there, distant yet unmistakable, a single speck of light.

Chapter 13

DRAEVENUS AND HARRIDAN Chant approached the entrance, a battered wooden door rimmed with frost and sealed by mud and stone. Chant began kicking his boots together in an attempt to dislodge the snow. Draevenus pulled to a stop as his escort put out an arm in front of him.

"Close your eyes and plug your ears," Chant said.

"Excuse me?" Draevenus said.

"It's a secret knock. I can't have you figuring it out."

Draevenus raised an eyebrow.

Harridan threw his hands up. "Oh, all right. Be that way. We'll just have to kill ya' then."

Chant turned to the door and rapped three times with his knuckles.

Draevenus waited a beat. "Is that it?"

A smile, then two more taps.

Then one.

Chant brought both fists to the door and began pounding out a chaotic rhythm. If there was any way to discern the pattern, Draevenus did not even know where to begin.

"All right, all right," a voice shouted from behind the door. He heard a squeal as the latch turned. The door jerked open, swinging inside and shaking loose white flakes from the frame.

"Shadow!" Chant said. "What took you so long?"

"'Bout to ask you the same thing." Shadow's eyes fell on Draevenus. "At least you didn't come back empty-handed."

Shadow, like Chant, was an old man. Old, yet his movements betrayed a strength that most young men would envy. And, also like Chant, Draevenus could swear the name was familiar somehow.

"Well, get in here," Shadow said. "Can't have you freezing to death before we even start this thing." He stepped back and waved them both inside.

A fire burned, warming the cavern, and Draevenus immediately began peeling off the outer layers of his clothing. A dozen men sat around the blaze. They eyed Draevenus but kept about their tasks. Some sharpened swords, other fit straps to shields, and one man was scraping the rust from his armor. It was the last that caught his eye because, despite its age and wear, it was still quite distinguishable.

It was the armor of an Elite.

Draevenus looked to Chant and Shadow. The names, in conjunction with this new context, sparked a memory.

"Captain Chant," Draevenus said. "Captain Shadow. And your third, Captain . . ."

"Daere," Harridan finished. He swept his arms to indicate his brethren. "All of Kael's old Fist. What's left of us, anyway." He set his fiddle case by the fire.

Further questions were set aside when someone mentioned a room with both privacy and a washbasin. Draevenus bolted towards it.

It been months since he'd had a proper washing, and a week since he'd even changed his clothes. The water had been warmed, and Draevenus found himself lingering, hands pressed to the bottom of the basin even after his body had been washed. Warmth. Cleanliness. *It's funny how your appreciation for things grows immensely when you are denied them.* Draevenus smiled to himself as he re-dressed and joined the others by the fire.

A hot bowl of stew and a foaming mug of ale were waiting for him when he emerged. He inhaled them, asking for seconds of both.

Chant reached for his wooden fiddle case. "Think she's about warmed up, now."

And true to his name, the old Elite captain began to play a tune, singing along. Draevenus barely heard the words, but the voice . . .

He had expected a tavern singer. Someone capable but forgettable. Chant's voice was, quite simply, the most beautiful thing he had ever heard. Perfect pitch, a range greater than the Andean Mountains, and every utterance dripping with authentic emotion. The notes scratched out from the beat-up fiddle, despite their rawness, matched the voice perfectly.

Draevenus lost track of time, listening to the songs, joining in occasionally, eating, drinking, swaying side to side along with the soldiers seated around him. Just for a while, he was able to forget about everything. He felt, for one fleeting moment, at peace.

Eventually, Chant put the fiddle away, and the soldiers, one by one, turned to Draevenus with expectant gazes.

He knew what they wanted.

"Thank you all for being here," he said. "What I hope to do is dangerous, and the chance for victory improves drastically with all of you to help."

"Of course," Harridan said, patting him on the shoulder. "Ain't none of us got any love for the empire. Not after what happened to Yandumar."

"I take it you know what awaits us then?"

"Verge," Shadow said. "I've been scouting. Can't see inside, but we've been able to piece together what goes on there."

Draevenus sighed. "Then you understand why I must stop it."

Everyone seated around the fire nodded in unison.

He turned an incredulous gaze on Chant. "Are you sure it was my sister that sent you?" Vashodia knew what went on at Verge. Knew but, unlike him, did not seem to care. Despite her efforts to seem indifferent, it seemed she had found a part of her that cared after all. Enough, at least, to send him help.

"Like I told you before," said Harridan. "She asked us. We agreed."

Draevenus smiled. Knowing her, it had taken a great deal of humility to stoop to actually *asking* for help, even if it was not for herself.

And he was glad for it. More so than anyone could possibly realize. This was not merely extra soldiers to assault a fortified objective. Draevenus was confident he could have been successful on his own. But there likely would be collateral damage. Deaths he could not prevent.

Maybe now, he could.

And more importantly, he would not now be forced to return to the place he had been so many centuries ago. A place where he didn't hesitate to act, to kill without mercy or pause, to throw all thought for the consequences aside and accomplish the mission, no matter the cost. A place where the very mention of his name brought his enemies to their knees with fear.

A place where he despised himself.

Even if you don't care about Verge, you cared enough about me to save me from the self that I hate. For that, dear sister, I love you.

And on the heels of that thought, another.

Just as you save me, someday I will save you from yourself. From what you have become. Even if you don't hate it now, fear it now, and even if you never thank me, I will see the darkness within you turned to light.

He turned again to Chant. "Now then, let us discuss how best to assault Verge and free those trapped within."

YANDUMAR LIFTED HIS head from his hands. He looked to the six men in front of him.

The fastest riders. He'd asked Idrus to send them, with spare mounts, to each of the nearest six cities. They had a simple objective. Now they had returned, and their reports were exactly as Yandumar had predicted.

Exactly as I feared.

"All the garrisons?" he asked again. "All empty?"

One by one, the scouts nodded. Again.

There was only one reason that the empire would leave the cities without even so much as a token guard left behind.

"They know," Yandumar said. "Somehow, those scorching mierothi know where our main forces are."

He looked south. Mevon was down there, somewhere, and so was Gilshamed. His son and his best friend. In danger.

Because of me.

"Mount up!" he ordered. The men around him jumped at the harshness of the command. Even the three captains. "Our allies are in need of our help."

He boarded Quake, and they headed south. All thoughts of stealth were abandoned in favor of speed, even so far as to ride on the roads. They made excellent time.

But Yandumar knew that it wouldn't be fast enough.

"What are we doing here, Gilshamed?"

Gilshamed glanced at Orbrahn. He'd grown tired of the boy's insolence. "We are here to complete the objectives of the revolution. To liberate this land."

Orbrahn looked from him to the city walls, just visible in the distance. "The plan was to make for Mecrithos. That's where our allies are expecting us. This?" He waved a hand in disgust. "This is a distraction we can't afford."

"Mecrithos is still a week distant. We've been idle for too long. The people need to know that we still fight for them."

"This is foolhardy, and you know it. Our position will be compromised."

Gilshamed smiled. "Not entirely."

"Is that why you had us steer west around that lake, rather than east, which made far more sense?"

Is that all you caught? For the past week, whenever they came to a possible split in their path, Gilshamed had been guiding them west every time. "Even if they pinpoint us, they'll have no idea where we are headed next."

"But this is—"

"Enough!" Gilshamed looked down on the boy. His rage must have been showing, for Orbrahn gulped and backed up a few steps. He said no more.

Gilshamed turned to several Elite, those not part of Mevon's Fist that had become troop leaders for his forces. "I will disable the forces at the gate myself. Once it is open, lead everyone through."

They exchanged glances. *You made your choice already. Do not think to defy me now.* "Aye," they said at last.

Gilshamed nodded. He unfurled his wings and ascended into the air alone.

He flew along the treetops, keeping the city's main

gate in the center of his vision. It felt good to once again be doing something. Taking from those that had taken everything from him. They deserved the fate he had in store for them, and Gilshamed deserved to be the one to deliver it.

The gatehouse passed beneath him. He turned around in midair, energizing, and came at it from inside the city. He sent a blast of power that knocked the gate from its hinges and collapsed the sides of the guardhouse in a shower of crumbling stone and mortar. As he reveled in the destruction, he noticed something strange.

He saw no bodies.

Where are the guards?

He looked around. The streets were abandoned. Not a soul was in sight.

Something is not right...

Nearly panicking, he hurled himself back towards his army. It was only then that the clamor of battle reached his ears.

"HERE," MEVON SAID, his hand outstretched. "I picked these for you."

Jasside smiled at him. She reached to grab the make-shift bouquet of wildflowers. "Thank you, Mevon."

"They grow along the cliffs here," he said, pointing to the deep ravine alongside which they traveled. "I've never seen them anywhere else in the empire."

"That was very thou—"

The flowers slipped from her hands and fell, scattering back down the cliffs on a gust of wind. Mevon looked into her eyes.

They had gone black.

He waited.

A mark later, she came out of it, blinking and trembling. "What is it?" he asked.

"From the scouts," she said, breathing heavily. "Imperial formation dead ahead. We ran right into them."

Mevon closed his eyes. *If my rangers were here, this never would have happened.*

But they weren't. He was on his own. And he would have to make all the decisions.

"What else did they say? Enemy strength? Disposition?"

Jasside shook her head. "I don't have any numbers, but it seems they were marching across our line of advance. They're just as surprised as we are."

Mevon nodded. He knew surprise. Knew how to use it. He turned to the sergeants acting as his commanders. "All forces advance forward. Strike hard and don't let up. We'll only get one shot at this."

Fear showed on their faces. None moved.

"We either take them down here, or we face them again outside the walls of Mecrithos. Now move!"

They moved.

Mevon ran forward. *Time to do battle once more.*

He smiled—glad to know that some things never changed—and unleashed the storm.

"STATUS!" GILSHAMED SHOUTED as he landed among his commanders.

"It's a pitched fight but numbers seem even," said one of the Elite. "Our casters are linked in trios and are keeping the daeloth at bay so far."

"That's the good news," another said. "Their formations are more cohesive than ours. Our lines are slowly giving way before them."

Gilshamed nodded. How had the Imperials found them? How had they approached unseen? These questions would have to wait. "Press the attack," he ordered. "I'll give you the push we need." He looked to the sky and flew once more.

He advanced quickly forward, keeping low until he heard the clash of bodies, the ring of steel, the cries of pain, smelled the blood and sweat and fear. Balls of blue flame and arcs of purple lightning danced back and forth as the casters dueled, and hails of arrows fell down upon both sides. Death clung in the air.

He had reached the front lines.

He rose, casting a blaze of light forward. This blinded the enemy and announced his presence to his allies. In a moment, the slow advance of the Imperials reversed direction.

A dozen spells launched in his direction. Rather than form a shield and waste energy, he dove forward to avoid them, and cast his own spells—raging red fireballs the size of a wagon—back at each daeloth he could see. One by one they exploded, consuming each half-breed and any other nearby soldiers in flesh-melting heat.

He rose higher once more, gaining a clear view of the entire breadth of the battle. As he had when the Hardohl and their Elite had raided them at the start of winter, he dashed here and there, guarding his allies by sending his sorcery where the enemy was strongest. But this time, his opponents did not have magic-deadening armor, nor a lifetime of experience fighting casters to aid them. This time, Gilshamed rained fire down from above, and none withstood his fury.

Not since the War of Rising Night had he felt this alive. Not since then had his potential been fully realized. It was, quite simply, glorious.

With the daeloth decimated and the Imperial lines in shambles, Gilshamed smiled to himself and withdrew to gather his strength.

As he turned back, his eyes fell upon the city once more. He watched, heart skipping a beat, as rank after rank of Imperial soldiers marched out of the city he had thought was empty.

LIKE A CHARGING bull, Mevon slammed into the Imperial platoon. Bones crunched beneath his shoulder, and three ranks collapsed outwards, their falling bodies rippling from the point of impact.

Mevon vaulted over them as his troops moved in, hacking and stabbing at the downed figures. Mevon moved on. He had more important targets.

He felt sorcery on all sides. As spells flew in every direction, the chaos of battle left him dizzy trying to sort out where his presence would be most influential. It didn't help that both forces were in disarray. But even as he spun Justice to strike at any that came near, he was able to focus his concentration on a knot of casting in the distance.

Too far south. Can't be ours.

He smiled and began pushing through the press of Imperial soldiers, few of whom had the courage to stand against him. Those who did, he cut down without slowing.

The tingling sensation intensified as he closed the distance, and he began to gauge where the castings were coming from. A low hill rested in front of him, a hundred paces away. He could see spells flying towards his troops from just on the other side.

All the daeloth clustered together? I don't recall that being anywhere in the Imperial tactics book.

It didn't matter, though. Mevon would make them pay for the mistake.

He crested the hill at a speed that would make a gazelle seem slow and took in the scene below him in an instant.

Threescore figures adorned in the armor of the daeloth stood facing north, to Mevon's left. Their hands intermittently thrust forward, releasing some sorcery aimed for the lines of Mevon's troops. He saw the counterspells from his own casters strike back. Often, two spells would meet in midair and annihilate each other in a concussive blast.

Without hesitation, Mevon spun into their midst. His

Andun drank deep from a dozen souls before anyone could so much as react.

The farthest daeloth spun towards him and jumped back. Those nearest turned to face him.

Mevon saw now what he hadn't on the hill. Their faces were pale. They wore the armor of the daeloth, but most of them were just as human as he.

Which is when bodies slammed into him from behind. Steel bit into him in what felt like a dozen different places. Pain blazed in his legs, shoulders, arms, and back.

With a scream of rage, he spun. Six daeloth lost their grips on daggers sticking out of Mevon and skidded along the ground, now slick with his blood. Their eyes widened as Mevon chopped at them savagely. None managed more than a single scrambling step of retreat before Mevon cut them down.

Must've followed me up the hill, shadow-dashed in as I became occupied with the decoys. How could I have been so careless?

But the decoys were still soldiers, and they were still a threat. At the commands from the few daeloth that were still hiding on the far side, they drew swords and converged.

Mevon arched his back, then bowed it quickly. All but one of the blades popped out of his body. The last was lodged deep, and he could feel it tearing at the lining of his lung. He coughed, spitting up more blood than air.

Mevon staggered backwards up the hill, fending off half a score sword thrusts in a matter of beats. *So thirsty.* The loss of blood had weakened him. His blessings burned as they began to reknit his damaged body, but not even they could restore everything.

He slashed sideways, cutting three men through the eyes. He punched left with Justice, impaling two men, even as he ducked, allowing several blades to pass overhead. He swung his legs out to knock down two more. They toppled, taking four more behind them to the ground, and Mevon danced across their forms with spinning blades.

The move exhausted him, though, and he had to retreat once more to catch his breath.

Even weary as he was, he still noticed the surviving daeloth moving into flanking positions. When they tried dashing in, this time he was ready for them.

They came in pairs. The first, jumping in from opposite sides, collided with each end of his blades. Their bodies were moving so fast that they met in the middle of his *Andun* and stuck there.

More came. Mevon abandoned Justice and met them with fists and elbows and feet, driving their dashing forms from the sky with a crunch of bones and a spray of blood.

He drew his own daggers from his belt and whirled among the remaining soldiers. He ignored the pain, the fatigue, the thirst, and let the storm finish the fight.

His last enemy fell. Mevon collapsed upon the hilltop. He reached behind and pried the dagger from his back, and, after half a mark, was able to take a breath without spraying blood.

He drained his waterskin. Then, he counted the bodies. What he found disturbed him.

Not enough. Not nearly enough. He looked around the battlefield but could not see or feel any more daeloth.

Where are they?

ANOTHER WAVE OF dark sorcery, like a molten river, screamed up towards Gilshamed. He didn't have the time to dodge. He threw all the power he had into his shield. The spell struck the barrier—popping it like a bubble—and bounced away. The force drove Gilshamed towards the ground.

Abyss take those daeloth! They had been ready for him this time, harmonizing in groups of at least a dozen. They had less control of their soldiers that way, but their raw, combined power was too much for Gilshamed to overcome alone.

He crashed down, landing on the backs of his own soldiers. Hands reached to help him to his feet. He shouted some words of encouragement to everyone within earshot, then took off toward his commanders.

Before his ejection from the sky, he had been able to glean the enemy's disposition. He would deliver his orders, catch his breath, and get back to the fighting. The enemy had surprised him by quickly reacting to a hopeless situation—namely, Gilshamed himself—but he knew of ways to punish them for their new arrangement of troops.

When he got to the command post, only Orbrahn was present. His eyes were closed. Gilshamed stepped up to him and shook his shoulders.

The boy gasped, opening his eyes. "What? What is it?"

"Where are the commanders? They are supposed to stay where I can easily find them!"

Orbrahn still appeared dazed. "They're . . . off. Fighting. Half went south to lead the retreat . . ."

"Retreat? What are you talking about? The first Imperial force is nearly destroyed and pulling back. The second has adjusted tactics to my presence, but I have a few ideas—"

"A third army just hit our northern flanks. That's where the other half went. To lead a volunteer force to hold them so we could get away."

"A third army? How big?"

"The scout that reported in stopped counting when he got to twice our size."

Gilshamed's mouth went dry. *Trapped. Our only route of escape is towards more danger. How the abyss did they know where to find us?*

His forces were moving. Fleeing. He marched in their midst. Just a few tolls ago they had been eager for battle, filled with ardor and zeal. Now, their faces held nothing but weariness and dejection.

This was, he realized, their first true defeat. *How easily is your enthusiasm blanched. How quickly your great purpose forgotten. Is this all it takes to break you?*

Gilshamed looked behind, eyes trailing to the small force locked in battle against now-overwhelming odds. They were the truest soldiers of the revolution, the only ones he was not hesitant to call his. And today they would die for those less worthy.

He sighed. *Such has always been the way, the blood of the brave and strong spilled to allow the weak and cowardly a few more wasted moments upon this world.*

Gilshamed glared at Orbrahn. The boy glanced his way every so often. Each time, Gilshamed could tell what he was thinking: *This is your fault, Gilshamed.*

Yes, my fault. My fault for believing the people of this continent were ready for freedom, were truly willing to sacrifice everything to achieve it. My fault for believing in any of you.

He laughed bitterly. "I'll fly ahead to make sure we are not running into any more traps."

Orbrahn glared but said nothing beyond a quick nod. Gilshamed unfurled his wings and took off, once more, to the skies.

He skimmed over the heads of his retreating formations. Soon, he came to the leading edge of his troops. He did not slow.

You said that you did not need me anymore, Orbrahn. Let us see how true that statement turns out to be.

Gilshamed rounded a hill and lost sight of all of his troops. He banked west, flying well out of the path that they would take, staying low. He continued another half a toll before landing.

Patience had always been one of his defining qualities. He had demonstrated it beyond any who had ever lived as he plotted how best to enact his revenge on the mierothi. This revolution was his first and greatest scheme.

But by no means his *only* one.

MEVON RAN. HIS troops scrambled out of his way as he plunged through their lines. The Imperial formation had started with less than half of their own numbers, and with the daeloth out of the way, their command and control had crumbled. The casters of the revolution shredded gaping holes into the Imperials, and his troops stepped in to break them wide open. His enemy was reeling.

Yet Mevon's stomach twisted in fear.

As he approached the rear of his own formations, where all the troop commanders and casters were positioned, his fear became realized. A new knot of sorcery bloomed in his senses, coming from the far side of his formations.

He had found the remaining daeloth at last.

Hundreds perished within a beat. Daeloth spells ripped through the unsuspecting, and unprotected rear. His sergeants and casters took the brunt of it, even now falling as the daeloth advanced.

Jasside!

He scanned as he sprinted, but he couldn't find her. He began cutting down daeloth, barely pausing to register their deaths. But there were too many. The damage had already been done.

He propelled forward, searching, slashing about in a rage. His control began slipping. *If anything happens to her. . .*

The daeloth reacted to his presence. Some drew blades and dashed at him. Some picked up rocks or trees with magic and flung them at him. Some, realizing their doom had come upon them, either froze or fled. Mevon cut them all down. The symphony of death sung by his blades had morphed into dissonance.

In the distance, Mevon spotted two daeloth burst into blue flames. A caster—one of his own—still alive, still fighting back. It had to be her. It *had* to be.

As he scythed his way towards what he hoped was the only woman he had ever dared to love, he saw several sorcerous arrows speed toward a group of daeloth. But the aim was off and they flew wide. The daeloth smiled and launched counterspells at the caster. The arrows, unseen by them, turned in the air and struck them all from behind. A series of pops announced the explosion of their heads.

Mevon came around a large boulder and finally spotted the caster.

Jasside!

Relief flooded through him as their eyes met. Sweat poured down her forehead, and her chest heaved with each breath, but she appeared unharmed, leaning against a waist-high stone on the edge of the ravine. They shared a smile as he walked towards her.

Mevon craned his neck to look behind him. Several hundred paces distant, the last daeloth were engaged with Mevon's forces. Too far for him to be any use. With the surety of victory entrenched in his mind, Mevon turned back to Jasside and allowed himself to relax.

His eyes swept towards her face, passing three shadows on the way. Those three shadows moved, coalescing into men as they stepped out from beneath the low-hanging branches of a nearby cluster of trees.

Daeloth.

Mevon's blood turned to ice. They were right next to Jasside. And judging by her eyes, still trained on him, she had no idea.

The shout of warning caught in his throat. Too late for even that. He dashed forward, moving faster than he ever had before.

The daeloth lifted their hands towards Jasside. Mevon felt a tingling as black fire flew from their fingertips. He flung himself the last five paces into the path of the sorcery. In midair, he dropped his *Andun* and—just as he had when he first encountered Jasside—threw his daggers at his enemy. The distance was near point-blank, and his two targets were stationary. This time, he hit exactly where he wanted to: dead center forehead.

His body intercepted first one, then—with outstretched fingertips—the second of their spells, voiding them into nothingness. His eyes followed the third as it passed him on its trajectory. Agony gripped him as he realized it would strike true.

Mevon's gaze found her. She stood with arm outstretched in his direction. A spell flew from her hand, but too late. Her sorcery met that of the daeloth less than three paces from her, each annihilating the other in an outward burst of air. Jasside flew backwards.

He watched panic grip her eyes as she disappeared over the side of the cliff.

VOREN, NOW A regular of the war room, stood in silence and looked out over Mecrithos from the balcony, letting the reports wash over him in a muffled flood of sound. Reports of victory for the empire and defeat for the revolution.

My doing. All of it. Their deaths are on my head.

He took the full weight of the burden, neither shirking from it nor attempting to justify it. He had made a choice nineteen hundred years ago—a choice to live, and live free. As free as was possible, anyway. It had never been easy, especially when constantly reminded of what he had sacrificed, but not once had he ever wished he could change his mind.

If there was a single word that could define him, it would be "survivor." Every action he had taken, even his choices during the War of Rising Night, had been rooted in self-preservation.

And it was the fear of death that drove him. Not just fear, either, but gut-wrenching terror. He had never met his god, never felt the supposed comfort of his presence, never had his prayers answered. Never had faith. The paradise that was promised by Elos to the valynkar was, to Voren, a sham. Elos could not even penetrate the Shroud, a construct of this world's mere dwellers.

Voren knew he was on his own.

He closed his eyes, pooling just enough power to pull him into communion. He made note of the relative position of Gilshamed's star and dropped back into the waking world once more. He made a mark on the small, rolled-out map on the table next to him, then resumed staring out over the city.

"That's not right," a voice barked at Voren's shoulder.

He looked up into Grezkul's face. "What do you mean?"

The supreme arcanod was peering down at the map. He pointed to the mark that Voren had just made. "Is this his latest position?"

"Yes. Why?"

"It can't be. My scouts are keeping contact with their main force, here."

Voren glanced down to see a finger far to the east of his mark. He stood. "I just checked. The position is accurate."

"You calling my best men liars? Or just idiots?"

The room became quiet. Voren ignored the stares. "What I'm saying is that Gilshamed must no longer be with that group of rebel soldiers."

Grezkul appeared perplexed. "Why would he do that?"

"Either he is running," Rekaj said, coming up behind them, "or he is linking up with another, previously unknown force. Wouldn't you say so, Voren?"

Voren's eyes widened. *Is he actually valuing my opinion? Or merely appearing to?* "Yes," he said before the pause in his response would be noticed. "We already know they have split their forces. The loss of your division along the Shenog Ravine is proof enough of that. I suppose it's possible Gilshamed could have any number of small units that he could bounce back and forth between."

"I suppose . . ." Grezkul said.

"Either way," Voren said quickly, "we should box him

in. Restrict his movement. I assume you want a quick end to this rebellion?"

"Of course," said Rekaj.

"Then, if he is trying to escape, it is imperative that we not allow him to do so. He has the patience of a mountain. If he sees this endeavor failing, I believe he will simply start over again."

Rekaj thought a moment, then waved the marshal adjudicator over. "Grezkul, you will push your troops into the towns, and along all major trade routes. Jezrid, instruct your people to watch the hidden paths, the roads less traveled."

They both nodded.

"Voren will tell you how to dispatch your men."

At this, both mierothi shot gazes of pure hatred his way. Once, and not too long ago at that, Voren would have wilted under such scrutiny. Instead, he stood tall, raising his chin slightly. "As you command, emperor."

Hearing this, both men's belligerence floundered. They muttered the same words though far more begrudgingly.

Rekaj walked away, leaving them to their arrangements. Voren acknowledged Grezkul and Jezrid with a grin. "Let's get to work then, shall we?" He gathered energy and returned again to the black void of communion.

Come to me, Gilshamed. Let us finish this. One way or another, let it be done.

Chapter 14

SUNLIGHT GLINTED OFF the ice fields far below. The jagged formations of crystalline cold swept as far south as the eye could see. To the west, the Shelf cut the land away like a cleaver. Wind whistled overhead, but they were sheltered from the worst of it by the cliff's edge rising on their left as they traversed the narrow mountain path.

Icy footing made the trek hazardous. A single slip, and a fall of several hundred paces awaited them, but this impromptu trail was the only approach in which they could remain unseen.

Draevenus had been inside once, centuries ago, then again a few decades past. He knew the layout. Knew how many guards there were, where they patrolled, when shifts changed. He'd shared this knowledge with his new allies. They hadn't balked when he'd told them what they faced. Instead, they had hunkered down and pounded out a plan.

Shadow, the only ex-ranger among them, led the way. As they rounded a bend of the path, he stopped. Draevenus looked past him and saw it.

Verge.

Crafted by sorcery and carved right out of the cliff side, it protruded into empty space, held up by nothing that could be seen. Squarish and blocky, and glistening beneath layers of ice and snow, not a mar could be seen. No gaps, no holes in the construction.

No way in.

There were only two entrances, east and north. Both hidden, both leading to underground tunnels, and both well guarded. Draevenus didn't plan to use either of them.

Shadow lifted a far-sight to his eye. After a moment's perusal, he turned to Draevenus. "I see the breach point. You got the trinkets?"

Draevenus lifted the band from around his neck and held it out to Shadow. "This will allow you past their wards without alerting them, but remember, you must move slowly."

"Aye," Shadow said, fitting the leather cord over his head. "And the package?"

Draevenus presented his back. Shadow reached into his ruck and withdrew a long, cylindrical object wrapped in linen. Once extracted, Draevenus turned and pointed at the end marked red. "Point this side towards the wall, then pull the string. You'll have five beats to get clear."

Shadow nodded. Without another word, he began his approach, staying low and slow. The package had taken him most of two days to create. This close to Verge, he couldn't risk using his full power, and so had only drawn a sliver of energy over and over again. Two hundred spells were stacked upon each other inside the device.

There was no explosion. No noise at all that could be heard. Draevenus smelled it though. Melting stone had a peculiar scent.

It took a mark to eat through the wall. Draevenus waited one more until he felt the wards wink out of existence. Shadow had taken out their handlers, and still no alarm raised. He smiled. All according to plan so far. He ran forward, Chant and the other twelve right on his heels.

They flowed smoothly into a circular hole—half a man's height in diameter—and into sudden darkness.

Shadow waited with blood on his hands and two dead daeloth at his feet. "Breach successful."

"Where to now?" Chant asked.

Draevenus took a moment, getting his bearings. The hallway was plain stone lit by lightglobes. He began down the left path. "Follow me." He didn't need to add "quietly."

He pulled two throwing daggers as he stalked towards his destination. He paused before each hallway intersection, thrust a blade out, and looked at the reflection on the mirrored surface to ensure it was clear.

They came to the last one. He peered towards the double doors leading into the barracks and saw two daeloth standing guard outside. He drew back, took a breath, then lunged out. His daggers flew. The two daeloth fell limp to the ground, hilts sticking out of their bloody temples. Draevenus cringed at the noise their bodies made upon contact with the ground.

The Elite took up positions on both ends of the corridor. Draevenus softly opened the doors.

Beds lined the walls, twenty to each side. Wall lockers separated them. In each, a sleeping daeloth. It was exactly in the middle of their sleep cycle, the time least likely for any to be up and about.

Draevenus energized. Here, in the heart of Verge, no one would suspect a little casting. His spell took effect, smothering the room in silence. His own breathing and heartbeat became as loud as explosions in his ears as all other noise ceased.

He turned and waved the Elite in. They began their grisly task. Daggers through the heart. No mess, no noise. Quick, efficient work. Draevenus dashed to the end of the room, drew his own blades, and began working back towards the center. It didn't take long.

"Halfway done," he whispered when they had all gathered at the exit. "With the easy part, at least."

They pushed out, still in silence, still undiscovered, but they would have to move quickly now. Routine check-ins would begin any moment. When the guards Shadow had killed didn't report in, the alarm would sound.

They split into five groups of three. Four groups headed to the perimeter to scour the rest of the on-duty guards. They would have to ignore those at the two entrances, but they were distant still, and—if all went to plan—would not know anything was amiss until it was too late. Draevenus, with Chant and Shadow in tow, had another destination.

It was only one passage farther on from the barracks.

They waited, giving the other groups time to complete their cleansing. Draevenus stared at another set of double doors. He paused and caught his breath. *So close. No mistakes now.*

Unable to wait any longer, Draevenus dashed towards the doors, flinging them open with a kick. He, Shadow, and Chant flowed into the room, weapons bared.

A half dozen daeloth, though caught off guard, quickly spun to engage. Draevenus shadow-dashed forward, gouging two as he passed but otherwise leaving their fate to his companions. He had more important targets.

Three mierothi females stood, eyes wide, as he approached. A glass wall slanted up from their feet towards the ceiling farther on, which looked upon a wide chamber below them. Draevenus didn't slow. He slammed the hilts of his daggers into the jaws of the outer two. Their unconscious forms sprawled backwards, knocking over the swivel chairs they had just vacated.

He lunged upward, driving a knee into the middle mierothi's sternum. She crumpled beneath the blow and fell. Draevenus landed atop her, both of them coming to a rest on the slanting glass.

Draevenus forced himself not to look at what lay beyond.

He brought the tip of one dagger to the woman's eye. "Hello, Samaranth."

"Draevenus," she hissed. "What the abyss do you think you're doing?"

"What I should have done a long time ago."

Footsteps approached from behind. Draevenus turned to see Harridan and Shadow, both covered in blood. Chant held a hand over a wound on his forearm, and the ex-ranger was limping, but there was no other movement in the room. He spied what he was looking for on a nearby table.

"Go fetch that pitcher for me, please," he said, nodding towards it. Shadow hobbled to retrieve it. He filled a cup and knelt next to Draevenus. "Fancy a drink, Samaranth?"

Her eyes bulged. "What? No! You can't! Don't you know what that stuff does?"

"Of course I do. It didn't stop you from pouring it down the throats of your 'patients' for all these years." He moved his dagger to her throat. "You drink, or my blade will."

She gulped. Nodded. Shadow dropped the cup to her open lips and poured in its contents, the smell of sage and cinnamon suffusing Draevenus's nose. A tear leaked out from Samaranth's eyes as she swallowed.

After half a mark, Draevenus stood, lifting her into a standing position. He had Chant and Shadow bind the other two women. Samaranth's head lolled, and her eyes took on a glazed look though she remained fully conscious. He supported most of her weight as they walked out of the room.

They descended a set of stairs, then waited. The rest of the Elite began returning. Two of the groups were missing a man, and a third had only one return. No one was free of bloodstains or injuries. Draevenus could do little for their wounds.

"It's all right," Chant said. "At our age, we're just looking for a good way to go. They couldn't have asked for a better death than this."

Draevenus nodded soberly. He gestured, and the remaining Elite moved to take hold of the "treatment room."

The doors opened. Draevenus stared down row after row of beds. Maroon curtains separated each one, and dozens of human women moved about the chamber. Nurses. They stopped and gaped as their sacred grounds were invaded.

Two Elite darted to the far end, securing the doorway. The others rounded up the nurses and pushed them to a corner and out of the way.

Draevenus put his mouth next to Samaranth's ear. "Take me to her."

She waved, the motion seeming to take enormous effort, and Draevenus moved in the indicated direction.

That same sage-and-cinnamon smell permeated the entire chamber. A pitcher of the liquid occupied every bedside table. Each patient he passed looked up at him with the same glossy eyes and slack faces, the same disinterest in the world. Three hundred in all.

Mierothi women.

"How could you, Sam?" Draevenus asked. "All this time, how could you do this and still live with yourself?"

She muttered incoherently. He'd only given her half a dose, but apparently even that much was enough to disable intelligible speech. He was glad, though. He didn't want to hear her excuses. Didn't want her to say she did what she did for the good of the empire. That she had to choose between becoming a phyzari or finding herself among those now interned in this place.

Mierothi could not have children; nor could they mate with either human or valynkar. A flaw of Ruul's design? Or, perhaps, it was intended. Draevenus didn't know. Not yet, anyway. But here, after endless experimentation, and countless sacrifices, the phyzari had discovered a way around mierothi limitations.

Men, just like the ones he had rescued, were brought and sent in, one by one, to lie with the mierothi women. And at the moment of release, one of the overseeing phyzari would cast a complex spell that would kill the man and bind his soul, his ineffable spark of life, to his seed.

And thus would daeloth be conceived.

All for the glory and might of the mierothi empire. *Right. As if any of these women volunteered.*

They came at last to their destination. Draevenus stopped and helped Samaranth down to the floor, far more gently than she deserved. He stood straight and approached the bedside.

The woman's eyes were like all the rest. But . . . perhaps there was the faintest glimmer of recognition. Or maybe that was just wishful thinking.

He stooped over and placed his hands on either side of her head, softly stroking her temples. He energized. Draevenus had never been very good at healing. Despite the centuries, it had never come naturally to him, digging around inside a person's body with sorcery. But this one spell he had practiced. And practiced.

Practiced until he could get it right blindfolded, drunk, and mostly asleep.

The sage-and-cinnamon drink had saturated their systems. It would take months, possibly even years to become fully cleansed. He did not have that much time.

His spell worked its way through her, slowly purging fifteen hundred years of poison. That was the easy part. The damage to her mind was far worse, entire sections atrophied from lack of use, others shut down to protect her from the horror of her own existence. Draevenus sweated with concentration, willing the harm to be undone.

After over a toll, straining all the while, he finished and pulled back.

Her eyes closed tightly, then popped open. She looked at him. Sat up quickly and sprang out of the bed.

Draevenus fell to his knees, suppressing all but a single tear from flowing out his eyes. "Angla," he said breathlessly.

She looked down and slapped him across the face.

Rage boiled behind her eyes. "What took you so long!" she screamed, voice cracking from disuse.

Draevenus barely felt the sting and heat from her hand. "I'm sorry. I'm so, so sorry." He closed his eyes, not bothering to fight the tears anymore.

After a moment of tense silence, her arms wrapped around his neck. "Draevenus," she whispered. "My boy. My sweet, sweet boy."

He hugged her back. "It's all right, mother. I'm here now. The nightmare is over. You're free."

SITTING ATOP QUAKE, Yandumar brought the far-sight to his eye. The broad cave mouth carved into the hill two klicks away sprang forth into his vision.

A sorcerous shield held over the opening, pummeled by endless waves of destructive spells from hundreds of daeloth at the base of the hill. Behind it, the clustered remains of Gilshamed's army.

As he watched, half a dozen formations surged up the hill, pushing forward from the mass of over forty thousand Imperial soldiers. The ground was already slick with blood from previous attempts, and their charge was slower than it needed to be. As they neared his entrenched allies, arrows arched up and fell on their heads. Only the front rows held shields, and those behind them suffered grievously. Closer, the revolutionary soldiers pounded the Imperials with rocks, crossbows, and thrown javelins.

Much reduced, and winded from the uphill sprint, the Imperial lines crashed into the pickets. The close-in, heavy fighting lasted all of a mark before the last of the Imperials were cut down. None retreated. He'd seen some try earlier, but they were executed by the daeloth before making it ten paces.

He could tell by their sluggish movements—how slowly they re-formed their barricades and lines—that his trapped allies were on their last leg, though. One, maybe two more Imperial assaults before they capitulated from sheer exhaustion.

He swept his far-sight down among the daeloth. Two-thirds of them were either sitting or lying down, and those that were actively casting moved as if underwater. A three-day siege had burned their energy reserves down to embers.

Perfect.

Yandumar drew his bastard swords from their crossed sheaths and held them up high. Early-morning sunlight shone down on his back, glinting off the bared steel. Tolvar on his right, and Ropes and Idrus on his left, each on the top of their own hill, couldn't mistake the signal. Without looking, Yandumar brought an arm behind him, then arced it forward. Nearly four thousand horses sprang into motion. The ground began to rumble.

He kept swords in hand as they closed the distance. Quake moved with perfection, needing no guidance from Yandumar. He could tell the horse was as eager for battle as he was. They crested a rise, and the full breadth of the Imperial camp surged into view. More than ten times their number. Yandumar smiled.

It is only in times of strife when the true measure of man can be found. No matter his intentions, his words, his morals even. When tested, what a man does is the only thing that counts.

And so, Yandumar led the charge.

The pounding hooves became a roar, like standing under a waterfall, as the gap closed from three hundred paces to two, to one. Some few soldiers turned, wide-eyed. Not enough. Panic spread among the loosely milling crowd.

From four directions at once, the revolution's cavalry struck deep.

Yandumar slashed down, first on the right into a flee-ing man's skull, then on the left where shoulder met neck. Quake crushed one beneath his hooves and chomped an-other man's face off with his teeth.

His horsemen plunged into the Imperial lines, barely slowing. Only four ranks deep, the charge used surprise and momentum to inflict maximum casualties. Yandu-mar continued forward, hacking at any who came within reach. His allies behind him would take care of any he couldn't.

The cries of frantic, dying men rang out, and the scents of blood and sweat and fear filled his lungs. Yan-dumar's vision tunneled. His next opponent and the tips of his blood-drenched blades became the whole of his existence.

A crossbow bolt zipped past his face, clipping his ear. Warm liquid spread down his neck, but he barely felt it. The press of Imperial soldiers suddenly thickened into a wall of shields. The charge stalled. Several men thrust swords up at Yandumar. He chopped at their wrists then turned Quake left.

His allies mimicked him. The straight charge became a swooping rake of claws across the Imperial face. Jav-elins lanced out, often finding gaps in the wall, but even one stuck into a shield weighed it down and rendered it near useless.

Yandumar spun away, taking stock of the battle. More than half the Imperials had been cut down by the charge, and his cavalry was still mostly intact. But now, the re-maining enemy forces had reacted, turning and forming tight square formations to counter them. The daeloth, one and all, had stood and were facing his direction.

Facing away from the hill.

A cluster of boulders overgrown with thick brush lay seventy paces beyond the daeloth. The ground was too rough and uneven, and the area had been ignored by the Imperial advances up the hill. Last night, Mevon's Fist had sneaked into it.

Now, as all eyes were turned towards Yandumar, ninety-two of the finest warriors in the land burst forth.

The rangers struck first with pinpoint strikes from their bows. Daeloth began dropping like stalks of grass before a charging boar. The Elite spread out and began hacking into the rest. Fast, efficient kills. It was over in beats.

They pulled back, leaving almost six hundred dead daeloth behind.

A battle cry rose from the hill—the remains of this part of the revolutionary army. Thousands rushed down, a flood of pent-up violence. Orbs of flame arced down towards the Imperials ahead of them. It was probably the last scoop of power many of the casters could summon, but it was enough. Fire and chaos erupted in the enemy lines, breaking the shield wall that held his horsemen at bay.

Quake drove forward once more, and the rest followed suit, crashing again into the Imperials from one side as the Elite led companies to scythe into the other.

The fighting became close, hot, desperate. The Imperials would not give. Though surrounded and now outnumbered, they fought on, clearly expecting no mercy.

And just today, Yandumar was not prepared to grant any.

It was twenty-five marks before the last of their enemy fell.

Yandumar dismounted. He staggered towards the group he had rescued, letting his battle fury dissipate with each step. He wiped the spattered blood from his face and hands in an attempt to appear civilized.

"Yandumar!"

He turned towards the voice. Orbrahn. Just whom he was looking for. The boy's pale face and unsteady gait told Yandumar how hard he'd been pushing himself to keep everyone from harm. Still, Orbrahn managed a smile.

"Boy are we glad to see you," Orbrahn said. "Another day—abyss, another scorching *toll*—and we would have been done for."

Yandumar narrowed his eyes. "Ruul's light, how'd you even get in this mess? And where's Gilshamed?"

"He's . . . not here. I think that answers both your questions."

Yandumar froze. "Dead?"

Orbrahn spat to the side. "Not yet. Once I get my hands on him though . . ." He shrugged, scowling.

Yandumar closed the distance in an eyeblink. He didn't strike Orbrahn though he wanted to. He merely put his face so close that they breathed on each other. "Regardless of your personal feelings, or your . . . other loyalties . . . we wouldn't have gotten this far without him. Scorch me, we wouldn't even have started!"

Orbrahn appeared thoughtful for a moment. Finally, he looked down and nodded. "Fine. But what do you think will happen to morale once everyone realizes he's not just on some extended recon? He started this, sure, but he also abandoned it!"

"This was never about him. As instrumental as he was so far, we'll just have to carry on the best we can."

"And you'll lead us?"

Yandumar gritted his teeth. "It seems I must."

Orbrahn considered this a moment, a look of acceptance slowly spreading across his face. "Think we have a chance?"

"That depends," said Yandumar.

"On what?"

Yandumar looked over the army—what was left of it anyway. Between them and Mevon's group—provided they could link up safely—they had barely thirty thousand troops. The outer-wall garrison of Mecrithos could muster almost that much by itself, and they had the benefit of the most fortified position in the empire.

"We'll need to bolster our support. Slick Ren and Derthon will be back soon, but that alone won't be enough. I'll need you to contact whoever you can that may be swayed to join us. Anyone. *Everyone.*"

Orbrahn lifted an eyebrow. "I see. And what will you be doing?"

Yandumar smiled. "I've got some old vows to collect on."

GILSHAMED ADJUSTED THE shoulder straps of his pack as he shuffled through the town, hunched over to hide his height, hood forward to hide his face. It was middling as far as towns went, and he moved along with the light midday traffic, mostly people on foot. Everyone seemed in a hurry. Eyes darted about. He rounded a corner and found out why.

A group of soldiers had set up a barricade across the road leading out of town. They were checking every person who tried to pass, inspecting faces and comparing them to a sketch.

Abyss take me! Again? Gilshamed knew exactly whose visage was displayed on that paper.

He faked coughing, slowed down, then ducked into an alley. He pressed himself against the wall of a butcher's shop and suppressed the urge to punch something.

Seven towns and villages, and in each the story had been the same. The empire knew he was coming, knew he was trying to travel north, and they blocked him at each turn. He could have flown over, or fought his way through with ease, but doing so would have pinpointed his location, something they had not yet done.

The faint aroma of sausages and bread wafted from his pack, reminding him why he had come here in the first place. Though centuries of wandering the world had gifted him with ample survival skills, the land here was barren, picked clean of most forage and game by the armies marching every which way. He had gone without food for extended periods of time before, but doing so now would weaken his body and his senses, both things he needed to keep in prime condition to escape this trap.

And it *was* a trap. He was sure of it now. He had been

forced farther and farther south with each passing day. It felt as if a noose were closing about his neck, and his only choice was to continue drifting away from his destination . . . right into the lap of his enemy. South, towards Mecrithos.

But how are they tracking me? He had been careful. No casting, very little speaking beyond terse bartering for goods, nothing to draw attention to himself. Yet, at every step on his path, the empire had been waiting for him.

"Impossible," he hissed.

He could understand if his army was eventually found out. Large groups of casters clustered outside of cities was nearly unheard of, and through communion . . .

His breath caught in his throat.

Shade of Elos. . .

Gilshamed closed his eyes, his mind racing through the evidence and arriving swiftly at the only possible conclusion. He was being tracked, funneled back to the capital. And there was only one person on the continent that could do it.

Voren.

I always knew you for a coward. But a traitor? Actually siding with the mierothi against your own kin? I never knew anyone to stoop so low.

Voren was trying to draw him into an ambush. To force a confrontation. He could see that now. But the best thing to do when one becomes aware of a trap is not to avoid it, no . . .

The best thing to do is to turn it on its head.

Gilshamed smiled. He stepped back into the avenue, heading the opposite direction, no longer worried about the soldiers and daeloth that sought to ensnare him. Vengeance would come. Soon, if a little different than he had originally planned. But that was the thing about strategy: Flexibility was the key to any successful plan.

Gilshamed hefted his pack on his shoulders and assumed his hunched, shuffling gait as he walked out the southern road of the town.

"DID YOU EVEN hear me, Mevon?"

Mevon looked up into Paen's smooth face. His mind had wandered, recalling Jasside's final look. Within the clarity of the storm, he had witnessed her surprise turn to terror as her body flung into open space. Terror, then, into acceptance. Acceptance into determination.

Even as inevitable death approached, still you retained your courage. Her final look humbled him, even as it filled him with despair. With her, a part of him felt whole, a part he had never even known to be empty. Now she was gone, and he felt the emptiness, like a gaping wound in his soul, and he feared it would never be whole again. Just now, he didn't want it to.

"Sorry," Mevon said, not meaning it. He flipped his hand towards Paen to tell him to go on.

"As I was saying, my family's distribution warehouse in Mecrithos has dropped supplies for us three days' south of here. We will meet up with our other armies at the location. And from there, we will be positioned to assault the city itself."

Mevon nodded. Jasside had always wanted to see Mecrithos.

"I've also taken the liberty to arrange for, shall we say, covert infiltration?" Paen leaned forward and handed Mevon a sheet of paper. It showed the five gates of Mecrithos, with circles around the outermost entrances. Names of contacts and pass codes were written beneath. "I assume we'll want to get people inside the walls before we try to take them."

"Yes," Mevon said absently. "Good work."

Calla Rymerhin cleared her throat. She had taken over as leader of his casters after the battle. After Jasside had fallen. "I've made contact with three different groups from the eastern territory. They are headed this way."

"How many?" asked Mevon.

"Six thousand in all, many defectors from their local military units."

More defectors. Without their daeloth masters driving them, many Imperials had switched over, bolstering the revolution. *They will be needed.*

Bellanis stepped forward. "The weapons and armor we recovered from our last battle will be sufficient to outfit these new recruits. There was some concern about using Imperial gear for our troops, though. Some said it would get confusing in the thick of fighting, and wanted to make sure we knew how to tell friend from foe." She smiled, bringing her helmet from around her back. "We think we've come up with a satisfying resolution."

The entire helmet gleamed, shining in the evening sunlight.

"Gold paint?" Mevon asked.

Bellanis nodded. "We were going to use tied golden cloth at first, but thought it might slip off or get sheared during a battle. This, however, will remain unmistakable. Once all helms are complete, we'll start working on pauldrons and gauntlets, too, if we have enough paint left over."

"Good thinking," said Mevon.

In truth, they had all been maintaining the army without him since Jasside became . . . lost. And they'd done a fine job of it. Better than he could have. Much better. The truth, as he saw it, was that they didn't need him at all. It made what he had to do next that much easier.

Mevon sighed. Loudly. "Anything else to report?" His tone made it clear that if they had anything to say, it had better be important.

Calla shook her head, already turning to depart. Paen leaned in close and whispered in his ear, "You need to take your mind off things. Find a woman. *Any* woman. Get it out of your system." He winked and shuffled off.

Bellanis lingered. She so pointedly ignored Paen as he left that Mevon knew the boy had something to do with what would come next.

She smiled at him, a look full of pity, yet laced with an unspoken promise. *Going to comfort me in my grief are you?* Mevon felt anger rising. At her, at Paen, at the mierothi. He was done with all of it. Still, the army needed her, and he could not afford to drive her away.

Bellanis took a step forward. Mevon stopped her with a single, firm look. She stiffened. The look in her eyes instantly became a glare.

"Was there something else you needed?" Mevon asked. Polite, but professional. She was no fool. She knew her chances had become nil.

She sighed. "She was a good woman. A brilliant caster. But in the end, she was a soldier. Like you. Like me. We all knew the stakes when we started playing this game, her most of all."

"I know."

She hesitated a moment longer, as if searching for something else to say. Apparently coming up blank, she turned and marched away.

The sun was nearly set. Mevon made for his tent.

He pushed through the flap. It was small, not nearly as roomy or ostentatious as the one Gilshamed occupied. He kept nothing in it, normally, but a bedroll and a small sack containing emergency provisions. Those were now pushed to one side. Dominating the cramped space was chest a pace long and half a pace wide and tall. Mevon knelt in front of it, unlatched the lock, and flipped open the lid.

A gasp rose from inside.

Mevon inhaled the scent of blood and old sweat and the man's stale, ragged breath, which was infused with the scents of sage and cinnamon.

"Come to give me my evening draught, then?" the daeloth spat. "Or is it more questions? Or just torture for its own sake, as you seem to enjoy."

Looking down into the eyes of the man who had killed Jasside, Mevon shook his head. "Not tonight." Mevon knew then that he had made his decision. "Tonight begins our reckoning."

He reached down a hand to the daeloth's throat and squeezed, gripping until long after the thrashing had stopped. He stood, not bothering with the lid.

Mevon moved to the side of the tent and knelt, rolling up the bedroll. He affixed it to his pack, cinching down the straps to secure it. Food and water were already in the ruck, and he could find more as he needed.

It seemed quick, but Mevon had always been ready for anything. And for this, he had been ready for a long time. Now that he was sure the army was taken care of, there was nothing holding him back.

"I am not a leader of men."

He sighed. Saying it out loud helped make it real. He had known what he was—had always known. But being thrust into a position of authority, finding himself suddenly among people who shared his blood, a father who had sacrificed so much to find him—all of that had make him forget.

"I am a killer."

The mierothi had forged him into an instrument of death. Even though he now turned his talents against them, nothing could change the fact of his existence. His purpose. His only true usefulness. Playing at leader had gotten too many killed already. Had gotten *her* killed. Mevon knew, for the good of everyone, he had to stop pretending.

There was only one thing left. He had only done it once before, and that time was only to ensure it worked.

Mevon pulled Justice into his hands. Now, more than ever, he realized how true the name was. His fingers and thumbs slid along familiar grooves, finding ten individual notches on the rod. Each a thorn. His fingers squeezed, his hands twisted and pulled.

His *Andun* slid apart.

Mevon folded the two halves together and tied them to his back. He put a cloak over himself, covering it up completely, then shrugged his arms through the straps of his pack.

He stepped out of his tent. Night had fallen, and no one paid any attention to the hunched figure walking out of the camp alone.

"It's working," Voren said to the council members gathered around the war table. He pointed to markers on the map that he had placed indicating Gilshamed's position. They formed a straight arrow aimed for Mecrithos. "It appears he was trying to head north. We still do not know why, but we do know that he is alone."

Rekaj nodded. "Jezrid?"

"I can confirm Voren's report. My men have been following him for days, keeping out of sight as you requested."

"It's for their protection," said Voren.

"So you've said. But he is only one man, and even valynkar have to sleep sometime."

"He's more useful to me alive," Rekaj said. "When we hang his body from the city walls as their armies approach, whatever spine they may still have will break."

Jezrid bowed his head, withdrawing from further argument. The emperor turned to the supreme arcanod. "Give me some good news about our forces."

Grezkul stiffened. "We have fewer than I'd like in any position to be a factor. The loss of an entire host was . . . unfortunate. But I am confident the city walls will repel any attack."

"How many are stationed there?" Rekaj asked.

"Twenty thousand, along with three hundred and twelve daeloth. We can double both those numbers if we move men away from the inner walls and foot patrols inside the city."

"Do it. And add sixty of our kin to your list of assets."

"What?"

The corner of Rekaj's lip curled up. "I've recalled our brethren serving at each of the territory capitals. Those twenty will link with two of the enlightened each and stand the outer city walls."

"That will be . . . most helpful," Grezkul said. "Their darkwatch, too?"

Rekaj shook his head. "Their guards will augment our own at the palace. A thousand darkwatch should be enough to protect us from anyone thinking to slip in during the chaos."

Voren saw what the emperor was doing. Sowing division among even themselves by proclaiming those in this room more valuable than the rest of their kin. He could tell that none of the others liked the notion. It meant that Rekaj alone had the power to decide which of them was worthy of life itself and that falling out of his good graces meant they could become like the rest: expendable.

I do not know what great purpose you and your god strive for, but shattering the already tenuous unity of your people is most certainly not the best way to go about it.

Voren smiled to himself, thinking he had discovered another dangerous side effect of absolute power—absolute blindness.

Rekaj turned to the high regnosist. "I trust your 'forces' will soon arrive?"

"Just in time," Lekrigar said. "Though I still don't see the need—" He bit his lip, choking off an argument he'd made before and knew he couldn't win. "I leave tonight to meet them."

"Make sure you hasten their steps. If they miss the battle, I would find it most . . . disappointing. It's long past time that we tested the effectiveness of your little experiments."

Lekrigar fought a scowl. "They wouldn't miss it. Not even for the world."

Truln, standing at Voren's side, muttered under his breath, "Stop trying to be so clever."

"Let's hope so," said Rekaj. He turned to the mother phyzari. "Anything to report?"

Voren realized that she had been quiet, not speaking during the entire meeting so far. She practically jumped when Rekaj called on her.

"No." Kitavijj shook her head as if waking from a dream. "I have nothing to say."

Rekaj gazed at her sharply for a few beats but said nothing further to her. "Well then, we'll meet here tomorrow at the same—"

"Wait!" Truln said, risking a glare from the emperor for the interruption. "Isn't anyone going to talk about the revolt of plantation workers on the Agoritha plains? Or the sudden and complete drop-off of bandit activity in four out of five territories? And why isn't there mention of our Hardohl assets?"

Voren laid a hand on the chronicler's shoulder. "Questions for another time, I think. Once more pressing issues have been dealt with."

"But . . . the Chronicles . . . I need accurate, timely information."

"And you'll get it," Rekaj said. "But not today." He looked around the room. "We'll convene in the morning."

Everyone muttered their acknowledgment and began filing out of the room.

"Voren," said Rekaj, wagging a finger at him.

Voren sighed and followed the emperor to the balcony. He shivered as the night air hit him, longing for his bed. Even throughout the night he was required to make a report every toll on Gilshamed's whereabouts. The disruption of any kind of sleep pattern was beginning to wear on him, and he had learned to savor the few moments of rest he could get. A yawn crept up as his thoughts lingered, and he failed to suppress it.

Rekaj eyed him sideways, seemingly amused. "In need of rest, Voren?" He chuckled. "Worry not. Soon, Gilshamed will be dead, and this rebellion will be swept away. We'll all be able to sleep better then and get back to more important matters."

"Like conquering the world?"

Rekaj grinned, revealing his pointed teeth. "So, you figured it out, have you?"

Voren shrugged. "It was not hard. Especially considering that you wanted me to find out." Voren studied Rekaj for any sign that he was mistaken. He saw nothing. "The only real mystery is why?"

"Why I aim to conquer the world? Or why I wished you to know?"

"Both, actually."

Rekaj paused, as if gathering his thoughts. Or, perhaps, just giving Voren time to conjure the worst possible explanation. If so, it worked.

"Before my communions with Ruul became exercises in silence, he made plain what he expected of me, of all the mierothi. I intend to fulfill his final guidance to us. It is . . . all we have left of him."

Voren's breath caught in his throat as realization dawned. "You actually miss the presence of your god."

"Of course. As do you, yes?"

So that's why I've become your confidant these past few months. You expect that I feel the same about Elos, that we share the same sense of loss. Well, I've got news for you, Rekaj—I don't even remember my god. He doesn't care about me in the slightest, a sentiment I return.

Of course, he could not tell Rekaj all this. Not and expect to live much longer. Their recent familiarity was tenuous at best. Voren knew it could all be shattered by a single wrong word.

Instead, Voren nodded, turning out to view the palace grounds far below them and the city beyond. "I understand," he said. "So, what was it?"

"Ruul's final guidance?"

"Yes."

"It was the same thing he said to us when he first created my people. When he first turned us into what we are today. He guided us in the construction of the first voltensus, then told us to cover the world in them."

"The sensor towers? Why?"

"He said they were needed for our protection. I always took that to mean the protection of the mierothi, but perhaps I was wrong. Perhaps he meant to guard *all* life on this world."

Voren suppressed the urge to scoff. *Altruism from the god of darkness? Right.*

Rekaj continued. "He actually apologized about them. About the sacrifices necessary to create them. Can you imagine? A god saying 'sorry' like he was answerable to his mere creations?"

"That must have been . . . confusing."

"Indeed."

Voren found himself tapping his fingers nervously on the stone railing. It seemed Rekaj was about to get to the point, and Voren was not sure he wanted to hear what was about to be said.

"I intended to use you, eventually," Rekaj said. "A bargaining chip with the valynkar. Keeping you and the others alive had its uses, but I knew one day you might become valuable to keep your people from our throats while we fulfilled our purpose."

"You wish to avoid conflict? That's wise, I suppose. After what happened the first time, war between our peoples would likely tear this world apart."

"Perhaps. More importantly, it would undo all of Ruul's work. That, we cannot have." Rekaj sneered at Voren. "Recent events have given me a new perspective, however. I believe Gilshamed will be far more potent in your place. To that end, we must capture him. Alive."

Voren gulped. "I see."

"The question then becomes, who will he come for first? You, or me?"

Voren chortled, expelling the nervous energy within him. "Do you really need to ask that?"

Rekaj shook his head. "I'll supply you with fifty darkwatch. When he comes for you, get to your chambers and stay there. The wards will render him impotent, and the guards will apprehend him."

"I understand."

Voren walked back to his chambers and fell into his bed, exhausted. But his mind would not turn off.

I understand perfectly, Rekaj. Even now, even after all my service, I am still . . . expendable.

Chapter 15

HARRIDAN CHANT APPEARED in the road ahead of them, a ceaseless grin plastered across his face.

"Good news?" Draevenus asked.

"All gathered and awaiting your arrival," Chant said.

Draevenus dipped his head. "You have my thanks."

"What's all this about, then?" Angla asked.

Draevenus turned to his mother, who marched at his side. Her face, pale as all mierothi, was pinched and smooth, with a narrow nose and pointed jaw. It was good to see it again after all these years. "A surprise, mother. You'll see."

"Oh." Her eyes fell to the dirt ruts paving their way.

Draevenus smiled at her, but inside he grimaced. The old Angla—the one he knew from childhood and the early days after the transformation—would have risen to his cryptic response, either showing mock delight over the very idea of a surprise or smacking the back of his head for not answering to her satisfaction. She showed none of that now.

His cleansing had done much to restore her but it could not completely undo fifteen hundred years of rape, poison, and endless pregnancy.

Draevenus glanced over his shoulder at the three hundred mierothi women walking behind them. It had taken him most of three days to heal them all. The spell was complex, requiring large amounts of concentration and power. He almost thought about asking some of the first ones he had cleansed to help him with the rest but decided against it. None, so far, had even tried to touch their power. He wasn't sure if they remembered how.

"You never answered my question, you know," Angla said.

Draevenus raised an eyebrow. "Which question would that be?"

"The first one I asked."

He thought back to when she first reawakened, replaying the scene. "Ah. That." He sighed, trying to think of the best place to start . . .

"Well?"

Impatient, aren't we? He smiled. It was a good sign. "As we speak, there is a revolution under way."

"Another one?"

"Yes, but this one is different."

"How?"

"Gilshamed leads them."

"Gilshamed?" Her face went blank as she accessed her

ancient memories. "Oh. Oh! So it's not just your usual band of bloodthirsty fools."

"Indeed."

She tilted her head, peering off into the distance for several beats. "Do you think they have a chance? Can they actually succeed?"

Draevenus shrugged. "Nothing is certain, even now. But their actions have drawn Rekaj's attention fully. It was only because of that that I was finally able to break you free."

Angla fell silent, twisting her lips in thought. "I . . . did not mean to be harsh with you, son. They were poor first words for our reunion. It was a long, trying time, and despite your best efforts, I'm afraid I'll carry scars—physical and otherwise—the rest of my days."

"I should have done better, mother. For you, at least, I should have—"

"No. You came. You did what you could, when the rest of the world had forgotten about us. Thank you."

Draevenus put an arm around her shoulder and hugged her to his side for a moment. When he looked at her face, she seemed to be holding back tears.

"So," said Angla, turning her head away. "How is your sister?"

Draevenus nearly teased her for changing the subject so abruptly, but thought better of it. *We'll get the old you back someday.* "Alive, last time I communed with her. Still seeking knowledge. Still thinking she alone carries the fate of all worlds on her shoulders."

Angla opened her mouth in a sneer, but rather than

spout the retort he was getting ready for, she merely pursed her lips for a moment. "I am . . . glad she is well."

"Don't be angry with her, mother. Please."

"I have every right to be. She obviously doesn't care one whit about me!"

"She does, though. She'll never admit it, but she cares a great deal. She just . . . spreads it too far, too thin. I've had to look hard, but I've learned to see the greatness in her, and even, on occasion, some goodness too."

"So she's a saint now?"

Draevenus looked at her crookedly. "I didn't say that."

The walked in silence for several marks. Finally, Harridan turned, and said, "Just up past the next bend in the trail."

Draevenus called his thanks.

"Is this your mysterious surprise?" asked Angla.

He nodded. "Listen, mother. Things are happening in Mecrithos. Events of dire import. I need to be there. I *must*. I can . . . travel faster alone."

A pained, frantic look entered her eyes. "You're leaving?"

He spread his hands, palms up. "I'm sorry. Don't worry, though. I'm not leaving you unprotected."

She stared at him quizzically until they rounded the curve and came to a moss-covered amphitheater nestled just off the trail. The stone benches were crowded with men. Draevenus watched his mother's face as she took a quick count of them. Three hundred. Just as many men as mothers.

Angla turned a sharp gaze on him. "Bodyguards?"

"Maybe. In time. Just plain guards for now. I'll let you get to know each other. When each of you is ready, you can choose a man to be your own." He smiled. "The first step in restoring your darkwatch."

She scoffed. "They don't look like much. And how do we know they can be trusted?"

"You are mierothi. I'm sure you can think of some way to form a mutually beneficial relationship."

She stared blankly at the men. After half a dozen beats, a smile began spreading across her face.

Draevenus remained stoic, but inside he was beaming. Asserting themselves, after so long a slave and prisoner, was a crucial step in their recovery. Based on her response, it was moving even more swiftly than he could have hoped.

Angla stepped into the center of the amphitheater and waved the rest of the women forward. She quickly explained the situation to them, taking the lead as Draevenus hoped she would. The other mierothi, though timid, seemed to take comfort that one of their own had hope for their future.

A pile of wood had been stacked in the fire pit but not yet lit. Angla stepped up to it, pushed her hands out in front of her, and took several deep breaths. The wood ignited.

"Still got it," Draevenus said.

Angla raised an eyebrow. "Was there ever any doubt?"

He shook his head. *Not anymore.*

The blaze soon became a roaring bonfire, and some of the men piled on even more logs. Others brought food and passed it out, firstly among the women. Draevenus saw no small amount of smiles as those long chained were finally able to experience the simple pleasures of life—a warm fire, a shared meal, and people who wished to spend time in their company without demanding anything of them.

Harridan soon unveiled his fiddle. Draevenus sat down next to him as he played and sang. Most of the men joined in the singing. Some even taught the words to the women, who had never heard the tunes. Someone brought out a set of skin drums and beat out an accompanying rhythm. The sun set, but the singing and swaying and smiling continued until deep into the night.

As Chant began to put his fiddle away, Draevenus spoke up. "You're a Ragremon, right?"

Harridan froze in the act of closing the case. Slowly, his movement resumed. "Aye."

"Do you . . . remember?"

Chant grunted. "That I do."

Draevenus nodded, losing his gaze in the embers. "Will your people rise for this?"

Chant remained silent for half a mark. Finally, he leaned back, exhaling loudly. "I have a nephew, Idrus. Good lad. Best eyes I've ever seen. Joined the army at sixteen along with several other boys from our village. By eighteen he was asked to join the darkwatch but refused. By twenty, all his fellow soldiers called him crazy for not trying out for the Elite.

"He was waiting, you see, for one particular Hardohl to graduate. The son of the best man I've ever known, and the first void in history to possess the blood of our people."

"Mevon Daere," Draevenus said.

Harridan nodded. "Idrus was just one of many. Will our people rise, you ask? The answer is no." He paused, chuckling. "We have risen already."

Draevenus shuddered, chills shooting up his spine. "I see." He stood, reaching for his pack. "Take care of my mother, will you?"

"'Course."

Draevenus energized and ran off into the night. Taking the trail until it met the main road, he began shadow-dashing, often reaching as far as a klick per jump if the path ran straight. All souls were converging in Mecrithos. He could almost feel the pull, like a beacon of destiny drawing him in, as history wove itself into the annals of time, playing out in the lives of so many blazing souls.

And I will be there—I must. After all, who else is willing to contain the chaos? Who else can?

CONSCIOUSNESS RETURNED IN minute, painful increments. Pain and darkness were the first bubbles to surface in the sea of awareness. Confusion quickly followed.

Where? When? Who, even? Panic rose as the answers to such simple questions eluded her. *Why can't I remember?*

A dull ache throughout her body and tingling numbness on skin pressed into a hard surface let her know she had been lying for a while. Days, most likely. The sound of her breathing grew louder as the fog cleared from her ears. She struggled to wiggle toes and fingers, stamping down her fear as her body refused to respond.

No. I am not paralyzed. I. Will. Move!

She felt a flush wash through her at the thought. She smiled, loosing a tear, as her limbs shifted in response to her mental commands. She briefly thought about trying to sit up but discarded the idea. It was only a matter of time now. Recovery was certain. She remembered . . .

I remember falling. . .

Her eyes popped open, vision swimming in shapeless, ever-changing objects on a backdrop of pure blackness. She blinked, trying to banish the images, but they persisted. The place she was in was truly dark.

Falling. Then . . . nothing. . .

She pressed her arms down and managed to shift her hips a few fingers to one side. Her whole body groaned at the motion, then seemed to exhale in relief. She counted it a victory.

No. Not nothing. I . . . I did something. The ground came up and I . . .

Thought. Motion. Remembrance. She focused on these things as the beats ticked by into marks. Tolls? Time seemed strange, a jumble with no clear beginning or ending, and no way to tell where on its wheel she fell.

Power flooded into me, through me. Outward. Down. I . . . I pushed. . .

Cold. Stone. The words drifted up, giving meaning to the object upon which she lay. Her fingers explored its edges. Smooth, right angles greeted her touch. Not natural, then. Something crafted.

I pushed . . . but it wasn't enough. I didn't even slow. No hope. No chance to survive. Had to try something crazy. Something impossible. . .

Her hands reached out to her sides. The right met only emptiness, but the left stopped short as it came to a vertical surface identical in feel to what was beneath her. A wall, then. A wall and a bed. She was in a room.

I made a barrier. Round. Hard. In the center was only air, but I knew I could change it. Make it something else. Don't ask me how I knew. . .

"It usually happens this way. Go on."

If she was in a room, then someone had brought her there. How many? Who were they? Were they still here? She held her breath, straining to hear. The sounds of multiple people breathing came from somewhere close. Her eyes were beginning to adjust, and she could just make out the shape of the room—low, square, featureless.

Air is not emptiness. I felt it then, as I fell. More importantly, I understood it. It's so full, bulging with energy, just like everything. I saw below me a million million million tiny specks, and around each, spinning so fast and tinier still, as many more.

"Few ever have the privilege to see as we do. Marvelous, is it not?"

Sorcery. Magic. Caster. Fire. She grunted in effort, recalling what she was capable of, and shaped her will into a ball of flame hovering above her hand. The enclosure sprang forth into her vision. Four walls, the stone glistening in the flickering light, and there . . . a doorway. Through it, she saw . . .

It was simple, really. I just had to pull the specks apart, reshape them as I needed. Simple, but draining. The power required was far beyond what I thought myself to be capable of. Still, the air changed, thickened. No longer air at all, really. I slowed.

"Efficiency will come with practice. And power? Well, something can be done about even that."

. . . three figures. Two stood in doorway, one man, one woman. The third sat in a chair beyond them. Despite the stern visages and diamond-shaped blades poking up from the backs of the two closest, she felt her gaze inextricably drawn to the small figure enfolded in robes, the cloth as dark as the void.

I hit the ground, but not hard. I tried to stand but felt light-headed, feverish, disoriented. Heat and darkness overtook me then. . .

"Enlightenment comes with a price. Even when it is woefully incomplete."

Recognition hit her like a hammerblow between the eyes. She knew them. She'd seen them before. The dark one years ago, when she'd learned something important, something useful. And all three much more recently—at the village eaten by darkwisps. She had looked through time, viewing past events. These three had been there . . . collecting . . .

The next thing I remember is waking up here. Clever, this place. Handy, too, having a shelter or barricade available at the flick of a wrist.

"Another bad habit I will have to break you from. That is, if I decide to let you live."

She cracked open her lips, surprised at how moist they were. Had they been giving her water? Her first attempt at speech resulted in a faint squeak, followed by hoarse coughing.

Oh? And what is the criterion for my continued existence?

"To start, you can tell me your name."

She cleared her throat.

~snap~

And time resolved itself. No longer a bouncing ball but once more a straight line.

"Jasside," she said. "Jasside Anglasco."

"Anglasco?' asked the robed figure, the voice that of a girl just shy of her teen years. "Anglasco?"

Jasside furrowed her brow. The girl had said it wrong the second time, emphasizing the first syllable rather than the second, pronouncing the "s" like a "z", and saying the last two letters as if they were a separate word. "I . . . yes. That is my name. Why?"

"Your father was a daeloth." Not a question.

"Yes."

"He killed your mother by the order of one of my kin."

"Yes. How do you . . . ?"

"What did you do next?"

Jasside gritted her teeth. "I talked my way into his chambers one night, posing as a bit of entertainment. Young and innocent, just like he preferred. When he was . . . sufficiently distracted . . . I stabbed him in the neck with a poisoned hairpin."

"He never recognized you?"

Jasside shook her head. "He never . . . never *saw* me. I was a stranger in his eyes."

The girl stood. "Good. It is important that you remain completely honest with me. I cannot have my new apprentice keeping secrets."

"New . . . apprentice?"

"It's been ages. So few these days ever prove themselves worthy. And I do not have it in me to help those who are not capable of helping themselves." She flipped back the hood of her robe, revealing a young, pasty face framed by scales.

Jasside sat up. "If you want me to be your apprentice, I have some conditions."

"Really, now? I *could* just kill you."

"You could. But you could have done that awhile ago, too. My demands are not harsh, but I would rather die than fail to secure them."

The young mierothi girl smiled. "Very well. Let us hear what the child has to say."

Jasside stood. "First, my friends. You will not harm them or ask me to do anything against them. Second, you will take me back to them and let me finish what we have begun."

"Done and done. Is there anything else?"

"One last thing. Tell me what your name is?"

Jasside felt a pulse of dark energy shoot out from the

young mierothi who was not young at all. The walls vanished into mists, and she became blinded by the sudden influx of sunlight. She blinked away the glare and found herself amidst a strand of trees in the middle of a vast, grassy plain. The two Hardohl moved away and began loading up a pair of oversized rucksacks.

"Vashodia," her new mistress said. "As if you didn't already know."

GILSHAMED STEPPED THROUGH the doors of the Silk Path, inhaling deeply of a rich, floral scent. White-marble floors met walls adorned with priceless works of art. Women entertained their male guests—albeit tamely—on furniture fit for kings, sipping Taditali private reserve from caster-spun diamond glasses. The opulence was almost blinding, particularly after years spent traveling the wilderness.

Looks like I have found the right place.

He stepped towards the concierge, expecting to find at least a handful of guards at a place like this. Instead, only a single old woman stood between him and the rest of the establishment. Gilshamed gave her a smile.

The old woman looked him over stoically, seemingly unperturbed by both his imposing figure and disheveled appearance. "Any weapons?" she asked.

Gilshamed had left his pack, which held several daggers and a hatchet, outside the city. He had been able to fly over the walls easily—almost too easily—hiding his incursion with a spell of light bending, but would not have been able to do so weighed down.

He unclasped his sword belt and handed it over. As the old woman's fingers brushed against him, he understood why no other guards were necessary.

"No casting," said the Hardohl, who obviously felt what he was when they had touched. "There are wards in every room. Won't harm you, just knock you out before you can blink."

"Thank you for the warning." Gilshamed struggled to refrain from laughing. He could see the wards affixed to the ceiling of the lobby. They were attuned for casters of dark energy only. Against him, they would be useless.

Gilshamed stepped past, presenting a purse to the concierge. Gold glittered as it fell open on the woman's podium. "A room, please. One with an unobstructed view to the south."

Unlike the rest of the women he could see, nearly every bit of her skin was covered, all the way up to her neck and down to her toes. "Very good, ser. You'll be wanting a bath, I presume?"

"Yes. And there should be enough there to get me new clothes." He quickly explained his requirements, which she must have memorized, for she wrote nothing down.

"Would you like to peruse our fine display of nubile—"

"No. Any will do."

The concierge clapped her hands, and a sultry-faced, curvy woman, wearing nothing but a few scraps of silk, came to take his arm. She led him to a lift, a sorcerous construct that raised them to the seventh level of the building. They passed several soundproofed rooms before stepping through an open door.

Here, red reigned supreme, suffusing every surface in a gaudy and unsubtle motif. Gilshamed ignored it all, heading for the balcony.

He was stopped by a tug on his arm. "This way, ser."

Sighing, Gilshamed let her shuffle him into the bathing chamber. A silver tub, already filled with steaming water, awaited them. The view could definitely wait—he had been looking forward to this for days. He quickly stripped out of his dusty traveling clothes and sank into the tub, gasping in near ecstasy as the hot liquid encased his skin.

The woman began scrubbing him immediately with a soapy sponge. He let her, failing to respond even in the slightest when her hands lingered in suggestive locations.

"You should relax," she said, squeezing his shoulders. "It will be better for both of us." One of her hands slid down to his chest, his stomach . . .

He grabbed her wrist. "No."

She stood back, and he let her go. "Very well, sir. Tell me what you *would* like, then."

To sit here . . . forever . . . and let my troubles dissolve into mist. "A bathrobe," he said. "And some quiet, if you do not mind."

He stood, letting the water slough off his body into a tub now browned by weeks of his filth. She held out a robe, and he shrugged into it, securing it about his body with a silken belt, and stepped out to the balcony.

Merely half a klick distant, separated by only a single wall and several low buildings, sat the Imperial palace.

So, this is where you have spent the last nineteen hundred years, old friend. I am afraid it does not look like much.

Gilshamed could tell, from the outside, that very little thought had gone into making the structure aesthetically pleasing. "Imposing," rather, was the word that came to mind. Built to menace and intimidate, not welcome or dazzle. The empire had no need to play host to foreign dignitaries, no need to impress. The only message sent to those that came here was this: *Look upon your rulers and quiver in fear.*

He peeled his eyes away, turning his head halfway around. "This is the finest establishment in the city?"

"Our rivals would argue that assertion, sir," she said with a smile. "But they would be wrong."

"Then may I assume your members are often called upon to serve in the palace?"

"Only the best for the masters of our land."

"You personally?"

She nodded.

"Good." He turned to her fully, giving her his warmest smile. Inside, though, he felt nothing. "I mean to visit an old friend who lives there. However, I have no idea where his chambers are. I was wondering if you could help me?"

A surge of alarm streaked through her features. "Perhaps, if you could describe your . . . friend . . . I might be able to help."

"He is nearly as tall as me, with midnight-blue eyes and hair to match. Last time I saw him—"

"He has a statue of you in his room, you know."

A stab of shock raced through him. "What?"

"Yes. And three others. The names carved into their bases were Analethis, Murathrius, and Heshrigan."

Gilshamed shuttered his eyes, feeling a blow of almost physical pain as she said each name. The three greatest failures in the history of his people . . . and himself. The association made his stomach twist.

He took a deep breath to steady himself. "I do not suppose you could tell me where it was you saw this?"

She tilted her head. "Is he really an old friend of yours?" Her lips were pressed together, drained of blood. So slightly that a lesser man would have missed it, he saw her entire body shaking.

"No," said Gilshamed. "Quite the opposite."

She nodded, gesturing towards the palace. "South side, above the gardens. There is a giant glass bubble sticking out from his chamber. You can't miss it."

One knot of tension unclenched but another took its place immediately. He knew everything he needed to in order to carry out his plan. Now, all he had to do was . . . execute.

Justice. Revenge. He could no longer differentiate between the two. He no longer cared. His love had been taken from him. First by zeal, then by recklessness, then, finally, by betrayal. It mattered not how, though . . . only whom. Voren had to be punished for his crimes, and cir-

cumstances had dictated that it be Gilshamed himself
who carried out the sentence.

*And who would blame me for taking what pleasure I
can from that?*

"Will you be needing anything else from me, ser?"

Gilshamed blinked. He had nearly forgotten the
woman was still there. "You may sleep on the bed, I will
not need it. You have been a great help to me. I think you
deserve a night off."

An appreciative smile decorated her lips. "Thank you,
ser. You are too kind."

"Kind?" Gilshamed rubbed his chin. "No. I am not
kind.

"I never have been."

YANDUMAR SOOTHED QUAKE into a trot as the outlying
buildings of the village came into view. He saw movement ahead through the trees—probably a runner gone
to report the approach of strangers. *Good. Maybe this
won't take all day.*

He pointed his chin over his shoulder, eying the four
men—his "honor guard"—riding behind him. Idrus had
insisted on them. He and Arozir had wanted to come,
which was understandable given his purpose here, but
he'd convinced them that the army needed them more.

Yandumar faced forward. "Let me do all the talking."

Maybe they nodded, but none responded in any way
that he could tell.

"Good," he said. "Just like that."

They continued for a few marks, passing longhouses that appeared devoid of life. Yandumar knew better, though, and could feel the hidden eyes on his back as they rode. It didn't take much longer until their mounts were stamping hooves onto the village square.

It was empty. Still. Quiet. A breeze blowing a few crinkling leaves was the greatest sign of life he could see.

They rushed out from everywhere at once. Yandumar didn't even hear the signal. A solid ring of flesh, armed to the teeth, sprang up around them in beats. Men and a nearly equal number of women, the latter by far the more ferocious, stared grimly up at him. For every pitchfork, woodsman's axe, and makeshift cudgel there were as many spears, pikes, swords, and shields. Youths on the rooftops had arrows nocked to bows, pulls steady.

And in the center stood a big man who was obviously in charge, hunkered beneath the low thatch roof of a stable. Yandumar leveled his gaze at him. "I take it you got problems with bandits in these parts?"

The big man rubbed his beard, burnt-orange flecked with grey. Sunlight glinted off his smooth pate. "Not bandits so much these days. Soldiers. Little squads breaking off from all the armies, thinking their uniforms grant them immunity. Thinking a backwoods village is the kind of place they can have any kind of fun they want. Thinking they can get away with it."

"Thinking wrong," Yandumar said.

"Dead wrong," the man said.

Yandumar raised an eyebrow.

The man mirrored him.

"Ha!" said Yandumar. "Ain't no other way to deal with 'em, is there Abe?"

Abendrol Torn stepped out from beneath the shadow of the stable roof. He had to duck under its lip to allow the handle of his greatsword, which was strapped to his back, enough room to clear through. "No, Yan, there is not."

Yandumar looked around. No one had yet moved to stand down. If anything, they looked even more ready to pounce. "So, what's it gonna be then? We getting the same treatment?"

"That depends," Torn said. "Why are you here?"

"Isn't it obvious? Or have our people taken to burying their heads in the sand?"

"We are well aware of the goings-on in the empire. But we've heard . . . disturbing rumors . . . about your loyalties."

Yandumar sighed. *Maybe I should have brought you, Arozir. Maybe you'd be able to talk some sense into your uncle.* "We've all taken vows. Perhaps I have taken more than one, but that doesn't mean they conflict with each other. And it certainly doesn't mean I've forgotten my people, or value my oaths to them any less."

"So . . . what? You think you can come back here after all this time and simply decide our fates for us?"

"Of course not. Our people's vow was not meant to force anyone to do anything. I came only to sound the call. Let all men and women decide for themselves if they wish to answer."

"And you honestly thought this . . . this revolution . . .

was enough cause to invoke it? Last I heard, you were on the brink of disaster."

Yandumar gritted his teeth. *Lying will do no good . . .* "Yes. We were. Are. We went up against the mierothi. Not everything went quite the way we planned."

"And you expect us to risk everything on an already failing cause?"

Yandumar shook his head. "You're right to think we have little hope of victory. As we stand, I doubt we'll even make it inside the walls of Mecrithos. But the rise of our people may just tip the scales in our favor. And let me assure you, this land will not see a better opportunity than this for a thousand years.

"This is not just the right time to invoke the vow. It's the *only* time."

Abendrol Torn stepped towards him. He paused, staring in silence for several beats, arms crossed. Finally, he said, "Before we decide anything, you gotta prove yourself worthy."

"What? That was never a condition of invoking our vow!"

"Oh? So you've been inducted as an elder then? Learned all about our most secret laws?"

Yandumar growled. *Forgot about that little detail.* "What do I gotta do?"

Torn pulled his greatsword from its scabbard. "You and me will fight. To the death. The winner will lead our people wherever he chooses."

Yandumar slumped, a knot forming in his stomach. "Is there no other way?"

"No."

He slipped off Quake, patting the horse's neck, then stepped towards the empty space between him and Torn. He closed his eyes, filled his lungs, and exhaled, looking around the circle of his kin, pausing a beat at each set of eyes his gaze fell upon. Everyone seemed expectant, with an edge of fear. He didn't know what to make of that.

Yandumar peered at Abendrol. "God views all sins equally. But man does not. And the title of 'kinslayer' is not something I wish to carry for the rest of my days. Nor," he said, as Torn began objecting, "would I force it on anyone else."

He drew both of his bastard swords in one swift motion. He stepped forward, then slammed the tips down into the ground, leaving them quivering.

"If this is the price for our people's soul, then I refuse."

Slowly, Torn slipped his greatsword back into its scabbard. He smiled. "That, my friend, was the right answer."

Yandumar frowned. *What . . . ?*

He looked around at his people again. The fear and tension were gone, replaced by . . . joy?

"I don't understand," Yandumar said.

Abendrol stepped up, patting him on the shoulder. "I said you had to prove yourself, and you just did. Only a true leader would refuse to shed his own people's blood to get his way."

Yandumar blew out his lips, letting his anxiety run out with his breath. "So . . . that's it?"

"Almost," Torn said. "This is just one village after all. We'll have to get the word out to the rest of us."

That will take too much time—time we don't have. His people had no casters among them. They rarely married outside of fellow Ragremons and never allowed outsiders to settle near their towns.

Torn whistled. "Hey, Celar! Your boy ready with them doves?"

"'Course he is, Abe!" the woman shouted back. A boy, maybe ten or eleven, stepped up next to her, limping slightly.

"Doves?" asked Yandumar.

"Birds, Yan. We've trained them to carry messages between towns. After your son was born, we knew we'd have to start preparing for this."

Message-carrying birds . . . genius! "Wait. You've been getting ready for thirty years? Why?"

"Mevon was something special. First void from our blood. When Harridan told us what had happened to you, we knew that you would come back someday, and that finding your son would be your top priority. We didn't know how it would all play out, but we figured this was an opportunity that only came around once in an age."

Yandumar nodded, head whirling with all the news. He still couldn't believe he had gotten what he came for.

He stepped towards Celar and her son. "Hope you're good with your letters, kid," he said.

Yandumar was stopped by a tug on his sleeve. "Excuse me?" said a voice.

He spun to face the man. "Yes?"

"Sorry, yes. I was wondering if I could draw you?"

"What? Who are you?"

"Oh," said Torn. "This here is our historian. Be nice to him, Yan. He means well."

"Historian, huh? Well, nice to meet you . . . ?" He stuck out his palm.

"Thress," the man said, shaking his hand vigorously. "Sarian Thress. I'd love to get your story down, if you don't mind?"

"Uh, sure. What's this about a drawing though?"

"Oh, that. Well, I try to include illustrations in my chronicles. I think it's important to capture the true essence of a moment."

"I've really got to be going. Lots to do. A war to fight . . ."

"No problem, I can ride beside you. I'm quite adept at working on the move."

Yandumar glanced at Torn, who merely shrugged. "Ah, I see. Well, that's fine I guess."

"You must leave nothing out." Sarian Thress pulled a blank journal from the pocket of his robe. "Now, start at the beginning . . ."

Yandumar groaned.

MEVON SNIFFED DEEPLY as the scent of woodsmoke hit his nose. He pulled back the hood of his cloak and shifted his gaze about the expansive plain, searching for its origin. He did two full circles before realizing where he was.

Mecrithos lay only two days away, directly south from here. He knew this land. He'd spent many a day sweating with exertion from dawn to dusk—and often beyond—right . . . there.

He spotted the depression hidden between two mounds too low to be called hills. The haze of smoke drifted up from the spot. Mevon shifted his pack straps and left the game trail he had been following to head towards it.

Memories of his final year in training lifted to the forefront of his mind. It was here that he endured the final lessons a Hardohl would ever receive, training his body and mind to kill. His reflexes sharpened to razors. His skill burgeoning from endless sparring bouts with the masters. Most students received one-on-one training. Mevon got a bit more than that.

Kael, as ever, was present. But the old man convinced a few of the other masters, and even some active Hardohl, to join their training. Kael matched Mevon up against several others, including himself, at the same time. Mevon would never forget how many near-death defeats he suffered in the first few months.

But he did get better. Two at once quickly became easy for him, and when facing three, he could often fight to a draw. Kael didn't let up, though. During the month before his eighteenth birthday, he was fighting five of the best warriors in the world at once . . . and getting thrashed regularly.

Mevon smiled to himself. *Some lessons, you never forget.*

As he approached the entrance, the smell of woodsmoke grew thick—too thick—and he heard the chatter of many voices emanating through the simple wooden door. He only hesitated a moment before pulling the handle and, back straight, thrusting himself inside.

The chatter ceased before the door had even shut behind him. He blinked rapidly, forcing his eyes to adjust to the suddenly dim environment. In three beats, he was able to make out nearly threescore figures staring at him. Some were strangers. The others . . .

"My brethren," he said to his fellow Hardohl. "It is good to see you."

Their responses varied. Some smiled or stood slowly, with shock on their faces. Others spat in the dirt or simply glared. At least none drew steel. That would not have ended well.

"Mevon," said a familiar voice. He turned, noticing a figure crouched on the far side of the nearest fire pit. Logs were stacked up within the circle of stones, but it had yet to be lit.

"Ilyem," he said, moving slowly towards her. "I see you kept your promise."

"As much as I could. Not everyone agreed to stay out of this fight."

He sat down on a log next to her, dropping his pack. All the others took their cue and resumed whatever they were doing before he had intruded. Mevon watched the smoke from half a dozen fires drift up through a gap in the roof of the enclosure. "Cave" wasn't quite right because the space was carved from between two hills and had no true ceiling. Still, it kept out most of the elements.

"How many in total?" he asked.

"Most of our peers in the eastern and northern territories, and all in the central. Minus, of course . . ."

"The Blade Cabal. I wouldn't have expected you to even try for them."

"I didn't."

Mevon nodded. "It should be enough. I . . . hope."

"Do you?"

"Do I what?"

"Hope."

Mevon sighed. *I don't know anymore.* "Of course I do."

"Then why are you here?"

He studied her face. "Would you answer that question if you were in my place?"

"It depends."

"On what?"

"On why you're here."

Mevon grunted. "Fair enough." He looked into the unlit logs in front of him, which were built over the embers of a previous fire. He wished it were blazing. He could have used some of its warmth right now.

"Well?" Ilyem said.

He sighed. "I . . . I don't know. They wanted me to lead, but that ended in disaster. We were never trained for that. Only for killing."

She nodded. "So, you . . . ran away?"

He opened his mouth to refute her, but stopped. *That's exactly what I did.* He pressed his lips together and remained silent. He could feel her eyes on his face, but refused to meet them. He didn't want to see their accusation. Instead, he said, "She's dead because of me."

"She? Oh. The convincing one. The two of you were . . . ?"

"Maybe. I think so. Beginning to anyway. Now we'll never know."

"How did she die?"

Mevon told her everything. When he was done, Ilyem remained quiet for a while, appearing to contemplate. At long last, she replied. "She was a soldier, Mevon. She knew what the stakes were when she got involved."

He nodded. It was almost exactly the same answer Bellanis had given him, and the kind of answer he had expected from her . . . and not at all helpful.

"You know," she said, "you've put all our kind in a difficult place."

"What do you mean?"

"Whether your cause is successful or not, there will be severe consequences for all voids in the empire. If the mierothi win, we'll never be trusted again, and I wouldn't put it past them to try to hunt us all down.

"But if the mierothi lose? Then, our kind will become—"

"Obsolete," Mevon said. "I know." *I've known for a while. Why did I ever think this could end any other way?*

"There may be an alternative, though."

Mevon locked his eyes on her, raising an eyebrow. "Alternative?"

"You said your father came from beyond the Shroud.

If that's true, then there must be a path. If there is a path, then all of us can escape the empire. For good."

Mevon's eyes widened. He'd never even thought of escaping.

"Think of it, Mevon," Ilyem said. "I've accepted the fact that the mierothi took our lives away from us, molded us into weapons for their wielding. By some miracle, you still have your father, but he is no Hardohl, and if your revolution presses on, he will likely die. Wouldn't it be better to find someplace new? Somewhere we can start fresh, without being someone's tool?"

Mevon pictured a life away from the empire. A life of freedom. Where his father could live out his final years in peace, and Mevon himself could do whatever he pleased. Not answering to anybody. Traveling the world. Seeing the ocean up close. Sailing.

He almost found himself smiling. *A good dream . . . for a normal man. Could I really leave the empire behind, knowing how many mierothi had escaped justice?* He shivered as he contemplated the answer.

Ilyem rubbed her arms. "I'm cold as well." She stood and raised her voice. "Hey, who built this fire but didn't bother to light it?"

When no one answered, she sighed and began rummaging through her supplies. Mevon assumed she was looking for a flint and tinder. "Is it so much to ask," she said, "for people to just nail the last plank on the bridge?"

Mevon froze, his gut twisting at the words. As it always did, the final part of the catechism sprang into his mind.

Too faintly for anyone to hear, he said, "Even when it's burning."

Ilyem called after him, but she was too late. Mevon was already out the door.

"KAEL!" VOREN SAID. "How good to see you."

"Whaddya want?"

Voren smiled. He had already known the old Hardohl was immune to any sort of charm, but a little civility never hurt to smooth the path for a difficult request. "I am glad you came. To be honest, I was not sure if you were still in the palace, what with the termination of your current assignment."

Kael glared at him. *Or is that just his normal look? I cannot tell anymore.* "Yeah. I'm still here," Kael said. "Something tells me I may still be needed."

Voren shrugged. "I hope not. Rekaj is many things, but I have not known him to break his word lightly. When he says my tether will be cut, I expect that it will be."

"Whatever you say. Now, tell me why you called me here, so I can get on with my day."

Voren sighed. Too much was riding on this. He could not afford to fail. "By now, I am sure you have heard of the little trap we are preparing for Gilshamed?"

"Not exactly a secret."

"Yes, well," Voren gulped, "I do not think it will work. Not the way Rekaj has planned. Intentionally or not, I am being put at great risk, and there are far too many ways for Gilshamed to slip out of the trap. I need your help, Kael."

"Help with what?"

"Nothing you have not already done before. I would do it myself, but I am ordered to stay here until after the trap has closed. If you could just—"

"No."

Voren's head rocked back. "But, I have not even said—"

"I know what you want, Voren. I won't do it."

"I assure you, this is for the good of the empire."

Kael puffed out his lips. "Right."

Voren stepped closer, lowering his voice. "I never did tell anyone about your insider information on the revolution. About your *true* loyalty. And I will continue to keep my lips sealed. All I ask is a little cooperation."

"Ha! You've no proof. And it would only raise questions as to how you knew. No, Voren, don't bother threatening me. You're a young man playing at an old man's game."

"Young? I am almost two millennia your senior!"

"And since when does age have anything to do with the number of years you've been alive?"

Voren jerked his head.

"Never mind," Kael continued. "You know, the only reason I even told you about that was because I felt sorry for you, and I didn't think it was right the way the mierothi treated you. If I'd known you'd become this, I would have just put you out of your misery."

Voren felt a chill as he realized he was just steps away from a man against whom he had no defense and whose allegiance was, more or less, opposed to his. He backed up, raising his hands.

"Fine," said Voren. "Fight for the losing side. Do not expect me to stand for you when the mierothi begin extracting their vengeance and are looking for people to blame."

Kael grunted. "I'd say 'abyss take you,' Voren, but it looks like it already has."

Voren watched in silence as his former keeper slammed the door shut on his way out.

He closed his eyes. Focused on his breathing.

This is not the end. Another solution will present itself. I am sure of it. He did his best to convince himself that everything would turn out all right. That he would survive the conflagration that was to come. If he could just do that, then freedom itself would be within his grasp. And with freedom, all the things that he had been denied for so long. Wealth. Power.

Vengeance.

He swept his arm across his refreshment table, knocking over several glasses and an expensive Taditali red. Glass and wine sprayed across the floor.

"You did this to me!" he spat. "You, Rekaj. And you, Gilshamed. Your arrogance made me what I am today."

"Is this a bad time?"

Voren whirled towards the voice. Someone stood in his doorway. He had not even heard it open.

"Chronicler Truln," Voren said, mustering as much etiquette as possible. "I must apologize. You caught me unprepared for company."

"I can see that." Truln scratched the side of his face, pathetically trying to hide his open stare at the mess.

Voren cleared his throat. "Was there something you needed?"

"Hmm? Oh, yes. I was hoping you had a moment to talk. I've been updating the Chronicles and would like to get your perspective on events."

"My . . . perspective?"

"Mm-hmm. I find that everyone has a slightly different spin on things. Helps me craft a more complete picture. You know, for posterity."

"I see."

"So," Truln said, "what can you tell me that no one else knows?"

I do not have time for this, you rambling idiot! Voren had to restrain himself from lunging for the mierothi's throat. *Want to know my secrets, do you?*

Voren stopped breathing. He *did* have secrets, secrets that would light a fire under the feet of the entire mierothi nation. But they were not his secrets.

They belonged to Rekaj.

He took a deep breath, steadying himself. *Can I trust you, Truln?* He shook his head. He had run out of options, and this was simply too good an opportunity to pass up. "I know some things, yes. Things that I believe you will find of great interest. Things that might very well change the course of history."

With each word, he witnessed Truln's eyes grow increasingly wide. The chronicler actually began bouncing back and forth on the balls of his feet in excitement. He pulled out a tome and laid it down on the table, preparing his inkwell and quill. Voren gathered from the expectant gaze, the rapid, shallow breathing, and the get-on-with-it gestures, that Truln wanted to hear every word *right now*!

"Patience," Voren said. "There will be time later. I would not want to rush the words. And besides, I do not think I can tell it right now."

"What? Why not?"

"I . . ." Voren hung his head, feigning shame. "I fear for my life. I believe Rekaj is trying to get me killed."

"But . . . but . . . why would he do that? I thought you've become somewhat of a favorite of his lately."

Voren shook his head. "Only so far as I can further his goals. Once I have done that, he has made it clear that my continued existence is . . . inconvenient to him. And it is the very knowledge I would share with you that has put me in such a predicament."

Truln twisted his lips, gazing at the ceiling in thought. "How can I help?"

Voren sighed, pouring on the show of relief. "My . . . friend . . . I was hoping you would say that. Do you know of the chamber where my kin are held? It is not a long journey, but you'll need some help from a void. I happen to know of a few retired Hardohl living right here in Mecrithos . . ."

PART IV

Chapter 16

WITH THE DISTANT walls of Mecrithos on his right, just visible in the haze of twilight, Yandumar rode between his armies.

Behind him, the army of his people. It numbered twenty-five thousand and counting, with several of the more remote villages slow to respond. He knew they would come, though. He knew his people, and he knew that no one would want to be remembered as the one who sat out the greatest moment of their collective existence.

He crested a mound and caught sight of the second army—the army of the revolution—still moving south towards the capital. Still alive. It looked bigger than he remembered its being when he last left it. Much bigger. The two groups must have merged together sometime in the past week, and picked up new recruits besides.

He smiled, urging Quake into a trot.

Yandumar rode at the very tip of the loose formation.

He had recalled the scouts a toll ago, not wanting there to be any mishaps between the two groups of armed men and women. As he came to the screen of the revolution's sentries, he pulled to a halt. One of the men stepped forward. Yandumar recognized him.

"Good to see ya', Ivengar," Yandumar said.

The ranger inclined his head. "Glad to have you back. And to see all your friends."

"My kin," corrected Yandumar. He jerked his chin over Ivengar's head. "I see our forces have reconciled. I need to get to our leaders as soon as possible."

"I'll escort you."

"No need. I know the way."

Yandumar turned as Abendrol rode up behind him. "Abe," he said. "Coordinate with Ivengar here and begin integrating our people into the defenses."

Torn smiled deviously. "As you command, Lord-General."

Yandumar looked at him, dumbfounded. "Come again?"

"Ha! One more thing you didn't know because you were never properly raised to Elder status. We all got together and voted last night. Some few gave a fit, but our bylaws never specifically state that the position *had* to be given to an Elder."

"Uhh . . . all right. What does it even mean?"

"That we'll follow you into the maw of the abyss without even blinking."

"Oh. So, pretty much like it already is?"

"Yeah. But now, you have a title!"

Yandumar laughed. But his merriment turned sour as he saw another rider approaching. Sarian Thress. The man had not stopped hounding him for information since they had met. It was bad enough posing for the man's portrait of him, but it seemed like his every waking toll was spent answering questions about the events that had led to their present circumstances. *If "annoying" and "persistent" are requirements for the profession of historian, then Sarian Thress might very well become the greatest who ever lived.*

Yandumar prayed for the sanity of Thress's future children as he urged Quake into a gallop and sped towards the center of the revolutionary forces . . . and away from the historian.

Soon, he came through the outer shell, a ring of battle-hardened warriors. Troops were digging in, preparing pickets for the night's defense, setting up tents and horse lines, staging the wagons, prepping weapons, and starting fires to begin cooking dinner—the last many of these people would likely ever have.

By tomorrow night it will be decided. One way or another, history will be written, and the soul of this continent will be bought by the blood of the victors.

Yandumar came to the command tent, slipping off Quake. He could hear muffled voices coming from within. The guards saluted him, and he returned it, pausing only long enough to take one deep breath before stepping inside.

"Ya' miss me?" he shouted.

The voices cut off abruptly. Then, several at once responded with, "Yandumar!"

He blinked, clearing his vision, and identified all those standing before him. Orbrahn, Arozir, Idrus, and Ropes were present representing the army that had once followed Gilshamed. Paen Taditali, the sorceress Calla, and the young commander Bellanis who must have been standing in for Mevon, wherever he might be. But Yandumar barely even saw them. Standing slightly apart from the others were a pair of familiar and much missed figures. Derthon, and . . .

"Slick Ren," he said. He ran to her, picking her up by the waist, and twirled her around. Her gasp only made him smile and laugh all the harder. He pulled her close—not quite setting her down—and pressed his lips to hers, feeling her hot breath against his face as she returned the kiss with enthusiasm.

At last he set her down, a few moments too late to avoid the awkward coughs and shuffling of feet performed by the others in the room. Yandumar didn't care. He held her by the waist, at last giving her room to breathe.

"Well," Slick Ren said, "if that is any indication of the ways things are to go in our relationship, I might just have to keep you."

Yandumar smiled. "Marry me?"

She wagged a finger at him. "Uh-uh. I asked first."

He laughed, pulling her close again and wrapping him arms around her. "You win," he said into her ear softly. "My answer is yes."

Looking over her head, Yandumar spied Derthon, who flashed him the hand signal for approval. Then, another sign, this one commending his bravery.

"Ha!" Yandumar said.

Slick Ren pushed away gently, then jabbed him in the kidney. Yandumar lost his air, bending over nearly double from the blow. "That was for the interruption, my dear," she said. "We were, after all, discussing important matters."

"Right," he gasped. He inhaled deeply and righted himself, waving his gaze across everyone else. "Where do we stand?"

Idrus cleared his throat. "We were just going over the numbers as you entered. Our combined base force, with recent recruits from the area, comes to thirty-five thousand."

"And," Slick Ren said, "if seeing me and Derthon didn't make you happy enough, perhaps I can give you fifteen thousand more reasons to smile?"

"Fifteen?" Yandumar said. The number was half again their most optimistic estimate. "How'd you manage that?"

"The bandit lords of the north and west provided half of their men to our cause. They were resistant at first, but after I promised to dedicate my life to dismantling their operations—followed by a lengthy explanation of precisely how I would do it—they proved amenable enough. That, and a promise of complete amnesty were we to succeed."

"What about the central territory?"

"Ah. The lords of this area did not take kindly to our quite reasonable proposal. Or should I say, the *former* lords."

"Oh, bloody abyss . . . What did you do?"

"Nothing, my dear. We just staged a little coup. No harm done."

He raised an eyebrow. "No harm?"

She smiled wickedly. "All right, maybe a *little* harm. I have new scar. When we're alone, I'll show it to you."

Yandumar tried his best not to blush. He failed.

"Since you returned," Arozir said, "I take that to mean your mission was a success?"

"Resoundingly," he said, then told them all how many of his kin had joined the cause. The excitement in the room grew, hope blossoming as they all realized they might actually have a chance.

"Let's not get ahead of ourselves," Yandumar said. "Despite the fact that we outnumber the city garrison by almost two to one, taking the wall will be no easy feat. You can bet the empire knows we're coming and that every last soldier and daeloth within a hundred leagues is marching towards us as we speak."

"And there are the mierothi themselves," Orbrahn said. "If they stand the wall in force, our numbers will count for little."

"We need an edge," Ropes said.

"As to that," said Paen, "I may have a solution."

Yandumar gestured at him. "Spill it."

"I've been in contact with associates of my family who reside in Mecrithos. They tell me that no guardsmen patrol the streets anymore, all of them standing the wall in preparation for our assault. This has allowed the seed of dissension to spread unhindered through the populace."

Yandumar waited, like all the rest, as Paen looked about the tent, letting his words sink in. Yandumar soon grew impatient. "Cut the theatrics, Paen. What does this mean for our strategy?"

"It means that, when the time comes, the Imperials will find the wall under attack from both sides at once."

Yandumar closed his eyes, picturing the lower district of Mecrithos as reconstructed from his memory of his time there. Picturing the wall. Thirty paces high and just as thick, full of narrow holes in the stone face for archers to fire out upon attackers, the top lined with ballistae and linked groups of daeloth.

"Feints will be no good," he said, opening his eyes and locking gazes with Paen. "Can you get word to your contacts before tomorrow?"

Smiling, Paen nodded.

"The central gate. Dawn."

"They'll be ready."

Yandumar turned to Orbrahn and Calla. "Organize the casters. I want one embedded with each commander and four with me. Let them know to send updates by commune every few marks and for every major development. The rest, get them practicing that linking thing you do. We'll likely need all of their combined strength to hold off the daeloth and break through the gate."

He turned to Mevon's captains. "We'll need your Fist to lead the central assault. Begin making preparations."

"Aye," they said together. Yandumar didn't need to say any more to them. They knew their business.

"Bellanis," he said, meeting her gaze. "Inform the

other commanders of our plans and get the troops started making ladders and overhead cover that is light enough to be carried yet still protect against arrows."

"Got it," she said.

"Slick Ren, Derthon . . . where will your forces be?"

"Most bandits aren't particularly suited to fighting on the front lines," said Slick Ren. "But everyone that came with me carries a bow. We'll do what we can to keep those on top of the wall occupied."

"Good. Have them start fletching more arrows."

"Until their fingers bleed, my dear."

Yandumar looked around the room. Satisfied, for the moment, with their preparations. "Ready or not, we assault at first light. We won't have time to meet like this again, so use your casters to send and receive messages. Let's get working."

They all voiced their assent and began shuffling out of the tent to their respective tasks. He closed his eyes once more. *God, please don't let me be forgetting anything.* The sound of shuffling feet ceased, and Yandumar sighed, turning towards his side of the tent, intending to retrieve the detailed map of Mecrithos. Tonight, there would be no sleep.

He opened his eyes, stopping short. Orbrahn and Paen waited silently.

"We need to talk," Orbrahn said.

Yandumar growled. "I don't wanna hear it. Not now."

"It's about your son," Paen said.

"Mevon? Where's he got to? There are all kinds of people I want him to meet. Distant cousins and such."

Paen and Orbrahn shared a look, and Yandumar felt a chill go up his spine.

"What is it? What's wrong?"

Orbrahn stepped forward. "Jasside is dead. Mevon had been getting close to her, and, well, he didn't take her death very well." He craned his neck towards Paen. "Show him."

Paen pressed his hand forward, a letter held within. "Yandumar" was written on the front. There was no seal.

Paen must have noted his frown. "Yes, we read it. He *left* us, Yandumar, in the middle of the night with no notice. I had to find out why."

Yandumar snatched up the paper and unfolded it. It read:

Father,

> *Know, first, that I will never regret the decision to join you. However, I now find myself at a crossroads, and am uncertain which path to take. I will continue to aid the revolution if I am able, and will contact you again once I have determined where my steps will lead.*
>
> *Keep yourself safe. I am glad to have known you, and I am proud to be called your son.*
>
> *—Mevon*

Yandumar read it again, uncomprehending, then folded it up and tucked it away.

"Look," Orbrahn said. "We need to—"

"Get out," Yandumar said, low, firm.

"But sh—"

"OUT!"

Never having witnessed his temper unleashed before, the two scrambled backwards, practically racing each other out of the tent.

Yandumar fell to his knees. *It was all for you. Everything I've done—every drop of blood, every vow, every deal with every devil—all to find you and bring you peace. Somewhere, I lost sight of that . . . and now I am lost.*

He bowed his head, closing his eyes. *God, please watch over my son, wherever he is, and guide his steps. Bring him back to me. Please . . . bring him home.*

THE STADIUM LAY quiet and empty, dark under the blanket of night, but the stench of death lingered. Mevon sat, hidden beneath his cloak, on the balustrade encircling the upper levels of the Ropes, feet dangling over the edge, looking down into the pit of tar swelled by the rotting corpses of its victims. He found no joy it in, only a sickening sorrow, and anger burning like the sun.

Getting into the city had been easy enough. Mevon used the contact information provided by Paen and met a man within the sprawl of ramshackle buildings outside the westernmost gate of Mecrithos. After providing the right passwords, he'd found himself tucked into a wagon beneath several layers of wine crates. Floods of the empire's citizens crowded through every gate, fearing the clash to come, and guards did not have enough time to perform more than cursory inspections.

Once inside the city, he'd come straight to the Ropes. He'd already made the decision to act—the atrocities committed here only served to fuel his fury—but he did have one more thing left to decide.

Mevon looked south over the lower tiers of the city. At the base of the slope rested the wall.

He looked north. Displays of wealth increased as his eyes trailed up the mountainside. At the city's crown sat the Imperial palace.

Should I aid the revolution by helping secure a foothold in the city? Or, cut straight to the heart of this empire's corruption?

Mevon looked south to north, back, and back again, frozen by indecision. Soon the sun would be up, and based on talk he had overheard from the guards, it looked like the end would begin with the dawn. He doubted he would have the strength for both tasks. He needed to decide soon.

"Mind if I join you?"

A lesser man would have jumped out of his skin. Mevon merely tensed, gripping the hilts of his daggers and jerking his head towards the voice. Beside him on the balustrade, twenty paces distant and unmoving, a figure stood. A black cloak covered his body, hood hiding its wearer's features. His hands were visible, palms forward—a gesture indicating that he did not wish to appear threatening. Mevon could tell nothing else of him but that he had a shorter than average height and a softly coiled stance.

Mevon felt a chill as he realized he hadn't seen or

heard the man approach. He himself had to scale a five-pace-high wall to ascend to his vantage. One couldn't simply stroll up.

Unless someone was very, very good at remaining silent and invisible.

Adjudicator.

Mevon relaxed halfway. If he was truly an Imperial assassin, then Mevon had little to fear. He knew the type—too reliant upon sorcery to be any serious threat to him.

"By all means." Mevon gestured to a spot of stone not too far away.

"Thank you." The man sat down roughly where Mevon had indicated, keeping his hands in sight. "Tonight is not a night to be alone, I think."

Mevon decided to play along. "Perhaps not. But I needed a place to clear my head. To think."

"I can see why you picked this place, then. I myself used to come here often, for much the same reasons."

Mevon nodded. A moment of silence stretched between them that might have been awkward had he not felt so disinclined to speak. At last, however, curiosity drove him to probe.

"So what brings you here now?"

"Fate," the other said. "But one of my own choosing. Which, I suppose, isn't really fate at all."

"No."

"Call it . . . the end of a road, then. A long road. Made longer by each deliberate and often painful step along the way." The man turned towards Mevon. "I'm sure you can relate."

"Yes," Mevon said, fascinated. "Someone can claim to hold your leash all they want. But as long as we are free to choose according to our beliefs, then the path we walk is our own."

"Well put," said the other. "And what path have you chosen?"

Mevon didn't have to think long. It could only have ever been one thing. "Justice," he said. "You?"

"Redemption." The man sighed. "It turned out more difficult than I thought it would be at first."

"How so?"

"Redemption for yourself is trying enough. But if you seek it for others? If the people you are trying to save are the very ones standing in your way?"

"Ah. Much like trying to impose justice on those who have declared themselves above the law and have the power to stay up there."

"Indeed." The man leaned back on his elbows, exhaling loudly. Mevon looked south. Then north. Back, and back again.

"I sense," the other said, "that you are struggling with a decision?"

Mevon frowned. "Yes."

"I understand, I think. Obligations pull you in too many directions at once, and you find yourself in the middle, grasping at threads, and more often than not, failing them all."

"Exactly." Mevon sighed. "Right now I have two responsibilities. One, to protect those I call friend and ally. The other, to cut out a source of corruption that plagues more than I could ever know. Alone, I will not have the strength to finish both tasks."

"What if you weren't alone?"

Mevon paused, considering. "What do you mean?"

"I believe our goals may not be all that dissimilar, Mevon. Why not help each other?"

"Perhaps. But first, we have a problem."

"What's that?"

"I never told you my name."

Silence. Mevon couldn't even hear the man breathing. Then, his guest released a terse burst of laughter. "Right you are. I'm not quite as sharp as I once was, it seems."

"If you ever were."

"Oh, I had an edge to me once that cut most anyone that came near. But it came with a price. I thought I would have to pay that price again recently. Luckily, someone I love saved me from that fate."

"An edge would help right about now."

"It would. But I think, even dull as I am, what I bring will be enough. So long as we work together."

Mevon stewed. "Convince me."

"I notice you looking from the wall to the palace. I assume your responsibilities rely in those two places?"

How the abyss could he tell where my eyes were looking? Mevon nodded.

"I, too, have obligations to . . . take care of . . . at both locations."

"What obligations?"

"On the wall are people who stand in the way of the redemption I seek. You see, I made them. Trained them.

Quite literally wrote the book that they now follow. And they use the power I gave them for the wrong reasons."

"And you seek to put an end to that perversion?"

"Yes."

"Who are they?"

"Adjudicators."

"Ah," Mevon said. "Then maybe you're right. Maybe our goals do coincide." He paused. "What about at the palace?"

"As to that . . . let's just say I have a feeling I will be needed there."

"What's that supposed to mean?"

"Just that some players still have choices left to be made. Based on those decisions, my purpose will likely change."

Mevon didn't think it much of an answer, but he didn't feel like pressing the issue either. "Very well."

"And your responsibility in the palace?"

"The primary target of my justice. And those that guard him. Those I feel compelled to deal with myself. My . . . peers." Mevon grunted. "I once wanted to become one of them. It seems like forever ago, now."

"It's funny, isn't it, how that which once seemed like the most important thing in the world can become so hollow once our priorities change."

"No," Mevon said. "Not funny at all."

"I know."

Silence descended, and they sat without speaking or moving for several marks. Mevon watched the eastern sky change from black to midnight blue. Time was running out. Without making any sudden movements, he stood.

"I have one request," said Mevon.

The man stood as well. "Name it."

Mevon smiled. "Try to keep up."

He threw off his cloak. In one swift motion, he reached behind him, grasped the two halves of his *Andun*, and pushed the pieces back together with a click.

The man hesitated only a moment before ripping off his own cloak, revealing blackened chain mail and bands of leather holding sheaths filled with daggers and throwing knives. Even in the gloom, Mevon could make out the pale, boyish face with lightless scales around its edges. Recognition bolstered the knowledge he already possessed.

"Come, Draevenus. We've some cleansing to do."

THE STAR WAS all that he saw now. The void beyond might as well have ceased to exist, for all that Voren could discern it. No, the star filled all his senses from the moment he stepped into communion.

All he could tell was that Gilshamed was close. Very close. And that he had not moved much in the past few days. He had begged Rekaj to begin searching the city but was refused. The emperor had not wanted to spook their prey into fleeing.

Voren knew that, when the time came, the trap would shut swiftly, and any options he might have had would expire. And that there would be no time for words.

This would be the only chance Voren had to say his peace. His only chance to defend his choices. And, maybe—if Elos answered even one of his prayers—to extinguish the fires of rage that had been burning against him for so long. He only hoped his old friend was of a mind to listen.

Never was his greatest strength.

Voren formed a body, took a deep "breath," and brushed his consciousness against the star. Such as he could, he pulled back and waited.

Almost immediately, the star began collapsing. Smaller and smaller it became, until shrinking to a point and vanishing without a sound. A few more beats, and a golden figure straight out of legend stood before him.

"Hello, Voren. It has been awhile."

Voren gave his most gracious bow. "Councilor Gilshamed, greetings."

He straightened, noting the look of fury upon Gilshamed's face.

"After all this time . . . after what you did . . . you dare to make your first words to me a mockery?"

Voren sighed. *So that's how this is to be.* "No mockery was intended, I assure you."

"Forgive me if your assurances bring no peace to my mind."

Voren reined in his anger. Loosing it would do no good and would only hinder his chance to . . .

Chance to do what? He still did not know what he hoped to accomplish. But arguing, surely, was the least productive way to get anywhere.

"Please," Voren said. "I did not want our reunion to be like this. I seek not a quarrel with you."

"You do not get to dictate terms, Voren. You lost that right when you led our kin on that foolish, dangerous expedition against my explicit instructions."

"I was young."

"You still are if you think hiding behind pitiful excuses will do you any good." It burned, how closely his words echoed Kael's.

"We were . . ." Voren paused, shaking his head. "It does not matter now, does it? We cannot change the decisions we made in the past, only strive to live as best as we can with their consequences."

"I *am* your consequence. One you have escaped for far too long."

"Is my death really so important to you that you would start a revolution, a conflict claiming tens, if not hundreds of thousands of lives already, just to see it done?"

Gilshamed appeared to soften slightly. "The revolution was not for me. It was for the people of this land, to help them escape the yoke of oppression laid upon them by the mierothi. Even you should be able to see the need for that. Or have you truly become the emperor's tool?"

"No. I just thought . . ." *I just thought to join you, once. But you made it clear that such a path was closed to me.* "I just thought it all seemed too convenient, that you were using it solely to further your own goals."

Gilshamed frowned. "Perhaps I was, for a time. Perhaps I still am." He chuckled, a sound holding no mirth. "Our kind have a tendency to do that."

"What? Use people?"

Gilshamed nodded. "Without hesitation. Without regard for the consequences they will suffer."

"I know. It is the greatest fault of both our people and the mierothi. It makes you wonder. Perhaps sentient beings were never meant to live as long as we do."

"Perhaps you are right." Gilshamed shook, as if remembering something. "But if there is one thing I have learned, it's that people will not allow themselves to be used forever. Eventually, they will figure it out, and either turn on their manipulators, or—in extraordinary circumstances—actually take ownership of their actions . . . and accomplish wonders."

Is that how you justify all you have done? Voren did now know whether to be awed or disgusted by that. Then, he did know. His stomach turned as he took stock of his own actions and realized he was no better. *We have more in common than you might believe, old friend.*

"I was going to stay," Gilshamed continued, "after this war was won. Stay and guide the people to a bright new future. I was going to reclaim this continent for the valynkar and end our long exile from this land."

"Do any, besides you, even still hold to such a dream?" Gilshamed eyed him sideways.

Yes, Gilshamed, I have been away that long.

"No," said the golden-haired man. "I alone carry the torch of such a hope. Carried."

"What changed your mind?"

"A good friend, the best man I have ever known. And an arrogant young bastard. Hearing the truth from either of them would not have been enough. But from both? Somehow, it became supplanted in my mind, and now I cannot ignore it if I wanted to."

This did not sound like the Gilshamed he knew. Voren never would have put it to him to give up on something he had truly set his mind to. And to do so for apparently selfless reasons? Whatever else had happened, the man had been changed by his experiences among the people of this continent. Changed for the better.

But is it enough?

Voren swallowed hard. There would be no better time than now to ask.

"What do you plan to do with me?"

Gilshamed's lips pressed together into a sad smile. Voren's heart broke. "This has been a nice chat, Voren, but there was never any question about your fate. The only question was *when*. And by aiding the mierothi in tracking me down, that timeline quickly shrank to nothing."

"There is nothing I can say to dissuade you?"

"Nothing," said Gilshamed, his voice cutting like a razor. "You took her from me . . . my Lashriel. You stole her loyalty . . . her heart . . . and finally, her life."

Voren closed his eyes. He did not know where to begin explaining just how wrong Gilshamed was. *Her loyalty was always to you, but she just needed a chance to escape, for a time, from the shadow of your legacy. Her heart—oh, how I wished she had given it to me, but she did not. Not even a little bit. Not even for a moment. And her life . . . ?*

He opened his eyes, but Gilshamed was already fading.

"When next we meet," the ethereal figure said, "there will be no words. Only reckoning."

With that, Gilshamed vanished.

Voren knew, now, that only one path remained for him to take.

JASSIDE SHUFFLED UP the dirt- and rock-strewn hillside, pausing at the crest as the camp first came into view. It had not been hard to find. They'd been able to steer towards it all night by the glow from ten thousand fires reflected off the clouds.

She looked down on Vashodia as the mierothi came up next to her. "You sure you want to come with me?"

Vashodia flashed a twisted grin—a smirk to show her amusement with all the lesser beings. She wore it ceaselessly. "I wouldn't miss it for the world."

"But our casters are constantly in communion, sending messages. If they haven't already, one is sure to notice someone as powerful as you approaching."

Vashodia waved dismissively. "I began dampening my signal days ago. It won't be a problem."

"Dampening?"

Vashodia sighed. "A lesson for another time, perhaps. For now, I think we should hurry along our way."

"But—"

Vashodia shot her a cold, dead look, and Jasside clamped her jaw shut. "I told you it was good to ask questions. It is. But not when I have made myself perfectly clear. Understood?"

Jasside nodded.

"Good. Now, shall we?"

Jasside—followed by a short mierothi in dark robes, and two Hardohl wearing the plain clothes of peasants and carrying heavy packs—led the way down into the war camp of the revolution. They were stopped three times. First, by the outer sentries, then by the perimeter pickets. Jasside supplied the proper passwords, and they were let by with little more than curious glances for a group bringing a child into what would soon become a battlefield. The third time, a woman stopped in her tracks as they approached her, eyes widening.

"Jasside?" called the woman in disbelief. "Is that you?"

Jasside smiled at her. "Yes, Calla, it is me."

"How are you still alive? I saw you fall."

"Clever application of sorc—" She stopped, glancing at Vashodia briefly. Her new mistress forbade the use of words such as "magic" and "sorcery," considering them superstitious nonsense. Instead, she continued with, "my energies. And a good bit of luck."

"Incredible," Calla said. "Oh, you've missed so much, I don't even know where to start."

"I'd love to catch up, but there's no time. Can you take me to the command tents?"

Calla ran a narrow sweep of her eyes over Vashodia and the two Hardohl before nodding and waving them all forward. "This way."

They walked along, barely able to stay out of the way of all the preparations under way. As far as she could tell, not a soul had gotten a wink of sleep. Jasside asked Calla, "Are we attacking today?"

"At dawn," Calla said. "Scouts have ranged in every direction and report Imperial reinforcements closing in. Yandumar wanted to take the walls before they arrived."

Jasside nodded absently, muttering something about a good plan. *We're lucky to have arrived now. Not a moment too soon, by the looks of it.*

She spotted Vashodia's swinging arms out of the corner of her eye. *No. Not luck. When it comes to her, I don't think anything is ever left to chance.*

They continued wending their way through the camp, which was far more vast than Jasside remembered, until Calla brought them up short with an outstretched arm.

"There," said Calla, pointing. Jasside saw the familiar tents a few hundred paces away. "I've got to go. You take care of yourself today, all right?"

"I will," Jasside said.

They parted ways, and their little group soon came to stand outside the entrance to the tent. No less than threescore soldiers stood guard nearby, several physically blocking the flap. This close to Mecrithos, Jasside could understand the need to guard against assassins.

She cleared her throat, making eye contact with the only guard that would return her gaze. "I need to speak with one of our leaders. Mevon is preferred if he is in, but Gilshamed or Yandumar will do as well. Tell them Jasside Anglasco is here."

The soldier gave her a quizzical look. "You haven't heard, I take it?"

Jasside's heart skipped a beat. "Heard what?"

"You find out soon, I suspect." The man sighed, jerking a thumb towards the tent. "Yandumar is busy. All the commanders just went inside for a meeting. It'll probably take awhile. You're welcome to w—"

The flap burst open and a flood of grumbling men and women poured out in a rush. Before the last had even broken the threshold, a voice barked out from inside. "Send her in!"

The soldier's jaw hung towards his chest. He motioned Jasside inside without a word.

"Stay here," Vashodia ordered, turned just slightly towards the Hardohl. The two took places next to the guards, facing out.

Jasside swallowed hard. Together, she and Vashodia marched into the tent.

An argument, low and strained, was ongoing in one of the side chambers. Left. Yandumar's room. Jasside headed towards the voices.

"You sure?" Yandumar. "Why hasn't anyone else noticed?"

"She's a clever girl, that's why." That oily voice could only be Paen.

"I'm telling you, I never forget someone's particular aura once I've communed with them." Few besides Orbrahn could stuff quite so much arrogance into one sentence.

"Yeah, but—"

Yandumar clamped his jaw shut as Jasside stepped through the cloth tunnel into the room.

Orbrahn waved a hand towards her. "Like I said."

Jasside opened her mouth to offer greetings, but stopped. None of the three men were paying the slightest attention to her. She craned her neck down and to the side, forgetting how to breathe as her gaze fell upon the top of Vashodia's head.

Her hood was already down.

"My boys," Vashodia said. "I am so very pleased to see you all."

Jasside could not look away from the mierothi. *You know them? They know you? Scorch me, what is going on?*

Her confusion only deepened as Paen dashed over and scooped up Vashodia into a close embrace. Their lips met, each opening and twisting against the other. Soft moans emanated from both their throats.

After a few long beats, Vashodia pushed away. "Enough for now, you naughty boy." He put her down, giving her a knowing, longing gaze as he stepped back.

Vashodia set her sights on Orbrahn. "Been enjoying your enhanced capacity?"

Orbrahn smirked, nodding. "Put it to good use, too."

"By which you mean, 'killing mierothi' I assume?"

Orbrahn shrugged, still smiling.

"You've done well, keeping me informed," said Vashodia. She turned to Paen. "And you, my love, your efforts have proven most useful."

"Always happy to be of service," Paen said.

"And how is your father?"

"Abyss if I know. No doubt he's throwing a fit over how many of our family's resources I've commandeered for your little civil war."

Jasside's thoughts whirled, unable to comprehend. *Civil war? I thought this was a revolution?*

Vashodia's face lit up. "Can I be there when you tell him? I do so love to watch grown men stammer."

Paen bowed. "Do I ever say 'no' to you?"

Vashodia giggled in delight.

Jasside looked at Yandumar. He'd been silent, still, the only sign of life a slow grinding of his lower jaw and his knuckles going white over the hilts of a mace and axe suspended at his waist. Now, as the diminutive mierothi ceased her laughter, he opened his mouth for the first time.

"I know why you're here."

"Oh?" Vashodia raised an eyebrow.

"There's only two reasons you would come. Either we're about to fail you, or we already have."

Vashodia shook her head. "Oh, Yandumar. My dear, sweet, misguided warrior. I always meant to enter the game myself at some point. I am, after all, my very own ace in the hole. But I knew that playing my hand too early would alert our enemies to the real stakes of this conflict."

"Don't talk to me about stakes. I've already lost Gilshamed, and . . . and Mevon." Yandumar lowered his head.

Jasside felt tears forming, a twisting clench in her chest. *No . . . not Mevon. Please. . .*

"I did the best I could," Yandumar said. "But I lost focus. Lost sight of the people that were most important to me . . . all because of my vow to *you*."

"When we came to you thirty years ago, the very night you learned about the murder of your wife and children, and the kidnapping of your newborn, we gave you a choice. Are you really going to tell me you'd make a different one?"

"No. But, scorch me, I wish I didn't have to owe anything to you."

A smile slowly crept across Vashodia's face. "Yandumar, I am pleased with all that you have done. I consider our bargain . . . fulfilled."

Yandumar's eyes widened.

Vashodia continued. "So I ask you: What will you do now?"

Yandumar exhaled loudly, slowly, then sucked in a deep breath. Held it. Closed his eyes.

"Ha, HA!"

Jasside could almost see the weight of his burdens sliding off of him. His back seemed straighter, muscles more relaxed, and his lips curled up seemingly without effort or thought.

"I'm gonna lead these people into battle," Yandumar said. "And do my best not to get them all killed."

"A wise plan," Vashodia said.

Yandumar chuckled again. "How 'bout a new deal then?"

Vashodia made a sound like *tsk tsk*. "Just beats from

completing one vow, and now you seek to bind yourself to another? I can't wait to hear it."

"Help us out. Lend us the full measure of your power for the fight to come."

"And in return?"

"I don't hunt you down when this is all over."

Vashodia giggled. "Stronger men than you have tried."

"But more dedicated? More persistent?"

She looked at the ceiling, as if contemplating his remarks. "Offer accepted, on one condition."

"What?"

"You keep news of my involvement strictly confidential, especially from those bandit friends of yours."

Yandumar frowned. "Why shouldn't they know?"

"Let's just say I have a rather unpleasant history with them."

Yandumar hissed in his next breath. "I almost forgot that was you."

"Afraid so. On the bright side, that particular experiment yielded fantastic results."

Jasside couldn't hold it in anymore. "What happened to Mevon?" she said all at once.

All eyes in the room turned on her, seeming to notice her presence for the first time. She had the feeling life would often be like this if she continued on as Vashodia's apprentice.

"He left," Orbrahn said.

"Left? You mean he's not dead?"

"Of course not," Yandumar said. "If I've learned anything about that son of mine, it's that he's one tough nut to crack." He sighed. "I do wish I'd heard from him, though."

"Your boy is fine," said Vashodia. "I sent my brother to help him. They are beginning their work even as we speak."

Jasside felt the twisting inside her subside. "That was kind of you."

"Kind? I just put two of this planet's best killers together and sent them into extreme danger. I intend to use their actions as a catalyst for all that is to come. No, my dear, kind has nothing to do with it."

Jasside, somehow, felt as if their statures were reversed. She nodded, trying to hide her blush.

"About Gilshamed," said Yandumar. "I gotta apologize on his behalf. It was my responsibility to keep him in line, and when we split forces, I failed him. Failed us."

"Fret not," Vashodia said. "He has fulfilled his purpose as I have intended so far, and even now may still prove useful."

"Useful? I thought he ran away?"

"He tried. Another player in this game—the wild card, if you will—stepped in to prevent that."

Yandumar began rubbing his temples. Jasside felt as if her own head were about to explode.

"I don't—" began Yandumar, but was cut off by a sharp gesture from Vashodia.

"Focus on your task, Yandumar. Let me worry about the big picture."

"Aye," he said, clearly relieved

"Good. Now, I believe I offered you my aid in the forthcoming battle. How about we discuss strategy? Paen, be a dear and get us some wine. Your father's best, of course."

Chapter 17

MEVON KICKED IN the door, stepping back as Draevenus shadow-dashed through. The sounds of death hit him before he even took his next breath. The scent of blood. Mevon smiled. He stepped through the portal, unleashing the storm.

The top layer of the wall came into view, murky in the glow of predawn. Ballistae crews were staging their enormous projectiles, and linked trios of daeloth stood on the raised lip of the wall, looking out towards the field where the revolution's camp stretched to the horizon. Three hundred paces distant, a stone bridge crossed over the central gate of Mecrithos.

It was here that the revolution would strike. And here where the mierothi had gathered the greatest of their strength.

Mevon saw them. Half again a score of sleeping pallets lined the rear wall, and upon each, a resting mierothi.

Most still asleep. Those few that weren't seemed not far removed from it, and slow to respond to the eruption of violence.

Mevon, with Justice at the ready, sprinted towards them.

His first victim never woke from her slumber, her head rolling as he slashed downward through her neck. His blades rotated around, the other dealing an identical blow to the next mierothi in line.

Step.

He cut upward, taking off the front half of a man's face as he sat up.

Step.

Side slash, bisecting two standing males at the navel.

Step.

Thrust, impaling one through the chest as his heel crushed in a sleeping skull.

Step.

He lost himself in the glory of death, moving with a speed that none of the groggy mierothi could hope to match, and reveling in the beautiful symphony of blood sung by his blades. A few managed spells against him, but he moved like a wraith in the gloom, and none recognized him for Hardohl. And if any did, none seemed able to utilize any other methods against him.

Do none of you know the spell to disable my kind? The thought gave him hope even as he vanquished the last in line, that the emperor might be just as ignorant.

He turned, just in time to witness Draevenus throw two daggers. The spinning steel struck the stone beneath two groups of daeloth and exploded. The wall collapsed, tumbling down, taking six daeloth with it. Their screams ended abruptly three beats later.

Mevon glanced across the rooftop behind them. Bodies lay strewn about, but nothing moved. His admiration for his newest ally grew.

Draevenus dashed, landing next to him. The mierothi viewed Mevon's handiwork, then nodded respectfully. "Good work. But the other side is alerted to our presence. Strategy?"

"Stay hidden," Mevon said. "I'll engage and draw their attention. Join the fray when it appears to be most advantageous."

Draevenus smiled. "I like the way you think."

Mevon returned the smile. "Go."

Draevenus waved towards himself and nearly disappeared. A living shadow, crouched low, moved away at speed that even Mevon could appreciate.

He turned towards the bridge. A wall of soldiers stood upon it.

Mevon ran straight towards them.

Fondly, he recalled all the practice sessions he had conducted with his Fist. Him against them. They'd shot countless crossbow bolts at him as he assaulted their position, ran across their line, retreated—every angle possible. They had become masters of shooting at moving targets, and Mevon, through much pain, had become a master of dodging those shots.

The soldiers now arrayed before him, at a voiced command, squeezed their fingers on the triggers of their crossbows. Mevon watched the twitch of their muscles and knew which would pull their shots, which blinked, which were trying to aim but couldn't draw a bead on him. In the end, only three projectiles out of dozens were in any position to do him harm.

Mevon ducked, throwing himself forward into a tumble, and the streaking bolts passed by without injury.

He righted himself and shouldered his way through their line. He didn't bother killing them. He had more important targets to deal with.

Mevon stomped down the opposite side of the bridge without slowing.

The mierothi, this time, were ready for him.

Ten stood in a line, facing Mevon with hatred in their eyes. Twice that many stood behind this first group, faces blank, shoulders drooping. He felt the tingling of the sorcery coming off the first line and saw scores of stone blocks, each the size of Mevon's torso, ripped from the very wall and floating in the air.

With a gesture from the mierothi, the blocks began hurtling towards Mevon.

He ducked, dove, and dodged, avoiding direct blows but unable to prevent the dull thuds of pain as several glanced off his body. He heard screams behind him as the soldiers on the bridge took the worst of it.

He tried to keep all the stones in sight, but he had to spin more often than not to avoid them. Before he could close even half the distance, one struck his hip with more momentum than he could absorb. Mevon went down in a heap.

In beats, half a dozen more struck his body. He felt himself being crushed as they pounded into him again and again.

Darkness closed in around the edges of his vision. Breath became a dream.

He saw a shadow move across the backside of the front mierothi line. Each fell as the shadow passed. And as they fell, the blocks they commanded became inanimate once more. All ten were down within the span of three heartbeats.

Mevon burned. The fire of his blessings worked to undo all the damage he had just sustained. It was half a mark before he could even breathe, and several more before he could stand.

He blinked, righting himself, and shook off the pain. *Draevenus . . . the other score mierothi!*

Mevon jumped to his feet, scooping up his *Andun*. What he saw made no sense.

Draevenus stood before his kin, head hanging. No one moved.

"What's going on?" Mevon asked.

Draevenus turned, holding out a hand as if to stop Mevon from coming any closer. "These . . . aren't our enemy."

"What do you mean? Do they not stand with the emperor?"

"Not by choice." Draevenus's shoulders slumped. "There must have been some on the other side as well. If I had known . . ."

"You didn't. And neither did I. Who are they?"

"Rekaj calls them the Enlightened. They are . . . simpletons. Their power is drained from them in a process akin to rape, all to empower your kind's blessings."

Mevon hissed in a breath. "Are you telling me they are not responsible for their own actions?"

Draevenus nodded.

"Then I declare them innocent." Mevon replaced his weapon onto his back. "My justice is not for them."

Draevenus smiled grimly, then turned. A group of soldiers and daeloth from the far side were edging closer. They seemed hesitant, however.

"My kin require care and escort," Draevenus called. "Which of you is willing to volunteer?"

The men froze. They looked at each other in confusion. Finally, a voice called, "What's going on, honored one?"

"Change," said Draevenus. "Keep up or be swept away." He accented this with a jerking wave of his hand. "Now, I'll ask again, but do not test my patience. Who will help these people to safety?"

A large group of the soldiers, wide-eyed, dashed forward. Mevon saw the looks of the daeloth. Felt them begin to energize as they stared at the backs of those men that had come forward.

Mevon lunged into their midst, spinning. Daeloth blood flew from the ends of his blades. None had gotten off a single casting.

The soldiers turned, fear evident on their features. Mevon cradled his weapon in one arm. "I do not suggest you make of me an enemy," he said.

A hundred weapons slammed back into their sheaths at once. Mevon nodded, relaxing his stance. Men moved to begin helping the mierothi to their feet as Draevenus walked over to him.

"Our work here is done," Mevon said.

Draevenus sighed. "So it seems."

"You're not satisfied?"

"No. I came here for one reason, and that goal remains unfulfilled."

"The adjudicators. If they're not here, then ..."

"Exactly."

Together, they looked out towards the field beyond the city walls.

JASSIDE HELD OPEN the tent flap and stared out at the eastern horizon, willing the sun to rise. The butterflies in her stomach were, to her surprise, as much from anticipation as from fear. This day would be hard—a test like no other—but with Vashodia involved, she had faith it would all turn out all right.

Someone gasped behind her. Jasside turned just in time to see Calla fall limp to the ground.

She dashed over, kneeling down and shaking the woman's shoulders. "Calla?" Jasside said. "Calla, what is it? What's wrong?"

Orbrahn and Yandumar drew close and hovered, concern writ on their faces. It took half a mark more of gentle prodding before Calla's eyes finally fluttered open. Tears formed in them, spilling down.

"What happened?" Yandumar asked.

Calla sniffled. "I was getting a commune report from Piran when . . . when . . ." She squeezed her eyes shut once more. "I think he's dead."

"Piran," said Yandumar. "Who was he assigned to?"

"Commander Bellanis," Orbrahn said.

Jasside looked up at the two men, and the three of them shared a silent moment of dread. Piran had been just a boy. They'd assigned all the youngest casters to the commanders, hoping it would keep them relatively safe in the coming battle.

They'd expected some sort of attack, but none of them had the foresight to see this coming.

"Give me a beat," said Orbrahn. "I'll check on the others."

Jasside felt a tiny pulse of energy as Orbrahn closed his eyes and entered communion. He returned a moment later. Slowly, he shook his head.

"Three others are missing, all assigned to commanders. I think we can assume the worst."

Yandumar turned to the table and pounded it with a fist. "Get the word out. Assassins in the camp, targeting our commanders and their casters. Tell everyone left to sound the alert and stay alive!"

Orbrahn nodded. Jasside helped Calla to her feet. While the two other casters returned to communion, Yandumar leaned in towards Jasside, lowering his voice.

"Jasside?"

"Yes?"

"See what you can do."

Jasside heard the unspoken plural in the "you" of his request. She dipped her head and turned away. A few steps led her into the chamber of the tent once occupied by Gilshamed. It had a new tenant now.

"I heard," Vashodia said as Jasside stepped in. She was seated cross-legged in the middle of the room, which was entirely empty. "Tell Yandumar that we will take care of the issue."

Jasside slipped back through the narrow cloth passage. "I'll handle it," she announced.

"You sure?" Yandumar said. "Just the t—just you?"

Jasside straightened her back, lifting her chin slightly. "Of course."

Yandumar sighed, then waved her away.

She returned to the side chamber. "What do you need me to do?"

"Be my eyes," said Vashodia.

"How?"

"Enter communion, then immediately return."

Jasside nodded. She energized, then conjured a black disc in her mind, turned it, expanded it until it filled the whole of her senses. Then, she stepped through. The white void appeared, occupied by hundreds of black stars, some larger than others. Much larger. And far too close for comfort.

Remembering her instructions, she exited communion, blinking in the dim light of the tent.

"Again," Vashodia said.

Jasside did so. It came with ease this time, and she sped in and out without pausing.

"Again. Faster, girl."

The black disc snapped into her mind. She was through and back in less than a beat.

"Too slow. Again!"

Again. And again. And again. Each taking less time than the one before. She had an idea what Vashodia had in mind now, and she learned quickly. She flashed in and out of communion half a dozen times per beat.

"Good," came Vashodia's ethereal voice. Jasside was not both in and out of communion at the same time—such was impossible—but she might as well have been. Images of the void and of reality superimposed themselves onto her vision. "Now, how are you with illusions?"

"Passing," Jasside said, her own voice strangely distant, hollow.

"Can you conjure an image of what you see in communion?"

Still flashing in and out, her mind strained as, in answer, she pulled in more energy and cast a spell of simple darkness. For each dark star she saw in the void, she created an identical image inside the tent. It stretched the limits of her control and concentration, but eventually the two sets aligned, until she saw the same thing— including location and relative sizes of each caster's soul—in both worlds at once.

"Excellent," Vashodia said. "Now, all I need is . . . perspective." A pause, then. "Hold on and don't stop what you're doing."

Jasside didn't even have time to answer before she

felt herself rising. Power rolled off Vashodia, energies directed to change the very ground beneath their feet, lifting it as layer upon layer in quick succession formed, each pushing the rest farther towards the sky. Another wave parted the roof of the tent, and they ascended into the glowing predawn air.

She sucked in a breath and looked down upon the sprawling army of the revolution. Here, standing on a pillar of stone a hundred paces high, she could see it all.

Vashodia pulled in power. And kept pulling. More and more, until Jasside was sure the small form would simply burst from holding so much at once. She'd held more herself, at the battle of Thorull, but then she had been linked with forty others. Vashodia, by herself, now met that strength.

Then, she summoned more.

There was a strange buzzing, and Jasside had a familiar sensation, as if someone were harmonizing nearby. She kept up her task, jumping in and out of communion and maintaining an illusionary image of what she saw—nudging the small bubbles of darkness to align with the new positions of the stars. A small part of her began to worry that the two of them wouldn't be enough.

Then it didn't matter. She witnessed Vashodia unleash—as promised—the full measure of her strength.

Eight orbs shot out from their position. They each traveled towards the largest stars, clusters of five that, by their size, could only be other mierothi. Jasside peered closer at the spells. No—not spells. Manifestations of will, empowered by the body's symbiotic energy manipu lators. Their design was genius. The outer shell concealed the rest, and what was held within . . .

They struck. Energy exploded forth from the shells, but with extreme discrimination, honing in on forty mierothi bodies. In the blink of an eye, they were reduced to less than ash. None were able to defend against it, yet not a single nearby soldier was harmed in the slightest by the blast.

"So sorry, dear brother," Vashodia said. "Looks like you won't have the privilege of crossing Jezrid off your list yourself."

Jasside ceased her bouncing and dissolved the conjured illusion. She felt the stone beneath them compressing, changing layer by layer, as they descended. In beats, they were back inside the tent. The roof returned to its original form, cutting out the sky just as dawn's first rays flashed down upon them.

She took a breath, reveling in what she had just witnessed. "That was . . . spectacular."

Vashodia smiled. "You'll be capable of even greater, soon."

"Me? You're serious?"

"Of course, dear. And together, just think what we could accomplish, hmm?"

Jasside's imagination began running rampant with possibilities. She had to force herself to rein it in, the needs of the moment not allowing her to indulge such fancies. "I'll go tell Yandumar."

She dashed into the central chamber. Smiling, she met Yandumar's worried eyes. "It's taken care of. You're free to begin your assault."

His jaw fell towards the floor. "What? Just like that?" Jasside stared blankly at him.

"Right." Yandumar looked to Orbrahn and Calla. "Give the order. Dawn's come. Time to take those walls."

DRAEVENUS RACED ALONG the alleyways of Mecrithos, Mevon following close behind. The walls on either side were close enough to touch with both hands at once, slick with grease and soot and other things Draevenus did not want to think about. The main streets would have been faster, but less inconspicuous. Besides, they were empty—too empty—as though the entire populace had decided to sleep in today, and Draevenus did not trust things for which he had no explanation.

A scent hit his nose. It was pleasant, especially after so many marks among the refuse of the city, and Draevenus slowed to a halt.

"Wait here," he told Mevon, then dashed through a nearby door. He emerged ten beats later with his prize.

Mevon showed confusion as Draevenus shoved a greasy sausage, a quarter wheel of cheese, a fresh-baked loaf of bread, and a skin of wine at him. "Eat up," Draevenus said. "You'll need it."

"For what?"

"Energy."

Mevon shrugged, but tore off a large section of the loaf and pushed it into his mouth. Draevenus resumed their run, sure that Mevon was following by the sound of his unsubtle footsteps.

"Don't you want any?" Mevon called, his words filtered through a mouth full of half-masticated meat.

"You need it more," said Draevenus over his shoulder. "Your body just had to repair itself from the brink of death. That takes a lot out of your kind."

"And all this will replenish me?"

"Well enough for such short notice."

Mevon fell silent for half a mark, the sounds of his thudding steps and loud chewing all that Draevenus could hear from him. Finally, he said, "You seem to know a lot about Hardohl."

Draevenus shrugged. "My sister did a lot of research."

"Research," Mevon said. "Don't you mean experiments?"

Draevenus cringed. He knew he couldn't lie. Not about this. Mevon had said the last word more like a curse than a question. "Yes. Not that I approved, of course."

"Did one of these experiments yield you the spell for disabling voids?"

"Yes."

Mevon went silent again. Draevenus braced himself for the reaction. He feared that now, after all that had come to pass, it would all fall apart based on this.

"I suppose," said Mevon, "that I should thank you."

Draevenus stumbled as they ran. "What for?"

"A young caster learned the spell by watching your sister. She then used it on me. If she hadn't, I never would have come to know my father, never questioned my place in the world, never done anything meaningful in my life. And . . . I never would have known Jasside."

Jasside? Why does that name sound familiar? He felt as if he had heard the name said, and recently. Someone Vashodia had mentioned maybe?

"I'm glad you see it that way," Draevenus said. "Especially since it would be easy for you to blame us instead."

"Been planning all this awhile, I take it?"

Draevenus turned his head and nodded.

Once decided upon this path, everything he had done had been for those he loved. His mother, his sister, his people. Whatever it took to get the freedom, the solace, and the redemption each so desperately needed. And Draevenus never dreamed that he would ever make it this far down his chosen road.

But there had been casualties along the way that still haunted him.

He glanced over his shoulder at the towering figure stomping effortlessly in his wake.

Mevon's mother and two siblings had been killed, and his father exiled. He had never known his people. He'd grown up as nothing but a tool of Rekaj, used to perfect the will of a power-hungry and paranoid emperor.

Yandumar, at least, had been given a choice—even if he'd had few logical options left to him. Mevon? He'd been a pawn of every side in this conflict from before he was even born. Draevenus was just as guilty as the rest of them.

And even now, we continue to use you. Perhaps the historians are right. Perhaps all this bloodshed will be pointless in the end, no matter if we emerge victorious or not.

"I understand," Mevon said, his words pulling Draevenus out of his reverie. "I think, from the beginning, I had a suspicion that Vashodia might be involved. Even if I never had a definite thought, the whole situation was plagued with coincidences, the kind that could easily be explained by her involvement." He paused, collecting breath. "But, knowing what I know now, I think I still would have made the same choices."

Draevenus wondered. After all they had been through, all the plots and schemes and coercions, could they have accomplished much the same simply by . . . asking? He shook his head, chuckling to himself.

"Something funny?" asked Mevon.

"No," said Draevenus. "Just realizing how right you are." *And you can be sure, Mevon Daere, that if anyone can claim to be free of the leash . . . it is you.*

The alley bent suddenly, ending in a high wall of black stone. Beyond it, the palace grounds.

"I take it," Mevon said, "we won't be entering through the front gate?"

"A thousand darkwatch might not take kindly to such an intrusion." Draevenus smiled. "Besides, I've always preferred of the road less traveled."

He faced the wall, energizing. It had been no random alley path they'd been traversing. It was this spot exactly that he'd been aiming for. And though he wasn't capable of the type of change-sorcery Vashodia employed, he did know a thing or two about covert infiltration.

Layer by aching layer, he scraped off the wall, using infinitesimal amounts of power. A caster would have to be right on the other side of it—and straining their senses—to feel anything. It would take time—time they didn't necessarily have—but he was confident this intrusion would remain undetected, and at the moment, that was more important.

In ten marks, he'd made a hole just large enough for Mevon to duck through. Beyond, nothing could be seen but darkness. Draevenus beckoned to his companion and, in silence, slipped inside.

The air was close, stale, like it had been sitting unused for centuries. Which it had.

"What is this place?" Mevon asked. Draevenus followed his gaze to myriad stalls set apart by stone crumbling to dust, vacant of all signs of what they might have been used for.

"This," Draevenus said, "was the Imperial dungeon."

"Dungeon?"

"We used to send criminals in here to rot to death, slowly losing all sense of what it was to be human, to be alive." *And far too many of them had been sent here by me.* "Once the Ropes were constructed, it was cleaned out and sealed off. Rekaj preferred playing to the crowd.

"I'm still not sure which would be worse . . . but I suppose that's what we're here to change."

They ascended several flights of stairs before coming to an archway. Here, they could see the vague outlines of a doorway, and beyond that a wall of bricks far newer than the others. Draevenus drew to a halt.

"What's on the other side?" said Mevon.

"The end," said Draevenus, "of the need for subtlety."

"Good."

Draevenus energized fully, enhancing his body with temporary blessings. Then he flung a spell at the wall. It shattered, debris flying backwards from the blast as vaporized mortar filled the air. Mevon was through before he could blink. Draevenus followed.

They emerged into a chamber fifty paces by thirty with a high roof. Unlike most rooms in the palace, the walls, floors, and ceiling were of unadorned stone. Weapon racks lined one side, and padded mats another. Bloodstains marred the open center in a thousand different patterns.

Two men, shirtless and sweaty, had been sparring with metal staves on one of the mats. They stopped as he and Mevon entered. Stared. A beat later, they ran out the only door in the room.

"This what you had in mind?" Draevenus asked.

Mevon smiled as ten men flooded into the room but moments later. They bore identical armor and weapons to each other . . . and to Mevon.

The Blade Cabal.

"Yes." Mevon reached for his *Andun*. "Exactly what I had in mind."

TWENTY THOUSAND BOWS snapped in near unison, their arrows arcing down upon the top of a half-klick stretch of the wall. Nothing answered. No shields formed by daeloth to protect the Imperial troops. No return fire from the ballistae.

Yandumar began to sweat. "Report," he ordered.

Calla, marching at his side, was the first to speak.

"Eastern flank advancing under moderate bow fire, but the mobile cover is keeping casualties low."

"Same in the west," Orbrahn said.

Yandumar strained his eyes, looking forward toward the center. Of the enemy, he could see nothing.

He took a breath. *This is not what we expected. I don't like it.* He pulled Orbrahn in close. "Tell the casters to keep defenses ready. We don't know what's waiting for us."

"Aye," he said.

He turned to Jasside. "Any idea what's going on?"

She smiled at him, holding up a finger. She closed her eyes as she walked. Matching pace fifty steps behind, were a man and a woman in peasant clothes, and between them, Vashodia, her features completely obscured by a hooded robe.

Half a mark later, Jasside blinked, meeting his gaze. "A good surprise, for once. We suggest you take advantage of it."

It wasn't the sort of answer he was looking for, but it was good enough. "All units full assault," he commanded. "No hesitating. No disengaging. I want all ladders in place within the mark!"

Orbrahn and Calla bowed their heads, a mock prayer, to deliver the orders. Yandumar wondered how many he had just sent to their deaths.

The center hit first. *Let's see what those Elite have cooked up.*

Eight ladders began rising, the ends lifting into the sky on the side farthest from the wall. Pushed from below and pulled by long ropes, they rose faster than Yandumar believed possible. They were thick, too, the shafts and rungs twice as wide as he expected. And swinging on each outstretched tip, a wooden cage.

The cages crashed down upon the top level of the wall. From the wreckage emerged heavily armored Elite. Yandumar could only make out flashes of sunlight off their helmets and didn't know what they saw, or whom, if anyone, they fought.

He was about to demand another status report when the gates split open.

His breath caught. A wall of armed figures stood on the other side.

Have we been deceived? Is this the trap that will kill us all?

"Got a message for you," reported Orbrahn.

"Out with it."

"Paen says: 'You're welcome.'"

"Huh?"

Orbrahn swung an arm towards the gate.

Yandumar watched as Elite converged on the opening. The figures opposite them did not move, and the Elite came to a halt before them. There appeared to be a conversation ensuing.

"Abyss with this," Yandumar said. He was sick of being so far from the action. He broke into a run. The casters, each yelping in surprise, raced to catch up. The men who had taken to guarding him—a mix of Ragremons and some of the original shepherds—struggled to keep pace as he threaded his way through the middle ranks. In two marks, he had made it to the gate.

"What's going on?" he shouted.

Ropes, Arozir, and Idrus turned at his question.

"'Bout to be a reunion," Ropes said, adding a keening cackle for good measure. "Best not get in the way." He gestured over Yandumar's shoulder.

He turned as Vashodia and her twin guardians stomped up, Jasside and Paen close behind. The two Hardohl stripped off the bulky peasant clothes, revealing the hard, crimson leathers beneath. Simultaneously, they pulled and assembled their *Andun* with a twist.

Yandumar turned back. Those that had been on the inside also began removing their outer garments. Beneath, the camouflaged leathers of rangers, and the dull green armor of Elite. There were nearly half a thousand of them. Vashodia's Hardohl stepped among them and began issuing orders. The Fists, as he now saw them, sprang into formations and began advancing up the main street.

He fixed a glare on Paen. "You couldn't have told me about this *before* we began our assault?"

Paen shrugged. "I did not expect them to be ready so soon. But I gather they met significantly less resistance than we foresaw."

Why is that, I wonder? Could the Imperials be preparing some kind of trap?

"We're off to the palace," Vashodia said, breaking his reverie. She stepped forward, still hooded. "Do be careful, though, Yandumar. You have such a bright future ahead of you."

He glared at the back of her head as she passed, hoping

she tripped and fell flat on her face. Just for once, he'd like proof that Vashodia was, in fact, fallible. But he doubted she had seen herself that way in a long time.

He grabbed Jasside's arm as she came near. "Find him," he said.

"I will."

He released her and looked around. Mevon's captains were gone, leading their men, as he should be doing. He dashed through the gate, sparing a glance for the group marching up the main avenue of Mecrithos, and entered the nearest door leading into the wall. He quickly found the stairs, taking them two at a time, and emerged onto the roof. He took stock of all he could see.

Signs of battle, but not fresh. *No wonder we met no resistance.* Thirty mierothi bodies lay on or near a line of sleeping pallets, their wounds caused by blades he had come to know well. He smiled. Mevon was still alive, still fighting for their cause. Despite her tendency towards blatant honesty, he could never quite bring himself to take Vashodia at her word. Proof he saw himself was much more comforting.

He viewed the battle. Soldiers of the revolution now swarmed over all parts of the wall that he could see. Resistance increased the farther out they went, as though what had taken place here at the center had reverberated outward, like ripples in a pond, and sapped the will to fight from the Imperial defenders.

It was not without cost, though. Flashes of sorcery spewed down from the wall in places. His caster cadre had less to contend with than Yandumar had feared, but still his allies fell. Answering spells silenced these attacks, however, and soon no one who did not belong to him moved in or on the wall.

The surviving Imperials scurried away from the wall like ants, seeking refuge in the city. They made it two blocks.

Hordes of civilians sprang out of every building in sight. They fell upon the fleeing soldiers, and—with cudgels, makeshift weapons, and even bare hands—began ripping them apart.

Yandumar recognized the gesture for what it was. Rekaj had held the city under a yoke of fear for far too long. This was its breaking.

It is a beautiful sight to see.

His guardsmen burst through onto the roof, escorting Orbrahn and Calla. They were out of breath, but Yandumar turned on them before they had a chance to catch it.

"Tell all units to push out," he ordered. "We've got five klicks of wall to cover, and every last finger of it needs to be guarded twice." He looked out at the field. On the horizon, as far east and west as the eye could see, ranks of men began marching into view.

Imperial reinforcements.

"*Taking* the wall," he added, "was the easy part."

GILSHAMED SQUINTED AS the sun peeked over the horizon. A new day dawning, and with it, the end of an age.

But will it also see the birth of the next?

He stepped up onto the railing of his balcony. In a

blaze of light that drowned out even the sun, he unfurled his wings.

Time to find out.

He leapt.

Gilshamed fell free for four beats, letting the wind rush past his face as he plummeted. Letting gravity takes its natural course. Letting himself, for one last moment, let go of all sense of control.

Then he flexed his back, spreading his wings, and swooped up out of his dive. He banked east. With the sun warming his left side, he made a lazy loop around the palace grounds. He spotted the bubble-dome indicating his destination in exactly the spot the girl had indicated. He wondered, briefly, what Voren had done to her to earn her ire but banished the thought. He had more important things on his mind.

Like how he was going to make his entrance.

Directly south of the palace now, he turned sharply to the right. Jagged rocks poked up from beneath him. He energized. A razor wave of power sliced through the base of one boulder, its twisted form reminding him of two oxen mating. With his will, he picked it up, propelling it ahead of him as he flew in a line at the glass dome.

I am the right arm of Elos. The avenger. By my actions, his will is complete.

The boulder slammed into the glass, shattering it into a thousand thousand pieces, each glittering like diamonds in the sunlight. It continued through, striking the base of a sloping ledge and causing a platform to crash down upon the steps below it.

His power spent, Gilshamed released his sorcery and dove through the wreckage into the chambers. He touched down, dismissed his wings, and skidded along the marble floor towards a set of ancient wooden doors.

He drew his sword and turned.

Silence. He took a step, glancing about, and found his eyes drawn to his own face. The girl had been right. The statue was a strikingly accurate depiction of himself. The other three, less so, but he assumed the makers had had only Voren's memories to draw from.

Gilshamed's gaze flick upwards. He froze. *Wards on the roof . . . attuned to our kind. What have I walked into?* He felt a twinge of ice wriggle through his body.

A burst of bright blue light made him squint. Gilshamed watched as a figure flew up from below, touching down like a butterfly upon a blade of grass. The light and wings vanished. There, less than thirty paces away, stood the most vile of creatures ever to step foot upon the surface of the world.

Voren.

Gilshamed set his features firmly. No joy. No hatred. No rage. He was here simply to exterminate the vermin.

He brought his blade up and stalked forward. True to his word, he uttered not a single syllable.

Voren smiled sadly.

Armed men burst into view. From four side chambers, up both curving stairs, and from the main double doors behind him. Weapons and shields held at the ready. At least a dozen daeloth, energized with hands extended, just waiting for him to make a move.

Gilshamed glanced once more at the wards on the ceiling and knew he was doomed.

His sword clattered to the floor.

"The emperor," Voren said, "has plans for you."

Gilshamed felt too numb to answer. After all this time and planning, waiting and hoping, killing and praying . . . he had failed.

Voren reached into the folds of his robe, extracting a small object. He rolled it in his palm. "Shall I let him?"

Gilshamed worked saliva into his mouth. "What does it matter now? Neither of us has the power to stop him."

"But his plans," continued Voren, as if he had not heard him, "do not include me." He fingers curled about the object into a fist.

Gilshamed hung his head, his eyelids drooping half shut. *Lashriel, my love . . . forgive me. At least now we can finally be together.* He bent over, reaching for his sword, finding a purpose for it after all. He gripped the handle and righted himself, with the tip of the blade pointed at his own heart.

Daeloth spells crackled at fingertips. The guards surged forward.

Voren, nearly forgotten, whispered, "No. I do not think I will let him."

With his free hand, Voren swiftly drew a small dagger across his palm, then contracted his now-bleeding hand into a fist. Gilshamed heard the faint sound of breaking glass.

He felt Voren begin to energize.

What are you thinking, Voren?

The wards triggered, shooting their stored spells at the offender faster than thought. They had enough power to render him utterly disabled.

But they didn't.

A wave of energy burst forth from Voren. The spells aimed for him melted. The wards shattered.

Impossible! It would take scores of full valynkar harmonized together to overpower such wards! How did he—?

He blinked, looking closer at Voren. Blood poured down from his hand. Far more than could possibly come from his small, self-inflicted wound.

Voren's face had become empty. A stab of ice hit Gilshamed's chest. Voren lifted his arms, releasing another wave of energy outward.

Straight through the clustered guardsmen.

Gilshamed's robes began smoking as the fire burned through every other living thing in the room. In a beat, not even bones remained. Not even ash.

He stared at Voren. No—not Voren. Not anymore. The creature standing before him, wreathed in molten fury and unmatchable power, had transformed into the very avatar of vengeance.

Gilshamed turned and fled.

ALL TEN OF the Blade Cabal stood across the long room from him. Mevon had hoped that some would stay to guard the emperor. This would make matters more difficult.

"Strategy?" Mevon said.

"I have an idea," Draevenus said. "But it will put you at great risk."

"Let's hear—"

The world cut out. Mevon felt a tingling such as he never had before. A casting, nearby. What he had felt on prior occasions, even in the midst of large battles, was as a trickle compared to the floodgates now pouring forth. For a moment he couldn't even see, and his entire being thrummed.

Mevon, involuntarily, took a step towards it.

A single word came to him: *Abhorrent*. Whatever it was, he felt a compulsion to stop it, to void the sorcery into oblivion. All other considerations became secondary.

This . . . this is what we were made for. This is our purpose.

Mevon shook his head, blinking to clear the haze. As his vision returned, he saw that all the other Hardohl were as disoriented as he was.

"Who is doing that?" asked Mevon.

"I don't know," said Draevenus. "But it is no kin of mine."

Movement returned Mevon's attention to the line of his peers. And beyond them, springing through the open door, he witnessed the return of an old friend.

Kael, somehow unaffected by the casting, dashed into the room. A sword in either hand chopped through the necks of two of the Blade Cabal. Twin heads rolled across the floor, leaving blood trails as Kael, spry as ever, came to stand with Mevon.

Before even a word of greeting could be said, the remaining eight lunged forward.

Mevon retreated, parrying and dodging a hail of blows. He took a cut on his right shoulder and left calf.

He cartwheeled back, seeking to summon the storm.

A voice shouted. Draevenus. "Keep them off me! Watch for the fall!"

The word sank into Mevon's mind somewhere. He was too busy fighting for his life against four other Hardohl. Two each had engaged Kael and Draevenus. It was clear who their priority was.

And still, the storm wouldn't come.

His *Andun* twirled in his hands, fending off blows. He had no room to counterattack. He took another cut just below his left elbow. Another on his right hip. The Blade Cabal drove him and his two allies farther and farther apart.

Mevon grasped Justice at one end and swung, wide and wild. His assailants all bounced back a step.

In that gap, small as it was, he had time to summon the storm.

Rage and chaos swirled around him, pushed through his limbs and out to his weapon. In the center, calm and focus. Here, he was untouchable. And no storm before could compare to what he had now conjured.

Draevenus's imperative sprang forth into his mind. Mevon reversed direction, spinning into his four attackers faster than he had ever moved before. Their blades bounced off his, and he landed his first blood, slashing across the upper chests of two men. He broke through their blockade.

He spared a glance for Kael. His old mentor was holding his own, twin swords flowing like water around the heavier *Andun*. Both his assailants were bleeding from several wounds.

Mevon sped towards Draevenus, leaving his own opponents in a wake of dust. The mierothi saw him coming and shadow-dashed across the room.

Mevon tossed Justice into the air, threw both his daggers at one of the Hardohl attacking Draevenus, and caught his weapon before it hit the ground.

The man paused in his pursuit of the mierothi, turning to deflect the flying steel.

Draevenus extended a hand towards him. A familiar pattern of sorcery engulfed the Hardohl.

The daggers flew over the figure as he crumpled. Mevon sprang over him, sweeping down with a blade and severing head from body.

The mierothi retracted the spell and pushed the same one into his other attacker as the man approached. Mevon lunged forward. His *Andun* split the prone Hardohl's chest through the heart.

Mevon twisted, spinning his weapon out to deflect the blows he was sure would fall on him at any moment.

His weapon swung through empty air.

His four attackers were on the other side of the room. All six now surrounded Kael. Mevon couldn't even see his old mentor behind the bodies of the remaining Blade Cabal. All he saw was the rise and fall of their weapons. And the figure between them go down.

Like the wind . . . Mevon was across the long chamber in two beats.

Draevenus was faster. He shadow-dashed through the line of Blade Cabal. His heavy daggers slashed across two necks as he passed. The wounds weren't quite fatal—not for a Hardohl—but they were distracting. Mevon's attacks were, though, as he chopped sideways, finishing them off before they could recover.

All four of the remaining Blade Cabal turned, readying their weapons defensively. Mevon attacked with cold, precise strikes. His strength flowed down his arms into the steel of his weapon and broke through their defenses, again and again.

Draevenus distanced himself with another shadow-dash. His spell shot out. One of the Blade Cabal crumpled. Mevon altered the swing of his blade and cut the man in half from shoulder to opposite rib cage.

Mevon could see the final moment of confusion and fear in their eyes as—one by one—they fell before Draevenus's sorcery and died by Mevon's blade.

As the last of his enemy faded, another wave of the abhorrent magic writhed through the palace. This one was closer. Mevon, again, lost all other senses and felt himself being pulled towards it.

"What *is* that?" Mevon said.

"I don't know," Draevenus said. "This . . . was not something we planned for."

Mevon nodded. Then, he looked down and finally saw Kael.

There would be no last words. If a Hardohl had the strength left to speak, he could recover from his wounds. Kael was slashed to ribbons, a heap of bloody flesh.

Still. . .

Mevon fell to his knees before the body. Jasside had woken within him the ability to feel. When she died, he thought that such a gift would die with her.

He was wrong.

A single tear dropped from his eye and flowed down his cheek. He placed a hand on Kael's forehead. "Thank you, old friend, for this one last gift. You've laid your final plank. And . . . it was a good one."

He stood. Another wave hit, even closer this time. Somehow, he resisted the pull.

Mevon looked at Draevenus. "Rekaj. Where is he?"

Draevenus closed his eyes. A few beats later, they sprang open again. "Into the hallway. Left. Up the first staircase. Right at the third corridor. Large double doors halfway down."

Mevon nodded. "Where will you be?"

"Me?"

The rampant sorcery again wracked Mevon's senses. The palace shook. Stones from the roof and walls exploded into the room. He and Draevenus sprang out of the way as the bodies of the Blade Cabal were crushed into pulp beneath the falling blocks.

"I," Draevenus said, "will be trying to stop *that*."

YANDUMAR DOVE FOR cover as another bolt of dark lightning crested the lip of the wall, snapping as it tore its way across the battlements. Calla, at what seemed to be the last possible moment, threw up a shield to deflect the spell from their position.

Yandumar scrambled to his feet. "Don't cut it so close next time, will ya'?"

"Sorry," she said. "I'm sending too many messages myself now that Orbrahn is occupied." She waved a hand towards the stone archway atop the gate.

Yandumar cast his gaze that way. "What's taking so long?" he shouted.

The boy held up a finger.

Yandumar cursed under his breath.

Finally, whatever it was that casters did to link their sorcery was complete. Orbrahn looked up, a glow of pure ecstasy on his face. "You can't rush perfection," he shouted.

Joined with the power of a hundred other casters, who stood in a cluster behind him, Orbrahn began laying waste to the Imperial lines assaulting the central gate.

Each of the five gates had an equivalent group of casters, but it had taken too long, by Yandumar's estimation, for them to become effective. Ballistae crews and Slick Ren's archers had decimated the enemy ranks as they came, but the wall was still under siege in a dozen places. With a quarter million troops—and thousands more of daeloth—the Imperials could afford the losses.

Yandumar's forces, however, could not.

We're spread too thin.

"They've broken through in sector fourteen," Calla said. "Same in sectors one and four." She paused, eyes going black. "And sectors seven through ten."

Scorch me!

"All casters hold their positions," Yandumar ordered. "Focus on driving back any Imperials who get too close. All other troops besides ballistae crews and archers will assault Imperial footholds and reinforce the space between gates."

Calla nodded, then began relaying the orders.

Yandumar rubbed his temples as he peered down at the ground outside the central gate. Orbrahn was catching his breath between spells. Like a boulder tossed into a pond, waves of devastation rippled outward from his position. Piles of armor littered the scorched soil, steaming husks empty of life. The sickly-sweet smell of roasted human flesh hit his nose, making Yandumar gag. Where a few moments ago had been ten thousand souls, there was now nothing but stillness and death.

Yandumar glanced again at the mierothi bodies, which had been pushed into a heap against the edge of the wall. He knew that, had Mevon not taken care of them, the revolution troops would have faced much worse when they had first assaulted the walls than Orbrahn was now unleashing. He shivered. The daeloth had the advantage in both number of casters and individual sorcerous strength, but they were slow to adapt. *If they realized what they could accomplish with large-scale links. . .*

He turned to his messengers. "Tell the ballistae crews to target Imperial commanders whenever possible."

They nodded their understanding.

He turned to Paen, who lounged nearby. "Do me a favor?"

Paen, who had been gazing up toward the palace, twisted around with a flourish. "What is it, old man?"

"See if you can organize those civilians." Yandumar pointed down at the crowds. After ambushing the fleeing Imperials, they'd simply milled about. It was time to put them to good use. "Take any that are willing and get them to plug up the gaps in our defenses."

Paen bowed low. "Anything for our esteemed leader."

Yandumar sighed. The boy dashed down the stairs.

He walked over to the edge, peering down on the field beyond the city. His troops had their orders, the best he knew how to give. Now, all he could do was . . . wait.

And so he did.

Ballistae and bows kept firing. The casters pushed back the Imperials from the walls. Armed civilians became soldiers of the revolution as they made their way up the stairs. Step by step, each bought with blood, his troops drove their enemy off the wall.

He listened as the reports came in. Each sector, one by one, retaken for the revolution. Then he heard the casualty lists.

Between the initial assault, and holding off the Imperial counterattack, his troops had been cut down by over thirty thousand. Imperial losses were more than triple that, yet they still outnumbered him.

"Imperial forces are . . . retreating?" Calla voiced the report as a question.

"What?" Yandumar said.

"They're pulling back everywhere," she said. "Why would they do that?"

"Yandumar!" called Orbrahn, gesturing wildly. "Look to the west!"

Yandumar pulled out his far-sight, adjusting the focus until he could see the land beyond the Imperial lines.

"What the Abyss?" he said.

"What is it?" asked Calla.

"Someone is attacking the Imperials from behind. Who could be stupid enough to try something like that?"

"Didn't I tell you, dear?"

Yandumar spun. Slick Ren and Derthon stood at the head of the stairway, covered in blood. He hadn't bothered to ask her to avoid the fighting. He knew she just would have ignored him anyway.

"Tell me what?"

"When seeking out the lords of the central territory, I came across another uprising, completely detached from ours. The plantations of Agoritha are a nasty place, after all. It's no surprise they used the fine distraction that is our revolution to stage their own."

Yandumar shook his head. He was reminded, once again, just how big the empire was. He did not envy whoever took control after this was all over. The job of ruling this continent was far beyond anything he could comprehend. "Any idea of their numbers?"

Slick Ren shrugged. "Last I heard, they were up to forty thousand, or so. That was a month ago."

"And they came to help us?"

"They're brave little soldiers, my dear."

He looked out over the retreating Imperials. He understood the move. He'd not want to face threats from two sides at once either. Best to cut your losses and eliminate one as quickly as possible.

He closed his eyes, breathing deep. "If they stand against the mierothi, then we must stand with them."

He was ready for resistance, but none came. All heads were bobbing.

"We've got fifteen thousand horses. The Ragremons will lead the cavalry charge. We'll ride double, with bandit archers behind who'll dismount before the final distance is closed. Leave ballistae crews and half the casters. Everyone else come by foot as quickly as you can."

No one opposed his orders. He rushed down the stairs and made his way to Quake.

"GATES," VASHODIA ORDERED. Gathered energy crackling the air around her.

Jasside, already fully energized, peered over the shoulders of the Elite marching before them. The palace gates stood stark against the dawn. Closed. The lack of guards made her nervous.

She reached out with her will, seeking the hinges upon which they swung. Once found, it was a simple matter of disintegrating the bonds of the specks—what Vashodia called "atoms"—that made up the mechanisms. All twelve hinges dissolved at her command. She used a pulse of crude power to topple the gate backwards.

Before the dust had even begun to clear, palace guardsmen charged towards them.

Vashodia released her power. A wave of hissing darkness rolled through the guards. It melted the flesh off every man it touched, leaving rank upon rank of skeletons. Still armed, they remained standing for a moment, a mockery of the life that so quickly fled, an undead army on the march. Then they clattered to the ground.

The two Hardohl signaled their commands, and each of their Fists poured through into the palace grounds. Jasside followed on the heels of Vashodia.

"That was well done," said Vashodia.

"Thank you," said Jasside.

"It took nearly all of your capacity, though?"

"Yes."

Vashodia sighed. "Next time, instead of dissolving the bonds, try simply changing them."

"Into what?"

"Something that will not support such a massive weight. It will take practice, but requires far less energy."

Jasside nodded, grateful—truly—for the lesson. Every moment with Vashodia was like the first breath of air after being held underwater, the first beat of coherency after waking from a dream. The life she had lived before seemed so hollow, so ignorant, that she had a hard time thinking it was not all a hallucination.

They marched now between rows of outbuildings, three to each side. Jasside peered into one, which was full of shelves holding books. *A library? Here? I didn't think the mierothi cared for such things.*

"Do something about those bowmen, dear."

Jasside looked around, energizing. "Where are—"

From the rooftops, figures revealed themselves. Hun-

dreds. They lifted their arms, showing the curved wood
of their bows.

Don't dissolve, just change.

With each hand she formed a tiny ball of energy.
Within them, just like she had seen Vashodia do
moments ago, a field designed to alter whatever it
touched. She pushed them up to the rooftops. Starting
at one end, they shot along the line of bowmen, passing through the center of their weapons, changing the
consistency of the very material. Weakening it.

The men flexed, fully extending their pulls.

A sound like a thunderclap echoed through the corridor. Every last bow had snapped in half. As if on cue, several Elite emerged onto each rooftop and began mowing
down the guardsmen. Though they had swords, most remained forgotten in their sheaths, and the bowmen died
trying to fight with broken sticks.

Jasside looked ahead as they came free of the buildings and entered Lightfall Square.

Here, the enemy hadn't even bothered with the surprise tactic. They were displayed in the full of their might,
spread out east and west, a wall of flesh standing between
the intruders and the palace proper. Jasside's heart fluttered as she realized they were outnumbered more than
ten to one.

From the large formations on the flanks, thousands of
arrows arced into the air.

Jasside gasped as the female Hardohl picked her up
by wrapping a single arm around her waist. The woman
dashed forward, carrying Jasside like a trussed pig under

the waiting canopy of Elite shields. As she was set down—noting Vashodia had received the same treatment by the male Hardohl—a sound like a hailstorm beating on a wooden roof filled her ears.

"There are some daeloth ahead of us," Vashodia said. "Take care of them."

"How many?" Jasside asked.

"Oh, less than a hundred, surely."

Jasside felt her mouth go dry. "How am I supposed to kill them all by myself?"

Vashodia giggled. "I don't expected you to *kill* them, just hold them off awhile. Try using this."

The mierothi floated a small field before them as they walked. Jasside studied it.

"You see?" said Vashodia.

Jasside, eyes wide, nodded.

"Spells incoming!" The shout came from someone ahead. Jasside snaked her way through the Elite, stopping just before the foremost line. Peeking through them, she witnessed dozens of castings flinging through the air. And now, dozens more.

Jasside energized fully. With her will, she formed the field that she had just been shown, spreading it out like a curtain before their formation. Two beats later, the daeloth spells passed through it.

One by one, they fizzled, falling apart into aimless strands of energy that struck the Elite but did no harm. Jasside smiled.

She maintained her shield as the Elite marched in lockstep, closing the gap. Vashodia, behind her, gathered power. The guards on the flanks fired one more volley of arrows, then readied their spears and charged.

Vashodia's power shot straight up into the air, then fell upon their advancing enemy. A jolt, like lightning, passed through them in an instant. For a beat, nothing happened. Then, men fell, gasping and clutching at their chests. Of the four thousand guardsmen, less than a hundred remained standing.

One last group remained. A thousand left. They stood directly before the entrance to the palace. They were close enough now that Jasside could make out three purple claws painted upon their uniforms. Darkwatch. *This will not be easy.*

There was no cry of rage. No frenzy. No chaos as men forgot themselves in the heat of battle, becoming animals The two groups of professional soldiers merely tightened their ranks, shields overlapping, swords thrust out over top, and closed the distance.

Jasside sank back, letting Vashodia come up next to her. "What do I do?"

Vashodia hummed. "Stay alive, of course."

The lines crashed together, reverberating like tumbling boulders. Short cries of pain sounded as men suffered wounds. Shorter ones as they died. Jasside did the only thing she could think of.

She squatted and encased her body in shadows, praying that no one would give her notice. She watched the battle unfold.

The Elite were outnumbered nearly three to one, but Vashodia's two Hardohl, spinning and chopping their way through the darkwatch, opened up gaps that eased the pressure. The daeloth, obviously empowered by self-blessings, crashed into her allies' lines. Wherever they did, however, Vashodia shadow-dashed in at nearly the same instant. With a pair of conjured whips in either hand—like liquid swords formed of pure dark energy—she sliced the daeloth into pieces before they could inflict too much damage.

Men died on both sides. Jasside wasn't sure, but she thought the Elite gave more than they got. *As long as the darkwatch don't have any hidden tricks up their sleeves, I think we can win this.*

A figure leapt through the air. Towering pauldrons. Spiked armor the color of midnight. A barbed sword in one hand and a half-moon axe in the other. Though she could not see his face as it was covered by his helmet, Jasside knew exactly who he was.

Supreme Arcanod Grezkul.

Fear leapt into her throat.

He landed in the thickest part of the Elite ranks, knocking several men over. Daeloth sorcery might have been too weak to be effective against the Elite armor, but his was not.

Power encircled him like a wreath, cooking eight of the nearest Elite where they stood. With movement like a blur, he dashed out, striking precisely for throats and hearts. Ten more men fell, never to rise again, all before Jasside thought to release the breath she was holding.

Both Hardohl appeared a beat later. Jasside felt dizzy, watching Grezkul's blades dance out only to be blocked by the *Andun*. The two voids parried and dodged expertly, but it quickly became apparent to her that they were not equal to Mevon . . . and maybe not to the supreme arcanod either.

Their adversary moved like a snake, flowing around them, blades snicking out to inflict wounds that would have dropped normal men. Yet the two moved together, as if a single entity. Grezkul changed stance, pouring the strength of an oxen into his strikes. Even blocking them, the Hardohl were driven back by the sheer force of the blows.

Jasside realized that they were going to lose. She looked around for Vashodia, but didn't see her anywhere. *She doesn't even know. . .*

She stood. Energized. Swallowed her fear. Enough power was being flung about the battlefield. Her small addition, she hoped, would simply go unnoticed.

Her first casting shot out. It struck the female Hardohl as she spun into its wake and vanished, jolting Jasside slightly. She tried again. This one passed through all three combatants, and she dissolved it before it could strike the Elite fighting beyond.

She closed her eyes, took a deep breath, and concentrated. *I need not make it a projectile. I can simply form it . . . right . . . there!*

The field crackled in the supreme arcanod's chest. He stumbled.

The two Hardohl pounced. Blades chopped through both arms and legs in less than a beat, and their opponent—now just a writhing torso and head—fell to the ground. The male dove on top of him, and the female readied her weapon for the killing blow.

Jasside dissolved the shadows around her and stepped forward. "Stop! Wait!"

They looked at her askance. But they waited.

Jasside moved up to the figure and knelt by his head. She removed his helmet. Their eyes met.

The mierothi man coughed. "Don't I know you, little wench?"

"Yes," she said, then leaned in, pressing her lips next to his ear. "This is for what you ordered my father to do to my mother."

She drew her belt knife, leaned back, and drove it through his forehead.

Jasside stayed, leaning over his body for a few marks. When she rose at last, Vashodia stood before her. The battle was over. Less than fifty Elite remained standing, but the darkwatch were no more.

"Ready?" said Vashodia.

Jasside nodded, a lightness coming to her step. Together, they marched into the palace.

VOREN FLOATED THROUGH the palace at the center of a sun. Power flowed through him, outward into a sphere that incinerated all it touched. Nothing escaped its wrath. Flesh and bone melted like wax. Wood and cloth turned into vapor. Metal burned. Even the very stones crumbled to dust.

Before, when he had used this power in the chamber

up in the mountains, it had been for a specific purpose. Now, he had none. All the fear and sorrow and loneliness, pent-up for centuries, bled out from him. The hope he had abandoned long ago, rekindled by the whispers of freedom only to be squelched once more, took with it everything that had once been recognizable as his soul. He had not passion nor dream nor joy nor love nor faith.

Voren now had only power. He *used* power.

And power, in turn, used him.

GILSHAMED DOVE AS another ray of power lashed through the hallway. His shield, into which he poured every last drop of his energy, writhed and screamed against him, nearly popping. The molten power had barely brushed against him.

He stood and continued running, glancing back over his shoulder. The walls were gone, as was the ceiling. He could see into the hallway of the floor above and the rooms to the side. At least what was left of them. Scorched swaths marked where this latest outpouring of fury had scythed through. Nothing remained in its path.

Gilshamed did not know if Voren pursued him. Nor if the creature now tearing apart the palace could still be considered "Voren" at all. He could not even think. He fled through the palace, heart racing, pitiful noises emanating from his throat, blinded by the unholy power that consumed all sense, all reason.

Another wave pulsed towards him. He shouldered his way through a door, stumbling into a darkened room.

The corridor behind him glowed as power raced through it, but the ray, this time, struck downward rather than straight through.

Gilshamed took a deep breath and peered about. Shelves lined the walls, filled with tomes and scrolls, inkwells and quills and blank parchment. Four writing tables sat evenly spaced in the center. In the far corner, several brown-robed youths crouched, fingers stained black. Fear was writ on their faces as clearly as words on a page.

Huddled between them was a small mierothi man, shaking. He had hugged to his chest a book not much larger than Gilshamed's open palm. He stepped closer until he could make out the title.

History of the Empire, vol. I.

"My fault," the mierothi said. "All my fault."

"What do you mean?" Gilshamed asked.

"I got it for him. Never thought he'd do this. Never thought . . ." He lowered his head and began rocking back and forth.

Gilshamed shivered, somehow recovering some small sense of himself. He quested toward Voren's power. Despite its abhorrent nature, he now realized that some small part of it was . . . familiar . . . like an old friend shouting from the far side of a crowd.

He shook himself loose as another wave began wracking the palace. He lunged forward and snatched the book from the mierothi, a pitiful gasp escaping the man's lips. He turned to the scribes. "Why aren't you fleeing? Can you not see that staying here is a death sentence?"

They each turned wide gazes to the hallway behind him, which was already brightening. None moved. Gilshamed, energizing, searched the room and found a blank spot on the wall opposite the door. He cast a spell towards it, blowing open a hole wide enough for him to pass through.

He dashed through the opening. A patter of steps sounded in his wake. He pushed the tome into the inner pocket of his robe and began running. A scream sounded as flame engulfed the room behind them.

MEVON PUSHED OPEN the double doors and stepped into the chamber. It smelled thickly of dust. Carpets, worn and grey, covered the floor. Tapestries hung on both walls, reduced to tatters by age. Sunlight streamed through a series of windows to his right. Weblike patterns hinted at what once might have been images, but the glass had sagged and warped so much that Mevon could not tell what they were intended to depict. Soaring archways reached their peak three stories up, supported by rotting, moldy timbers.

Mevon, at last, focused on the far end of the room, some hundred and fifty paces distant. There sat a wide, high-backed chair, sharply carved from pure obsidian. It shimmered in the dawn. Lurid reflections danced on the floor around it, marring the raised marble dais with its antilight.

Upon it slouched the emperor.

He shifted upright as Mevon entered. "You?"

Mevon marched forward, his footfalls echoing throughout the hollow chamber. He said not a word.

"Ah . . . of course," Rekaj said with a sigh. "Even now she fears to face me."

His long strides overtook another, shorter set of footprints in the dust. The emperor's.

Rekaj stood and began ambling down the steps before his throne. "I do not blame her, though. It's not as if she could win."

Mevon reached behind him. As the cold steel of Justice slipped into his grasp, he became one with the weapon.

"How does it feel, Daere, knowing you're just a pawn?"

Mevon shook his head. *I've been your pawn my entire life. Now, I've finally found a purpose I can call my own, and I do all in full knowledge of who benefits from my actions.*

And I have never felt more at peace.

Perhaps Rekaj deserved an explanation. Perhaps not. Either way, Mevon did not feel like sharing his thoughts. He broke into a sprint. The distance between them melted away.

A look of resignation passed over the emperor's features. In a whisper, he said, "What a waste."

Mevon sprawled on the ground with a thump. His *Andun* fell from his grasp. His face was turned away and he did not know where it landed. It might have been fingers away, or paces.

Only after experiencing the effects of the spell did Mevon feel the tingling that announced casting nearby. Rekaj's sorcery made lightning seem slow. He understood, now, how the man had gained his power. How he had kept it all these long centuries. Why anyone would fear to become his enemy. Against such speed, such power, how could anyone hope to stand?

The realization that the emperor knew this spell did not surprise him. Nor that the man had hoarded such knowledge from even his closest allies. In this moment, as a man about to die before no witnesses, Mevon knew that he was seeing Rekaj's truest self.

He heard footsteps drawing near. The snick of a dagger being pulled from its sheath. "Another sacrifice to the gods," said the emperor, his voice full of sorrow. "Will you not ever be satisfied!"

Mevon, slowly, stretched out with his hand, searching with his fingertips. After a few beats, they brushed against something hard and cold.

The footsteps drew closer.

Closer.

Stopped.

Mevon summoned strength of will from the depths of his soul. Strength beyond anything physically possible. His hand shot out, gripping the rod of his weapon. He swung sideways across the surface of the floor.

Twin thunks sounded as a blade passed through flesh and bone. Blood sprayed across the floor, pattering dully, turning instantly to mud in the dust. A cry of surprise and pain gurgled from Rekaj. He fell.

The spell holding Mevon dissolved. He jumped to his feet and dove on top of the emperor.

Crazed eyes glared up at him as Mevon planted a knee

on Rekaj's chest, cracking ribs. He took hold of the mierothi's wrists and held them down. The move brought their faces so close, Mevon could feel wheezing breath on his cheeks. The emperor hadn't even bothered to empower himself with blessings. If he had, he could have thrown Mevon off him with ease. Now, however, Rekaj was completely in his control.

"How?" croaked the emperor.

"A woman," Mevon said. He smiled, remembering her. "The first time she used the spell on me, it made me question everything I thought I knew. And the more she used it, the more I came to understand the effects."

Mevon shifted his left knee onto one of Rekaj's wrists, freeing his arm.

"You see," he continued, "the spell only cancels the effects of our blessing. All the speed and strength and perception granted us is negated backwards, and we experience—all at once—the peeling back of those benefits."

He reached to his belt, extracting a dagger. He brought it up, with no haste, to rest on the emperor's throat.

"The more she practiced on me, though, the less the effects became. The more I was able to fight past them.

"And she practiced a lot."

Rekaj began coughing, which turned into a sardonic laugh. "So what now? You kill me and take my throne?" He glanced at the obsidian chair. "You think you know how to govern an empire? Ha!" He broke into more coughing, wheezing. "You know nothing."

Mevon sighed. "I know one thing."

He pushed down and slashed sideways.

"I know justice."

Black blood spurted from Rekaj's grinning throat.

Mevon stayed atop him for several marks, watching until the life faded from those red eyes. He pressed his head to the emperor's chest, listening for the intake of breath, feeling for a heartbeat. Nothing.

It is finished.

Mevon stood, dusting himself off. He thought he'd feel better, maybe even whole, but something was still missing. Some*one*. And nothing he had done could bring her back.

He recovered his *Andun* and trudged out of the lifeless chamber.

DRAEVENUS DASHED AWAY as another arm of fire lanced across his path, obliterating the place he had just been standing. He turned, treading forward once more.

These were easy enough to avoid, at least. His senses were honed, able to predict their movements, and he himself was nimble enough to dance out of their way. Still, after several marks of trying, he could not get any closer to his target.

Draevenus was moving in from behind. For every two steps he took forward, his target moved away one, and he was pushed back another by a pulse of energy flowing outward like a wind.

What are you thinking, Gilshamed?

He didn't know where the man had conjured such

power. Likely some hidden valynkar weapon he'd kept hidden all this time, just waiting to be unleashed until he could get into the palace. A reminder that while the empire had remained stagnant in most things, the rest of the world had continued to advance. He should have seen something like this coming. And if not he, Vashodia.

Or, perhaps she did see it but chose to do nothing.

As much as he loved his sister, she was capable of anything so long as it furthered her own goals. More and more, he was coming to see just how little she shared with him.

Draevenus felt another arm cutting towards him. He shadow-dashed sideways into another hallway, letting it pass by. Gaping holes, edges charred, marked where Gilshamed had gone before. The palace was being gutted. He could see into places that should have taken half a toll to travel to by foot.

A group of figures crept into view. Crouching, they wended through a path of crumbling stones and scorched debris. He looked closer. Recognizing one of them, he drew his daggers and ran to intercept.

An arm of fire came towards them as well, chopping down from above like a cleaver. They didn't see it. Hapless, they continued their too-slow movement through the wreckage.

A few of them, servants, managed a scream before the living lava fell into their midst. The one figure managed to form a shield just in time. But only for herself. The rest vanished into smoke in an instant.

Draevenus shadow-dashed over to the mierothi

female as soon as the spell had passed. He stopped, standing over her crumpled form. He smelled roasted meat.

Her legs were gone from the knees down, ending in cauterized stumps. The flesh up to her waist was cooked. Draevenus felt a twinge in his stomach.

Mother Phyzari Kitavijj looked up at him through tormented eyes. "Mercy . . ." she squealed.

Draevenus stepped closer. "You don't deserve any. Not after Verge."

"I know," she said. "Please . . ."

Draevenus sighed. Finally, he nodded. His dagger found her frantically beating heart. It stopped, and the mierothi woman slumped to the floor.

He turned from her, facing the maelstrom once more.

And prayed for a miracle.

"VASHODIA," THE MALE Hardohl said. "Let us go. This is getting out of hand."

He didn't need to specify. Jasside could feel the raging fire of power whirling around inside the palace. She felt it before they'd even stepped foot inside and was surprised when Vashodia did not lead them straight to it.

The mierothi now waved absently toward the two Hardohl. "Oh, very well. Do what you must. I will be along shortly." Without another word, they sprinted away, disappearing around a bend in the corridor in two beats.

Jasside stayed a few steps behind Vashodia as they walked. They made several turns. Everywhere she looked displayed signs of devastation. Death. She had been expecting resistance here, every step contested. The eerie silence unnerved her.

Vashodia rounded another corner then stopped, stepping back. Jasside halted before the turn, unable to see what lay beyond. The mierothi peaked her head around the corner, and Jasside heard heavy footsteps. After half a mark, the steps faded to obscurity, and Vashodia continued forward once more.

Down this hallway, they turned right into a double set of doors. Jasside's eyes widened as she saw what awaited them.

"Ah," Vashodia said. "Still fresh."

Emperor Rekaj lay in the middle of the room. Dead. His feet were severed from his legs. A pool of blood surrounded his neck. Jasside realized she had stopped moving, and trotted ahead to catch up with Vashodia. Together, they came to stand over the body.

Vashodia motioned her backwards. "Not too close. We don't want the samples mixing."

"What?"

The mierothi ignored her, bending over double to inspect Rekaj. "The throat was it? Fitting, I suppose. Yes, the symmetry will be quite nice, and the scar will be a constant reminder. Would you not agree?"

Jasside's head spun. "I have no idea what you're talking about. Why are we even here?"

Vashodia stepped closer, reaching up to pat Jasside on the cheek. Her claws pressed dimples into her skin. "Why, girl, this is your reward."

Reward?

Vashodia's hand moved across her face in a blur.

At first, Jasside felt nothing. Only confusion. Then, fire and pain bloomed in a line across the front of her neck. She heard the trickle of blood—*her* blood—as it dripped down onto her chest.

Jasside fell to her knees, hands grasping for her throat. Darkness closed in on her vision.

YANDUMAR YANKED HIS head back as the tip of a spear jabbed toward him. He swung upward with one of his bastard swords, pushing the spear away. His other sword thrust forward. The Imperial soldier, a man almost as large as himself, gritted his teeth as the blade plunged into his chest. His bloody hand reached up on towards the hilt, scratching at Yandumar's fingers.

A sudden shift in the battlefield drove Quake forward. Yandumar could either hold on to the blade and risk losing his arm, or let go.

Reluctantly, his fingers uncurled. He pressed his knees together to keep upright atop the horse.

Scorch me, I loved that sword!

He'd had it since his days as an Elite, over thirty years ago. Harridan Chant had given the pair to him upon the announcement of Kaiera's third pregnancy. He felt a twinge of pain at its loss.

He looked up and realized what had caused the shift. Imperial forces were retreating. The lines before him melted away to the northwest, and for the first time, he found himself looking upon his newest allies: the rebels of Agoritha.

A cheer arose, echoed on both sides. It warmed him, somewhat, to see that his efforts had not been in vain. Though the rebels had lost nearly half their number, the revolution had been there in time to save them from annihilation.

The archers had been able to fire from horseback, loosing a few dozen volleys as he maneuvered into position. They hadn't been very accurate, but then they hadn't needed to be. The Imperials were in pursuit of the rebels, and few even turned to thwart the revolution. And when only one man in four carried a shield, the tactic had proven quite effective at thinning their numbers.

He rode forward over the field of dead as the Imperials raised dust in their retreat. They still outnumbered them heavily, and the revolution support coming on foot was still at least a quarter toll out. They had no reason he could see to pull back now.

Something doesn't feel right.

Eventually, the dust cleared. Yandumar, mounted far in front of his own forces, was the first to see them.

The Imperial army split around another group, this clustered in a mob with a dozen figures standing before it. Yandumar fished for his far-sight, then brought it to his eye. The dozen figures were mierothi, and the mob behind them was another army.

But this was not an army of men.

They were . . . creatures.

No—not creatures. Monsters.

Thirty thousand beastly forms stood stamping and growling on the field. Their bodies were twisted amalgamations—half-man, half-beast, all nightmare. He could see no pattern to their appearance. Some seemed formed from bears, others from bulls, still others from lions, with a dozen more varieties. The only thing they had in common was their grotesque nature. And their size. Each was easily thrice the mass of an oxen.

Yandumar's chest tightened. Memories surfaced of his trips through the tunnel. Memories of tormented screams that emanated from side chambers, chilling him to the bone. Whispers of experiments performed there in the deep, in the dark. Unholy growls of things not made by any sane god.

Those same growls sounded now.

Yandumar wept.

The mierothi all gestured forward, and the mob surged into motion. Yandumar gasped as he took in how fast they were closing.

He turned, looking to the city wall. Turned back to the creatures. Closed his eyes.

We're not gonna make it.

But it's our only chance.

He wheeled Quake anyway, galloping toward his army. He pulled in as much breath as he could hold, then let it out in a shout.

"RETREAT!"

GILSHAMED CASTED, BLASTING another hole in the wall before them. He gestured at the figures behind him and dashed through.

There were two dozen now. He picked them up wherever he went. He found them—stewards, servants, bed slaves—all mostly huddling in groups, too frightened to even move. His charisma was enough to get their feet shuffling, but few were able to mutter anything coherent. He had to find his own way.

Voren's power pushed out all thought, all reason, and all Gilshamed could do was revert to instinct. He was surprised to find that instinct meant to protect and to lead. Even now, as annihilation pressed down from every corner, he was glad to find a part of himself he had thought lost. A part of which he was not ashamed.

He glanced back at the figures following him blindly.

I just wish I knew where the abyss I was going.

But he had no choice. He could not turn back. He could only charge forward, praying that the old military mantra was true.

That any decision was better than no decision at all.

He entered a place that looked to have been barracks for the palace guardsmen as the writhing chaos closed in. The long chamber was full of beds and footlockers. He led his party to the far end. He energized and threw a spell at the wall.

Stone and mortar crumbled, filling the room with dust. Gilshamed looked through, expecting to see into the chamber beyond.

Instead, all he could see was bedrock.

His heart skipped a beat.

He realized, then, his mistake. At first, he had sought to go upwards, for he could fly to safety himself. But as soon as he'd taken responsibility for the scribes, he had unconsciously sought the ground floor. It appeared he had gone too far down.

A burst of power knocked against the wall opposite, like a harbinger of doom. Another, and the wall tumbled inwards.

Gilshamed cast his gaze over his sorry-looking followers as they huddled together against the wall. "I am sorry. I . . . I tried."

The looks they returned were not as he expected. There was no hate, no anger, no accusation. Only thanks. And . . . pity.

I do not deserve such from you. I, who have led you to your deaths, deserve only scorn.

A ray of power snaked through the room. Gilshamed summoned all the power he could, casting a protective net over the group. He knew, though, that it would eventually fail.

Heat intensified on his back as death drew closer.

And now, my love, we can be together again. I am so sorry it took this long for me to join you.

He closed his eyes, welcoming the end . . .

The heat and light vanished. Gilshamed turned.

Two figures stood in the room. A man and a woman. By their weapons and armor, he recognized them for what they were.

Hardohl.

Gilshamed had never been so glad to see one.

As they stepped towards Voren, voiding another ray, Gilshamed saw the door on the side wall from which they had entered. Normally hidden, it was visible now only because the door had been left open.

He turned to his wards, pointing towards the opening. "Up! Move! Let's go!"

It took them a moment to realize what was happening. That their deaths had been postponed. Gilshamed reached a hand to help the last few to their feet, then led them, scrambling, towards salvation.

He nearly tripped as he felt Voren's power change. It contracted, falling in on itself. The rays shooting out in all directions vanished. Gilshamed looked towards his old friend and found himself frozen.

A tidal wave of catastrophe marked his path. Standing in the center, alone, looking so tiny, so pale, stood his kin. A man he had once called brother. Gilshamed realized that not an ounce of sorcery flowed from him. Voren was completely vulnerable.

Then, with a trembling hand, Voren reached into his robe. He extracted another vial of blood and crushed it into his palm. Gilshamed had missed the implications the first time. Now, however, he recognized exactly what was happening.

Blood scything! But that requires living *souls to power. How the Abyss . . . ?*

Then . . . he knew.

And everything changed.

Power flooded into Voren with renewed vehemence, but its flavor had changed. No longer was it chaotic, unfocused. It now growled with intent.

A hundred thousand infinitesimal strands latched onto

stones and bricks, pieces of wood and broken furniture, bit of metal and glass. A cloud of debris lifted into the air.

Only two beats had passed. The Hardohl, quick as ever, had closed half the distance to Voren. But it did not matter. Objects began flying into the room at speeds to make the wind howl in jealousy. The two figures had no place to dodge. Projectiles were everywhere.

Gilshamed threw up another shield, this one kinetic. The Hardohl took the brunt of the attack, but hundreds of object still sailed towards Gilshamed and his wards. The shield held, each object bouncing off and clattering to the ground, but he strained with each passing beat to keep it in place. All thoughts of escape vanished as he poured everything he had into staying alive.

He spared a glance for the Hardohl, feeling a stab of agony in his soul. They moved forward, towards death, even as shrapnel ripped their bodies to shreds. Blood spilled from each of a hundred wounds, spinning sickeningly through the air. And still, step by step, the two advanced.

They cannot take much more. When they die, the power will be free to resume its cataclysm. We will not last a beat past their final breaths.

A small part of him chuckled at the thought. Somehow, Voren and the power he wielded had become separate entities in his mind. The latter he hated, for no matter its source, it had taken a mind of its own. A mind with evil intent.

For the former, however, he had at last found the kinship that he had once felt, so long ago now it seemed a dream.

You did not kill her, old friend. You saved her. For that, I love you. For that, you will always be known as the greatest of our people's heroes.

Gilshamed clung to the thought as both Hardohl stumbled to their knees.

A slight motion—barely discernible in the chaos swirling around the chamber—caught his attention. It was a figure, stepping through the side door. She stood barely up to Gilshamed's waist and was dressed in dark, flowing robes. In her hands she held a pair of metal objects. They appeared to his eyes as spheres cut in half and splayed open with hollow centers.

Around her swirled a maelstrom of darkwisps.

Sorcery shot out from her, a shield across the face of the room, protecting the two Hardohl and everything behind them. The figure giggled, then looked over her shoulder at him.

"It's been awhile, Gilshamed," Vashodia said. "Did you miss me?"

Gilshamed, despite her aid, cringed in dread.

Vashodia turned back and began marching towards Voren. Somehow, impossibly, her sorcery began pushing back at the other.

And where the two powers met, even gods would fear to tread.

MEVON STUMBLED THROUGH the palace, feeling as if gravity had shifted sideways. The abhorrent sorcery was now joined by another, point and counterpoint in a debate from which there could be no clear victor. No longer in waves, the twin powers pulled at him ceaselessly. Mevon did his best to ignore them both. He silenced his instinct and trudged away from the clash of magic.

I did it. I won. My justice is delivered, and my nemesis is no more.

The thought was supposed to bring him peace. It did not. Victory had always accompanied a surge of joy, but this time was different. He had known it would be but hoped otherwise. Hoped that he had changed enough that he would no longer crave blood and death inflicted by his own hands. Hoped that the justice he had served would stand in the gaping hole he had created himself.

What, now, is the point of me?

His mind ran through scenarios of an empire at peace. In none of them could he find a fitting place for himself. His kind existed, he now realized, for the sole purpose of keeping rampant sorcery in check. The purpose that the mierothi had subverted for the last nineteen hundred years.

The purpose that, even now, he resisted.

It is not enough. Such things will balance themselves out in the end.

Mevon did not bother to direct his feet, electing instead to let them wander where they willed. He was not surprised to find himself back in the chamber where he had faced the Blade Cabal, standing a step inside the doorway. He could still see bits of their armor sticking out of the rubble, flashes of dead skin, the glint of their weapons.

All the while, the palace writhed under the pressure of the competing powers.

Wind swept by his face, brushing back his hair. He looked up. A wound in the roof exposed the exterior of the palace, and through it streamed bright morning sunlight. Mevon closed his eyes, inhaling deeply, cherishing the taste of clean air and the warmth of the light on his face.

He thought of all he had lost. All he had gained. All the evil he had done, and undone. All the good he had destroyed and helped to flourish.

On the scales of his life, he judged himself.

His body went numb.

Justice fell from his limp fingertips, clattering onto the floor.

None, save the gods themselves, are more guilty of wrongdoing than I.

The clashing powers reached a crescendo, and a quake rocked his entire world to its foundation.

A stray beam of power scythed through a wall high above him, turning it molten. Mevon lifted his eyes as it exploded into countless white-hot fragments, falling down on the room like lava . . .

JASSIDE OPENED HER eyes with a gasp, the gesture proving that she was, in fact, not dead.

Again.

Gods, I hope this doesn't get to be a habit.

She sat up, groaning, and rubbed her forehead. A

wave of dizziness warned her not to ascend another hand higher. She felt cramped and bloated. Itchiness pervaded everywhere, seeming to come from within her body, but even as she sat to clear her head, the sensation evaporated. A few marks later, she had finally composed herself enough and wobbled to her feet.

In a flood of panic, she recalled her last moments of consciousness.

Her heart sped up, and her breath came ragged. She stroked across her neck, feeling a line of uneven skin: scar tissue. She looked down, remembering the blood.

Her dress was clean, as were her hands. Not a spot of red. She looked to where she had lain. The expected blood pool was absent.

Did I imagine it all?

Her gaze shifted to the body of the emperor.

Jasside distinctly remembered the dark stain beneath his head when she had first come in. It, too, was gone. The corpse had changed as well. Pale, shriveled, features sunken, his wounds clean and dry, Rekaj appeared as though every last drop of fluid had been sucked out of his body.

Where it had all gone, though, Jasside could not say.

And now, just as her body's senses came to in increments, another sense rushed to its renewal. The powers that raged seemed to slam into her like a hammer. Still quite disoriented, Jasside felt as though they were right on top of her. On instinct, she energized . . .

. . . and staggered as alien power flooded into her.

Jasside's lips parted, a sigh of pleasure passing through

the gap. She pulled in more power. As much as she could hold.

Her father had not been considered strong among the daeloth, and she'd inherited less than half of his capacity. The weakest of full mierothi possessed at least twenty times her natural strength.

What she held now was a hundredfold what she could before.

"Vashodia."

The word came out not as a curse but as a whisper of adoration. Veneration, even. Jasside drew the line before worship, however. Such a sin, even in a moment such as this, would be unforgivable.

Jasside knew what Vashodia had done, and by that act she understood the mierothi girl better. Perhaps not fully—*can anyone but God ever truly know someone?*—but enough to know that she would follow her to the ends of the world. And beyond.

She remembered the promise she'd made to Yandumar as they entered the city. She skipped out of the room and began searching for Mevon.

DRAEVENUS STUMBLED FORWARD as the power that held him at bay suddenly winked out of existence.

It can't be over. Not so easily as that.

Rather than rush forward, he crept, wary for the trap he was sure would spring at any moment. He stalked in silence, not casting, not even energizing. Nothing to draw attention to himself. The perfect hunter. In two beats, he was within the sphere that had been pushing back at him.

No going back. . .

The power returned. Angry. Malicious. Blinding. Draevenus braced himself for the wave that would, at the least, knock him back. At worst, kill him.

It never came.

Draevenus felt the morph. The power no longer writhed outward in all directions. It was, instead, focused. Away from him.

Another power joined the first. This, if not quite its equal, was smarter. And familiar. Vashodia, at last joining the fray. It was exactly the distraction he needed. He resumed his advance.

Step by step, he approached. In half a mark, he rounded a surprisingly intact wall and came, at last, to view his target. The figure glowed like the sun. Draevenus could not even look directly at him for fear of losing his sight.

He paused, readying his daggers in both hands. Gilshamed's attention, his power, were all focused forward. His back was completely exposed.

It was a mistake ever bringing you into this. A mistake to think we could rely on you. A mistake to believe we could control you.

A mistake that I will now remedy.

Draevenus energized. Stood upright. He kept his head down, not needing to see to pinpoint his target.

Daggers held rigid before him, Draevenus shadow-dashed forward.

Blades sank into flesh. They both tumbled forward, crashing to the ground in a tangled heap. The power sputtered. Died.

Draevenus looked over his target's shoulder into his sister's eyes as she withdrew her own sorcery. Beyond her, the two Hardohl, and . . .

No . . . !

. . . Gilshamed, standing protectively over a group of people. And if he were there, then . . .

The scream that erupted from Draevenus's throat echoed the anguish of generations. And the sound held not a single raindrop before the storm of sorrow wracking his soul.

My friend . . . what could have driven you to this madness?

He quickly withdrew his daggers, knowing it to be pointless. Ever the perfect killer, his blades had struck true. The body slumped to the ground. Motionless.

Voren was dead.

QUAKE'S HOOVES THUNDERED beneath him, tearing up soil as the horse galloped across the field. Yandumar was sure his mount had never moved faster.

He led all eighty-two Elite in a long, single line, dashing westward across the front of the advancing horde. His hope was that the monsters' animal instinct would prevail over orders, and that they would pursue the nearest targets. It was a desperate move, but the only one he could think of. If it worked, it would allow the rest of his troops the time they needed to make it back to the wall, back to safety.

Yandumar peered over his shoulder.

All of Mevon's men had gladly volunteered for this, a testament to their dedication. Captain Arozir Torn insisted on bringing up the rear. The fastest of the creatures had closed to within striking distance of him.

A dark lion's paw swiped for Arozir's head. He ducked, striking back with his sword. The blade plunged into his opponent's eye, causing it to scream in fury as it staggered back.

Two more rushed in. Bear jaws closed upon the horse's rear legs, and the mount crashed to the ground. Arozir leapt from the saddle, just avoiding the thrust of a boar's tusks. He fell into the creature, slamming his sword home in its chest.

The boar-thing went limp, falling dead atop the captain, pinning him to the ground.

Three more monsters swooped in, devouring both Arozir and the creature he had killed in a flurry of snapping jaws.

Yandumar forced himself to watch, to witness their final moments, to honor their sacrifice, as another of Mevon's Elite fell. And another. And another. Each man followed the example set by their captain, and took at least one monster with him into death.

Looking past them, Yandumar tingled with mixed dread and hope as the horde swung westward in its entirety. The tactic was working. His allies would live. For a little while longer, anyway.

An old saying came back to him, a favorite of Chant's. *We couldn't have asked for a better death than this.*

Yandumar, now fully prepared to meet his maker, looked forward with a smile. He still remembered old Harridan's face, could see it right now.

He could see it . . . *right now!*

A shadow covered the grasses in front of him. Hundreds of figures in dark clothing. Standing foremost among them, Captain Harridan Chant himself.

With a woman—a mierothi—at his side.

His emotions and thoughts were too tangled to make any sense out of them. He slowed Quake and stupidly called out. "Chant?"

The man smiled and waved. Yandumar was sure he was hallucinating.

Then the mierothi woman pressed out a hand, and all other thoughts ceased. Energy crackled at her fingertips. Even Yandumar, who had no sensitivities to magic, withered before the conjuring. A storm cloud of darkness formed at the woman's calling, then shot out, churning up dirt as it whizzed past him. Yandumar craned his neck to follow it.

The Elite saw it coming, and drove their horses south. The cloud writhed, spitting with vehemence, straight into the charging horde. Beastly screams erupted as darkness engulfed the monsters. Screams that were quickly stifled.

As the storm moved on, Yandumar could see the blood and bone and scattered hides. All that remained of his pursuers. The cloud pulsed, expanded, now covering nearly a klick-wide swath of land. The remaining monsters reeled in all directions to avoid it.

The cloud sought their flesh, and finding it, consumed.

Yandumar turned back as Quake slowed to a halt alongside his old comrade. This close, he could make out the age lines that hadn't been there the last time he'd seen him. "You real?" Yandumar asked.

Chant smiled. "Real as ever, I'm afraid. Surprised to see me?"

"*Glad* to see you. *Surprised* to be alive." He looked over the crowd. "How the Abyss did you come by this company?"

"Oh, just a deal with a devil. I've heard you're familiar with the concept?"

"Aye."

He turned back in time to witness the demise of the last of the monstrosities. The cloud, then, broke into pieces, the sections snaking along the ground toward each of the dozen mierothi who had fled in as many directions. Though they shadow-dashed away in spurts of incredible speed, the clouds moved faster, catching up in beats. Death came wherever they touched.

Yandumar sighed. "It's over."

"No," the mierothi woman said. "It has only just begun."

The storm cloud re-formed. This time it banked toward the milling Imperial army.

Yandumar peered down at her, noticing for the first

time her features. He was surprised to find they were familiar to those of another mierothi he knew. "Is that really necessary?"

"They stood with Rekaj. As he has died, so will they."

Yandumar jumped off Quake and tromped towards her. "But it's *over*. Don't you see? If Rekaj is truly dead, then there's no need for any more killing. It time to start thinking about mending bridges, not burning them."

Yandumar could see she wasn't listening. The Imperial army shivered in panic as the storm cloud neared their lines.

He peered over the crowd. None of the other women were so much as budging. *Their power must be linked. And this one woman is the conduit.*

His speech rang hollow as he stepped forward, drawing his lone bastard sword.

Harridan moved between them, his own sword held at the ready. "Not another step, Yan."

Yandumar froze. "This isn't the way, and you know it."

"Maybe. But I took a vow to defend Angla. You, of all people, should respect that."

Angla? Sweet bloody abyss . . . Yandumar was, of course, familiar with daeloth naming patterns, and knew exactly what this woman's half-breed children would be named. And, by extension, her grandchildren.

He advanced another step. He knew he could not reason with Chant. Even if he convinced him, a vow taken by any son of Ragremos was not something that could be broken. Ever. But Angla . . . she stood in position to destroy all that *he* had fought for, the fulfillment of *his* vows.

Yandumar's soul twisted in agony as he realized that either he or his old friend could survive this day, but not both.

Idrus dashed up to his side, twin shortswords in hand. "I stand with the Lord-General, uncle," he called to Harridan. "We all do." The shuffling of feet announced the arrival of the surviving Elite.

More relics out of memory joined Chant: Shadow, and five others from his old Fist. And behind them, three hundred armed men stalked forward. Yandumar closed his eyes.

God, please, not like this. Forgive me for my sins, and find for us a way out of this scorching mess.

As he opened them once more, he felt Idrus shift his gaze to the right. Yandumar followed, seeing what the ranger had a moment later.

A tiny figure dashing through the grasses. Coming in from behind the mierothi.

He looked again towards Chant. "I said I wished for no more bloodshed. Now, I'll lead by example." He thrust the tip of his sword back into its sheath on his back.

The rest of Mevon's Fist did the same. Chant breathed out heavily. He and the others with him visibly relaxed.

The figure in the grasses sprang forward. A smooth, hairless head revealed itself. Familiar armor and weapons . . . and face.

Ilyem Bahkere reached out, laying a hand on Angla's shoulder

The thrumming sorcery dissipated, and with it, the battle.

Thank God.

"It's over," the Hardohl said firmly. Then, turning to Yandumar, she added. "I'm sorry I did not arrive sooner. Your son showed me the way days ago, but I took too long to act on it."

My son . . . Yandumar nodded to her respectfully. "You'll never know how much your arrival means to me. Thank you."

Yandumar turned, trotting back to Quake and mounting quickly. His obligations here complete, he felt himself being pulled south towards Mecrithos.

Towards Mevon.

He feared, however, that he was already too late.

GILSHAMED BRUSHED THE tangled hair back from Voren's face as he knelt beside the body. The man had aged since he had last seen him. No longer young. In memory, both recent and ancient, Voren's visage had always been full of strain and frustration, as if he had something to prove to the world but possessed not the cleverness to pull it off.

Looking upon him now, Gilshamed at last saw a measure of serenity. That only death could grant him such drove an ache of compassion through Gilshamed.

A muffled sob brought his head up. Close enough to touch sat Draevenus.

Names such as Vashodia and Rekaj had been shouted

as curses by men and women alike from his armies of old. But the name Draevenus had only been murmured in hushed tones, accompanied by a wary glance around and a shiver up the spine. To see the source of grown men's nightmares reduced to anguished weeping renewed his own sorrow, his own rage.

He bent down and kissed Voren on the forehead. "May Elos shelter your soul and guide you into paradise." Even as he said the words, though, he could feel the hollowness of the catechism. Elos had abandoned Voren. Him, and all the rest.

A patter of steps approached from behind him. Gilshamed stood, turning to face her. "Where are my kin?" he demanded.

"So," Vashodia said, "you've surmised that much on your own. Perhaps you're not as hopeless as I assumed."

Gilshamed set his jaw and repeated his question.

Vashodia giggled. "Why so demanding? You cannot honestly believe you're in any position to bargain."

"They are my blood, my responsibility. You have no right to them."

She raised an eyebrow. "You speak of responsibility, yet you abandoned the revolution at the first hints of failure." She sighed. "Not at all how I planned. What a disappointment you turned out to be."

"How *you* planned?" Gilshamed closed his eyes, his mind flying through the implications. "Yandumar. You sent him for me."

"Of course I did. And you were supposed to lead the revolution right up to these palace gates, announcing your victory for the valynkar people. At which point, your own followers would have tried to kill you." She giggled again. "And if they failed, only then would I have stepped in."

Gilshamed felt a twinge of guilt, for that had, at one point, been exactly his plan. He shook his head. "This land does not need me. And it certainly does not need *you*. Now, will you lead me to my kin? Or will I be forced to scour the land for years in search of them?"

"As if I'd allow that." Vashodia's eyes narrowed. "You don't deserve a happy ending."

"I know," said Gilshamed. "But they have suffered enough."

"Perhaps they have. But you . . ." She energized. " . . . have not."

Gilshamed pulled in his own power. She had embarrassed him the last time they had fought, but he had learned a thing or two since then. With her darkwisps spent, he would not prove such easy prey.

"Enough!"

Gilshamed turned at the shout. Draevenus stood behind him, eyes full of sorrow and rage.

"Enough," Draevenus repeated, softer this time. "Sister . . . please . . . no more."

"We cannot trust him," Vashodia said.

"That doesn't matter anymore. He is a member of the Valynkar High Council. If we kill him, they will know. And once the final stage of your plan is complete . . . ?"

She tapped her claws across her chin, contemplating. After several beats, she discharged her power. "Very well."

Gilshamed, reluctantly, did the same. He peered at Draevenus, nodding with respect. "Thank you, but I do not understand why you show me such kindness."

"The corruption at the heart of our people has been excised. I look now to the future. To draw the enmity of the valynkar is the last thing I would wish for—enough valynkar blood has been spilled," he said quietly, looking down at Voren. Straightening, he said, "If the mierothi are to survive, we must make peace."

Peace? I hardly know the meaning. It will be good, I think, to discover it. Gilshamed exhaled. "Will you show me to them?"

Draevenus glanced past him towards his sister. "Can I borrow one of your bodyguards?"

Vashodia waved, looking bored. "Fine." The male Hardohl stepped forward.

"Come, Gilshamed," Draevenus said. "I will lead you to your kin."

JASSIDE STOOD BEFORE the doors, which were forced open by debris, and stared around in confusion.

She'd sent pulses of energy outward. Hundreds in all directions. Such would have been impossible just a toll ago, but now she could perform the cast without even straining. Wherever they winked out of existence, she knew she would find voids there. She ignored the two that were with Vashodia. Instead, she had followed the trail here.

The pulses sent this way, however, had been . . . strange.

Rather than disappear like a popping bubble, they had dissolved like mist before the rising sun. Now, she knew why. It appeared as though a volcano had erupted in this chamber. Nothing here could possibly be alive.

Mevon wasn't here. But her probing had revealed no other sources in the palace. "Where are you?"

She turned to leave. A spot of sunlight streaming through the collapsed roof glinted off something near her feet. She stopped, bending to inspect it.

Sharp steel. Triangular in shape. Sticking out of the rubble and half-covered in a crust of recently molten stone. There was lettering on it. Her heart skipped a beat.

Shaking, Jasside wiped her hand across the flat of the blade.

YANDUMAR THUNDERED THROUGH the city gates. A cheer arose at his arrival. His bodyguards, now mounted themselves, fell in around him, offering escort up the main avenue of the city.

Crowds grew thick around them. Cries of joy and adulation sounded. Shouts of "Lord-General" and "savior." Some, foolishly, even began chanting "emperor." Yandumar ignored them all. There was only one title he wished to hear right now.

"*Father.*"

Nearer the palace, the crowds thinned, and he was able to pick up speed once more. Quake soon outpaced the horses of his guards, and Yandumar rode through the palace gates alone. The gutted husk that once housed the heart of mierothi power stood before him. He vaulted off of his mount, entering without a moment's hesitation.

His feet sprinted forward of their own accord, pulled by an instinct he dared not ignore. The last time he had felt it had been at the battle of Thorull. There, he had been just in time to save his son, the child of his blood.

As he cut round a corner, he knew this time would be different.

Jasside knelt before an open doorway, scrambling frantically in a pile of debris. Grey soot covered her from foot to head, clinging to the tears that carved rivers down her cheeks. It took him a moment to realize what she was doing.

She was digging.

Yandumar stumbled forward. He stopped over her prostrate form, watching as she paused between each lifted stone, overcome with heaving sobs. He knelt next to her, reaching tenderly for her shoulders.

"What is it, child? What's wrong?" Even as the words left his lips, he knew he didn't want to find out.

But also knew he had to.

She shook her head, peering with red-rimmed eyes into his face. She pointed down. Yandumar's gaze dropped to follow.

There, sticking out from the wreckage, lay the exposed blade of an *Andun*. Etched into the steel was a single word.

"Justice."

Yandumar slumped into her. They embraced. His own tears flowed now, joining hers, and between them flooded an ocean of grief.

Chapter 18

VASHODIA HAD MADE the announcement herself. It had been a simple matter to broadcast to the entire city. Less simple—but far more important—to repeat the message within communion to every carrier in the empire. It had been this:

Rekaj's regime has been purged. The conflict is over. The people have won. All surviving mierothi and daeloth are hereby ordered to extricate themselves from the continent. We meet, in two months' time, at the Taditali estate in Namerrun to stage our departure.

A flood of questions, from a thousand sources, had crashed upon her not moments from the message's end. She'd been forced to mask her signal entirely. The most pervasive query had been in the form of a single word: *How?* Few, of course, knew of the tunnels leading to the lands beyond this continent.

Vashodia, however, did not plan on using them.

"Ready, mother?" she said.

Angla cut a sharp glance her way, saying nothing. She did not need to. Vashodia could tell exactly what she was thinking. *You can feel as well as I that our harmonization is still in progress, so hold your tongue and let me finish in peace, you impatient little tart.*

Vashodia smiled to herself. Her life had been dedicated to the pursuit of knowledge. In all her research, she'd found the study of people to be the most vital. Dissections had revealed to her the pathways within the mind, and the little grey cells that controlled thought and memory, emotion and motivation, impulse and instinct. Fascinating. As such, she could, through careful analysis, narrow down the likely choices a person would make. It was as close to seeing the future as any would get.

She sighed, looking out over the crowd that had gathered. The tar pit in the center of the Ropes had been dismantled—one of Yandumar's first decrees—and Vashodia sat cross-legged on the sand that now covered the arena floor. Three hundred of her kin stood nearby—females freed by her brother. The seats were nearly filled. Some had come out of curiosity. Others out of fear. Most, however, had come simply to witness.

The frequencies synced together at last. The crowd felt it, taking in a communal breath as the disparate vibrations became one. Vashodia energized. The five spheres in a circle around her popped open, and thousands of darkwisps sprang into the sky.

The symbiotic organisms, which clung to the identity strands in her blood, shifted into action, drawing upon the energy that bound the universe together. They touched their disembodied brethren, pulling more and more.

Vashodia directed them with her will. The darkwisps formed a funnel, its wide mouth facing down. On top, this conduit broke into smaller channels pointing out in all directions.

"Now, mother," she said. "All I need from you is raw power. Do not bother forming it. Just send everything through the opening, and I will do the rest."

"Are you sure we can make this work?" Angla asked.

Vashodia nodded.

Her mother frowned, softly adding, "Are you sure we *should*?"

"It has been long enough. This veiled empire can hide no more."

With a sigh, Angla pushed her ocean of gathered energy through the funnel.

Power poured through the large conduit and into the tight channels, shooting out their ends like water from a fountain. The sky came alive at the intrusion. Vashodia hummed to herself as the dark energy strands traversed hundreds of leagues to their destinations.

Over the last few decades, she had placed her machines around the edges of the continent. Five hundred of them. Within each were housed thousands of darkwisps, the gathering of which had taken centuries. She had programmed them all with a single imperative. Now, as the power formed by Angla and directed by herself came crashing home . . . they awoke.

The lingering symbionts of the last two millennia

pulsed as one. Their purpose was unified. Up and out, they spent themselves against the accident of ages past.

The sundered world shook to its very core.

The Shroud . . . shattered.

Like pressing a boot upon a saturated sponge, the darkwisps squeezed outward in all directions, finally free from their artificial constraints. The pressure had built up to its breaking point—much longer, and they would have begun devouring towns, and soon, cities. Then . . . everything. And even her own efforts to stymie them would prove insufficient.

Fly away my pets.

But now they were free to float across the oceans and seek out their cousins of the light. Free to find and annihilate each other. As they were meant to. From the information she had recovered from Ruul, their behavior of seeking living flesh was completely aberrant. The original makers had not designed such functionality.

Then again, a little degeneration is to be expected after fifteen thousand years.

Her mother, picking herself up off the ground, released her power, breaking the sync. "All the world will have felt that," she said with awe.

"This world, yes," said Vashodia. "And so much more."

Angla gazed at her with bewilderment. "What?"

Vashodia giggled.

GILSHAMED POURED HIS will into the construct, sweating with effort. He had not slept in a week, and only ate when his body screamed at him for sustenance. This project had become the whole of his being, for it was the only thing in his life over which he had control. The only thing that made any sense.

His arms dropped as his current pool of energy was consumed. He reached for his canteen and squeezed the last few drops into his mouth, then tossed the empty skin away. He energized once more.

The design was one he had learned from the Panisahldrians. Gilshamed had scoffed when he first saw it—what valynkar would ever use such a thing?—but now, he wished he had paid closer attention. His seemed crude in comparison; a child's attempt to mimic the adults. But, for his purposes, it would be enough.

And now, finally, it was finished. Gilshamed turned away.

The hill fort was only two klicks from the cave, and the lone squad left behind as stewards had—after some persuasion by Draevenus—brought wagons to help transport his kin. Gilshamed eyed the barracks door through which they now rested. His labors completed, he had nothing else to do but wait.

He blinked. The door opened. The sun, though hidden behind grey clouds, had shifted noticeably in the sky. Draevenus stepped out from the doorway. The mierothi looked towards him and slowly shook his head.

Gilshamed felt a hammer strike his soul.

He should have been prepared. Draevenus had told him he was not much of a healer. Had said not to hold out hope. But he could not help himself. Could not stop from dreaming dreams he had not dared to entertain in centuries. And the pain of fresh wounds, slashed across the festering of old, nearly drove him to his knees.

"I'm sorry," Draevenus said. "I did all I could. Your people will undoubtedly have greater skill than I."

Gilshamed nodded, grateful that this man whom he once called enemy would seek to comfort him. The sincerity of the gesture brought tears to his eyes.

"Remember this," said Draevenus. "When you are back among the valynkar, tell them that not all of our kind are without mercy or compassion. Tell them that those responsible for the crimes of our ancient war have been punished. As my people go now to find a new place among the nations of the world, please remember that we wish only for peace."

"I will."

They stood facing each other for a long moment. The silence that stretched between them could not be called companionable, but still, a measure of respect persisted. Despite the despair he felt, Gilshamed had a glimmer of hope for the future.

Draevenus glanced past him. "Is it ready?"

"Yes. Please bring them out."

The mierothi disappeared through the doorway. A mark later, carried on cushioned pallets by pairs of local soldiers, came his kin.

Gilshamed stepped into his construct, a rectangular, wagon-like vehicle, and guided the pallets into place as they came. Most of his kin slept. Some few, though, looked about lazily. He did not know what their minds perceived as their glazed eyes roamed, but it was certainly not reality. Whatever nightmare they had been trapped in all this time had taken everything from them. Not a one had any response beyond what could be expected from an infant.

He counted them as they were mounted into place. At thirty-nine, his heart began racing.

Two final pallets were lifted into his carriage. In one, the body of Voren. His pale form, so peaceful now, had been preserved within a sorcerous ward.

I take you back to our people now. You will buried on the hill of Elos's Gaze, an honor only gifted to the greatest of the valynkar. An honor you have earned with your sacrifice.

Gilshamed guided Voren's pallet into position, then turned to the last.

Lashriel lay atop it. Her arms rested on her stomach. Her eyes were closed. Her feet canted slightly to either side. Violet hair spread in a tangle beneath her head.

My love. . .

Gingerly, he moved his hand to her brow.

. . . I started a war to avenge you. . .

His fingers began combing through her hair.

. . . but now, I would tear down the heavens just to release you from this prison. . .

A sigh escaped her lips.

. . . and sacrifice anything, just for the chance to take your place.

His fingers snagged on a tangle, jerking her head slightly. Her eyes popped open. They stared directly into his.

Gilshamed sank into his ancient memories. All the times she would look at him. The love that poured forth. The joy he felt in her presence. The peace when they embraced.

He saw none of that now. Her eyes held no recognition. Soulless. Blank.

Gilshamed extracted his fingers. Lashriel's head lolled, facing away from him, and her eyes—blessedly—closed.

He placed her pallet closest to the front, then began strapping himself into the harness.

"Will you not rest first?" Draevenus asked.

Gilshamed shook his head. "This land and I need to be separated, and yesterday is not soon enough." He unfurled his wings. "I cannot rest until we are gone."

He energized, then pushed a hair of power into the control mechanism of the wagon. It lifted into the air, becoming weightless. He rose with it.

Gilshamed surged forward, slowly accelerating as he pulled the mass behind him. Soon, the land beneath him was passing by in a blur. He aimed eastward.

With his kin in tow and the wind in his face, Gilshamed flew for home.

JASSIDE SHUFFLED ALONG quietly, just another mourner waiting for her turn to pay respects. The line stretched back behind her, all the way to the city gates, and before her just a few more steps to the raised platform overlooking the newest addition to the landscape.

A mound rose like the back of a slumbering giant, marking the mass grave that held all the fallen from the battle. The dead, from both sides, were honored here for their sacrifice.

Many women in line wore the full accoutrements of widows in mourning: lacy black fabric covering every bit of skin, and a veil hanging over the eyes. Jasside had considered donning the same but discarded the idea as being presumptuous. She'd settled instead for a plain black dress.

Her hands were held together at her waist, carefully cupping a small object as she stepped closer to the platform. It was almost her turn. The man who now stood upon its edge tossed a coin onto the mound, lingered a moment, then turned to make way for the woman behind him.

A pile glittered in the dirt. Not just coins either, but also trinkets and baubles, statues and knives, anything people had that held significance to them. All given away freely. Thousands of pieces already, with thousands more to come. A squad of soldiers stood guard to prevent their theft.

Jasside had thought long about her own show of respect. And with the power she now possessed, *show* indeed it could be. She'd pondered any number of grand gestures, from erecting a statue to summoning a permanent rain cloud above the barrow. But she'd dismissed them all. Such an act would only draw attention to herself, not the dead, and accomplish the opposite of her purpose in coming.

With a start, she realized no one else stood between her and the platform. She took a deep breath and walked up the wooden steps. Capping her emotions under a tight lid, she peered down upon the barrow.

Over two hundred thousand bodies lay interred beneath the soil. But the pain lancing across her soul was only for one.

They'd found only charred flesh beneath the crust. Not a single body from the chamber could be identified, and even the bones had been scattered. Only by the presence of each *Andun*, which had all escaped unmarred, were they able to know for certain who had perished there. Still, they'd scraped together what they could, placing the remains at rest alongside these fellow fallen.

Mevon. . .

Tears came to her eyes. Unbidden, but not unwelcome.

You gave to me, for a short while, a gift that I will cherish forever. A gift that I did not deserve. A gift that I had long since given up on ever finding. For that, my heart will always belong to you.

Jasside opened her hands, revealing the smelling-box trinket. It was the first device she'd ever made, beautiful for its simplicity and its purpose.

She tossed it forward.

Jasside turned and walked down the steps, and another took her place. A single thought ran through her mind, repeating itself over and over:

I have nothing left.

Her mother was dead. Her brother, too. And the man she would have loved lay in pieces beneath the dirt.

But the thought cut both ways.

Justice had been done to those responsible for her mother's death. Her brother's sacrifice had been justified by the victory of the revolution. Mevon, though gone, had awakened within her the ability to connect, to care for another, to love.

Everything tying me to this land has been severed. There is no longer any reason for me to stay.

Vashodia had extended the invitation. Jasside decided, then, to accept. For despite all her power and knowledge, the mierothi still needed someone at her side to be both conscience and temperance. Someone to, when necessary, plant her feet back on the soil.

And besides her ancient eyes, Vashodia still reminded Jasside of a certain little girl who, at too young an age, had lost her mother and her childhood in one grisly act. For that, Jasside would stay at her side, and in every way she knew how, show her love.

So, she would learn all she could, and attempt to kindle her understanding of Vashodia. In time, it would be enough to do what was needed—for the light in her own soul to balance out the darkness that held her mistress in its grip.

And together, she knew, they would accomplish wonders.

IN THE ROOM that had seen the death of the previous emperor, Yandumar stood before the crowd, still not quite believing what idiots they all were.

Everyone was present it seemed. At least, everyone who mattered. All the Ragremon elders in one group, the guild and enterprise representatives another. Sarian Thress sat, already scratching his quill across the parchment of an open tome. The commanders of the revolution and the rebellion and the surviving ranked soldiers of the Imperial army mingled together, none too happy about standing shoulder to shoulder with those who, just a week ago, were trying to kill them. Yandumar paid no attention to their grumblings. They would get over it. He would make them.

Mending bridges . . . easier said than done.

A squeeze on his hand brought his attention to the figure at his side. Slick Ren. His wife.

The elders threw a fit when he announced his intentions towards her. "*She is not of our blood,*" they had said. He remembered well the speech he'd given to shut them up.

"*The vows of our people are complete. There's no need to stick to traditions designed to keep us separate from the rest of the world. And every need to show this empire that I don't intend to play favorites.*"

Of course, that had also been the moment when he had inadvertently agreed to this asinine course of action. Yandumar sighed, looking into Slick Ren's eyes. For her, the price was worth it.

At least, it had better be.

Abendrol Torn cleared his throat, raising an eyebrow expectantly at him.

Yandumar sighed. "Let's get this over with."

Torn took out a scroll and ran his eyes over the contents. He inhaled deeply, then began his oration. "On this day, the thirty-fifth of Quarsis in the year 11,712 A.S., we, the victors over tyranny, do crown as emperor Yandumar Daere, and as empress his wife Elrenia Daere."

That was it. Simple, pointed, sturdy. Just like the clothes they wore, the thrones they would sit on, the crowns now being placed upon their heads. Many had insisted that the ruler of an empire as great as this should display the power and wealth of his station at all times. They'd written up toll-long speeches, designed garments and thrones and crowns that were more gold and jewel than anything else, and generally intended for his life to be filled with all the things he hated.

A single word had come to mind at their suggestions: Ostentatious. *And yes, Gilshamed, I do know what it means . . . now, anyway.* He'd told all the sycophants to bite him.

In *exactly* those words.

With the crowning complete, his title became official. He began his appointments without another shred of ceremony. Derthon became the crown's protector. Idrus, the supreme general of their army. Orbrahn, the minister of sorcery. Numerous people among both Ragremon elders and others to fill in governing positions left vacant by the departing mierothi.

Yandumar paused, looking over at a small figure hovering near the wall. She was his last appointment. "Ilyem Bahkere, will you accept the position of void master?"

She stepped forward. "I will."

Yandumar nodded, turning his gaze over the crowd. Unlike the others, this one deserved an explanation. "The old system of Hardohl is abolished. As void master, she will have three tasks before her. First, to re-form the voids now serving into a new combat unit, one that is capable of responding to any kind of crisis."

Heads nodded around the room. This was expected.

"Second, she is to gather whatever force she needs and escort the mierothi and daeloth out of this empire, ensuring they never return."

More nods.

"Third," Yandumar paused, "she will eradicate the Hardohl academy, and return all students to what family of theirs can be found."

At this, eyebrows shot up around the chamber, and a flurry of whispered conversations sprang to life. This, he had not discussed with anyone but Slick Ren, Derthon, and Ilyem herself.

For you, my son. The best that I can do. The best I know how.

Yandumar thought he'd shed all the tears he would, but he was wrong. His chest tightened as they carved their way down his cheeks and dripped silently to the floor. Everything he'd done had been for Mevon. To have come so far, and lost him anyway, seemed the cruelest sort of punishment he could think of.

So, right there in the audience chamber in the ruins of the palace, he made a new vow—one that only he and God would ever know—to honor his son's memory, and his sacrifice, above all else.

He led Slick Ren back, and together they sat on their new thrones, beginning a reign that would, he hoped, remove the oppression and persecution and sorrow and blood from the land and replace it with freedom and acceptance and joy and life.

Our veil has been lifted. Now, it's time to see who we truly are.

Epilogue

DRAEVENUS STROLLED, ENJOYING the last of the day's sunshine as it streamed through evergreen boughs. He breathed in the unmolested scent of a spring breeze. Leather straps squeezed on his shoulders, his pack shifted in rhythm with each step upon the verdant forest floor.

He carried with him everything he would need. Food and water, spare clothes, coin, tools for a life on the trail. Besides a hatchet and a skinning knife, he possessed no other weapons. He'd rolled up his blades inside his chain mail and left them behind. Where he was going, he would not need them.

He'd said his good-byes to his sister and mother. Vashodia knew, of course, what he was getting up to, calling him a fool. There had been no embrace to mark their separation nor words of encouragement, but he could tell from the sparkle in her eyes that she wished him well. Angla, though, had practically squeezed the life out of him. She warned him to be careful. Staying within the empire's borders after all their kind had been ordered to leave presented hazards, both to himself and the tenuous peace that kept the populace from their throats. He'd told her not to worry. He was, after all, very good at hiding.

My disguise could probably use some work, though. More than ever before, he would need to interact with people, hear their stories and tales and legends. A hood to hide his face would not be enough. He needed a wig, paste to color his skin, gloves that more thoroughly concealed his claws, and a convincing story about his identity.

These thoughts and others swirled gently around his head. There was no urgency, no strict timeline, no lives or souls at stake. The quest before him would likely take years, if not decades, yet Draevenus had never felt more content with his life. Never felt more at peace.

Night soon fell. Draevenus knew the forest well, and trudged towards a place nearby where shelter could be found. A hill loomed before him. On the other side was an alcove protected on three sides by stone and trees. Treading through the game trail, Draevenus circled around to the entrance.

An orange glow illuminated the place.

Instinctively, he halted and began turning away. But he stopped himself. *I've got to start thinking differently sometime. Might as well begin now.* He began humming and shuffling his feet, making noise to warn the alcove's occupant of his approach.

He stepped into the firelight and paused. A big man sat on a log, his face turned slightly away from the flames and concealed by a raised hood. Draevenus smiled. "Greetings, traveler. I see you have found the best shelter within a league of here. As night has already fallen, would you mind if I shared your fire?"

The man gestured at his makeshift bench of wood. "Be my guest."

"Thank you." Draevenus sat down at the opposite end of the log. He shrugged out of his pack and laid it before him, digging through to find his cooking pan. He put it on the fire, then unwrapped a slab of salted venison. After a moment, he took out a second. "I have plenty, friend. For the gift of your fire, I would gladly share."

The man dipped his head. "That would be most welcome."

Once the steaks were sizzling and their savory aroma filled the alcove, Draevenus turned to the man. "So, where are you headed?"

The man shrugged. "West, I think."

"Any particular destination?"

"For now? No. Not really. What about you?"

"I am heading west as well, towards the Andean Mountains."

"Ah. I hear they are quite beautiful this time of year."

"Quite. I hope to get there by summer, when the snows are least, and make my way through one of the passes."

"You seek the far side?"

Draevenus nodded as he flipped over the meat.

"It's a dangerous trek," continued the man. "What lies beyond the mountains that is worth such a risk?"

"Perhaps nothing. But I seek stories, and the people settled there may have some that no one else has heard."

"Stories? About what?"

Draevenus sighed. "About the fall of a god."

The man grunted. "You seek Ruul." It was not a question.

Draevenus nodded. "He and I have some unfinished business. And it is long past time that we met."

The steaks finished cooking, and Draevenus retrieved them from the pan. The man skewered one on a long dagger and began taking bites straight off the blade. Draevenus, rather than retrieve a plate and fork, laughed to himself and did the same. The man produced a skin of wine, took a drink, then passed it to Draevenus. They ate their meal in silence, washing down each bite with a swig of wine and wiping the grease from their mouths with the backs of their gloves.

When finished, the man slumped to the ground with his feet towards the fire and leaned his back against the log. "It occurs to me," he said, "that your journey will be a lonely one."

"I suppose it will be," Draevenus said. "But that is something I've grown used to."

"Used to, perhaps. But not fond of."

Draevenus shook his head.

The man leaned forward. "Your quest seems a noble one, friend. It has . . . purpose. Something I find that I am lacking at the moment. Perhaps we can help each other out?"

"You mean, solve the problem of my loneliness and your aimlessness at the same time?"

"Precisely."

"Then, my friend, I cordially invite you to accompany me on my journey. What say you?"

The man stayed silent for several beats, drumming his fingers in the dirt. "Before I say yes, I have just one question."

Draevenus waved his open palm towards him.

"Will there be blood?"

Draevenus did not need to think long. He slipped to the ground and hugged his knees to his chest. "Not if I can help it."

The man flipped down his hood. In the flickering firelight, Draevenus watched as Mevon Dacre curled his lips up into a smile.

Glossary

Locations and Terms

Abyss—slang term for death

Adjudicators—mierothi and daeloth sorcerer-assassins, led by Marshal Adjudicator Jezrid

Agoritha Plains—the breadbasket of the central territory

Andean—long chain of mountains on the extreme west end of continent

Andun—weapon used exclusively by Hardohl, a metal rod with long blades at each end which are bent into the shape of open diamonds

Beat—unit of time equaling approximately one heartbeat (.86 seconds). A hundred beats in each Mark.

Blade Cabal—group of ten Hardohl who serve as the personal protectors of the emperor and his palace in Mecrithos

Brightwisp—hovering swarm of particles held together by pure light energy, released from the body of a caster (valynkar-blooded) upon death

Caster—generic term for a wielder of magic/sorcery. Male: sorcerer—Female: sorceress

Cataclysm, the—event marking the end of the War of Rising Night, in which the continent was broken, raising the elevation by almost a kilometer in most places, and erecting the Shroud

Chasm, the—a deep canyon formed on ground zero of the Cataclysm, forms three-way border between the central, northern, and eastern territories

Daeloth—half-human half-mierothi, bred by nefarious means to act as commanders in the Imperial army

Darkwatch—zealous and skilled group of humans and daeloth, assigned as personal bodyguards to each mierothi in the empire

Darkwisp—hovering swarm of particles held together by pure dark energy, released from the body of a caster (mierothi-blooded) upon death

District—one of five regions divided from each prefecture

Elite—best of the best, assigned to a Fist under a Hardohl, wear heavy armor that is enchanted to minimize the effects of direct sorcery

Energize—to gather energy before casting a spell, also called charging, pooling, gathering, etc.

Evervine—bioluminescent vine that was cultivated in old valynkar dwellings

Fist—small unit led by a Hardohl and his/her selected captains, consisting mostly of Elite with a smaller number of Rangers, specializes in hunting down rogue casters

Frozen Fangs—a chain of long, sharp peninsulas jutting out into the icy southern sea

Fyrdra—the westernmost prefecture of the southern territory

Godsreach—chain of mountains in the eastern territory

Hardohl—humans who are completely immune to direct applications of sorcery, they wield an *Andun* and lead a Fist into battle against rogue casters

Lightfall Square—the ceremony grounds outside the palace in Mecrithos

Mark—unit of time equaling approximately a minute and a half. Fifty marks in each toll.

Mecrithos—capital of the empire, located in the central territory

Mierothi—humanoids covered in dark scales, with pale faces and claws, masters of dark magic, rulers of the veiled empire

Namerrun—prefecture in the northern territory

Panisahldron—nation outside of the empire

Prefecture—one of five regions divided from each territory, ruled by a mierothi prefect

Ragremos—nation that existed before the mierothi conquest

Rashunem Hills—foothills in the easternmost section of the Godsreach Mountains

Sceptre—nation outside of the Veiled Empire

Shelf, the—the massive cliff that marks the entire border of the continent

Shenog Ravine—southern offshoot of the Chasm

Shroud, the—a magic barrier around the entire continent, erected as a result of the Cataclysm

Silverstone—shiny stone that the valynkar used to build their floating cities

Taditali vineyards—landmass covering nearly all of

the Namerrun prefecture of the northern territory, owned and operated by the Taditali family of wine merchants

Territories—names of the five geographical and political segments of the empire (north, south, east, west, and central)

Thorull—capital city of the self-named prefecture in the eastern territory

Toll—unit of time equaling approximately seventy-two minutes. Twenty tolls in a day.

Valynkar—humanoids defined by typically tall height, hair all colors of the rainbow, ethereal wings that can be summoned at will, masters of light magic

Veiled Empire—unofficial title of the continent ruled by the mierothi

Verge—prison/medical facility on the southern tip of the Andean mountain range

War of Rising Night—the conflict between the mierothi and their subjugated allies (notably the nation of Ragremos) against the valynkar and the nations of men nineteen hundred years ago

Dramatis Personae

The Fist

Arozir—Elite captain
Idrus—Ranger captain
Ivengar—Ranger lieutenant

Mevon Daere—Hardohl (magic void), leader

Ropes—Elite lieutenant

Tolvar—Elite captain

The Revolution

Bellanis—former Imperial sergeant, commander

Calla—sorceress

Derthon—bandit king, former Hardohl

Gilshamed—valynkar, leader of the revolution, "Golden Man"

Jasside Anglasco—sorceress, knows the secret weakness of Hardohl

Orbrahn—cocky young sorcerer

Slick Ren—bandit queen, sister to Derthon

Yandumar—Second to Gilshamed, former Elite captain

The Mierothi Council

Grezkul—supreme arcanod

Jezrid—marshal adjudicator

Kael—elderly Hardohl, Voren's warden

Kitavijj—mother phyzari

Lekrigar—high regnosist

Rekaj—emperor

Truln—chronicler

Voren—valynkar prisoner

The Outcasts

Angla—captured mierothi, mother to Draevenus and Vashodia

Draevenus—mierothi assassin, brother of Vashodia

Harridan Chant—former Elite captain, uncle to Idrus
Paen Taditali—son of wine baron, Vashodia's lover
Shadow—former Ranger captain
Vashodia—puller of strings, keeper of secrets

Others

Abendrol Torn—mayor of Ragremon town, uncle to Tolvar and Arozir
Brefand—Jasside's half brother
Hezraas—mierothi, prefect of Thorull
Ilyem Bakhere—Hardohl
Kaiera—Yandumar's wife (deceased)
Lashriel—captured valynkar woman, life-mate to Gilshamed
Masri Gensrasco—daeloth, general of the Thorull Host
Naeveth and Mosnar—Hardohl
Samaranth—mierothi, phyzari in charge of Verge
Sarian Thress—Ragremon historian
Tursek—daeloth, in charge of Verge tribute caravan

Historical Figures

Analethis—valynkar champion
Elos—god of light and the valynkar
Heshrigan—valynkar arbiter
Murathrius—valynkar mediator
Ruul—god of darkness and the mierothi

Acknowledgments

FIRST AND FOREMOST, I want to thank my wife Kathryn, who stood by me with endless support and patience as I set out on this crazy journey into authorhood. Truly, this book would never have been written if not for the countless times she looked me square in the face and said, "Go write."

I'd also like to thank my family: My sister Rachel, whose strength and determination served as inspiration for turning the females of my early drafts from caricatures into actual characters. My sister Emily, who was my sounding board for ideas and gave me someone to pace against on our race to the publishing line. My father, for always believing in me and providing encouraging yet useful feedback on my novel. My mother, for instilling in me a love for the written word. And my cousin Christy, for turning a passing interest in fantasy into a lifelong obsession.

Thanks also to my agent, Nicole Resciniti, and my editor, David Pomerico—two tiny "yeses" amidst an ocean of "no's"—for taking a chance on me and my book, just when I had all but given up hope.

And finally, thanks to Randy Ingermanson, Larry Brooks, K. M. Weiland, and numerous other writers and bloggers, whose advice and insight helped demystify the whole storytelling and publishing processes one piece at a time.

About the Author

Born in 1983, NATHAN GARRISON has been writing stories since his dad bought their first family computer. He grew up on tales of the fantastic. From Narnia and Middle-Earth to a galaxy far, far away, he has always harbored a love for things only imagination can conjure up. He counts it among the greatest joys of his life to be able to share the stories within him. He has two great boys and an awesome wife who is way more supportive of his writing efforts than he thinks he deserves. Besides writing, he loves playing guitar (the louder the better), cooking (the more bacon-y the better), playing board/video/card games with friends and family, and reveling in unadulterated geekery. *Veiled Empire* is his first novel. You can follow him on Twitter at @NR_Garrison.